REIGN
OF
PAWNS

BOOK 1:
THE PARIEUR'S PLAY

BY V. S. EDWÁR

REIGN OF PAWNS - 1: THE PARIEUR'S PLAY

First edition. November 21, 2025.

Copyright © 2025 V. S. EDWÁR.

ISBN: 979-8-9931749-1-4

Written by V. S. EDWÁR.

To my mother—my first hero and eternal role model—who always placed me above all else.

To my wife—who patiently embraces the quirks that come with loving a writer.

To my grandmother—whose love was served in every plate of her unforgettable cooking.

To my elder sisters—who stood by me through life's toughest moments, unwavering in their support.

And last, but never least— To my precious daughters, the radiant lights of my life.

*"We dream of thrones among the stars,
yet drift as leaves in a current we cannot see."*

TABLE OF CONTENTS

CHAPTER
1

An Unlikely Ensemble

Somewhere in the world

Hope faded from the air like light from the downing Sun. There was no way out. Ojoré's frail and bruised body was trampled under the weight of the menacing beast. The brute was massive. Hungry and murderous, it vanquished his thin frame.

The pressure on his chest felt like a bench press he could not lift. Gasping for air, he held onto the hyena's neck while it tried to dig its canines into him. The animal's claws scratched his skin, opening elongated wounds that oozed blood.

Ojoré withered by the second. It seemed as if the hyena sucked all his energy through its ravenous mouth.

This is it; this is my final moment. I am going to die.

Scenes from the past flashed in his mind. His brain could not think straight.

Ojoré turned his face away from the hyena's champing mouth and saw several bubble-like objects floating across the vast landscape.

Giant bubbles floating in the air? Am I going mad?

Mist transuded from the bubbles and lingered a few feet above the ground.

"Aaaaaahh," Ojoré shouted. His grip on the hyena waned.

I can't hold it any longer.

Finally, he closed his eyes, let go of the hyena's neck, and waited for its teeth, for the pain, for his flesh to be torn apart.

But no such thing happened. Ojoré didn't feel a thing on his neck or any part of his body for that matter.

A blinding flash of white light shot toward him from the bubbles.

Am I dead? There was no pain. There is no pain.

He blinked his eyes a few times. It made the light bearable. His vision cleared. The light's source glided toward him.

His eyes narrowed to focus on it. *Wait a minute, it's a person.*

A humanoid figure slowly drew close. As it approached, an outline of a beautiful, curvy woman came into focus. Her presence filled the surroundings with misty vapors of fragrance. Sometimes it had floral notes with hints of jasmines, pine roses, plumerias, and kewras. Other times it smelled of musk and sandalwood and vetiver. She had skin that dazzled as if embedded with tiny jewels. Her attire was magical, unworldly; he had not seen a fabric like that before. It appeared as though water was woven into clothes. When she sauntered, the dress twisted, swirled, and more mist diffused the fragrance into the sultry air. It was heavenly. She appeared to walk into a slow catwalk, carrying the dress elegantly.

Her smile soothed, healed, energized. Ojoré could feel the strength return in his arms. Her eyes stared into his. There was no struggle, no hyena, no pain.

Angel?

Suddenly, the next second, she picked up a rock and... *Slam!* She banged it on his head.

"Aaaaaah!" he screamed. Pain soared through his skull. It felt as if his brain was going to explode.

It knocked him out of his dream.

For a moment, Ojoré was in shock, unable to comprehend that he was awake. But when he did, he composed himself. It was not the first time he had had this particular dream. The woman had visited his dreams over and over again, although the story in the dream changed every now and then.

As Ojoré slowly regained consciousness, a faint melody hit his ears. This was immensely confusing.

The pain made it hard to concentrate. *Where am I?*

He opened his eyes gently, and his vision went from blurred to clear as he blinked. The room was dimly lit. The ceiling behind the cobwebs was made of stone, while a dull and dirty tube light flickered above him, adding to the gloom. It looked like a basement with small windows at the top of the walls, protected by iron bars to prevent anyone from entering or leaving. They were covered with thick plywood sheets to block light, allowing little sound to pass. Though covered from all sides, the room was big. The air smelled stale and damp with hints of mold, stone, and dust.

Drums, lots of cheering, and clapping. The melody seemed to come from outside through the plywood-covered windows.

In the next second, he shouted, "What? Noooo—" He found himself lying on a hospital bed, a transparent tube injecting a clear solution into his arm from an intravenous bag hanging on his bedside.

Was I in an accident? I can't remember anything. This doesn't seem like a hospital.

Ojoré took a deep breath. He tried to remember everything about what had gotten him into this situation. He tried to move his limbs, but nothing happened. The only thing he could move was his neck. Everything below was numb.

Panic struck like a terrible hangover. It pushed his mind to the next level of paranoia.

The head side of Ojoré's bed was lifted a little on an incline. He slowly lifted his neck to look at his body. His arms and legs were restrained with chains and tied to a thick iron bed.

The pounding in his chest intensified. He could not understand what was going on. He tried to move his limbs vigorously and exerted all the strength he could muster, but nothing worked.

"Where am I? What's happening to me?" Ojoré shouted in his rhythmic Kenyan accent.

No answer.

"Who is doing this? Why have you chained me? Help! Someone, please help!"

Silence.

A few seconds later, a male voice spoke. It seemed to come from the opposite side of the room and had a sing-song Finnish accent. "Calm down. It'll only make it worse," the voice said. "You're not the only person in this room. Look around."

In his panic, he failed to notice the other occupants in the room, who were all in the same predicament.

"None of us can move our limbs either," the Finnish voice said.

This time, he lifted his head and looked clearly at his surroundings. Five iron beds in the room were fastened to the floor, strong and sturdy. One big bed—about two feet longer than a standard California king but as wide as a twin—sat beside him, while the other three twin-size beds were in front. Additionally, the beds were restrained to the wall through heavy-duty iron chains. At the end of this basement were stairs made of stone that went upward, leading to an old but solid-looking iron door.

Ojoré turned his head. An enormous man occupied the big bed next to him. He was tied with more chains than the others and seemed deep in sleep. He lifted his head as much as he could. The three men in front of him seemed to be of average height as compared to the one beside him. All were injected with IVs as well.

"You're the last one to wake," the man from Finland said.

"Why can't I move my arms, my body? What's happening to me?"

"I don't know," the man replied. He had ash-blonde hair, almond-shaped sky-blue eyes, and a small nose on a round face. He was on the center bed in front of him. "I gained consciousness only a few hours ago."

"Why are we kept like this?"

"We don't know," the man on the opposite left side bed lifted his face, wearing an equally tense expression. His accent had minor tones of Chinese. Parts of his silky black hair fell over his narrow eyes. He had a slender nose over an oval-shaped face.

Ojoré still kept on asking questions. "Were we in some kind of medical emergency? Why have they chained us?"

"Does this look like a medical emergency to you? Not a single bit. If it were, they wouldn't have put chains on our bodies." The Finnish man jerked his neck to point out the shackles on his body. "We all have the same questions."

The intensity of music in the background increased, followed by the intensity of clapping. They all listened carefully, expecting to find some clue about their captivity. A few seconds later, the symphony reached its climax. Cheers and shouts followed. A few minutes later, everything died down, and all they could hear were muffled voices.

"Help!" Ojoré shouted. "Somebody, please help us!"

The others followed suit. "Help us, please," one by one, they screamed.

Silence.

Everyone lifted their heads and looked at each other in expectation, waiting for something to happen. They hoped someone would come running and explain what was going on.

However, much to their disappointment, no one came. They continued to wait silently for several minutes, staring at each other.

"Where are we? Is this still Nairobi?" he asked.

"Nairobi?" the man opposite to him said. "The last I remember, I was in Kourtane... Finland."

Ojoré did not speak.

"I'm Aarno, Finnish." The wrinkles on Aarno's forehead constricted. "What about you guys?"

"Ojoré," he replied. "Last I remember, I was in Nairobi, Kenya. I'm from there."

"Liang," the man on the opposite left bed from Ojoré replied. "Chinese. I was in Shanghai last; that's what I recall."

"I'm Diego," the man on the opposite right side spoke for the first time. "From Brazil." He coughed a little. "I had just arrived in Old Trafford, England. But now, where we are, I do not know." He had a thick Paulistano accent, which sounded nasal, crisp, and fast. He had dark, curly hair, a chiseled jawline with prominent cheekbones, and prominent eyes. Ojoré had not seen a man more handsome than him.

Ojoré glanced at the enormous man beside him. "Where's he from?"

"No idea," Aarno replied. "He was awake for a few seconds, murmured something, then passed out."

"D... D... Darren. F... from the USA." The man creaked his eyes open. He struggled with every word he spoke. "Was in H...Houston last. C...came back to senses before y'all, and by senses, I ...m...mean only my f...f...freaking face." His midwestern accent was sturdy and sharp. He had a wide and pronounced jawline, thick eyebrows, a broad nose, and prominent eyes. His long hair was golden blonde, while his skin was rough with a hint of tan.

"Aaaaahhh." Darren stretched the muscles on his face wide as he finished, trying to induce some movement in his arms. But he was just as incapable as everyone else in the room. "Tried to get up for hours. Screamed at this goddamned ceiling until I passed out."

"Where do you think we are?" Ojoré asked

"Anywhere," Aarno replied. "We could be anywhere in the world. Look at us. All of us are from different countries."

"Not just different countries, different continents," Liang added.

Silence hung in the room like the smell of a rotten egg. No one liked it, but no one had anything to say. Their minds tried to make some sense of this information.

Liang broke the silence. "Think about this, why are five people from five different continents restrained, drugged, and held in this freaking room?" He deliberated on each part of the question as he spoke, as if to make it sink into everyone's head. His question, however, was silenced by the squeaking of the metal door. Their heads turned in the direction of the sound.

A man wearing a long white coat entered. Standing about five feet seven inches, he was skinny, with shiny copper hair, blue eyes, and a freckled face. A stethoscope hung around his neck.

He plodded in Ojoré's direction, came to a halt next to him, and pulled out a small wooden hammer from his coat pocket. Ojoré's eyes fell on his right thumb, which was more tanned than the rest of his hand, dark brown from the thumb joint to the nail.

The man slid aside the bed sheet that covered Ojoré's legs, exposed his knees, and tapped the right knee gently with the hammer. On seeing no reflex action, he looked satisfied.

"Hey! Who are you? What are you doing to us?" Ojoré shouted. "Where are we?"

The man did not answer but repeated the same procedure on his left knee.

"He's asking you something, dimwit!" Darren's voice echoed.

The man ignored them. He tapped everyone's knees one by one and confirmed the lack of reflex action.

"Why are you holding us?" Darren shouted. He tried to move, free himself, and get out of there. Nothing worked. "Goddammit, answer the freaking question."

Silence.

"Please," Ojoré pleaded. "Please, tell us what's going on."

The man stopped. He considered for a while. Finally, after a few long seconds, he spoke in a thick accent. "I can't tell you anything, mate. I'm here against my will, just like you all are." His voice had that unmistakable Australian twang.

"Don't kid the hell with us," Darren screamed as loudly as his weakened throat allowed.

"Are we in Australia?" Liang asked.

"Sorry, I really can't say anything. My hands are tied."

"Please, tell us something," Ojoré pleaded. "Anything, please."

The man in the white coat darted toward the stairs to avoid more questions, held the doorknob, and paused. He stared at the knob for a few seconds as if pondering whether to speak. At last, he turned around. "Mr. Odingá, Mr. Heikkinen, Mr. Li, Mr. Swanson, Mr. García." He looked into each one's eyes as he addressed them. "I'm sorry, but the only thing I can tell you right now is that—"

"Is that what?" Ojoré asked, not waiting for him to finish.

The man swallowed, looked at them, and suddenly looked away. He stared at the floor as he spoke. "All of you have been taken hostage,"—he stumbled on his words—"and from what I've been through here, I can tell only this—you will be here for a long, long time."

CHAPTER

Connecting Dots

The man in the white coat closed the door behind him. Two metal ceiling fans made a rhythmic clunking sound as they recirculated the damp air through the massive basement. The boarded windows at the top of stony walls allowed neither light nor freshness inside. The faint melody that came through them earlier was gone, too. The sharp, antiseptic odor of the spirit that the man rubbed onto their limbs replaced the smell of dirt and dust from the stone-tiled floor.

The five hostages—Aarno, Darren, Ojoré, Liang, and Diego—stared at it for a long minute, dumbfounded.

Panic struck the room like a bullwhip.

"Ungh!" Darren labored all the strength he could muster, trying to move. The drugs repressed his sizable biceps, beefy thighs, and girthy calves, which he often relied on for strength and attitude. The redness in his bulging eyes showed his rage. "Let me go, you piece of shit, let me go." He bellowed toward the ceiling. "I swear—I swear you'll regret this when I get out of these shackles."

The other four hostages tried to get up, but the only thing that moved was the muscles on their faces.

"Help!" Ojoré shouted. His prominent brown lips quivered as words left his mouth. His dark skin shone from the sweat that rolled down his forehead from his black curly hair. "Please help us! Please let us go."

"Oh meu deus. Oh meu deus, taken hostage? Why?" Diego screamed. Despite the hospital gown and the screams coming out of his mouth, Diego looked handsome. His perfect, white teeth shined as his chiseled jawline, and cheekbones showed the struggle on his face. "What do we do now? What do we do?"

"Who are you people?" Liang shouted. The veins on his slender neck protruded through his fair, smooth skin. His dark brown, silky hair fell here and there when he shook his head. "What are you going to do to us?"

Their voices circled the basement like winds from a ceiling fan. But none were answered. They kept staring at each other in search of answers.

Aarno was the only one who composed himself from the shock. *We have to think ahead.* He waited for the commotion to pass, for others to finish expressing their fright. "Friends, calm down. We are not going to gain anything if we panic." He waited for a few seconds. "The real question is what they want from us."

"I don't understand," Liang said. "Who are they? And why would they take us hostage?"

"Money, I'd say," Ojoré replied. "Most abductions are for money."

Aarno nodded. "I agree, but why five people at the same time? And from so many different countries."

"I'm the son of an ordinary farmer," Darren added. "We ain't no millionaires."

"I'm no *rico* either," Diego said. "It cannot be money. If they are after money, they wouldn't have kidnapped me."

"Well, count me with you and Darren, Diego," Liang added.

Aarno kept quiet. The eyelids on his sky-blue eyes did not move as he concentrated hard on the question. "Then what can it be?" he said.

"Revenge?" Diego suggested.

"But how? We don't even know each other. I don't recall crossing paths with you folks anywhere. How could it be revenge? We have nothing in common. Besides, I never wronged anyone for them to seek revenge."

"The more I think about it, the more I wonder..." Liang said. "Is there something that connects us? Something that makes us valuable to them?"

"Or something that threatens them," Darren added.

"We don't know who they are," Ojoré said. "How do we find the reason? And as Aarno said, we don't know each other. What can possibly be common between us? We are not from the same parts of the world, let alone the same country."

Silence seized the room like a fire takes wood. It felt as if the light from the flickering tube lights had dimmed some more, and the color of stone on the walls, pillars, and arches appeared darker than before.

"Maybe if we know more about each other, we can connect the dots," Liang suggested. "Find a common thread that links us all."

"That's a good start," Aarno concurred. "We should talk about our backgrounds, our lives."

"I agree," Diego chimed in. "Who wants to go first?"

No answer.

"Liang, as it was your idea, why don't you go first?" Aarno asked.

Liang waited for a few seconds. "I'm not sure where to begin, what to tell."

"Do you remember how you were abducted? What were you doing that day? Anything?"

"I remember, but only faintly. Maybe I'll remember more as I tell."

"Great, let's hear it."

Liang closed his eyes and sighed. After a long pause, he began his story.

CHAPTER 3

Liang Li

Hostage 1
Shanghai, China

Liang Li and his companion Sun stood waiting on the sidewalk next to the Chinese-style archway of the Yuyuan market on Renmin Road. Liang sported dark blue jeans, a black t-shirt, and a brown jacket. A grey backpack hung behind his shoulders. Sun looked stunning in her white thigh-high dress, which hugged tightly to her slender hourglass figure, displaying a generous amount of cleavage. She held a sky-blue denim jacket in her right arm. Her waist-high hair was silky black, her skin smooth as a baby's, and her pink lips soft like rose petals.

The weather was delightful: no clouds, good sunlight, and no rain. It was a haze-free day with clear skies.

"How about these guys?" Sun nudged her head toward a group.

"No, we need someone who is visiting for the first time, someone alone." Liang gazed ahead. "Never try this con on a group."

"How about this one?" Sun pointed her eyes toward another tourist.

"Good. Foreigners are easy. But look closely, this is not his first visit."

"How do you know?"

"Experience and intuition." Liang smirked. "Look at his body language; he's not looking at a map or phone, not asking for directions, not taking pictures. "

Sun stared at the guy.

"Does he look nervous, confused? Is he over-courteous to everyone on the street?"

"No, he looks confident."

"Exactly. He seems like someone who knows his way around the city."

"Suǒyǐ, bù qù." Sun nodded.

They surveyed the crowd around them.

The streets around the Yuyuan Garden were swarmed with shoppers and tourists. Everyone who visited Shanghai, whether for business or pleasure, paid a visit to the pristine garden located in the heart of Shanghai's old city neighborhood. This was especially true of foreigners.

The 16th-century garden housed many ancient cultural relics—wooden furniture, Buddha paintings, wood-carved dragons, stone-carved lions, scarlet tassel decorations, jade sculptures, and ginkgo trees. Small ponds inside its walls were packed with orange-colored koi. Visitors watched as the tangerine fish rushed toward the latest piece of crumb touching the water's surface.

Surrounding the garden was the Yuyuan bazaar. The aroma of local cuisine rode the air. There were dumplings, steamed buns, meats on sticks, ice cream, and countless other snacks.

"Try this." Liang bought two sticks of roasted chicken, handed one to Sun. Sounds of bargaining between vendors and shoppers, sellers advertising their products, and music from street performers surrounded them.

"Hěn hào chī, delicious." Sun ate from the stick. She gazed at a streetside vendor showing off an attachment made of small wheels, which, after fastening to shoes, transformed them into roller skates. "That's awesome."

"Shh, concentrate."

"Why are we here? We're unable to find anyone." She dumped the meatless stick in the nearby trash can. "There are tourists inside; let's go in."

"Patience, Sun. It becomes more difficult and obvious inside. Trust me. This is the best spot. You'll find out why soon."

After about ten minutes, a big bus halted on the opposite side of the road. It was the dedicated Yuyuan Garden stop on the red route of this open-top, hop-on-hop-off bus that ferried tourists all around town. After offloading, the bus left. Visitors waited at the traffic light to cross the road toward the archway at the entrance of the bazaar.

"Look over there," Liang whispered. "One of them is our catch."

He studied the approaching lot one by one. There was a family of four, then a group of friends, a couple, and a single man. Liang eyed the last. Short and beefy, he wore shorts, a half-sleeve shirt, a hat, and sneakers. A DSLR camera hung from his neck through a broad belt with a bold Nikon written over it. An expensive-looking pair of sunglasses shaded his eyes.

"That's our guy, the one by himself." Liang tilted his head gently in that direction. "Do you remember what to do?"

"Shì." Sun nodded.

"Good. Let's get started."

The man crossed the street, halted, and began taking pictures of the archway. After a few clicks, he returned the cap to the lens and walked again.

"Excuse me, sir. Would you take a picture of us together?" Liang extended his phone.

"Absolutely." The man picked up the phone and snapped a few pictures of Liang and Sun while they posed. Drops of sweat slid from his broad forehead onto his chubby cheeks and over to his double-chinned neck as he moved and extended his arms to capture the best frame.

"See if they look good," he said, returning the phone.

"Yes, they're excellent. Xièxiè."

"You are welcome."

"I'm Liang, and this is my friend Sun. We're visiting Shanghai from Beijing. What's your name?"

"Doug."

"Where are you from, Mr. Doug?"

"Umm, St. Louis, USA."

"Oh, from America. Welcome to China. Is this your first time?"

"Yes, arrived just yesterday." Doug smiled an awkward smile.

"Sun and my first time in Shanghai too."

Sun grinned at Doug. He smiled back.

"If you are going to the Yuyuan Garden, you'd better wait," Liang said. "It's very crowded right now. We were just in there; it took us about one hour at the ticket counter. I suggest you wait for some time till there are fewer people."

"It's all right. I've nothing else to do. My bus has left." Doug extended his arm toward the bus stop. "It won't be back for thirty minutes, so I'll wait in line."

"Well, we are going to a tea performance. It's close to here. Why don't you join us?" Liang said with a wide smile.

"What's a tea performance?" Doug narrowed his eyes curiously.

"It's where they let you taste all the different traditional Chinese teas."

Doug considered for a few seconds. "Well, I don't want to intrude on your time together. It's all right. I will go by myself to the garden."

"No, no, you wouldn't be intruding. It's not every day we get to make friends with foreigners. Please join us, I insist," Liang said and waited eagerly for Doug to take the bait.

"I don't know, man." Doug hesitated.

"Please, Doug, I insist as well." Sun tilted her head a little and smiled her widest smile.

"If you insist." There was a hint of blush on Doug's pink cheeks. "Where's the tea performance?"

Liang pulled his phone out and pretended to look it up on the map. "It's close from here. Straight on this street and then a left."

The three of them walked through the archway to the sidewalk and continued on the street toward the Yuyuan bazaar.

The bazaar and its streets were full of traditional Chinese architecture buildings - wooden walls painted in blackish red, glazed clay tiled roofs with pointy edges curved toward the sky. The buildings sparkled spectacularly at night, with lights running along the edges of roofs and walls.

Countless souvenir shops were harbored inside. Laughing Buddha statues, beautifully carved wooden dragons, Chinese opera characters, and other objects peeped out from their glass exhibits. Also displayed were Chinese jewelry, silk dresses, and teapots so delicate they seemed they would break with the slightest touch of a finger. Rows of scarlet lanterns with golden laces hung from ropes running along the streets, adding a festive ambiance to the entire area.

"To be honest, I'm overwhelmed. Trying to navigate through a new town and unable to communicate in Mandarin is intimidating." Doug jumped over a puddle of water. "Having a native Mandarin speaker like you guys showing me around is a godsend. Thank you."

"It's our honor." Liang smiled. "So, what do you do in America?"

"I'm in sales, here on business," Doug said. He removed a handkerchief from his pocket.

"We are students at Beijing University."

"Oh, good. What do you study?" Doug wiped the sweat on his face.

"I'm studying English, and she is studying Physics." Liang paused to step over another puddle of water. "That's why I can speak English."

"Yeah, your English is excellent."

The street was packed. The three of them dodged the passersby coming up to them from everywhere.

"Thank you. Her English is not so good, so she's too shy to talk to you."

"That's all right. I don't speak Mandarin either." Doug smiled at Sun. Sun's soft lips broke into a cherubic smile that displayed her perfect teeth.

After a long walk, the three entered a small shop. The panels of the saloon door swung several times around their hinges behind them before closing. There was a reception desk opposite it, beside which was a narrow hallway. On either side of the hallway were small booths. The saloon door, reception desk, booths, and other furniture were made from oak and stained a deep maroon. The hostess behind the reception desk had short black hair, a round face, and a small nose. Her petite frame was covered with a scarlet Qipao gown. She bowed, led them inside a private booth through a sliding door, and asked them to take the bench on the opposite side behind a table. They crammed into the small bench, with Liang sitting in the middle. On the tabletop, a black metal teapot sat over a small gas stove through which vapors puffed out. Several glass jars holding various types of teas lined the rack shelves on the booth's left side.

As they assumed their seats behind a wooden table, Sun asked questions through Liang's translations about life in America and reciprocated with Chinese customs. Almost all things translated by Liang, as coming from Sun, were compliments.

A few minutes later, a tea pourer entered the chamber and slid the door behind him. He wore an off-white cotton tunic and trousers with a round Tang cap that matched his tunic. A thin tapering mustache occupied the center of his oval face. Wearing a blank expression, he spoke in Mandarin.

"He is talking about the history of tea in China," Liang translated.

The tea pourer began his performance by placing a frog statue in the front and pouring hot water over it.

"That's supposed to be the tea god. We must thank him by offering him the first tea before we start. It brings good health."

Doug stole a glance at Sun. She grinned, batting her eyelashes as if she were interested.

The tea pourer pulled out six different types of clear jars from the rack and placed them on the table. Each contained a different kind of tea. He put four small China cups in front of them, opened the first jar, scooped some tea, and added it to the teapot. The delicate teacups resembled something similar to shot glasses in size but had detailed artwork framing their sides. He poured hot water over it and let it brew. After a few minutes, he poured the tea into the cups and handed them to the three. Liang showed Doug the correct way of holding the cups.

"After you, my friend. Ganbei!"

Doug gulped. It was refreshing and relaxing. The tea pourer described the benefits of this tea, and Liang translated them for Doug. One after another, they tasted all the different kinds of teas on the table.

"Nǐ xiǎng mǎi nǎ zhǒng chá?" the tea pourer asked with lazy eyes.

"He is asking whether we'd like to buy any tea," Liang told Doug.

"I'll go with Jasmine," Doug replied. He closed his eyes to take in the crisp aromas of brewing teas.

"Green for us," Liang said, looking at Sun.

The tea pourer went inside and brought two sealed packets. Sun spoke to him in Mandarin. He went inside again and brought another one. Sun handed the packet to Liang.

Liang placed the packet in front of Doug. "She wants to gift you this tea."

"Are you sure?" Doug asked Sun.

She nodded. Doug smiled and bowed.

"Shall we ask for the bill?" Liang asked

"Sure." Doug nodded.

The tea pourer left to fetch the check. Liang, Sun, and Doug meanwhile exchanged emails and phone numbers. The tea pourer returned and presented them with the bill. Liang looked at it casually, as if it were nothing, and passed it on to Doug.

"It's a custom not to let the lady pay. Is it all right if we both split it?"

Doug was still looking at the number. It was 2500 RMB.

"Umm, about three hundred and fifty dollars. Wow! That's quite expensive." The smile on Doug's face vanished while the lines on his broad forehead became prominent as he struggled to come to terms with the amount.

"Yes, but that's what it costs. Besides, you are taking tea with you as well."

Sun looked and smiled at Doug uninterrupted. Dough glanced at Sun, then handed his credit card, still unable to digest the number. Liang paid in cash.

After settling the tab, the three left.

"Let's take you to the ticket counter," Liang said as he pocketed his receipt.

Doug followed the two. The crowd increased on the streets of the bazaar as they treaded past the oncoming people.

It took them about fifteen minutes to reach the ticket counter of the Yuyuan Garden. There was no line at all. "See, I told you to wait. Now, there is no line," Liang said with a smile.

Doug did not complain about the cost of the tea performance again, but he did not smile either.

"Sorry, but we can't accompany you inside; we already visited in the morning," Liang said. "Enjoy the garden."

He and Sun waved, turned around, and walked in the opposite direction. In seconds, they disappeared into the crowd, leaving Doug behind them, staring in confusion.

Rushing through the same street they had taken before from the tea shop and passing by the same shops they glanced at on their way, Liang and Sun returned to the tea shop.

"And that's how it's done." Liang counted their share of cash from the owner as they stood in the back alley next to the rear door of the tea shop.

"But I played my part well, too. Remember, he was into me. That's why he paid the money."

"Ya, ya, whatever, but it was my plan." He smiled. "Now tell me, how do you want to spend it?"

"I always wanted to go on that cruise by the river. I have seen people go there but have never been on one myself." Sun put on the denim jacket she'd carried in her arm, pulled out a scrunchy, and tied her hair. She held Liang by his arm. There was excitement in her voice. She stared at the clear, blue sky as she spoke. "I want to enjoy tonight."

"My lady, tonight, all your desires will be fulfilled."

They both kissed.

☙❧

Dusk lights on the futuristic Shanghai skyline appeared like jewelry on a bride.

The metal, glass, and concrete jungle dazzled with reflections of copper and gold. As the Sun dipped, city lights popped to life. Sun and Liang stood in line to board the cruise, which sailed across the Huangpu River, offering prodigious views of the riverfront. With its aluminum railings and blue-white lights, the cruise terminal looked marvelous.

It was packed. Some came here to wine and dine in the backdrop of the magnificent ambiance, while others wanted to sail for the fresh breeze.

Sun and Liang dressed fashionably. Liang wore a black tuxedo that he had stolen by conning a man from a dry cleaner. Sun wore a beautiful shiny, black, one-piece satin dress which was stolen in a similar manner.

"Top deck, fast; let's take the best spot before it's gone," Liang whispered into Sun's right ear.

In one minute, they reached the top deck. Sun stared at the artificial turf on the deck's floor and multicolored lights that ran all across the taffrail in amazement. "Wow," she whispered, "it's wonderful."

"Wait here." Liang went inside. Minutes later, he returned with two beers. "Ganbei!" He raised his glass. They emptied their drinks.

"Today's count at the tea shop was ten, the most in months." Liang grinned. "I think the tea shop is way better than the traditional medicine shop. It is harder to con tourists by getting them to buy fake herbs. Glad we're not doing that anymore." He rested his back on the taffrail. "Tonight, we have a lot of money to spend."

The boat sailed onto the calm waters of the Huangpu River. The night sky was clear with twinkling stars.

Sun closed her eyes and untied her hair. Liang turned around, rested his elbows on the taffrails, and sipped from his glass. The gentle breeze caressed his face, taking the day's tiredness with it. The beer and the vibes set the mood. The buildings along Huangpu's banks lit up one by one, the water majestic with reflections.

Liang kept buying more beers one after the other.

After half an hour, the cruise made a U-turn for the terminal. Halfway down the route, the captain announced, "Ladies and gentlemen, in about one minute, the Oriental Pearl Tower lights will be illuminated. So be ready with your cameras."

Liang and Sun pulled out their phones, ready for the pictures.

The tower dazzled from bottom to top. Flashing colors with fancy patterns filled the night sky, and it appeared as if the entire Shanghai skyline had been transformed into one gigantic discothèque, with music on the cruise ship complementing the display.

"It's amazing, I have never seen anything like this," Sun said. "Oh, Liang, I love you so much."

"Anything for my love." They kissed.

The light show played for several minutes.

"I hope it never ends," Sun said as the cruise retreated toward the terminal.

"Don't worry, the night is still young."

Liang and Sun disembarked the ship with many pictures and a lot many beers in their bellies.

"Where are we going next?" Sun asked as she held Liang's arm on their way toward the taxi stand.

Liang kissed Sun again. "Okay, beautiful, let me show you the time of your life."

They took a cab to a five-star hotel on the Bund, one of the city's most popular areas. As it halted, a neatly dressed doorman opened the cab door. "Welcome," he greeted.

Sun scanned the glass building along its length. Liang read the expressions on her face. "Don't worry, we won't spend our hard-earned cash on this. I have a way," he said.

Receiving his tip, the doorman rushed to open the lobby door. "Thank you," he said.

Liang nodded a privileged nod. They entered the lobby. It was tall, like an atrium, with huge, circular pillars and a shiny, beige granite floor. Beautiful, golden chandeliers hung from the ceiling with warm yellow lights.

Liang turned toward Sun and sat her on a plush upholstered chair near a corner. "Wait here, I'll be back in a second."

"But—" Sun moved uncomfortably on the edge of the chair.

"Trust me, I've been here before." Liang turned to face the lobby. "Where was the housekeeping staffroom?" He scanned the area. "There."

Slow and stealthy, he walked toward the housekeeping staffroom. Making sure nobody was watching, he slid inside and waited. A lady walked in, hung her coat, and went to the toilet. He quickly went to the coat, searched the pockets, and found the master key. Score! He looked at the housekeeping schedule for rooms that requested evening service. A few minutes later, he returned to the lobby and dialed the first number on the list from the courtesy phone. No one answered. He dialed the same room a second time, but again, there was no reply. Liang didn't believe his luck. He returned to Sun; they both took the elevator to the twenty-second floor.

"What are we doing?" Sun asked, jumping on her toes in excitement.

"Wait and watch." Liang smiled

The elevator door opened. Plaques on the opposite wall, printed with room numbers and directions, greeted them. Wine-red carpet with designs of flowers covered the hallway floor, while a line of warm yellow lights fixed every few feet on the sidewalls followed them along the way. Liang found the room, swiped the master key, and slowly opened the door.

"Score!" Liang screamed in excitement.

He held the door open for Sun and winked as she looked into his eyes. The door closed behind them. As they entered the room from the entryway, floor-to-ceiling windows greeted them, presenting magnificent views of the Huangpu and the skyline along its banks. A gentle fragrance with notes of orange, jasmine, and white tea hit their senses. The room twinkled with the rhythmic beating of lights from the Oriental Pearl Tower through the spotless glass.

Sun jumped on the bed. The linen was clean and crisp.

"Oh my God, it- it's—" The lights, the décor, and the alcohol over-whelmed Sun. Liang jumped on her. "Mmm," she moaned. Their hands clasped each other's; their bodies intertwined. Their lovemaking roared like there was no tomorrow.

Just when they were about to climax, *click*! The doorknob turned, and a man walked inside, standing at the edge of the entryway. The light show from the tower outside paused, leaving the room in darkness.

Liang and Sun covered themselves with the bedsheet. They could not see his face.

The man pulled out a gun, screwed something on its tip. *Swoop, swoop, swoop* came the sound of projectiles. The needles at the tips of them pierced Liang and Sun on the shoulder and chest.

"You think you're so smart?" he said. "You thought you conned me, huh?"

The man stepped forward, and the shadows of the room shifted to reveal Doug's face with a grin spread across it. "Well, as it turns out, the reality is just the opposite, Mr. Li."

"I've tailed you since morning. I had to ensure it was you, so I played along in your con." Doug leaned forward. "Do you think you got the house-keeping key downstairs by luck?" He approached Liang's left ear. "I am the predator, Mr. Li, not the prey," he whispered. And I came to China just to hunt you."

In the next second, the tranquilizer kicked in, and Liang passed out onto the bed.

A few weeks later, he woke up in a basement, tied to a bed next to four foreigners, unable to move.

CHAPTER

4

Lucas Sánchez

Boston, Massachusetts, USA
Two years before the abduction of the five hostages

D r. Lucas Sánchez placed the keys of his Toyota Prius into a bowl atop a side table by the door. At five feet five inches, he was middle-aged with an average build, a peculiarly elongated nose, brown hair, and gray eyes. Sánchez held a Ph.D. and worked in the Computational and Systems Biology department at M.I.T. in Boston. He'd taught there for many years and conducted considerable research for the university.

Sanchez closed the door behind him, sat on the bench in the entry foyer, and placed his laptop bag on the side.

"Lucas, honey, Mark called again today." Martha, his wife, inserted her hand inside a well-cushioned oven glove. "He was very convincing. Why don't you at least go and visit the place?"

Dr. Mark Blanchard was Sanchez's good friend and ex-colleague. Together, they authored many academic papers that were published in world-renowned scientific journals. Their collaboration on research in genetics, machine learning, and data warehousing worked perfectly. This, however, lasted only until Dr. Blanchard accepted a new job in Las Vegas at a new research lab called the National Medical Research Laboratory.

"Martha, we talked about this. I don't want to move from Boston; I love my job; all our extended family and friends are here."

"Well, regarding that," Martha paused to retrieve the apple pie from the oven. "David called this morning; his next assignment is at the Nellis Air Force Base near Las Vegas." She placed it on the kitchen counter and examined the crust. "He said his project could go on for several years."

"Hmm," came the reply. *Finally, after so many years, my son has an assignment that's inside the country.*

"And—"

"And?" Sanchez raised his eyebrows.

"Michelle's application got accepted."

"That's wonderful news." Sanchez stopped midway from untying his dress shoes. *I have seen my daughter's scores.* He shook his head.

"Which school?" he asked.

"University of Nevada in Las Vegas," she said. "The admission comes with a handsome scholarship, too."

"What? I didn't know she applied there," he said.

Something doesn't add up. Michelle got into UNLV with those scores? Sanchez wondered as he removed his shoes and socks. He walked past the staircase to the second floor and entered the kitchen.

The kitchen had a semi-open layout with an L-shaped counter with light-brown granite, which housed a gas stove, an oven, and a ceramic sink. There were windows above the kitchen sink and behind the breakfast table on the other side. They kept the room well illuminated with natural light and allowed fresh air to come in on cooler days. An island in the middle was where Sanchez often tasted Martha's delicious cooking.

"This cannot be a coincidence; it has to be Mark. I'm sure this is his doing."

"You make it sound like it's a bad thing. Even if he did pull some strings, what's the harm? He just wants you by his side; he trusts you." Martha finished cutting the pie into pieces, lifted a piece from the pan, and placed it on a floral porcelain plate. "Why don't you reconsider it with an open mind? You have three good reasons to move now: David, Michelle, and Mark—your best friend." She nudged the plate toward him. "The kids will be there at least for four years. Who knows, maybe they'll stay longer. I'd love to be close to them."

As Sanchez pulled a stool from underneath the island, Martha slid open a drawer, fetched a fork, and handed it to Sánchez with a wide smile.

He sat down, cut a bite with the fork. As he relished the warm, sweet goodness of her baking, he realized that the situation was too perfect to ignore. They both wanted to be closer to the kids.

"I'll take it. Let's move to Vegas."

☙⟡❧

After two months of back and forth between Boston and Las Vegas, Sanchez and Martha settled into their suburban house. It took them two more months to feel at home in the new city, but eventually, they did. The house was two-storied with a beige stucco finish and brown Spanish terracotta tiled roof. A mesquite tree, surrounded by small cacti, stood in the front yard, surrounded by red lava gravel. The entry porch had a small metal bench beside which were pots of pink roses.

"The institute is amazing, the work is extraordinary, I have no limits on funding for my research, and I have full autonomy." Sánchez beamed as he entered the living room from the entryway. It had an open layout with the kitchen, dining, and living area all seamlessly integrated.

He had returned from his first day at the NMRL.

The NMRL was funded by the U.S. Government from the revenue collected by implementing a new tax on the casinos. Someone in the higher echelons of the capital wanted this project to go through without hurdles, and so it did. The Nevada government and the American Gaming Association publicized it in the media as a step to convert some of the "sin" in Sin City to goodwill.

"Didn't I tell you this was a good decision?" Martha replied from across the kitchen island, wearing a lime green apron.

"Thank you, my love." He beamed at her from the other side, removing his navy-blue coat jacket, and unbuttoning his shirt cuffs.

"I'm happy too, honey; having the kids home on weekends is so good."

He went into the kitchen, took her in his arms. They kissed.

Sanchez's next several months went repainting the bedrooms, redoing the backyard, hosting house parties for neighbors and collogues, and exploring the nearby national parks with his kids. Before he knew it, it had been almost a year for them in Las Vegas.

One morning, the alarm clock squawked as usual with all its vigor. Sanchez woke, and so did Martha. He went to the shower, and she to the kitchen.

"Honey, breakfast is ready," she shouted after several minutes.

Sanchez dried himself, covered himself in bath robes, and went into the kitchen. His usual three eggs, sunny side up, bacon, and potatoes were ready on the kitchen table, along with a glass of freshly squeezed orange juice. "I'm blessed to have you." He kissed her on the cheek as he sat down in a chair. She blushed.

After breakfast, he got ready for work while Martha packed him a sandwich for lunch. They kissed on the front porch again before he left in his silver Toyota Prius. NMRL was on the outskirts of the city. Therefore, Sanchez did not encounter any traffic on the way, and in about twenty minutes, he parked his car in the garage and swiped his access card on the reader at the entrance of the building.

Good morning, Dr. Sánchez," Steve, the security guard, greeted with a wide smile as he entered.

The reception area behind Steve was wide and tall with chandeliers hanging from the top, sitting areas made of small sofas, pots of indoor plants here and there, pictures of Nobel laureates on each wall, and a big reception desk in the center. However, the hall and the entire building, for that matter, were windowless.

"Good morning, Steve." Sanchez shook his hand with a smile. "How're you?"

"I'm good, sir. How about yourself?"

"It's been quite busy lately."

"You don't have to tell me. For the last two months, you've been the last one I see when I make my evening rounds."

"Well, today won't be any different either." Sanchez patted Steve on the shoulder. "See you in the evening."

"Sure, sir, have a blessed day."

"You too, Steve."

Sanchez went past the reception desk and took the first of the five long hallways. After five minutes of walking past closed doors on either side and some more pictures of scientists in between, he reached his door. Sanchez scanned the badge and entered. The lab was sophisticated, with lots of computers, servers stacked inside racks, displays, and switches. It looked more like a computer data center than a medical research lab. Sanchez's work was developing AI algorithms to detect patterns in genes from vast quantities of data.

Sanchez went through his routines of checking the equipment, ensuring preventive maintenance procedures were complete, safety procedures were followed, and, most importantly, all the data was backed up properly the previous night. Later, he moved to check the models his team had worked on the previous week, testing and re-testing every scenario, and before he knew it, it was late. He was the only scientist still at the NMRL.

Sanchez had wrapped up his work and was about to leave when the monitors, desks, and chairs before him blurred. The screens on the walls and the server racks around him swirled as if he were stuck in a carousel.

Sanchez blinked his eyes and shook his head to get out of it. But it continued. He could feel his chest rise and fall fast as his breathing became heavy.

With his eyes closed most of the time, feeling his way by touching here and there, he hurried outside to get some air. He realized he could not run; he could only limp.

When he exited the building, he took a deep breath and opened his eyes. Giant bubble-like objects appeared and floated around him. Their boundaries shone red, orange, and black, like holes burned in a stretched cloth when touched by a lit incense stick.

I need to call 911.

His dizziness worsened. He searched his pockets for the phone. *Shit, it must be in the lab.* He rushed inside, opened the lab door, and collapsed.

Pain soared through his head as it rammed the hard floor.

All Sánchez could see was dazzling light; all he could feel was a sense of speed. In a few minutes, his eyes gave in, taking him into darkness.

CHAPTER
4

Continued-Part 1

Las Vegas, Nevada, USA

The sun had set into the arid Nevada desert on a hot summer evening, but the sky was still trying to hold on to the remnants of the sun's rays. Their dance spewed magical shades of red, yellow, orange, and purple onto the distant horizon.

After sweating it out for almost an hour on the treadmill in his basement gymnasium, Dr. Mark Blanchard doused himself in a cold shower and decided to relax with a beer on the patio of his expensive suburban house. It was a quiet neighborhood. The house had five bedrooms, a swimming pool, a private gym, a bar, and a huge backyard. The terrain was a little hilly, but the design of Mark's house perfectly hugged its contours. In fact, this elevation offered the property magnificent views of the distant Las Vegas Strip.

Mark opened the refrigerator, pulled out an ice-cold pint of Corona, cut a piece of fresh lime on his spotless marble kitchen counter, and placed it into the bottle. With gentle pressure, he pushed the piece against the resisting orifice of the bottle. It went straight into the cold one, like a diver plunging into a swimming pool and coming back up with all the fizz, bubbles, and freshness.

Mark slid open the kitchen door that led onto the patio deck. He perched in his armchair, gazing at the distantly lit skyline of dazzling casino buildings. On one side, a bright beam of white light shot upward from the apex of the Luxor pyramid, while on the other side, the stratosphere tower's spire changed colors in a quick, rhythmic fashion. Between these two, one could distinguish the faint silhouettes of the Eiffel Tower at Paris, Paris, and the Manhattan skyline at New York, New York.

As Mark returned inside to fetch another pale lager, the phone rang. He quickly followed the sound, picked it up. "This is Mark."

"Th—th—this is Steve, Dr. Blanchard." Steve's voice sounded shaky.

"Hello, Steve, how are you, my man?"

"Th—th—there was an accident, Dr. Blanchard. Dr—Dr. Sánchez is lying on the floor."

"What? What happened?" The calm on Mark's face vanished.

"I don't know, Dr. Blanchard. I just got here, found him like this."

"Is there blood? Is he breathing?" There was tension in Mark's voice.

"No, no, there's no blood, and yes, he is breathing, but his belongings are all over the floor."

Mark sighed. A long pause followed. Composing himself, Mark deliberated on what to do next.

"Dr. Blanchard, you still there?"

"Yes, yes, I am here. All right, here is what I want you to do, Steve. Move Dr. Sánchez from his lab into the lobby, and only then call 911. There is a lot of classified information in that lab. Nobody can know the lab exists. Understood?"

"Yes, sir."

"I'll break the news to Martha." Blanchard hung up the phone.

He immediately dialed Mrs. Sánchez.

"Hello?" she answered.

"Martha, this is Mark."

"Hey, Mark. Lucas is not home yet. I thought you were with Lucas at work."

"I had a meeting downtown this afternoon. So, left early today."

"And you're making my husband work late instead." She chuckled.

"Listen," Mark said in a severe tone, "I have some bad news. I just received a call. Lucas met with an accident; he's in the hospital."

"What? How?" Martha's voice trembled. "Is he alright?"

"I don't know yet." He swallowed; his voice subdued with guilt. "They took him to the Desert Springs Hospital. I'm driving there right now; I will pick you up on the way."

It took Mark thirty minutes to reach Sánchez's house. He saw Martha waiting on the driveway, impatiently, her face covered with sweat. She rushed toward his SUV, opened the door, and sat in the front passenger seat.

"What happened to Lucas?" she asked, pulling out a Kleenex from the box on the dashboard.

"We're still investigating. But right now, let's focus on Lucas. Here, have some water." Mark handed her a bottle.

The rest of the ride went in silence. They arrived at the hospital forty minutes later.

Mark followed Martha through the parking lot as she rushed toward the emergency room entrance. The automatic sliding doors opened into the reception, where patients waited in rows of chairs. They went straight to the reception desk, where an old woman stared at them. A plastic name tag on her scrub read Kimberly.

"Kimberly, I am Mark Blanchard. We are here for Lucas Sánchez," Mark spoke before Martha. "I talked to Dr. Aguilar earlier over the phone."

"Yes, he's waiting for you. This way, please."

Kimberly led them through a series of doors and hallways that were brightly lit with white lights and smelled of bleach. Mark saw Martha grab her purse tightly as she walked.

In a few minutes, they entered the CT scan room.

"Dr. Aguilar? Mark Blanchard. This is Martha, Dr. Sánchez's wife."

"Dr. Blanchard, yes, please come in." Dr Aguilar turned away from the monitors before him to face them. The hair on his head was grey. A pair of glasses sat on his nose, and a stethoscope hung around his neck over a white coat engraved with his name.

Across the glass window on his right, Sanchez lay on the examination table of an enormous, donut-shaped scanner. Martha placed her right hand on the glass, staring at him, tears rolling down her cheeks.

"What happened to my husband? Is he going to be alright?"

"We're still running some tests. Initial results do not reveal anything we expected," Dr. Aguilar replied. "It doesn't seem anything cardiovascular, no stroke, no heart attack. No other obvious things."

"Well, that's good news, isn't it?" She wiped her tears with a facial tissue and turned to face the doctor.

"I can't be sure yet," Dr. Aguilar replied with a straight face.

"What's wrong, Doctor?" Martha's face showed her anxiety.

"I know this is hard, Mrs. Sánchez," Dr. Aguilar said sympathetically. "The patient is in a coma."

"But why?" Martha was confused. "How?"

Dr. Aguilar stepped forward. "At this point, we don't have an answer. We're trying our best to find out just that. I have requested some of the best specialists from all over the country to fly down to Vegas to work on this case. But, I'm—I'm..."

"What is it, Doctor? Tell me straight." More tears rolled down Martha's cheeks.

"I'm afraid you have to be prepared for the possibility that it might take a very long time for your husband to come out of the coma," he paused. "If he does at all."

Mark came next to Martha and put an arm around her. He rubbed her shoulders, trying to calm her down.

"Doctor, there must be something you can do, please," Mark said, his hands still trying to pacify Martha.

"I'm sorry, but right now, all we can do is pray and hope for the best."

ᝯᝍ

Six months went by as slowly as the clouds on a windless day.

One morning, on his way to work, Mark stopped by the Desert Spring Hospital to check on Sanchez. As he entered Sanchez's room, the fresh, fragrant lilies in the vase on the side table told him that Martha had come before him. He sat in the armchair next to the bed, talked to Sanchez for a few minutes, though he knew that Sanchez probably couldn't hear what he said, and left the room. As his SUV left the parking lot, he called Martha.

"Martha, this is Mark. How are you? I went to the hospital this morning."

"Hey, Mark, I am good. Looks like I missed you by a few minutes. I was there, too."

"Yes, I saw the lilies. Hey, listen, I was thinking of stopping by after work to catch up with you."

"Yes, please come. I will make something good for dinner."

"Awesome."

Mark finished his work early that evening and reached the Sánchez residence around six o'clock. When Martha opened the door for him, an appetizing aroma of baking hit his nostrils.

"Wow, that smells amazing. Can't wait to taste it."

"It's pecan pie, Lucas's favorite." Martha smiled a sad smile.

Mark did not smile.

"Anyways, come in. Will you drink something?" she asked.

"Do you have any sparkling water?"

"Yes. Have a seat." Martha went to the kitchen, fetched a bottle, and returned to the living area. She paused. Sounds coming from the study got her attention.

"What was that?" Mark asked.

"Not sure."

Mark and she went inside to check and were flabbergasted by what they saw.

There he was, Lucas Sánchez, in a hospital gown, searching frantically for something in the drawers, the cabinets flung open haphazardly. He behaved as if he were possessed, as if on a mission.

Martha gazed with an open mouth, disbelief on her face as she watched her husband—conscious again. Mark's eyebrows narrowed in confusion.

Martha jumped with excitement. "Lucas!" she shouted.

Sanchez ignored. He was still searching.

Mark spoke next. "Lucas, my friend, can't tell how happy I am to see you."

No reply. Sanchez pulled out a drawer and turned it upside down. Its contents fell to the floor.

"When did you wake up? The hospital didn't call us." Mark took a step closer.

Sánchez emptied two more drawers.

"Lucas? Are you all right?" Mark asked. He turned toward Martha, who, too, looked confused.

"You know you were in a coma, don't you, Lucas? Mark asked

Still no reply. Sanchez moved his hands through the shelves above and pushed all the boxes and folders toward the floor, where they joined the contents of the drawer.

"Honey, what happened? I was there this morning, you were—you were—" Martha stumbled on her words.

Again, there was silence. Mark and Martha stood there for several minutes, staring at a man who looked like Lucas but behaved utterly differently.

"Lucas, honey, how did you get home? What are you searching for?"

Sánchez ignored the previous questions, and a frustrated voice answered the last, "Where is my access card for work? I have to go back RIGHT NOW!"

CHAPTER 4

Continued- Part 2

Somewhere

Right when Lucas Sánchez roused from a coma, at that exact instant, thousands of miles away, a figure arose.

The slumber had been long and deep. He was tall and slender. The white dreadlocks on his head resembled large dirty ropes drenched in mud. His body looked ancient, devoid of fat and muscle, his skin cracked and wrinkled as if frostbitten, his teeth broken in parts, and the nails on his bony fingers were long like twigs from an old branch.

Although he was human, he was known as the White Ghost in this area.

The figure cracked open his eyes slowly.

It took him a while to cast aside the dense spider webs in which his body was cocooned. Dirt painted his robes in various shades of black and grey. With a hand gripping the stone platform around him for support, he hoisted himself up. Each step was a struggle, his frame shaking with the effort. It seemed as if he would collapse at any moment.

With an intense effort, he limped to the entrance. Outside, lush green vines hung from the gnarled trunks and moss-covered branches of trees while ferns and bushes sprouted on the ground. Dense patches of slender bamboo stood tall here and there. Calls of nightingales and peacocks echoed from all directions. The air was fresh with the fragrance of flowers and grass.

The sun kissed his face for the first time in centuries. His lungs ballooned broad to take in the crisp air. He breathed like he had never breathed before.

His fingers touched his forehead where an ancient scar lay.

There was only one thing on his mind. The thing he suffered for, waited centuries for, roused for.

His time had come.

And so, it had begun AGAIN!

CHAPTER 5

Diego García

Hostage 2
São Paulo, Brazil

The stadium went berserk.

"That's foul!" a fan of the Corinthian soccer team screamed—a Corinthian faithful. "Give him a red card."

"Porra, é um cartão vermelho," the other added.

It was the Paulista Derby, a match between the Corinthians and Palmeiras football clubs. Theirs was the most famous and oldest rivalry in Brazilian soccer. Arena Corinthians, the venue of the spectacle, had marvelous landscaping, beautiful water fountains, and huge LED screens.

The Corinthians—the host team—wore white shirts with thin black stripes, black shorts, and black socks. The Palmeiras team donned white shirts with green shorts and green socks. Every time these two clubs played against each other, the atmosphere was electrifying. The century-old rivalry brought forth strong emotions from the fans. There were some good moments, some bad, and also a few horrific ones, sometimes going as far as shootings and murders. Despite this, the people of São Paulo eagerly awaited the encounter, which was the pinnacle of competition for them.

At the edge of the technical area of the Corinthians, behind the seating, Diego García was in conversation with Larissa, a beautiful cheerleader, running his fingers through her long blonde hair. She wore a fitted crop top of black and white with accents of gold featuring the Corinthians logo over a matching pleated miniskirt and black sneakers. She seemed smitten by his charms.

"Droga! I missed what happened." Diego turned his gaze from Larissa to the big screen above the Corinthians' goalpost.

The Arena was filled with amplified boos of the Corinthian fans. The Palmeiras fans, on the other hand, were not complaining. A Palmeiras defender had collided with a Corinthian striker about to score a goal.

The replay ran over the two big screens on either end.

"That's definitely a red card," Diego told Larissa. "What do you think?"

She nodded and smiled, looking into his eyes.

The referee approached the defender, who also acted like he was hurt. He dug into his pocket and pulled out a yellow card.

"Boooooo," echoed through the stadium.

"I can't believe it; that's absolutely nuts. How can he give a yellow!" Diego protested.

The referee spoke to the fallen striker and signaled to the physio.

The physio rushed toward the striker.

"That was a deliberate collision to knock our striker and prevent him from scoring," Diego said, still staring at the screen.

As another replay panned, the booing doubled. Displeasure from the faithfuls was visible in broken chairs, cussing, plastic bottles, and small fires. Fights broke out.

"Well, it's part of the game. Sometimes there are good decisions, sometimes bad ones." Larissa shrugged and pulled him close.

"Yes, but at this stage of the match, with both teams leveled at 3-3 and forty-five seconds left on the clock, it is ridiculous. It's the difference between winning and losing. Not only that, it was also an opportunity for us to surpass their all-time-wins score tied at one-thirty to one-thirty against our archrivals."

"Yes, baby. That's very unfortunate indeed." She stroked his hair.

The medical crew rushed onto the field near the injured striker and transferred him to the stretcher.

"Diego, Diego. Where the hell are you?" Coach Roberto shouted.

"Over there, by the cheerleaders." Roberto's assistant pointed his index finger before Diego could reply.

The coach stormed behind the seating area. "Oye, there's still a game going on here." Roberto pointed his right hand toward the field, his face intense with anger.

"Oh shit. *Desculpe treinador*. I was—somehow the girls just find me, you know?" Diego ran toward him.

"When it's time to work, it's time to work; I need a hundred percent, no matter if you are sitting in the technical area. Now, kick the Casanova in you out of the stadium. You are going in."

"What? But I have not played a single major league game. You're sending me at this stage?"

"You don't trust your abilities?"

"I do, *senhor*, but it's only forty-five seconds left on the clock."

"And that's why I need you. Pull your brains out from those bosoms and concentrate. You are taking the free kick."

"Are you out of your mind?"

"Do I look like I'm joking?"

"But, Roberto," the assistant coach interjected, "it's his first game. It's a pressurized situation in such an important game. This is a big risk."

"I believe he can do it," Roberto said. "Diego, don't you believe it?"

"I do, *senhor*."

"Good. Off you go then."

Minutes later, the medical crew was on their way, carrying the striker off the field. An assistant referee signaled his substitution with an electronic board a few feet from where they crossed the boundary.

Diego stood ready to take the field. He tapped the outgoing teammate on the stretcher and sprinted toward the captain.

The ball was placed in its position.

The Palmeiras made a wall of four players in front of the goalpost and waited for the kick.

Diego repositioned the ball for the kick and walked back to take his stance. Loud cheers poured from the Corinthian stands. The Palmeiras fans responded with equal vigor and energy. With only forty-five seconds left on the clock, every faithful knew this was their last chance to win the game and claim the lead.

The goalkeeper jumped and clapped nervously. Tension hung in the air.

It was time. Diego concentrated on the ball, the human wall, and the goalpost. He looked for a weak spot.

There was none. There was no straight, unobstructed path toward the goalpost. The only way to score was to make an impossible curved kick toward the net. The distance was enormous.

He observed and observed. In his mind, he calculated the precise force and direction he needed.

Freeewwww, went the referee's whistle.

Diego sprinted. With all his strength, he kicked the bottom left side of the ball, putting several hundred revolutions on the sphere. The ball shot like a bullet. It missed the leftmost player's head in the human wall by a whisker and curved spectacularly along its path.

The goalkeeper dived toward the top right corner where the ball was headed, his two palms stretched.

But the ball beat him. It bolted through the narrow gap between the corner and his palms and hit the net behind.

"Goaaaal!" Coach Roberto shouted

"Oh, my God," his assistant screamed.

Euphoria took the stands like wildfire. Teammates sprinted toward Diego and jumped on him.

The faithfuls knew they were home. They screamed, danced, and waved their shirts in the air. The referee resumed the game. A few seconds later, the final whistle blew.

Corinthians win and take the lead in the rivalry, flashed on the big screens.

There were festivities everywhere. Diego was their hero.

"Diego, Diego," the fans cried his name from the stands. A few lit fire-crackers. Some sang songs.

"That, my friend," Coach Roberto told Diego, "was one of the best kicks I have seen in a long, long time."

CR8O

Celebrations continued the next day. Coach Roberto threw a party for the team at his place.

"Diego, Diego, Diego," the teammates chanted as they lifted him on their shoulders, carried him all the way toward the pool, and tossed him inside. One by one, they all took the plunge. One of the coaching staff opened a humongous bottle of champagne and showered it all over the players.

After Diego had come out of the pool and dried himself, Coach Roberto pulled him to the side and guided him to the next room. As both entered, he turned, closed the door, and locked it from the inside so that no one could disturb them. The room was finished with polished mahogany furniture. In front of them was a wooden desk across which was an office chair with its high back facing them. Several Cabinets lined the walls holding trophies of various sizes and colors. A glass chandelier with bulbs of warm light hung from the ceiling.

"How do you feel, Diego?"

"Sobrecarregado; didn't expect to score in the first match, or the winning goal. I...I still can't believe it."

"It's real, *amigo*, it's real." The coach patted his shoulders. "Anyways, have you checked the social media? It's not yet twenty-four hours, and you are the most talked-about person in the country. And it's not just about that goal." He pulled out his phone and handed it to Diego. The screen showed several threads. *#DiegoGarcíaSoHot* was the top trending tag on X. One headline read, *'Is this miracle goal striker the sexiest man alive?'.*

"You're an overnight sensation. In just one night, you have developed a tremendous following among the ladies. They're calling you the national crush."

Diego smirked. "Well, like I told you in the stadium, they just find me."

The back of the chair across the desk rotated, and a pale man wearing an expensive tuxedo appeared. He rose from the chair and spoke in a very elitist and pompous manner, "Hello, Mr. García, congratulations."

"*Obrigada.*"

"Diego, this is Mr. Castello."

Castello moved his gaze from Diego to coach Roberto, made a subtle gesture to leave the room. Roberto obliged.

Castello cleared his throat and spoke, "Mr. García, I must say I was very impressed with you. What you did yesterday in the game was absolutely fantastic."

Diego smiled.

"You must be surprised to hear this, but it was not the first game of yours that I've seen."

"Umm, I don't understand." Diego's face looked puzzled.

"Well, Mr. García, allow me to come straight to the point. I'm head of talent acquisition at Manchester United." Castello waited for this to sink into Diego's brain.

Diego's face lit up.

"My job is to go all around the world and find talent. My team has followed you and your game for many months. We should have approached you earlier when you were playing in the minor circuit, before Coach Roberto drafted you for the derby." He shook his head. "Anyways, here I am now."

Castello came around the wooden desk, supported his back on its edge, leaned forward, and stared directly into Diego's eyes. "Mr. García, I would like you to come to Old Trafford and join our academy. We would like to coach you, develop you, and eventually have you play for us."

He paused for a few seconds to make sure Diego took in what he said. Diego stared back toward Castello like a deer in headlights. He could not believe it. He had dreamed of playing for a professional football club in a world-renowned league, and the English Premier League was among the most prized.

"So, what do you think? Would you like to come play for one of the best football clubs in the world?"

"I would be mad to say no."

"Very well, very well indeed." Castello paused. "There's one thing, though."

"What, sir?"

"We must leave tonight. The season's over here anyway, and we are starting a camp for new recruits in a few days. Is that something you'll be able to do?"

"Absolutely." Diego was not going to let go of this opportunity.

"Wonderful!" Castello cast a wide smile. "Now, let me return you to your celebrations. Enjoy your time while you're here, Mr. García. Come tomorrow, it'll be a different life."

Castello left the room. Diego went out and hugged Roberto. They both returned to the pool and celebrated with the team.

Diego came home, told his parents about the opportunity, packed his bags, and waited in anticipation.

Later that night, he boarded the flight to England. Onboard the aircraft, he napped.

When he woke up, he was in a basement-like room with a needle in his arm, staring at four new faces from different parts of the world.

None of them were remotely connected to football.

CHAPTER

6

State Opening of Parliament

London, England

A pleasant morning dawned along the banks of the Thames in central London. After a terrible winter, everyone in the grand old city was enjoying the arrival of warm weather. At the end of spring, the town was full of tourists from all over the world.

Alexis Birdwhistle, a tall woman of medium build with straight, shoulder-length, dark hair, was getting ready in the dressing room. Ms. Birdwhistle worked for the BBC at their London studio. She was thirty-two years old with a square face and a prominent British accent. She had inherited the color of her hair, her light-brown complexion, and a unibrow from her Indian mother. However, her deep blue eyes, the shape of her face, and her slender nose came from her Caucasian father.

Today, Ms. Birdwhistle was asked to cover a very important ceremony as a lead anchor. She was about to host the State Opening of Parliament.

Several big screens occupied the broadcast studio. Cameras across the city provided an uninterrupted feed, while field correspondents deployed inside and outside the three venues that were a part of the day's extravaganza gave Alexis real-time coverage of the activities. Behind her was a big transparent glass window. It overlooked the main venue of this event, the Westminster Palace. Apart from her, three guests from various factions of the British political circle were to appear on the show.

"Alright, Alexis, you'll be on air in one minute. I will give you a countdown."

Alexis took a deep breath.

The cameraman shouted, "On-air in...ten...nine... eight...seven... six...five... four... three... two...Go."

"Good morning, ladies and gentlemen. Welcome to a special presentation on this year's State Opening of Parliament, broadcast exclusively on BBC." Alexis stared into the lens. "I'm your host, Alexis Birdwhistle, and I will try my best to bring you a comprehensive, well-rounded coverage of this event. I will take you through the details of today's ceremony as it unfolds. We will discuss its historical significance, particularly this year, in light of the dramatic events that took place in the last few months."

Although Alexis had done this a few times as a fill-in anchor, nervousness filled her today. Her gut told her that despite the extensive planning, something was amiss. Still, she had no idea of what was about to unfold.

"Before we begin with the coverage of today's ceremony, let us go over to my colleague Annabel Corbyn, who will explain the ceremony." Alexis turned and faced one of the TV screens beside her. "Good morning, Annabel. Please tell our viewers what we will see today."

"It's a good morning indeed, Alexis. Warm and Sunny. It seems like a perfect rain-free day." She held a microphone in her hand, accompanied by a vibrant smile on her beautiful face. Her shiny, dark hair was styled neatly with clips, while her prominent cheekbones were rosy red. She had a slender nose and soft pink lips. The shirt inside her suit jacket matched her green eyes. Carrying that smile, she explained in her sweet, clear voice, "Today's ceremony, the State Opening of Parliament, marks the beginning of this year's session of the British parliament. This particular ceremony has been taking place since the fourteenth century. However, the present sequence of the rituals is quite different from back in those days. It takes place in the Palace of Westminster, which you can see behind me."

The camera focused behind Annabel.

"It consists of an assembly of the two houses of parliament where the monarch delivers a speech on the Government's plan for the year."

The camera covered the iconic palace from the outside. Rolling shots of Richard Coeur de Lion, the clocks of Big Ben Tower, the Elizabeth Tower, New Palace Yard, and various other sections of the palace appeared on the screen.

"Our monarch travels from Buckingham Palace while the royal regalia, consisting of the imperial crown of state, the sword of state, and the cap of maintenance, is brought from the Tower of London by the royal jeweler."

"Annabel," Alexis interrupted, "since we are talking about the Palace of Westminster, let me bring in Ethan Collingwood to walk us through this building and its various ornate rooms for our viewers. Ethan, what do you have for us?"

"A grand welcome to all our viewers inside the Palace of Westminster. Alexis, it's the first time we've had access to the entire palace just before a ceremony. You will see live-action of the preparations as I cover this venue," Ethan said excitedly. He was a tall man with an oval face and dark hair. A pair of gray eyes sat above his long nose, while a chevron mustache sat above his wide lips.

"This palace was first built during the eleventh century as a residence for the King of England. There are close to eleven hundred rooms in this building, spread across four floors, and all of them have a specific purpose," Ethan explained as he walked. The camera followed.

Alexis watched as Ethan gave a tour to the viewers, describing the details of one room after another. It went on for several minutes.

"This is where His Majesty will prepare for the procession." Ethan entered the Queen's Robing Room speaking in a very excited tone. "And on this elevated dais, under this beautiful canopy of gold and velvet, on this enchanting chair of state, his Majesty will don the royal robes and the Imperial State Crown." Ethan exited the room and continued his talk.

"Before entering the Queen's Robing Room for the procession, the Sovereign will be received in this Royal Porch. We are directly under the

Victoria Tower now. It's the second most famous tower of the palace after Big Ben." The camera zoomed out to get a wide angle.

"The Life Guards and Blues and Royals, belonging to the household cavalry, will line up on this staircase between the Royal Porch and Queen's Robing Room. Let me tell our viewers another interesting fact, Alexis. Apart from Yeomen of the Guard—his majesty's personal bodyguards—only these soldiers are permitted to bear arms inside the palace," Ethan said with an expression of pride. "With that, Alexis, our tour ends, back to you."

Alexis Birdwhistle once again occupied the screen. "Thank you very much, Ethan. That gives us a good picture of the palace."

"Ladies and gentlemen, let's take a few minutes' break. But don't go anywhere. After the break, we will bring you details about the sequence of events of today's ceremony."

Seconds after Alexis finished speaking, frames from last year's State Opening played on the broadcast. A few seconds later, the commercials followed.

CHAPTER 7

Darren Swanson

Hostage 3
Houston, Texas, USA

Winter was not quite ready to ebb in the northern parts of the country, but here in the world's oil capital, it was springtime. Houston was a place where NASA astronauts inspired human imagination, curiosity, and the quest for other stellar worlds alongside cowboys, farmers, and ranchers that nurtured the relationship amongst humans, cattle, and the earth.

Darren Swanson was a student at the University of Houston. He had moved from a small town in Kansas and was admitted on a football scholarship. He liked it here. Muscular, tall, menacing, nobody dared mess with him. His height and strength made him famous across the campus. With him on the team, opponents dreaded facing the Cougars—the university team.

The weather at this time in H-town was spectacular, with pleasant temperatures for the outdoors. Trees that had stood naked for weeks donned a coat of fresh green. The skies were a bright, Sunny blue. Flowers bloomed, lawns were manicured, crawfish were put to boil, and the smoke and aroma of barbecue filled the backyards.

March was also the time for the Houston Rodeo and Livestock Show, an annual affair. Spanning over twenty days, it was the world's largest event for livestock and live entertainment.

"Look at the goddamn traffic." Darren sat behind the wheel of a lifted suspension Ford F-150, looking at the long line of vehicles waiting to take the exit. Passengers had to climb to get inside this custom-heightened vehicle, but it came at the right height for Darren.

"Where the hell will we park?" Darren expressed his frustration to his friends in the truck.

'Parking Full' signs popped next to the *'$25 Parking'* ones as he tried to merge from the exit ramp onto the frontage road.

The city of Houston was shaped like a bicycle wheel. Beltway 8 and Interstate 610 were its two concentric rings, while several other freeways emanated from the central downtown to the suburbs like spokes. NRG Stadium—Rodeo Houston's venue—was south side of the inner I-610 ring.

"I knew this was going to happen. That's why I didn't want to come," Darren shouted. He and his friends were stuck on the Interstate's frontage road, where traffic moved at a snail's pace. "We should have come on a weekday." He slammed the steering wheel with his right hand.

"Think of all the food you can eat there, Darren." Katie, Darren's friend from college, chuckled. She was tall, slender, and of blonde hair that was fashioned into a ponytail. She displayed her perfect white teeth when she smiled, and her sky-blue eyes matched the color of her denim. "Besides, there's a special event today; it's the first time they are hosting it instead of the concert."

"So, there won't be any celebrities?" Darren raised his bushy eyebrows. "Well—"

"You're killing me, Katie." He shook his head.

"There'll be celebrities." Katie smiled. "Just a different kind."

Trucks, trailers with cattle, SUVs, and sedans packed the roads while scores of people hurried down the sidewalk toward the Arena, resembling a gathering of ants making a beeline toward their colony.

Darren spotted a cop in a fluorescent green vest with a uniform underneath standing beside the road. "Officer, hey, officer. Where can we find parking?"

The officer signaled them to drive toward El Paseo Street, located all the way on the other side. After about half an hour of searching, a parked car ahead of them pulled out and vacated a spot.

"Woohoo!" Katie hooted. "Finally."

Katie and Jason had to jump out of the truck, but Darren's feet touched the ground with ease. Jason was about five feet nine inches with a dark complexion, a big nose, bushy eyebrows, and curly black hair. He was chubby and wore jeans underneath a Houston Texans team t-shirt. He was on the university's football team along with Darren.

The three rushed toward the east side gate behind the metro station and joined the long queue. The walkway zig-zagged several times, like an airport security check, at the end of which were several officers checking bags and scanning visitors with metal detector wands. People surrounded them from all sides. Groups of friends, couples holding hands, and families with kids, all wearing cowboy hats and high western boots, cheered, laughed, and hooted as they waited.

Darren wore denim, a sleeveless t-shirt, a leather vest, a cowboy hat, and western boots. Katie and Jason were ahead of him in the queue.

"Aaa," he shouted, rubbing his exposed left shoulder. A drop of blood oozed from a tiny dot on his skin. He screwed his face in irritation.

"What?" Katie asked. She turned to look at him

"Someone pricked me," he said, and looked around. It was packed.

"Must be a bug," Jason told him.

"Does this freakin' look like a bug bite to you?" Darren showed them his shoulder.

"Umm—" Katie hesitated.

"Your damn right it does not. I know what a bug bite feels like. Look, my skin ain't red."

He scanned the crowd once more, but slowly this time. "Someone's monkeying around. I swear, if I find—"

"Forget it, Darren; it was probably unintentional. Let's go." Katie pulled him by the arm.

Darren continued to look around, rubbing his arm, grunting.

In about thirty minutes, they scanned their tickets using the electronic reader and entered. A sea of carnival stalls and adventure rides welcomed them. Hot dogs, corn dogs, and jumbo dogs greeted them at the food stalls. For sweet-tooths, the stall that came next was a wonderland. Fried Twinkies, fried Oreos, fried cakes, fried Snickers, fried cookie dough; anything imaginable was served fried there. The air was heavy with the scent of fried sugar. Next to the food was a Ferris wheel.

"Guys, I'm hungry." Darren gaped at the barbecue stall on his right. The aroma of charred meats was tantalizing. Four pitmasters wearing cowboy hats and leather aprons worked on ribs, brisket, lamb chops, and other cuts of meat on the grill, basting them with sauces and marinades. Other crewmembers sprinkled freshly fried waffle fries and potato twisters with salt and seasoning.

"For once, say something else, Darren," Katie joked, "You're always hungry." She laughed and pinched Darren in the stomach as they joined the line to place their order.

"Don't mess with me, I ain't in a good mood." Darren flared his nostrils.

"That's not news either, Mr. Grumpy." Jason chortled. He stood behind Katie and Darren.

"Look, the only reason I came here is for the food, and right now, I'm starvin'." Darren's stomach made a rumbling sound.

While they waited their turn, a young beefy man wearing three-quarter jeans under a Houston Astros tank top and a baseball cap jumped the line and stood two places ahead of Darren.

Darren tapped his shoulder. The man turned around. He had a round face, small nose, and big eyes.

"Did you just do that?" Darren went closer to him. "You think we're fools waiting in line for the last fifteen minutes?"

"Dude, I was here the whole time," the man replied nonchalantly and turned back to face the stall.

Darren tapped his shoulder again. "What's your name?"

"Rick," he replied over his shoulder but did not turn this time.

"Listen, Rick, I know you weren't here. Now, go back and stand at the start of the line."

Rick ignored him and hid behind his phone.

Darren stormed to the man, grabbed the back of his collar, and pulled him out. "Do you really want me to say that again?" Darren stared into Rick's face. He stood three feet taller than him. The next second, Darren watched Rick walk back and stand behind an old lady in a wheelchair. She seemed exhausted.

Darren's anger dissipated at the sight of her. *She looks tired; I should help her.*

He went to her. "Are you hungry, ma'am?" he asked.

"I'm sorry?" she said, looking up at him from her wheelchair.

"Are you hungry?" Darren asked again, leaning close to her.

The women nodded.

He grabbed the handles of her wheelchair. "You can go ahead. Do you mind if I help you?"

"No, no. It's all right. I don't want to jump the line," she said, looking at Rick.

"Don't worry, you can take my spot." He moved her to his spot and went back to stand behind Rick.

Katie and Jason looked in amazement. They came back and stood next to him. "I thought you were hungry," Katie asked with her hands on her hips.

"I am. She reminded me of my nana." He shrugged. "Besides, the young should look after the old, shouldn't they?"

"Darren, I don't get you. One second, you are angry as a bull; the next second, you are such a sweetheart." Katie smiled as she held him by the arm.

The line moved ahead. Once reaching the cashier, Darren looked at the menu banners. "Four baby back ribs, jumbo fries, and a king-size soda."

"Hmmm. You ordered for us too?" Jason jumped before Darren, tilted his face, and asked, holding his chin between his index finger and thumb. There was a playful smile on his face.

"Don't even look at them; all four are mine." Darren pushed him aside gently.

"But aren't you on a diet?" Jason jumped back before him.

"That's how much I eat when I am dieting," Darren growled. "Now shut up and let me eat in peace." He pushed Jason to the side again.

Darren was a huge man. Sometimes, the big and tall outlets had difficulty finding clothes that fit him. His appetite was even bigger. He could finish three or four pigs alone if only his folks allowed it. Despite the enormous intake of calories, he was always in shape and sported a toned and muscular body with eight-pack abs. Today, he was the tallest person in the crowd. People stared at him in amazement as he devoured all four ribs and fries without giving out a single burp.

They finished their food and cleared the table. "Which way is the goddamn stadium?"

"We're not going to the stadium, Darren."

Darren rolled his eyes. "What now, Katie?"

"We're going to the Arena."

"Arena? But the rodeo sports are in the stadium."

"Like I said, we're going to an event which is part of the rodeo for the first time."

Darren shook his head. They walked toward the NRG Arena, where a long line greeted them. Darren turned and stared at Katie.

She shrugged. "Hooray, let's go." She grabbed him by the arm and pulled.

They stood in line for a long time. The doors to the NRG Arena were still closed. A large crowd gathered behind them, several holding placards.

'Blackrose, You Rock!' read one. 'We Want Paco,' read another.

"Ah!" Darren shouted, trying to rub his arms as he felt two pricks along his biceps. "Son of a bitch, that's it. I've had enough of it." Darren's face was red with anger. He closed the fingers of both hands into a fist and frantically looked at the crowd around him.

"What happened?" Jason asked.

"Someone pricked me again. Both arms this time." Darren's gaze landed on a well-built man standing behind him. He held a large soda in one hand and a placard in another.

Darren grabbed the drink, emptied it on the man's head, and held him by the neck. "You thought you would get away with it again, huh?

"Daddy, what happened?" A little girl emerged from behind the man. The sight of Darren holding her father by the neck frightened her.

Darren let go. "I'm so sorry," he said, looking at the girl.

"Dude, it wasn't me; there was a short man ahead of me. He pricked and ran away."

Cracking his knuckles, Darren surveyed the sea of people behind.

The next minute, the doors to the Arena opened, and people rushed inside.

A central performance area in the shape of a rounded rectangle greeted them. Rows of orange-colored seats at several levels surrounded the performance area. Seats closer to the action at ground level were expensive and got cheaper as the levels went higher and farther. In the center was a square wrestling ring, the surface of which was made of red clay. Four wooden posts stood at the corners holding thick brown ropes, which marked the ring's boundary. Four big screens hung from the ceiling in each direction to display live action and replays.

"You gotta be kidding me! Wrestling?" Jason closed his eyes as he complained.

Katie giggled. "It's not what you think it is; it's not WWE. This is dirt wrestling."

"No, no, no. It ain't gonna happen." Darren turned around. *I didn't come all the way, in this traffic, to watch a bunch of guys in undies, covered in dirt, fake wrestle.*

"Darren, please, for me." Katie stared into his eyes like an innocent puppy.

"Look around you. We ain't kids no more."

Katie nudged Jason.

"Yeah, it'll be fun, Darren," Jason said. "I have seen some of it on TV. It's intense."

Darren shook his head. "If you weren't my friends—"

Making their way through the crowd, Katie, Jason, and Darren grabbed their seats. The lights dimmed.

"Ladies and gentlemen, welcome to Rodeo Houston," the anchor announced. "I thank you all for coming. It's the first time we've partnered with the World Dirt Wrestling Federation. For the uninitiated, it is a trendy sport in many countries. In this country, too, its popularity has skyrocketed in the past several years. Now, I know you don't want to listen to me for long. So let me ask you all, are you ready?"

"Yes," the crowd echoed.

"I asked, 'Are you ready?'"

A 'Yes' roared through the Arena.

"Alright, let's get started."

Lights flashed around the wrestler's entrance. A focus light scanned through the audience and settled there. A tall and robust man walked out wearing a crimson brief. His dark skin shimmered in the lights. As he stood at the entrance and stretched, his muscles bulged on every side. His curly black hair was trimmed, and he screwed his oval face showing his bright white teeth.

"Ladies and gentlemen, I give you Blackrose." The wrestler sprinted toward the dirt pit, high-fiving on his way. "To fight him, we have none other than... any guesses?"

Another tall wrestler emerged from the second entrance.

"That's right, it's none other than Mr. Paco."

Paco bowed on his way to the ring, removed his shoes, and jumped into the red clay. His oiled, pale skin shimmered in the lights. He wore briefs of fluorescent green, and his silky black hair fell all over his eyes.

Both wrestlers stood face to face, grunting at each other.

"It's boring," Darren told Katie. "It's gonna be fake, just like the wrestling on TV."

A boy in front turned around. "It's not boring! You're stupid."

Darren snatched the Sharpie from the boy's right hand and his 'Blackrose, You Rock!' placard, turned it around, and wrote 'Wrestling is Fake!'

He held it high without leaving his chair. Boos echoed through the Arena. The focus lights moved and zeroed in on Darren and his placard.

Blackrose grabbed the microphone and pointed his finger at Darren. "Why don't you come over here, my friend. I'll personally show you whether it's real or fake."

Paco tilted the microphone toward him. "Yeah, country boy, let's see what you got."

Darren shook his head with a smirk. His face was defiant. *They want me to be part of this circus, as if I care.*

"Scared, are you? You smartass," the boy in front screamed at Darren.

"Yeah, he's a smartass, isn't he?" Paco laughed.

"Go, Darren, show them what you got," Katie shouted.

"Yeah, you go, Darren," Jason cheered.

When Darren stood up, the entire Arena went mute. He was taller than both his challengers by a foot and a half. He walked toward the pit, removed his shoes, and jumped inside. The wrestlers stood short, face-to-face.

"Kids, move aside. Let the adults play," a thick voice ran through the Arena. A gigantic man came walking out from the wrestler's entrance. He was about the same height as Darren, perhaps an inch shorter, but with a menacing face, nonetheless. As he grunted his steel-capped teeth and screwed his face, his bushy eyebrows curved, and his beefy nose twisted.

The focus lights settled on him.

"Balee! Balee! Balee!" echoed through the Arena.

Balee stormed into the ring. He pushed Blackrose and Paco aside and stood facing Darren. There was only an inch between their noses.

The referee parted them by placing his arm between them. "One, two, three!"

Freewwww, the whistle sounded.

Balee grabbed Darren by the neck. Darren held his wrists and pushed them aside. Balee turned swiftly, went behind Darren, and tried to close his arms around Darren's torso. He missed by a whisker. In the next moment, he bent down, moved his right arm between Darren's legs, and tried to lift him. Darren moved his own leg over his arm, went behind him, put his arms between Balee's legs, and... he lifted him above his head.

The Arena went mute. Spectators marveled at this sight.

No one had ever lifted the four-hundred-pound Balee before.

"Darren, Darren, Darren," Katie and Jason cheered.

The next second, Blackrose charged toward Darren and pushed him back with brute force. The following second, Paco came from the front, and his two hands pressed on Darren's chest.

Darren's frame didn't move an inch. Holding Balee above his head, he screamed, "Aaaaah."

Darren threw Balee outside the ring. Balee lay there motionless. Next, he held Paco and Blackrose by the neck, lifted them simultaneously in each hand, and walked to the ring's edge. Over the edge, he threw them outside.

Not a body moved. The referee whistled. He held Darren's arm and raised it. "Ladies and gentlemen, the winner," the anchor announced.

"Darren, Darren, Darren," the entire Arena cheered his name. Jason whistled in delight. Darren walked out from the ring and fastened his shoes, his back and chest bloody with blows from his opponents.

An attendant approached. "Sir, we need to take care of your wounds," he said. "Please follow me." He escorted Darren outside the Arena and ushered him into an ambulance.

The attendant made Darren lie on an oversized stretcher that was too small for his size and examined his eyes with a flashlight. "Do you have any pain?"

"Not much," replied Darren.

"I am going to inject a painkiller into your veins, just in case. Then I will take care of these wounds."

Two vials' worth of clear liquid went into either arm. A few minutes later, everything faded. The ambulance's top spun, and so did the windows. His eyes felt heavy as if he had not slept for weeks.

"You were a tough cookie to crack, Mr. Swanson," the medic whispered in his ear. "I pricked you twice, but nothing happened to that giant body of yours." He patted Darren's right cheek lazily. "Nonetheless, you are ours now."

Darren's eyesight became hazy, and next second, he passed out.

When he woke, Darren was still on a bed, but this was a different one. He had no clue how he got on it, but based on his beard growth, several months had passed. This bed, however, was several thousand miles from Houston and inside a dungeon-like basement.

Alongside him were four men he had never seen before.

CHAPTER 8

The Royal Regalia

London, England

The broadcast resumed after the commercial break. Alexis Birdwhistle's face filled the screen once again. "Welcome back, ladies and gentlemen, to the live broadcast of the State Opening of Parliament. I am your host, Alexis Birdwhistle. We have Diane Baker on the ground, who will explain the sequence of events in today's ceremony and their significance. Off to you, Diane."

A petite blonde woman appeared on screen. "Alexis, the ceremony plays out according to a well-rehearsed script consisting of a fixed sequence of events. It starts by searching the cellars, which the Yeomen of the Guard do. This is a tradition followed since the gunpowder plot incident of 1605, when a failed assassination attempt was made on King James I," Diane explained hurriedly. "This is followed by an assembly of Peers and Commons, where members assemble in their respective houses wearing appropriate clothing.

The Commons wear ordinary clothes while peers wear traditional robes of scarlet and gold." An image with screenshots of the Lords Chamber and Commons Chamber appeared on the screen.

"The next step, Alexis, is the delivery of the hostage. In this step, a member of the House of Commons is delivered to Buckingham Palace. This is done to guarantee the safe return of the monarch. Today, it is just a ceremonial step, and the Member is not really treated as a hostage. They are sent back after the safe return of the monarch," she continued. "Then follows the arrival of the Royal Regalia, where the Imperial State Crown is brought to the Palace of Westminster in a state carriage from the Jewel House at the Tower of London. Alexis, after everything is ready, it's time for the arrival of the monarch. The monarch travels in a royal carriage from Buckingham Palace and is received at the Royal Porch. The Sovereign is brought into the Queen's Robing Room, where they get ready and later proceed to occupy the throne in the House of Lords. After settling into the throne, the Sovereign orders the house to sit by saying, 'My Lords, pray be seated.'" Diane's explanation was swift and sounded as if she read off a teleprompter.

"When everyone takes their seat, the next step is the summons to the Commons, followed by their procession. A speech scroll is delivered and read by the Sovereign, addressing all present in the room. Finally, after this, it is time for the departure of the monarch and the Royal Regalia." Diane finished, wearing a relieved expression, "Back to you, Alexis."

Alexis' face returned to the screen. "Thank you, Diane. That was a fast but a good overview indeed."

Alexis turned to face the second camera. "In this next section, our expert guests will join us in discussing the significance of this ceremony in light of the recent political climate in England. But before that, let's go to Benjamin at the Tower of London, ready to tell us more about the Royal Regalia."

Benjamin, a young and good-looking correspondent, took over the screen. He had short, blonde hair, fashioned neatly with a generous amount of gel. Frames of brown glasses sat on his nose, covering his gray eyes.

"Alexis, firstly, let me tell you that security is extra tight here at the Tower of London. Only a few days ago, a very tall, hooded individual tried to break into the Jewel House around midnight. It triggered the alarms, and he vanished. Police are still looking for him. Thankfully, nothing was stolen," he said, looking into the camera without a smile.

In the studio, Alexis was intrigued by the news of the hooded individual who tried to break into the Jewel House. However, she did not interrupt Benjamin.

"Now, to talk about the regalia, I am with Mr. Williams, the royal crown jeweler at the Tower of London," Benjamin continued. "He is responsible for all the crown jewels of the British monarchy. He will explain the details of the Imperial State Crown to us." The camera moved from him to Mr. Williams.

"Good morning to all. I pray you are in good spirits," Mr. Williams greeted. His bald head was covered with a fedora hat, and on his double-chinned, round face sat a copper walrus mustache. He wasted no time and began, "Although used since the fifteenth century in many of its earlier forms, the current version of the Imperial State Crown was remodeled last year for the coronation of our new king. There is not much difference between its previous look and the present one. It's just given a more masculine look to suit its new possessor as per his wishes."

As Mr. Williams spoke, the camera moved away from his face, and a beautiful crown materialized. The crown's design included a base consisting of four cross formées, and four fleurs-de-lys arranged alternately. From the base rose four half-arches that met at a small globe on top, on which was mounted a small cross. A purple velvet cap was lined inside this metal frame. Diamonds, sapphires, pearls, emeralds, and rubies were embedded on the outside. Among them was the Black Prince's Ruby. It occupied the frontmost cross formée.

"This is the Black Prince's Ruby. It is one of the oldest crown jewels and has been in the royal jewel collection since 1367," Mr. Williams added. Although passed on during war from ruler to ruler, the actual origin of the gem is said to be in Tajikistan, near Afghanistan. We have no clue when it was discovered, perhaps thousands of years ago."

He shifted from the crown to the other two items in the Royal Regalia and once again continued his elaborate explanation. It took him a while to talk about them.

"Thank you for that great explanation, Mr. Williams, and thank you, Benjamin, for the excellent coverage of the regalia," Alexis resumed.

Three older guests sat next to her in the studio.

"I have three guests with me today who will talk to us about the significance of today's ceremony in light of the political climate in Britain. On my right is Mr. Patrick Millburn, a former Member of Parliament. On my left is Ms. Nicky Robinson, former Speaker of the House, and on her left is Mr. Matthew Wilson, BBC's political editor." The three guests smiled at the camera as their names were called.

"Now, before we hear from these extraordinary people, if you are someone who has just returned from abroad after a long stay with no access to British news or just did not care to follow it until today, let me give you some background." Alexis smiled.

The guests beside her chuckled.

"The last year in Britain has been odd. Exactly one year ago, the present king, a prince then, was abroad. During that time, calls for Northern Ireland's independence from Britain after the No-deal Brexit, which imposed hard borders between Ireland and Northern Ireland, took root. Certain people from Scotland also decided to join the protests, and a joint struggle emerged." Alexis cleared her throat.

"Massive rallies in Northern Ireland and Scotland were organized, and the streets of London were overwhelmed with demonstrations. In Scotland, various polls indicated that more than half of the population wanted independence. This time, more than independence, it looks like the supporters wanted to be a part of Europe rather than stay with the UK." She paused and swallowed.

"An independence referendum was called in both the protesting areas. However, wild rumors of intense lobbying from corporate groups, several close to the royal family, spread over social media. After all, the vote was canceled, citing violence in the region."

"Since then, countless threads popped up on the internet, increasing the bitter divide, blaming the royal family. Online users, some real, many fake, targeted their wrath at the royals. Riots broke out on the streets of Scotland and Northern Ireland. Foreign interests exploited the narrative. The nation was divided like never before. Many families and groups of friends split from within, fighting on opposite sides of the online and on-field battles. Parliament decided that the environment was unstable enough to reconsider a referendum."

Alexis paused again. This time, her face was severe. "To everyone's dismay, the discontent manifested into the worst day in the royal family's history. The present king's father, elder brother, and family were assassinated by a horrific bombing."

All three guests shook their heads in sadness as he continued, "Although he had relinquished his throne, the surviving sibling was called from abroad and crowned the new king. It was a somber ceremony indeed."

Alexis turned the pages of her notes as she spoke, "Even after all this, the rioting didn't stop. Parliament was hung on the vote to allow another referendum. Calls to abolish the monarchy echoed. Exercising his ultimate authority as the ruler, His Majesty called off the referendum and crushed the rebellion with the brutal use of force. Many say his personal loss and attack on the monarchy and its businesses enraged him enough to make such a harsh and unpopular decision. Democracy in Britain has been shaken since then."

Alexis sighed, as if replaying the past several months in her head. "The past few months, however, have seen some return to normalcy."

She kept staring at the camera for several long seconds. "So, with that in context, let's ask some questions." She turned to face the guests. "Gentlemen and lady, what do you have to say about today's State Opening?"

"Alexis, this event has been only ceremonial for more than a century now, more like a formality. However, with the new king this year, it will all be a show of royal authority," Millburn replied. "Just think about it; this time last year, we didn't even consider him to be someone who would get a chance to occupy the throne. And then, suddenly, the queen passes away, followed by the king's father and the whole family in that hideous attack, and here we are today with this very unexpected king."

"Ms. Robinson," Alexis said as she glanced at her notes before asking her question. "What do you think about some of the actions he took after assuming the throne?"

"I think it was a very emotional response from the king, and most people in England don't agree with it. However, it seems to have brought some calm after all the violence in the last two years," she said. "And that's why today's ceremony is so important. Through the subtle things in his highness's speech and actions today, we will find out if he plans to continue his stance of executing royal authority in the future or if he will take the monarchy back to dormancy, which we were used to in the queen's era."

Outside the studio, the sun rose through the clear sky, casting a magical spell of colors on the Elizabeth Tower of the Westminster Palace. The hour hands on the four dials of the humongous clock on the tower, more commonly known to tourists as Big Ben, moved in unison to indicate the beginning of a new hour. As the arms stopped moving, all the bells rang in unison, spreading their chimes far and wide.

Across Westminster Palace, on the opposite bank of the Thames, the London Eye, an enormous Ferris wheel, stood like a behemoth. This massive structure, resembling a giant bicycle wheel, with spokes made of tensioned steel cables and the circumference of solid steel, was packed with tourists.

The atmosphere was charged with anticipation, with the ceremony a few hours away.

"Thank you, Ms. Robinson, for your insights," Alexis said as the camera focused back on her. "Now, let's look at the preparations underway inside the palace. As we all expect, tradition reigns supreme in Westminster." She moved in her seat as she spoke. Live visuals from inside the palace appeared on the screens.

"The police are not permitted within its walls, but we see that the Yeomen of the Guard, the Life Guards, and the Blues and Royals are taking their positions." A wide smile appeared on Alexis' face. "These are the only armed groups allowed inside the palace today. Their presence is a testament to the weight of tradition and the solemnity of the occasion."

Alexis paused.

"Next, to talk security, we have Commissioner Rattlehouse joining us through video call," Alexis said. The screen split, with one half continuing scenes from the palace and the other half showing the commissioner's face.

"Welcome to the show, Madam Commissioner?" Alexis greeted Commissioner Rattlehouse. "Will you please update our viewers on the security arrangements for the ceremony?"

"Good morning, Alexis. The officers of the metropolitan police of London are strategically deployed across the city, around the two palaces, at the Jewel House, and along the route. Only a few days ago, someone tried to break into the Jewel House at the Tower of London. So, we're being extra careful about the regalia as well. More officers are remotely scanning a web of CCTV cameras, ensuring the entire ceremony is under their watchful eyes."

Rattlehouse's plump, round face was stern as she spoke. "Not just London, but other cities are also on high alert in the wake of last year's attack. We are in close coordination with our counterparts in other cities and Scotland Yard. Security in the main cities of Scotland and Northern Ireland is significantly bolstered. British intelligence is closely monitoring all activity in and out of the two regions, ensuring a comprehensive security net is in place."

"Thanks, Madam Commissioner," Alexis said hurriedly. "I am afraid that's all the time we have. The ceremony has begun."

The split screen went back to single with visuals of the palace.

"Ladies and gentlemen," Alexis spoke to the viewers, "we will be back after a short break."

CHAPTER 9

Ojoré Odingá

Hostage 4
Nairobi, Kenya

The day was bright and blithesome. The mood in the suburban mansion of the Odingá family, though, was quite the opposite.

The Odingás were one of those families that had been wealthy for generations and were among the most affluent families on the continent. Mr. and Mrs. Odingá were a devout Catholic couple and contributed heavily to faith-based charities. Their house was enormous, considering only two people, Mr. and Mrs. Odingá, lived there. Though many keepers occupied the servant quarters on the property, it still felt lonely. Perhaps the emptiness was more in the heart than in the dwelling.

For Mrs. Odingá, the house was emptier than ever.

"I- I'm sorry, b- but I'm not sure if I can do this," Mrs. Odingá sobbed. She stood on a dais behind a polished mahogany coffin. "I- I can't think of 'im in the past, I- I can't imagine my life without 'im." The coffin was placed in front of the altar. Above it was a big cross. The church was part of Odinga's twenty-acre property. A stained-glass window let multicolored rays of light enter the church, while candles added their light, resting on golden votive stands. Flowers of various colors and fragrances were arranged around the coffin.

More tears cascaded from those miserable eyes. "'e was a good 'usband, an excellent companion, and treated me with utmost love and affection. I was married to 'im for twenty-six years and enjoyed every day of it. We built our lives togetha', piece-by-piece." She paused and snorted. "When we got married, we- we didn't 'ave any money. We- we both worked two jobs to provide for oaselves." She turned her head toward the coffin. "'e erected this business empire from scratch with 'is hard work and determination. To many of you who worked with 'im, 'e often appeared strict and steadfast, but- but 'e was just as soft and kind inside. What more can I say? I can't- I can't——-" She stopped speaking, unable to control her emotions.

Relatives and friends helped her out of the dais and onto the nearest seat. One by one, others offered their own eulogies. The house was full of people who came to pay their last respects to Mr. Odingá, who touched their lives in many good and noble ways. One person, however, was absent, Mr. & Mrs. Odingá's only child, Ojoré.

"He should have shown up at least on this dreadful day," an old lady whispered to the woman seated beside her.

"They say he hasn't come home in years. No one knows where he is, not even his mother," the second woman replied.

"But what caused the rift between father and son? After all, he was going to inherit all this wealth. Was he into drugs or some other ungodly thing?"

"No one knows the reason; they say he had some illness. Mr. and Mrs. Odingá showed him to many doctors and tried religious treatments, but nothing made him better. And everyone knows how strict Mr. Odingá was, so things got progressively worse, they say, and I heard he ran away one day. No one has heard from him since."

The pastor took the dais and offered funeral prayers. When he was finished, the casket was lifted, and people carried it to the gravesite. All rituals and customs were performed, and after returning to the church, one by one, all those present bid Mrs. Odingá goodbye.

As the last of the lot left, Mrs. Odingá's eyes fell upon a young man standing at a distant corner of the hall, leaning beside a cabinet. She rose from her chair and ran toward him. When she was close, she couldn't control herself, threw her arms around him in a tight embrace, and cried like never before. "I knew you would come. Oh, Ojoré." She was uncontrollable. "We searched for you everywhere. You should 'ave come back, you should 'ave thought of yoa miserable motha', you knew 'ow much I love you, 'ow it would 'urt me if you left."

Ojoré patted her back gently. She ceased crying. Snorted. "Yoa father loved you too, my son, you know it, 'e just couldn't understand it, but 'e loved you."

"Ma, let it go. I'm here now; let's not talk of the past." Ojoré wiped her tears with his hands. He put an arm around her.

The smell of candle smoke filled the air as the candles went out one after another.

"I missed you so much, my son. I was so miserable. I don't 'ave anyone else. Please, please don't go back. I won't let you go back." Mrs. Odingá wrapped her arms around him.

"I missed you, too, Ma."

"You'll stay?"

Ojoré nodded.

She smiled for a second and cried some more.

രു൸Ꮆ

Pages turned on the calendar like things in a time-lapse film. Ojoré did not return to the village where he had dwelt for the past few years. He talked to nobody about his time there with the local Bángá tribe. Some of his cousins learned about his homecoming and came to see him. They invited him to hang out several times, but he politely declined. However, on his mother's relentless persistence, he went. After a few times, he enjoyed his time out as well. Things had changed around him; things had changed for him.

"Let's go to the new mall," Samuel—his first cousin—said over the phone. "There's this cool place that has bowling, pool, and other stuff."

"But what if someone recognizes me? I don't want to be hounded by the media and people." Ojoré lay on the bed in his bedroom. He walked up to the window as he talked on the phone and slid the sheer curtains.

"Don't worry. Hardly anybody remembers your face," Samuel replied.

"Are you sure?" Ojoré opened the window to let in the fresh air. He saw a gardener working on a flower bed through his window. It was a beautiful day with clear skies, gentle sunlight, and a cold breeze running through the grounds.

"Absolutely." Samuel's voice on the phone sounded confident.

"What time?"

"Seven thirty."

"Alright, see you there." Ojoré hung up the phone.

Ojoré had to wait for fifteen in the car before his cousins arrived in the parking lot. He wore a red hoody over a V-neck t-shirt and blue denim jeans.

Samuel called Ojoré from the parking lot. "Where you at, Ojoré? We are at the west entrance."

"In my car, near the east entrance."

"Why are you hiding there?" Samuel chuckled.

"The paparazzi. They attack like a group of bees."

"Don't worry, we'll come get you."

Samuel and the rest went to Ojoré's car.

"Problems these famous people' ave, I tell you." Samuel smirked. "Anyways, let's go to the bowling place first."

A few minutes later, they were tying their bowling shoelaces inside the arena. Ojoré took his time, meticulously working his fingers on the lace.

"Over with it already," Samuel said, tapping Ojoré's shoulder

"You know I take my time to get things in order." Ojoré shrugged.

"Seriously? I thought you must have outgrown that habit." Samuel placed his hands on his hips.

Ojoré ignored and finished.

"No groups, every man for himself. Ojoré, you want to go first?" Samuel said, pulling Ojoré by the arm and pushing him ahead toward their lane.

"Sure." Ojoré inserted his thumb, index, and middle finger and picked up a purple-colored number twelve ball. He observed for several long seconds holding the sphere. His left arm extended all the way back, his focus unshattered. He took a few quick steps and released the ball.

Smack! Not a single pin stood. Ojoré walked nonchalantly to his seat.

"I forgot how good you are at aiming, cousin. I shouldn't have let you go first."

"That was only the first shot, Sammy."

"Alright, alright, let's see how it goes,"

They took turns as their names popped up on the monitor. In every single attempt, Ojoré scored a strike.

"We're no match for you, Ojoré. Let's play something else."

The party moved to a pool table. Samuel arranged the frame, took his stance to break.

"Wait, I won in bowling. I get to break the frame first." Ojoré pushed Samuel aside and took his stance. One by one, the balls made the pockets. The frames finished in no time on every occasion. Ojoré's aim was spot-on.

"Let's go somewhere to eat, man. There's no point playing against you." They laughed.

Ojoré covered his face again with the hoodie. They strolled through the mall, looking for a place to eat. "God, so many people. Someone will recognize me."

After a fifteen-minute walk, they were out of the entertainment section of the mall and entered the food court on the ground floor. The food court was packed with people.

"Don't worry, pull your hoodie a little more. We will sit and cover you from the sides and front."

They settled down at an empty table with Ojoré in the middle.

The food court had a variety of options. There was a shop with sand-wiches, another with an Asian fair, a Pizzeria, a burger joint, and a coffee shop. Carts, big and small, were parked in the arena. Some sold cassavas—roasted or fried, sprinkled with chili flakes and a squeeze of lemon. Others sold mshikakis, bhajia, chips, samosas, and all sorts of Kenyan street food delicacies.

Each one got a dish of their liking. Ojoré bought himself some roasted cassavas and a few samosas. They ate in silence, listening to the cacophony of sounds reverberating through the arena.

As they finished eating and were placing their trays above the trash cans, right at that instant, there was a loud *Bang! Bang! Bang!*

Sounds of bullet shots echoed through the mall. People scattered here and there, not knowing where the sounds came from. They hid wherever they thought was the best place. Some took shelter behind the counters of food stalls; some went to the fire escapes, some to the restrooms, while others hid beneath the furniture.

"Terrorists! Terrorists! Hide, Hide." A mall security guard sped through the hallway. He went on running through the food court before hiding behind a counter.

In this confusion, Ojoré and his cousins ran inside an appliance store, which was nearest to the food court. On their way, running past refrigerators, washer, driers, televisions, music systems, and going through various sections of the appliance store, Ojoré got separated and landed in the kitchen section of the store. There, he hid beneath a counter and waited in silence.

Bang! Bang! Bang! came the sound once more. Screams followed.

"Please, don't kill us, please," Ojoré heard.

The victims were close by. That meant the terrorists were, too. He slowly peeked from the side of the counter to see how close he was. There were two terrorists, both with AK-47s.

The next set of victims fell dead to the floor before his eyes. His heart pounded, his adrenaline pumped, and his breathing became heavy. The terrorists moved ahead and searched for anyone hiding. They dragged some out and, one by one, shot them. Point blank. One body among those that fell was that of Samuel, Ojoré's cousin.

Ojoré watched helplessly as it unfolded before him. Tears rolled down his cheeks, but he made no sound.

The terrorists approached another counter in the linen section next to the kitchen section, snatching a few more shoppers. The action was happening very close to Ojoré.

I am not going to die like this. I survived worse with the Bángá. I will not go down like this. He had earned his place as a fighter in the village, a warrior.

Ojoré looked for something he could use as a weapon. He searched and searched. Luck! Right next to him was a collection of kitchen knives, sharp as razors.

"Please don't kill us, 'ave mercy, please 'ave mercy, at least let my son go," victims pleaded, "please, I beg you."

The gunman raised his gun. Ojoré took aim.

"Please, not him. Please kill us instead."

Ojoré saw the gunman smile as he pointed his gun at the child. Right when the gunman was about to pull the trigger, he launched a knife toward him. It pierced his chest. Red gushed on the white floor as he collapsed. His comrade turned around in the direction from where the knife came. Ojoré launched a second blade toward him. The second gunman dodged, raised his gun, fired several shots. They missed.

Both Ojoré and the second gunman hid behind opposite counters. The terrorist shot intermittently.

Ojoré peeped after the fire died. The terrorist stared from his counter. His body was behind the counter, and only a part of his head and one eye were visible. Ojoré picked another sharp, pointed knife. All his concentration focused on the terrorist's eye. The eye—that was all that mattered. A vision of a sparrow's eye flashed in his mind. He did not understand what it was. He did not understand why it came to him. He shook himself out of it.

In a single movement, he launched the knife and... "Yes!" The knife pierced the terrorist's exposed eye. The body hit the floor.

Ojoré was relieved. What he did not notice, however, was a bleeding arm. Right when he had launched the knife, the terrorist had shot a bullet that scraped Ojoré's other arm. The wound was not severe, but blood oozed from it, painting his white shirt red.

Ojoré ran toward the fallen terrorists, picked up their guns, and ran toward the counter where the security guard was hiding. He gave a security guard an AK-47. "Let's go save the others."

The remaining gunmen were scattered across the various sections of the mall. One by one, going from one floor to another, from one side to another, Ojoré shot at the remaining gunmen. The terrorists were no match for Ojoré's perfect aim. It took Ojoré one more hour to finish them off. But by the end of it, he had saved many lives.

As the hostages exited, ambulances lined the mall. Ojoré walked out of the mall and fainted.

When he awoke, he was in a strange bed thousands of miles away from Nairobi, in a strange basement, along with four strangers beside him.

CHAPTER 10

An Irish Party

Wexford, Ireland
Three days before the State Opening of Parliament

On the outskirts of Wexford was an enormous ranch. Surrounded by a dense cover of tall trees, an old stone house did an excellent job of hiding itself at its center. It was impossible to spot the things that transpired inside. A vast underground bunker was built beside it during World War II with a massive iron door and strong concrete walls that protected and prevented anyone from escaping.

Tom Ashe—the ranch owner—finished inspecting the property, came inside, picked up the home phone, confirmed its dial tone, and placed it back. It was the fifteenth time he had done so since morning.

Why is it taking so long? Why hasn't he called yet? He paced the room, went outside, returned, and sat on the couch.

Something was wrong. He stood again. *I hate delays. We have prepared for so long for this plan.*

Tom was the grandson of an Irish nationalist who was killed more than a century ago in the Irish War of Independence by the British military. Like his father, he was anti-British and sympathetic to the Scottish-Northern Irish cause.

The phone rang. Ashe answered. "Where were you? Been waiting donkey's years. Is it canceled?" His concern showed up in his voice. "Remember, we won't get this chance again."

"It's not easy to collect everyone in secrecy. We couldn't catch all at the same time; we had to hold them here as we captured them one by one. And it is altogether another job to ship them across the sea, especially with this kind of security," replied the voice on the phone. "Our phone lines were compromised. I had to find a secure line. It's not like I can text you, can I? Anyways, we'll arrive tonight."

"What about Birdy?" he asked. "Mucker got the hosting job?"

"Yes, Birdwhistle will be anchoring. She'll make sure we get a live feed of everything. She has sneaked in a few of our blokes amongst the BBC camera crew. They have cameras at locations strategic to our plan."

"Fierce Birdy made it possible after all. We couldn't have managed this without her resources," Ashe said.

"I don't deny that she's sympathetic to our cause. But what she really wants is the crown. Remember her condition?"

"Yes, I remember it quite well," Ashe said. He paused for a second. "Alright, crack on, and be careful. See you soon." He hung up.

The time is right. It's now or never. He walked toward a picture frame hung on the nearby wall. It was a portrait of a middle-aged man wearing a khaki uniform and a wide-brimmed black hat. The man's clean-shaven face was elongated with a slender nose in the middle and long, blonde sideburns by the ears. "I'll avenge your death in a way the world will remember forever." Ashe stared at the picture of his grandfather. He had waited for this opportunity for a long time. Now was the time for his plans to bear fruit.

After several impatient hours, ten men accompanied by women and children arrived on his property. The women and children were gagged with pieces of cloth, their hands tied tightly behind their backs with ropes. The men covered their faces with hoodies.

"Take them inside, quick," Ashe shouted. "Nothing should seem out of place."

The hostages were brought into the basement, ungagged, untied, and given a sleeping bag and food to eat.

"We don't intend to kill any of ya. No one will be harmed. Well, that's if your men carry out our mission correctly," a middle-aged man with a thick Scottish accent said.

All the hostages in the basement were family members of the Blues and Royals and Lifeguards. Ashe and his Scottish mates took the soldiers' families hostage with Alexis' help and blackmailed them to assassinate the king and take the Imperial Crown of State. It was no ordinary effort, kidnapping so many people, especially with so much surveillance. But the plan that Alexis Birdwhistle devised was expertly executed. Everything was on track.

Hundreds of miles away, the soldiers from the two groups were about to take their positions inside the Westminster Palace, poised to shake the monarchy.

Alexis Birdwhistle held the strings of an act that was about to unfold in London.

CHAPTER

II

Aarno Heikkinen

Hostage 5
Kourtane, Western Finland, Finland

It was the end of November in the lakeside town of Kourtane. As autumn caved into winter, the colorful canvas of red, orange, yellow, and green on trees disappeared, and a monochromatic white of snow and ice transpired. The days became shorter as the nights became colder. Streets were filled with tourists carrying skis, ice skates, snowboards, and other winter gear while locals began preparations for the upcoming holidays.

Away from it all was the Heikkinen manor. Inside the manor, Aarno uncovered himself from the sheets, stepped out from his bed, fastened the belts of his woolen robes around his waist, and slid his feet inside a pair of cushioned slippers. A distant grandfather clock in another room sounded seven chimes to announce seven in the evening. He picked up the remote, turned on the television on the opposite wall from the bed, and left it running. The news played on it.

The room was big, with a king-size teakwood bed in the middle, long windows covered with maroon curtains, a fireplace in the corner, and mahogany flooring. The door to the walk-in closet was beside the bed, while the bathroom door was next to the television.

Aarno walked to the bathroom sink, applied toothpaste to his brush, and cleaned his teeth.

Knock! Knock! Knock!

Aarno finished gargling and went to answer the door.

"Up, are we? Why so early?" an older man asked. The expressions on his face were halfway between disappointment and anger. He donned a long, dark-gray winter coat over a grey suit with a navy-blue tie. He placed his left hand on the polished birch door, trying to push it open.

"What do you need?" Aarno asked lazily, holding the door against the push.

"Here, this came from the University of Pennsylvania." Aarno's father handed him an envelope. "They will unenroll you if you don't return this semester."

Aarno ignored him.

"It's been months since your mother's demise, Aarno. Put yourself back together. You can't go on this way." Aarno's father looked into his eyes. "You were my brightest son. My best."

Aarno smiled a halfhearted smile. The two stood in silence for a few seconds. Only the sound of the television from inside Aarno's room came out.

Aarno's father pushed on the door with force and flung it open. He entered the room and shook his head at the sight of empty liquor bottles on the floor. "You drink morning, noon, and night," his father shouted. "Your brothers and I personally took you to counseling sessions. I paid for your rehab, provided everything there is, but you don't show any improvement at all. You're not even trying, Aarno. On the contrary, you're getting worse. Instead of bars, now we find you drunk, passed out in casinos." He stared back into Aarno's face. "I've not worked hard over these years so that you can gamble our wealth away. I'm fed up with you."

Aarno smirked.

"What's that?" His father tilted his head. "You think we're fools running after you to help? If I'd not promised your mother—" He paused. Aarno's father removed his glasses and wiped his eyes. "It would've pained her to see you like this."

At that moment, Aarno's face appeared on the television. His father turned to face it. "Look, the media calls you a wealthy, spoilt brat, no regard for the family reputation."

Aarno entered the walk-in closet and closed the doors in his father's face. He changed into a pair of joggers and a sweatshirt and sheathed himself inside a puffer jacket with gloves and a woolen cap.

"Where are you going now?" his father asked when Aarno reemerged from the closet.

"You know where I'm going."

"Aarno, please." His father placed a hand on his shoulder.

"I am sorry, Father." He slid it aside, walked out of his room.

He took the winding mahogany staircase at the end of the hallway to the expansive living area on the ground floor of the mansion and rushed outside. A navy-blue Range Rover waited for him in the portico.

"The usual place?" the driver asked as he opened the door for him. He nodded.

Aarno scrolled through his phone on his way to the bar, shaking his head as he glanced at the negative pieces in the media about him. When he closed his eyes, flashes of the fateful night when his mother passed away came rushing in, driving hard the need for a drink. The car came to a halt. Aarno stepped out and opened the doors to a sports bar lined with several big screens. It was the only place that played American college basketball games.

The place was packed. Only one seat at the bar counter was vacant. He took it. The TV screen in front showed a basketball game between Penn Quakers and Princeton Tigers.

"The usual?" The bartender placed a coaster before him.

"Yes."

A few minutes later, the bartender served him Scotland's finest whiskey on a spherical ice cube that occupied most of the glass.

"You have good taste in poison," the man on the seat next to him said. "You look familiar." He had neat, grey hair, a chubby face, and ice-blue eyes. At about five feet five inches, he was a little plump with a shaved face but a walrus mustache. He wore a black sweatshirt engraved with a golden shield-shaped logo over a pair of blue jeans. Kourtane Sports Institute was embroidered inside the logo.

Aarno looked away from him, trying to hide his face.

"You are him, aren't you? Aarno Heikkinen."

Aarno gulped his drink in one go, placed some cash on the counter, and stood up.

"Wait." The man placed a hand on his shoulder. "Please, sit back. I won't bother you like the Paps. I promise."

"This place is frequented mainly by North American expats. They play mostly basketball on screens. I don't expect or like people chasing me down here." Aarno returned to his seat.

"Again, I'm sorry. Let me get you your next drink." He gestured to the bartender.

The bartender returned with two drinks. "Here." The man lifted his glass and moved it toward Aarno. "Cheers."

They sipped a few sips in silence. The alcohol calmed his nerves.

"I'm Matias Laine, by the way." The man extended an arm.

Aarno shook it. "What do you do, Laine?"

"I'm the director of the Kourtane Sports Institute. It is very famous, although I'm quite new to the institute. We've produced many athletes who excelled in the javelin throw. As you must know, Finland has a long list of Olympic gold winners in the track and field category, especially in the javelin throw. Most of them have trained at our Institute. In fact, we are hosting the World Javelin Conference in a few months. Athletes, coaches, and training staff from across the world will attend. You play any sports?"

"I used to play basketball when I was in the States," Aarno replied among the cheers and hooting of other patrons watching the game.

"Oh, so you've come to enjoy the game." Laine nodded as he finished his drink.

"Yes, this is the only place that plays them," Aarno said. He rotated his seat toward the bartender and gestured for a refill.

"Nice. Well, I must get going. I have to pick a few things from the shop next door before it closes. Enjoy the game. Good night."

"Good night."

The man left. Aarno enjoyed the remaining quarters of the game on TV, but the result left him disappointed. The Penn Quakers had lost. He finished his drink and left the bar.

"Home or casino, sir?" his driver asked as he held open the door for him.

"Casino." The Range Rover exited the bar and drove through busy streets. Halfway to the casino, he told the driver, "I want to take a leak; can't hold it until we reach there. Pull over here for a minute." The driver obeyed.

It was a narrow lane with old brick houses and shops lining both sides. Most of them looked broken and abandoned. The paved curb was dirty and damaged. Weeds grew on it through cracks and crevices. Most street lights were out, with only a few flickering intermittently.

As Aarno emptied his screaming bladder, he heard, "Empty your pockets."

A man was pointing a knife at a middle-aged fellow. One more stood behind him. He could only see their silhouettes. They were far, about one hundred feet, but as the street was quiet, he could hear it all.

"I'm not seeking any trouble. Here. It's all yours; take it and let me go, I won't call the police." The victim handed them his wallet, watch, phone, and jewelry. Only the ring on his finger remained.

"I want that ring as well," one holding the knife said.

The victim remained silent.

"I said I want that damn ring."

"No. You can have everything else, but not this. This is my wedding ring." The victim moved his hand behind his back, hiding the ring. "My wife is no more. It helps me feel that she is still around. I cannot part with it."

"Now listen, man, you don't want to join your wife, do you? Be a good lad and hand it over. We'll let you go without harm."

"What part of 'No' did you not understand?" The man did not budge.

"Here's the thing. I'm going to count till three, and if I don't have it by the end—"

"Let's not escalate this; you have enough in there. More than enough, if you ask me. You didn't come to kill; you don't want the police on your tail. Just take all that and let me go."

The second mugger pulled a gun from his pocket. "You trying to act smart, old man? Hand us the ring."

Aarno didn't know what to do. He had nothing on him.

"One," the man with the gun counted.

Aarno decided to run toward them, but what could he do against a bullet? Besides, it was quite far.

A gust of wind went through the alley, carrying a biting chill. Not a single light was on in the houses or shops around.

"Hey! Leave him alone," he shouted, but his voice didn't reach the muggers.

Aarno looked beside him. Nothing.

He looked and looked. No luck.

"Two," he heard.

Finally, he spotted a fence in a nearby house. It was made of iron rods with pointed ends. A segment was broken with one loose rod sticking out, almost like a spear. Rust and withering had made it sharp. Aarno picked it up.

Suddenly, he felt control in his arm, as if the spear and his hand were one.

"Three."

The victim was still defiant.

The gunman sighed. Shook his head, ready to pull the trigger. Aarno raised the rod, pulled it back, and launched it into the air. Right when the gunman pulled the trigger, the rod sped like a rocket and struck him on the hand holding the gun.

The bullet missed. The other robber stood in shock for a second, then darted.

Aarno ran toward the victim through the potholed street, stooped down, put his arm under his shoulder, and helped him stand. The victim's face came into focus under the flickering of the street light.

"Laine?"

Blankness.

"Are you all right? Remember me? We just met at the bar."

Laine's eyes widened. "Yes, Aarno. I've never seen a throw like that in my life."

☙❧

Over the next few weeks, Laine relentlessly chased, cajoled, and pleaded with Aarno to visit the Kourtane Sports Institute. Aarno initially avoided him, but when Laine continued to show up at one of the casinos he frequented, he finally agreed to give it a go.

"He's our hidden jewel. Hand him the javelin, and you'll have no doubts that we have an Olympian," Laine introduced Aarno to his coaching staff.

The coaches obliged and watched with delight as Aarno displayed his talent. To his astonishment, Aarno enjoyed it too. From that day, he became a regular at the academy. He practiced hard. All his depression, anxiety, and addiction channeled into a passion for this sport. Whenever he threw a javelin, it felt like he had done it for ages. He won several awards and international competitions. Aarno's attitude changed. He was Laine's poster boy and the media's sweetheart. The news about him went from bashing to praising. There was nothing like a comeback story, and his was one the people adored.

Time passed. The World Javelin Conference was in full swing at the Kourtane Sports Institute. On the last day of the conference, the Institute organized a session for kids, young adults, and their parents.

Mr. Laine handed the microphone to Aarno. They were standing on an auditorium stage with hundreds of faces staring at them. A huge banner with the words '5th *World Javelin Conference*' written over it hung behind them. The auditorium's side walls had several pictures of current and past athletes.

Aarno dived into his speech. It was fabulous. He mentioned his past, his struggles, and his grief after his mother passed away. He talked about how the cycle of addiction and gambling trapped him, and how sports helped him overcome it. "The key to being a successful leader is to listen to every point of view and believe in yourself and your team. But honesty, fair play, and always doing the right thing are the most important things in the end," he said.

"When all's said, all's done, your trophies won't mean anything if you got them by deceit. History won't remember you."

When he finished, applause echoed through the auditorium.

"That was excellent," Mr. Laine told Aarno, "I'm so proud of what you have made of yourself, Aarno."

"It was you who turned things for me, sir. I was a train wreck when you picked me up."

"I am just the means. You are the star that shines." He smiled. "Anyways, I have something for you. Let's walk by the lake, shall we?"

"Sure."

They strolled across the banks of the lake and soaked in the fresh air. The sun had set with faint dusk lights coloring the sky. An army of pine trees surrounded the shores of the lake on most sides while gentle waves brushed the sand on which they walked. The smell of pinecones and acorns filled the gentle breeze that ran along with the waves.

"It's wonderful here, isn't it?"

"It's always excellent. This is where I found solace when I first came to the Institute," Aarno said. He took a deep breath to take in the sweet fragrance.

They walked for quite a while until they were far away from the crowd. Laine halted. Aarno continued a few more steps, then stopped as well. He turned around to face Laine. "I'm sorry, Aarno." Laine's face was stern.

"Sorry? For what?"

"For this." Laine pulled a gun from his jacket pocket. "It was never about the Institute or the sport."

"What do you mean? I don't understand."

"The night you saved me from those robbers several months back—" Laine paused.

"What about it?"

"It- it was all staged. I hired those robbers myself."

"What are you talking about?" Aarno's face showed his shock.

Laine ignored. "I had to be sure you were the one we sought. That's why I took so many months, made you come to the Institute, spent time with you."

"Who are we?"

Laine did not answer. He raised the gun. *Swoop! Swoop!*

Pain shot through Aarno's abdomen. "Aaah!" It crept to his chest. He looked down. Not a single bullet pierced his torso, nor was there any blood. Instead, a pointed needle stuck out from the area of pain. Seconds later, he found himself losing consciousness.

When he could resist no more, Aarno closed his eyes, only to open them again in a bed hundreds of miles away. Alongside him were Darren, Ojoré, Liang, and Diego.

CHAPTER
11

Continued-

A s Aarno finished telling them how he was abducted, the dungeon went silent but for the creaking of the ceiling fan and the flickering of the tubelight.

"I was shocked beyond belief to find Doug, the man I had conned that same day, abducting me," Liang said to the room. "However, it's nothing compared to what you must've felt." Liang turned his face toward Aarno.

"It all happened so fast. I couldn't understand anything at the time. But when I regained consciousness and remembered it, yes, it broke my heart. I trusted Laine and looked up to him. After all, he did help me get out of depression." Aarno shook his head. "But it is what it is."

"You two were tricked. In Darren and Ojoré's case, the circumstances were such that they didn't have a choice. But in my case, I willingly walked with that guy Castello. How stupid was I?" Diego closed his eyes, shook his head

"Don't blame yourself, Diego," Aarno replied. "I would have done the same thing in your place. They deceived us all."

"I wonder if it was just one guy," Liang said, staring at the ceiling.

"What the heck do you mean by that?" Darren raised his voice in frustration.

"I mean, were Doug, Castello, Laine, and the medics who took you and Ojore the same person?"

"That's an interesting thought, Liang." Aarno turned his face toward Diego. "How did Castello look? How did he sound?"

"He was tall, lean, pale in color, had black hair, and a thick Spanish accent. I think from Spain. Probably in his late forties."

"Not the same. Mr. Laine was nothing like that. He was older, short, and medium built with white hair. Spoke English with a heavy Finnish accent."

"Yes, definitely different people. Doug was about five-seven, quite heavy, blonde hair, and had a clear American accent."

"So, it's a team, it seems," Aarno added.

There was silence. Everyone was trying to make sense of what they had heard. Sharing their stories, however, had settled the mood in the room.

"Thank God I never went to Shanghai and ran into you." Diego lifted his neck and smiled at Liang. "But I must say, that was a smart con, the tea performance. Not unlike how I charm the ladies. The only difference is that I don't con my senhoras."

"I'm not proud of it." Liang smiled back. "But I had to do it, to earn my living somehow. Shanghai's a tough place to survive."

"Well, at least one of us is *extraordinário*." Diego turned his head toward Ojoré. "You saved all those people from the terrorists."

"I wish it had never happened. It haunts me even today." Ojoré's face dimmed. "I lost my cousin Samuel that night."

"I'm so sorry, brother." Aarno struggled to lift his head. "I understand how it feels to lose loved ones."

"I'm sorry too, *amigo*." Diego's smile was replaced with guilt. He sighed, looking at the ceiling fan. "I thought I'd be playing for Manchester United, but ended up here instead. The last thing I remember is Castello taking me to a bar soon after I landed in Old Trafford."

"I was aiming for Olympic gold," Aarno added.

"I just wanted to eat at the goddamn rodeo and return to my dorm. Now, I am freakin' kidnapped," Darren bellowed. "Look at my size. Would anyone believe that I was abducted?"

The others lifted their heads to look at Darren and laughed a hearty laugh. Darren joined them in the laughter.

It was the first time they had laughed since they woke up. It felt good despite the struggle to stretch those facial muscles.

CHAPTER 12

Imperial Crown of State

London, England

"Welcome back," Alexis Birdwhistle greeted the viewers. "The ceremony has started. As you can see, there is a strict and rehearsed sequence. It's been followed for centuries. The members are assembling in their respective houses; the hostage has already been delivered to the palace." Alexis' face was replaced by visuals from inside and outside the palace. "There's the king's royal carriage; he is getting a grand welcome on the porch."

One by one, Alexis' voice described the dignitaries who lined up to receive the king. "His Majesty is now advancing toward the Queen's Robing Room where he will don the Royal Regalia."

The king reemerged from the room and proceeded to the House of Lords.

"Look at that Imperial Crown of State on his majesty's head," Alexis commented. The camera zoomed in on the crown. "Beautiful, isn't it? Dazzling with all those gems. Oh my, can't get enough of it, can you?" Her face lit up at the sight of the crown.

After entering the House of Lords, the king occupied the throne. He unraveled the speech scroll and uttered, "My Lords, pray be seated."

No sooner did he speak those words than there was a long, loud, echoing scream through the hallway.

"What was that? What was that sound?" Alexis asked, looking into the camera.

The Blues and Royals and Life Guards had launched their attack. The men broke themselves into two groups as instructed by Ashe's comrades over the microphone. One group secured all the doors and entrances to the palace so that the police and military could not enter, while the other proceeded to the House of Lords.

"I can't believe my eyes, this is terrible. The Blues and Royals and Life Guards are killing people. No, this can't be, can't be true." Alexis brought her right hand to her forehead as she spoke into the camera.

Visuals from different cameras and angles played on various screens, each covering a different side of Westminster.

"But why? I don't understand." Alexis asked. She acted her part well.

People scattered haywire from the attacking men, screaming for help. Few resisted with whatever they could find: vases, candle stands, belts.

"They're killing anyone who is standing up to them. Oh no, it's awful. No, beyond awful." In her heart, Alexis was elated. Her plan was unfolding before her eyes.

"Looks like Yeomen of the Guard, the king's personal bodyguards, are forming a circle around him. God bless them!" Alexis spoke. "As long as they're around him, the king has a chance." She paused. "I'm sorry, I'm not sure if we should air this, but we can't stop now; our viewers need to know." She made sure the coverage went uninterrupted. Her plants in the newsroom forced all her superiors to continue streaming.

When the attacking men reached the king's circle of protection, a great fight commenced between the Yeomen and the attacking men. The Yeomen were outnumbered almost four to one. Their attackers formed an outer circle and faced them with swords pointing toward them. There were no shields to defend. The men from the outer circle attacked the Yeomen from four different directions. Bending, charging on the front foot, rotating the swords to deflect the blows, both sides displayed exquisite skills with the sword.

After a few minutes, one side of the protective circle weakened. The two Yeomen defending this side succumbed to their wounds.

Wasting no time, the remaining attackers plunged in and broke the symmetry. The defense disintegrated. The Yeomen dispersed. One by one, they fell.

"I can't believe we're witnessing this live. This is dreadful." Alexis shook her head in front of the camera.

Ashe and his comrades watched as their plan played out in real-time as they gave orders to the soldiers on the ground through their earpieces.

One of the Yeomen managed to escort the king to another room as others provided him cover.

A few Blues and Royals soldiers pursued the king and reluctantly held him from behind.

"No. No. No. This can't happen; this is beyond imagination. This can't happen on British soil," Alexis screamed into the microphone.

The soldier gripped his sword tightly, closed his eyes, and brought it near the king's throat.

Take the crown first, you idiot! Alexis wanted to scream at the soldier. Her primary goal was the crown.

"Oh God, please no," she said instead. "Only a miracle can save the king; only a miracle can save this country."

There was no way out. The world was about to see a horrible assassination of a monarch on live television. The soldier was about to obey the orders.

Just then, *woooushhhh!*

Copious amounts of water gushed inside the Palace of Westminster, flooding the entire building.

"Wait a minute, what the heck?" Alexis shouted. "Pardon my language, but this is unbelievable. How is all this water coming in?"

Her question was answered when the visuals on the television screen split to show the outside of Westminster along with the inside.

Outside, something had broken loose across the river, something humongous, something massive. The London Eye had come apart. It had rolled down the banks of the Thames and finally, tilting toward the right, collapsed into the river. It caused a small tsunami into the river that stormed toward the palace and flooded the insides with eight to ten feet of water.

The attackers, the defenders, the spectators; everyone tried hard to stay afloat.

At this opportunity, one of the surviving Yeomen guards swam toward the king. He grabbed the monarch by the hand, pushed him up, and carried him into the adjoining room. There, the king hid behind a huge statue.

"Oh, thank God, thank the mighty God, as bizarre as it seems, it could not have come at a better time. It's a miracle, it's a miracle," Alexis said, clenching her fist under the table, trying hard to hide her disappointment.

Alexis was dumbfounded. For the next several minutes, she did not speak but only watched the visuals on the studio screens in disbelief.

All my hard work of the last several months has washed away. She tried hard to hide her anger from the camera. *The Parieur will be so disappointed in me.*

Slowly, after several hours, the water subsided. Police entered the palace and arrested all the surviving attackers.

Several people lost their lives, but the king survived through the utter luck of his own and because of one Yeomen's courage. But the crown was not on his head.

The monarch was escorted to Buckingham Palace while the police searched for the crown. After hours and hours of searching, they found nothing.

The Imperial Crown of State was gone!

CHAPTER 13

Black Prince's Ruby

Somewhere

Thousands of miles east of London, inside a jungle too vast, was an old cave. A cluster of Banyan trees with intertwined branches and aerial roots covered every inch of it, while thick vegetation surrounded the neighboring area, making it almost invisible. Many dangerous animals—tigers, leopards, sloth bears, and rhinos—called this area their home. The forest department officers had restricted public access in this area. They hardly ventured here themselves and did not know of the cave's existence. It was not the wild beasts; something else filled their hearts with fear.

"Speak not of that place. It's cursed. No one should go near it," the native tribes warned. "It belongs to the White Ghost."

Their ancestors told them stories about its presence. Some had seen the shadow of this so-called ghost, while several others did not return at all. The ones that did were left with little mind of their own.

There was good reason for this rumor, indeed. The cave was not empty. A tall, old, hairy, and ghastly figure lived within. The White Ghost woke up from several years of deep slumber right when Sánchez came back from a coma thousands of miles away in Las Vegas.

For the past several days, though, The Ghost had been away, miles away from his cave, into a different type of jungle, a jungle of people, traffic, and buildings, in the city of London. On his mission in those foreign lands, he managed to remain unseen. He was there to get what was rightfully his, a part of his body that he had lost centuries ago.

Night spread its dark cloak over the jungle. As the figure entered his dominion, trees, branches, and roots untangled, making way for him to return to the cave—his den, his home for so many centuries. Here, he had hibernated, deep in sleep, lifeless. Ghostlike.

From the second he roused, only one thing occupied his mind: *find it, take it back.* But now, there was nothing to worry about. He had gotten it back. All these years, he endured his punishment, but now he could make it right.

Now, he could redeem himself.

The Ghost entered the cavern. Formed in rock and stone, the cave was dusty, with dried leaves, grass, and gravel covering the floor. An extended, stone platform covered with several layers of animal skin formed a bed in one corner, while a glass lantern hung from a post beside it.

From his robes, he removed the sparkling Imperial Crown of State that he had taken from his adventure abroad in London.

That was the difficult part. I can't believe I pulled it off with most of my powers gone. He closed his eyes and relived his adventure in England. He had tried to break into the Jewel House a few days before the State Opening of Parliament but was unsuccessful.

They almost saw me that night, nearly caught me. He sighed.

The Ghost recalled how he had used the London catacombs to reach the London Eye, how he used his diminished powers to let the Ferris wheel loose, and how he swam with the tsunami caused by its collapse to enter the Palace of Westminster during the ceremony.

If I were even a minute late, the crown would have been gone. He recalled how the crown fell off the King's head, sank to the flooded floor, and how he went underneath the water to grab it.

The White Ghost opened his eyes. He plucked the Black Prince's Ruby from the crown, clasped his hand around it, and carelessly tossed the crown to the floor. It circled like a trompo and settled on the stony floor.

They call that piece of metal the royal crown? He smirked.

The White Ghost placed the Black Prince's Ruby on the stone table and caressed it with his fingers. His maroon eyes stared at it with awe. He kissed it countless times as if reunited with a lost child. He didn't care about the Imperial Crown of State and all its gold, diamonds, and jewels. He only cared for the Black Prince's Ruby, his ruby.

The White Ghost placed the red gem in his palm and lifted it toward his forehead, where a big scar in the form of a cavity waited impatiently. The scar matched the shape of the ruby precisely. The ghost positioned the ruby in this cavity.

No sooner did the ruby touch his scar than a beam of light shot from his forehead, lighting up the entire jungle.

Loud animal calls echoed throughout.

Wrinkles on his body faded, and his muscles pumped up. The brown and dirty dreadlocks on his head fashioned into an elegant braid, and he transformed into a young man of strength, grandeur, and brilliance.

At that exact moment, a few extraordinary individuals in different parts of the world passed out. Aarno, Darren, Liang, Diego, and Ojoré were among them.

It was several months before their abductions. Aarno at the card table in a casino in Finland, Darren on his dorm bed at the University of Houston, Ojoré inside his hut in the Bángá village in Kenya, Diego making out with a soccer teammate in her room at São Paulo, and Liang at the Bund in Shanghai sitting on a bench holding Sun's hand.

They went into a brief slumber of their own with flashes of the White Ghost and his red gem on the forehead, only to arise again and realize their destiny.

CHAPTER 14

The Common Thread

The laughter in the dungeon died, and the room went mute once more. Thoughts from each other's stories went through the five hostages' minds again. They spent several long minutes staring at the ceiling. Shadows of the ceiling fan flashed on it as the tubelight flickered along.

"Well? Did anyone find the link? We heard everyone's stories; what do you think connects us?" Aarno asked.

No one answered.

"Liang?" Aarno turned toward him

"Our stories were as similar as the five fingers in my hand," Liang replied. "I can't find anything I can point to."

"There's no smokin' gun," Darren said.

"Anyone else?" Aarno asked.

They shook their heads.

"We are at the same darn place where we started," Darren squawked.

"There has to be something." Aarno stressed his brain. "There has to be a common thread. There has to be something that connects us all."

Aarno's mind dived into deep thought. He held something inside for a long time, something he never told anyone before, something he thought no one would understand or believe. *Shall I mention it to them? Shall I share that incident? Maybe that's what connects us all.*

He hesitated for a few minutes, but when he could no longer hold it, he spoke. "Gentlemen," he paused for their attention. "Have you guys experienced something weird in your life? Something that you would think does not make sense? Something—" he hesitated, "Magical? Paranormal?"

He waited.

"Have you guys ever passed out with visions of a man with a red gem on his forehead? Would you guys think I'm mad if I told you that I saw huge bubble-like objects floating midair all around me, that they had views of a mystical place within, and- and right after that, I had an out-of-this-world experience."

What Aarno said sparked an explosion inside their brains. They had all seen the bubble-like objects in their past, and right after that, they had all experienced something paranormal. It was as if a fire was lit. Everyone was galvanized.

Looking at their expressions, Aarno knew it was time to tell what had happened to him many years ago.

CHAPTER 15

The Golden Labyrinth

Philadelphia, Pennsylvania
Aarno's Story — A few years before the abduction

"This referee is terrible," Chris shouted as he gathered around his teammates at halftime. "They're playing extremely rough, making fouls one after another, but he has not called a single one yet."

They were in the middle of an intense basketball game between the Penn Quakers and Princeton Tigers. It was a fierce rivalry. Chris was with the Penn Quakers, the University of Pennsylvania basketball team.

"We have to play the same way, kick some ass." Chris shook his fist.

"No, we will not," Aarno countered. "We play by the rules; we play the right way."

"We're losing the game; your principles are not going to help us," Chris bellowed.

"Win or lose, how we play the game and whether we give our best is what matters. Trust me, we'll come through."

Aarno was the point guard and manager of the Penn Quakers, the only person to do so in the University's history. The team was abysmal in the previous years, so the school trusted him with both responsibilities at his insistence. That year, Aarno's leadership and on-court contribution helped them rise.

"All we need to do is execute our basics right, play to our strengths. We've dominated the entire season. We'll not be intimidated now. Trust me, when we score a few points in a row, they'll worry. We just have to get into our rhythm. So, tell me, who is the best?"

"We are," the team shouted.

"And who will win the game?"

"We will!"

"Now, let's go and show them what we got."

An intense quarter followed. The Penn Quakers struggled but later recovered.

"Team. We did great, still lagging, but we didn't let their lead increase. We have one full quarter. Let's close this out."

A few minutes into the fourth quarter, Aarno scored a couple of three-pointers in a row, and the momentum shifted in their favor. As he had said, the Tigers panicked.

At the final whistle, the Penn Quakers triumphed. Euphoria filled the stadium, and the Quakers' fans lifted the players and paraded around the arena.

Chris hugged Aarno. "You were right; they panicked when we started scoring. That referee couldn't do a thing."

Aarno smiled. "Just because the opponent stoops low doesn't mean we do the same. I knew we had it in us to win." He patted Chris's back.

The celebrations followed at the University.

As the bus entered the campus, the expensive piece of glass on Aarno's wrist came to life. Red and green icons for accept or reject popped up on the Apple Watch edition, along with his father's face.

Father? At this hour? It's 3:00 AM in Finland.

Aarno was the eldest of the three Heikkinen brothers. They were an affluent family and among the richest in Finland. Before coming to the United States for his MBA, Aarno finished his bachelor's degree in paper and pulp manufacturing from the University of Helsinki and joined his father in their family business. Their company, Heikkinen Private Ltd., was the biggest manufacturer and seller of paper-based consumer products and personal care items, ranging from printing papers to facial tissues in Europe.

"Aarno, my boy, I am so happy. You make me so proud. Your leadership and entrepreneurial skills impressed everyone at the company," his father had said one day. He had a balding head of ash-blonde hair and was a few inches shorter than Aarno, but his eyes were the same shade of blue, and the nose on his round face was small like his sons'. "You have inherited my knack for leading. That's what I love." Aarno's father took him in a tight embrace. He was elated to find a worthy successor in his eldest son.

Aarno worked with his father for three years. Despite the short span, shadowing his father and learning fast, he impressed everyone in the company.

Aarno had two younger brothers who looked like him. One brother was a senior in college, while the other was a sophomore. They both loved him and looked up to him. Aarno pushed them to intern with the company during semester breaks and mentored them in each aspect of their business.

But slowly, Aarno's interest in the business waned. He yearned for something else. Something he had not found yet. He didn't tell his parents any of this, but his mother felt his struggle.

"I want something else, Mom," he finally told his mother. "I don't know what yet. I just want to be away for a while, to gain clarity."

"But your father will not like it," his mother told him. She was shorter by a foot and had a thin frame with blonde hair over an oval face. "He believes in you so much, Aarno. He even mentioned retiring to me." She held him by the shoulders.

"I doubt that will happen anytime soon. He loves his work."

"That I agree. But he did say that, though he might not do it immediately. He talks about what a good job you are doing, how well you are grooming your younger brothers."

"But it no longer interests me, Mother."

"But what about your father? He will explode."

Are you with me or not?"

"Have I ever left your side, son?" She placed her right hand on Aarno's cheek.

"Thanks, Mom. You're the best." Aarno hugged her tightly.

A few months later, without his father's knowledge, Aarno moved to the US for his master's.

His father was furious at his decision and never missed an opportunity to remind Aarno about that. This always came up in their phone conversations.

Months passed with seasons. His father seldom called these days, and when he did, Aarno never answered. They only talked when he called his mom, and his father was around. The call usually ended with his father criticizing his decision, and him hanging up the phone.

Father and Mother never call this late.

He let it go to voicemail. The next minute, his father called again.

He never calls back if I don't pick up; it must be important.

After staring at the watch for a few more seconds, he answered the call. "Yes, Father?"

There was no reply for a while, only faint sobs. After the brief silence, there was a clearing of the throat and a deep breath. "Y- y- your mother is in the hospital. I have sent my jet to get you. My secretary Richard is on it, he will accompany you back. Son, it's serious." His father sobbed more.

"But why? What happened?" Aarno asked. He could not comprehend it.

"My secretary will tell you everything. Be at the airport in four hours."

In four hours, Aarno was packed up and ready at the airport. When he saw Richard, he ran toward him. "What happened?"

"Heart attack. The doctors are performing surgery right now. It was all so sudden," Richard replied.

It was as if a rug was pulled from under Aarno's feet. He couldn't comprehend how to react. He was not ready for this. The thought of his mother, the strongest person he knew, his favorite in the world, being so weak, so vulnerable, never occurred in his mind.

He boarded the aircraft, which took off and cruised across the Atlantic. It was a seven-passenger jet with plush leather seats, polished wood accents, and warm lights. After several hours of fear and anxiety, the flight descended. In a few minutes, which seemed like hours to Aarno, the aircraft landed. The next moment, Aarno was on a chopper that took him to the hospital, where his mother was admitted.

No sooner did the helicopter touch the ground than Aarno unbuckled and jumped out. He sprinted toward the hospital, went past the reception desk, took the elevator, got out on the third floor, ran along the hallway, and found his two brothers near the doors of the ICU. "What room is she in?"

His youngest brother, Aarvo, hugged him. The other brother, Aarto, came and embraced both of them. There, like that, the three brothers sobbed in a huddle.

"Don't worry. We will get through this. She will be fine. I am here now. Everything will be fine," Aarno consoled Aarvo and Aarto.

After some time, his youngest brother gathered himself. "I'm sorry, *veli*, y- you just missed her; *äiti* is no more." He broke down on Aarno's shoulders.

Aarno didn't shed a tear. He couldn't. It was as if the tears had dried up. "What room is she in?"

"The ICU; that door."

He walked toward the ICU, opened the door, and went inside. There she lay, lifeless, his father standing next to the bed, sobbing. He approached Aarno. "All she wanted in her last hours was to see you, Aarno."

Aarno came near his mother, kissed her on the forehead, and stared at her face. Memories flooded his mind. But he still found himself incapable of crying. He stood up, went out of the room, and ran. He ran out of the hospital onto the parking lot, on the sidewalk, alongside the lake, into the woods. He ran for a long time, miles away from the hospital. The forest took him in with open arms.

It was predawn, there was not enough light. Following the faint outline of a loam trail sided with tall coniferous trees, Aarno climbed high atop a hill and stopped only when he could go no further. He stood at the edge of a canyon, staring into the vast, dark abyss below. He could hear the sound of a gushing stream coming from the canyon beneath.

Cold air gushed around his ears. Lifeless, he stood, unable to think.

Finally, there they were. A few tears trickled, and the floodgates opened. He cried loudly, shouting into the damp air. "I couldn't even say goodbye." The thought ate him like termites.

Suddenly, several bubble-like objects appeared around him. They floated midair and resembled soap bubbles but did not break. A golden light emanated from inside them, making them visible in the darkness. He looked over the cliff, found several of them floating between him and the abyss.

Lack of sleep, jetlag, and sadness made Aarno dizzy. He had run for hours. His vision became blurred, his foot slipped, and his body free-fell off the cliff into the canyon below. The pressure of the air rushing past his body brought him to his senses. He knew what was coming. Any moment, his body would hit the rocks of the flowing stream, and his bones would be crushed into pieces.

He readied himself for the inevitable.

Instead of the crash, however, something unusual transpired. Aarno was directly in the path of the floating bubble, and his body collided with it. Nanoseconds later, he felt his entire body pass under an ice-cold waterfall, but it did not make him wet. He did not understand what was going on, but he knew he had entered the bubble-like object.

All of a sudden, there was a blinding light everywhere. His body landed on soft tree branches, slowing his momentum.

The next moment, his bottom touched solid ground. It took him a few seconds to gain clarity. When he finally looked around, his eyes lit up in wonder.

In front of him was an endless tree structure. The branches, leaves, and other parts of the trees were interwoven like fabric to make a gigantic labyrinth that seemed to go on for miles and miles. Light emanated from between the base of the trees and illuminated this transcendent place in the most spectacular manner. Aarno stood up and looked in detail. The source of the light was bioluminescent roots.

The light was amplified by something that blew his mind. In between the hanging, entangled branches were strands of gold. The entire network was full of these enchanting strands that seemed to extend infinitely within this maze.

After recovering from this wonderment, Aarno walked ahead. "*Hei?*"

The structure was not random. The tree-covered, tunnel-like paths extended in all directions, resembling the bylines of a busy neighborhood. The tunnels intersected randomly and organically.

As he walked further, rocks and boulders appeared in some places between the trees. Slowly, the path inclined downward, and a cave-like structure emerged above the mesh of branches.

Gold, gold, gold. It was everywhere.

A few steps ahead, a river rushed on the side. The current was strong. Aarno was tired and thirsty. He jumped off his path onto the banks and quenched his thirst. No sooner did he do so than panic replaced his awe. Paralysis slowly overtook his body. His vision became blurred again.

Almost instantaneously, the sound of hurried steps alerted him. He, however, could not see who it was.

The owner of these feet was a short, dwarf-like figure. It stared piercingly at Aarno's face. The figure pulled out a rope, tied Aarno's limbs, and picked him up like a bundle of a rug. The little bugger had strength.

"Kuka sinä olet?" Aarno shouted.

No reply.

"Who are you? Where are you taking me?"

No reply.

A few feet away, from out of nowhere, a second figure jumped in front and struck the one carrying Aarno.

Aarno's body landed on the hard, root-and-dirt-covered surface. In his paralyzed state, he was still aware. Blurry outlines of the two figures fought fiercely in front of him.

The struggle lasted several minutes and ended only when the figure carrying Aarno fell into the river and was washed away by the strong currents. The surviving figure picked Aarno up and moved him.

"Wait! What's going on? Where am I? Who are you?" he shouted again.

Again, there was no reply.

After a few minutes, the figure stopped and stuffed something in Aarno's mouth. Instantly, sensation returned to Aarno's limbs.

Once again, a bubble-like object was in front of them. However, this time, there was no golden light inside; it was dark.

The figure untied Aarno, stared at him for a minute, and pushed him forward into the bubble.

Aarno once again felt as if his body had gone under an ice-cold waterfall.

The next moment, his vision cleared, and he found himself standing at the edge of the same cliff from which he had fallen.

CHAPTER 16

The Correct Answer!

Paris, France

The airplane descended, cutting through patches of white clouds, and a beautiful city appeared.

"Ladies and gentlemen, we will land at Charles de Gaulle International Airport shortly. In preparation for landing, please make your seats upright, secure your tray table, and fasten your seatbelts," an attendant announced into the PA system. It went on for a few minutes.

"Let me take that for you, sir," another attendant extended a hand to a middle-aged man in seat 28A. He had a pale complexion, lean body, elongated nose, brown hair, and gray eyes. A golden necklace wrapped around his neck, holding a pendant made from two dice. They displayed six dots each.

He handed his trash to the attendant. The next attendant handed him forms for immigration and customs. He completed the forms and placed them inside his passport.

Although he had visited other parts of Europe, he had not visited Paris. His wife always demanded a vacation here, but it never materialized. They had planned several times, but his work kept him busy. Even today, she was not with him. This time, it was neither vacation nor work. This time, he was on a different mission.

That was in another life, he closed his eyes. *I am the Great Gambler, the Parieur, as they call it here.*

The flight dived. The Parieur could see Paris through his window seat—a beautiful city. He tried spotting the tourist attractions he read about, but succeeded in locating only two: the World's Wonder, the Eiffel Tower, and the golden dome of Les Invalides.

As the altitude dropped, there was discomfort in his ears. In a few minutes, the airplane's wheels touched the tarmac, and the attendant again announced into the PA system. The flight's doors opened in a few more minutes, and the passengers disembarked.

The Parieur followed the signs for immigration. After a long wait in the line, an officer called him. "*Bonjour*, passport please." The officer extended his left hand through an opening in the glass partition of his counter with a blank face and lazy eyes. A neatly trimmed French beard covered his triangular face. He wore a dark blue jacket with epaulets on the shoulders and a crisp white shirt underneath. A peaked hat sat on his wide head.

The Parieur handed him his passport.

"What's the purpose of your travel?" The officer asked without looking at him as he typed something into his computer.

"Tourism." The Parieur's left leg shook nervously. He stopped it at once. *Control your body language,* he said to himself. *Relax and focus on the task.*

"Are you traveling alone?" The lazy eyes focused on the Parieur.

"Yes, sir." He looked at the officer confidently.

"Married?"

"Yes."

"Why are you traveling alone then?" The office leaned forward.
Just be cool.

"My wife couldn't get the time off from work," the Parieur lied. "I really wanted to attend this exhibition." He handed the officer a brochure. "I love photography."

Does he suspect anything? Will he catch my lie?

The officer went through the brochure. Handed it back. "Where will you stay?"

"Here." The Parieur showed him his phone through the glass partition. "That's my hotel."

Forget your past; it's a new life now. You are the Parieur; you have to do great things.

The officer asked him about his job, where he lived, how long he would stay in France, etc. When satisfied with all the answers, the officer stamped the passport with an entry date, handed it back, and greeted him with a *"Bienvenue en France"* without a smile.

Now was the hard part; everything depended on it. As the Parieur walked past the immigration counter, he nervously rubbed the dice pendants hanging from his necklace with his left hand, while his right hand pulled his carry-on bag.

The Parieur advanced to baggage claim, collected his luggage, and proceeded straight toward the cargo area of the terminal to collect his special package.

You have prepared for this, don't worry.

The cargo area was a ten-minute walk from the baggage claim. It was a big hall with several lines of X-ray machines where officers were busy looking at scans of packages on their computer screens. They wore light blue shirts with epaulets on the shoulders over navy-blue trousers with matching navy-blue peaked caps and shiny black dress shoes.

Boxes and packages of all sizes and shapes were placed in an orderly manner throughout the hall. The Parieur followed the signs on the ceiling and reached a corner where he collected his items.

A customs officer in the cargo area directed him to place his luggage on the X-ray machine's conveyor belt. Her lean, oval face was stern.

The items came out of the machine, and another officer at the other end asked him to come forward.

She opened the bag's zipper to inspect it. "What's this?" She was looking at a long cylindrical object.

"That's a professional telephoto lens for my camera."

"Are you a photographer?"

"No, just a hobby," he said with a wide smile.

The officer inspected the lens thoroughly and examined the clothes, medicines, and other small packets in the bag. The Parieur was nervous, but it did not reflect on his face.

"What are these?" she asked, looking at tiny two-ounce bottles made of plastic with sealed caps and colorful stickers.

"E- Energy drinks—caffeine." Parieur's voice was shaky.

The officer moved on to the second item.

Phew.

A black cloth tied by strings to the protruding metal parts covered the item. It was big. The officer untied the cloth and pulled it away. Two separate metal cages welded together contained a golden eagle inside each.

"Birds?" Surprise struck the officer's face. "What for?" She had seen pets passing through the security machine before, but never had she seen such extensive and magnificent birds of prey at the airport.

"Th- they- are my pets," the Parieur stumbled. "They are golden eagles—"

The officer continued to stare.

"Couldn't leave them alone at home. They don't behave if I'm not around to take care of them," he added hastily.

"And these?" The officer inspected the two cages in more detail. She pointed at two matchbox-sized electronic gadgets tied to the birds' legs.

The Parieur's palms began sweating. "Tracking devices, so that I can find out where they are." He cleared his throat. "It's a new city for them, you know, just want to be sure."

"Do you have a transport permit for the eagles?" she asked.

"Of course; here." The Parieur pulled out a folded piece of paper from his jacket pocket and gave it to her.

She examined the permit carefully and handed it back with a nod.

The officer scanned the two cages along with the birds through the machine again and consulted her colleague. "*Que voulez-vous que nous devrions faire?*" she spoke asking him what they should do about the birds.

"*Son okay, laissez-le aller,*" he replied, giving her his okay. He was too busy with the long line of items behind the Parieur's.

After a few minutes, she returned, "You may go."

"Thank you, thank you very much, officer."

The Parieur spent little time collecting the bags, repacking them, and following the signs for ground transportation. A pleasant, sunny day greeted him as he exited the terminal building. A gentle breeze caressed his face. He removed his jacket and breathed the fresh air.

The taxi bay had several parallel pull-over spots where taxis parked to load customers. He looked for a taxi and spotted one. The cab driver came to a halt in a spot near him. He opened the door for him and threw his bags and packages into the trunk while the Parieur occupied the rear seat.

"*Bonjour, Où allons-nous monsieur?*" the driver asked him his destination.

Before speaking, he closed his eyes, sighed with relief, and calmed himself. This was the most challenging part of his mission; he had planned well and was confident about everything else. In a few seconds, he opened his eyes and, with a sense of determination, replied, "Marriott, near La Santé"

•••

La Santé was a prison in the Metropolitan of Paris.

Built in the eighteenth century, it was famous for imprisoning many renowned inmates in its exclusive VIP and high-security wings. In its recent history, however, the media and critics have termed it the prison from hell. Contrary to its name, which meant prison of good health, many infamous stories broke out, placing it in the middle of a significant controversy. Some of these stories stated that prisoners had to live in cells infested with rats and lice.

These horrible conditions of overcrowding, lack of sanitation, and sexual assaults drove many inmates into madness. There were suicides. The media covered it extensively. Questions were asked. This made the French government pay attention, and a massive renovation project was approved. In a few days, the last phase of the renovation was scheduled for completion, and inmates were temporarily moved from the high-security wing to the other side.

The prison was located in the fourteenth arrondissement of Paris on the left bank of the Seine River. It was built on a spoke-and-hub design, with a central portion connected to spoke-like arms and an adjacent trapezoidal section. The prison was well inside the city limits of Paris, located on the east side of the Montparnasse district, close to several famous Parisian landmarks. Among these were the Cimetière du Montparnasse, a vast cemetery, and Tour Montparnasse, a lonely skyscraper.

After about forty minutes into his ride to the hotel, most of which was through the speedy Parisian autoroutes, the taxi halted briefly at a pet boarding center where the Parieur dropped his birds. He had prebooked this arrangement before coming to Paris after a long search for suitable places. It was not easy to find a place that could care for golden eagles.

Satisfied with his choice of the boarding center, the Parieur left for the hotel. It was nearby. The taxi reached its destination in ten minutes. The driver dropped him off at the entrance of the hotel. It was a tall building with a glass façade and a wide portico. A bellhop wearing a red standing collar jacket over black trousers and a pillbox hat greeted him at the entrance and carried his luggage inside the hotel on a baggage cart. The lobby was small, with white faux leather seating, warm lamps, and chrome chandeliers.

After spending about fifteen minutes at the marble-topped reception desk to check in and collect the key card, he went straight to his room. The Parieur's jetlag overpowered the two espresso shots he had on the flight and forced a brief nap. When he awoke, he took a cold shower, dried himself, and stood in front of the fogged mirror. Taking a deep breath, he wiped the mirror with his hand and stared at his own reflection.

"You are a different person now," he said to the reflection. "Your past is gone." He rubbed his fingers on the two dice pendants of his golden necklace again. "Only your future remains. Only your mission remains."

Condensation ran down the surface of the mirror in tiny droplets.

"You have come far. Your comrades have succeeded in their missions following your counsel. Now, it's your turn. This is it. This is the beginning of the next chapter." The Parieur smiled a determined smile.

Next moment, he dressed himself, packed his backpack, and departed from the hotel to survey the area. The prison was first on his list. He walked around its surrounding streets, observing its walls and entry-exit points, trying to spot any weaknesses. Satisfied, he made some notes in his diary and walked toward the main entrance. He passed through the gate, entered the visitor's area, and sat at the end of the room. Several visitors talked to the convicted person they had come to meet. They spoke through a phone across a glass wall.

"*Bonjour*, right this way monsieur." An officer appeared out of nowhere. "Sorry, we can't let you meet him like this," he said, pointing at a woman talking to an inmate across the glass. "He is a high-risk prisoner. We've arranged a room for you. It's heavily guarded to ensure he does not escape."

"I understand," the Parieur replied. "He has that reputation for a reason."

They walked inside the prison alongside a dirty, old hallway with dim overhead lights and polished gray concrete flooring.

"But before we do that, the geôlier would like to meet you," he said, referring to his boss, the jailor.

The jailor must wonder how I got permission to meet the fiercest drug lord of the continent. The Parieur's thoughts forced a gentle smirk on his face. *Or perhaps he is curious about why I am meeting him.*

After walking for a few minutes, they entered the jailor's office. It was a small cabin with expansive glass windows covered by white plastic blinds. The door was half glass and half wood. A small wooden desk, four chairs, and multiple filing cabinets occupied the room. A computer screen on the desk displayed CCTV footage of the prison.

"*Bienvenu!*" greeted the jailor. The handlebar mustache on his square face rose with his cheeks as he smiled. His dark hair was neatly combed. He wore a navy-blue coat over a sky-blue shirt, a plain, black tie, and navy-blue trousers. "Please take a seat," he said. "Before you meet the prisoner, I have a few questions. You see, monsieur, we have been asked not to let anyone meet this inmate."

The jailor waited a few seconds for a reaction.

None came. Parieur's fingers nervously held the dice hanging from his necklace.

He continued, "But it seems you have contacts with very influential people. They had this arranged for you." The jailor paused again. "Nonetheless, I have to ask you, what's the purpose of this meeting?" He stared at the Parieur as if trying to read his thoughts.

"Monsieur Geôlier, firstly, I would like to thank you for the hospitality," the Parieur replied. "As for the purpose of this meeting, I'm a journalist doing a story on Mr. Drágoslav. I want to interview him, get some facts and timelines correct."

The jailor considered for a minute. "Very well. But be careful; he is very dangerous."

"I will, *merci*."

A few minutes later, the guards escorted the Parieur into a secure room. The door was made of metal with a small, rectangular glass panel above the handle. The room had a heavy table and two chairs, but no windows. A bright, long, suspended light hung from above.

The Parieur took a seat on one of the chairs and waited.

The door opened, and two guards escorted the prisoner. His tall frame, muscular body, rough skin, and oblong face made him look intimidating. His dark, curly hair fell to his shoulders. He had prominent, dark brown eyes, a big nose, and thick lips. Over the khaki uniform that looked like scrubs, heavy chains restrained him.

The guards made him sit on the opposite chair and fastened his chains to the table. Afterward, they stood in the room corners with their hands on their weapons.

"I need some privacy, please," the Parieur requested.

One went outside asking for permission and returned a few minutes later.

"We generally don't leave him alone with a visitor," the guard said, "but the geôlier gave you special permission. You have twenty minutes."

"*Merci*."

The guards left the room. The door slowly closed behind them as the pistons of the overhead door-closer pulled it toward the frame.

The Parieur turned back to face the prisoner. "Hello, Mr. Drágoslav, how're you doing?"

"I've no interest in your story, and I don't want to be interviewed," came the reply in a thick Ukrainian accent.

"I'm not here to interview you." The Parieur walked across the table, stood behind the prisoner, and whispered in his ear. "I'm here to break you free."

Drágoslàv probably did not expect this reply, at least not from a stranger.

"You think you are funny? You don't know who you're messing with. I'll—" Drágoslàv threatened.

The Parieur interrupted him before he could finish. "I perfectly understand that there is no reason for you to trust me. I understand you have many enemies. It's natural to suspect my intentions," he said. "You must be wondering why a stranger like me would help you. I'll answer all your questions shortly. But right now, Mr. Drágoslàv, tell me one thing." The Parieur paused, waiting for Drágoslàv's full attention. "Have you ever wondered if there is something more to your life than what you ever did or are doing now?"

"If it's some kind of a joke, I'll have you killed the minute you walk out of this prison."

"Have mysterious things happened to you in the past, things that are impossible in this world?" The Parieur ignored his threat. "Did you ever feel that you're waiting for something? Something bigger, powerful, and bizarre?"

The Parieur saw on Drágoslàv's face that fireworks were bursting within him. Despite its absurdity, the Parieur knew what he said had struck a chord. He could feel that Drágoslàv had waited for this for a long time. Drágoslàv's facial expressions, pupils, and eyelids moved fast, as if everything was slowly coming back to him from the past.

"I don't know what you're saying, but—" Drágoslàv stopped mid-sentence. He paused for a second. "I remember an incident that happened in my youth." He closed his eyes as he spoke. "It happened so long ago that I almost forgot about it." He sighed. "It is so weird that, perhaps, I chose to forget it. But back then, someone told me that a person would come in the future and answer all my questions."

"I have the answer to the question you've waited to ask all your life." The Parieur smiled and patted Drágoslàv's shoulders. "But first, we've got to get you out of here."

"Do you think I'm sitting in this prison for fun? My people have tried to break me out several times. The security here is unbreakable."

"No prison is unbreakable." There was confidence in the Parieur's voice, arrogance on his face. "The hard part will be after I break you out. For that, I will need help from your people. Please tell me where I can find them."

"I can arrange for that easily. They will find you if I tell them."

"Very well."

"But before I do that, how do I know this is not a set up? Trap to arrest my people?"

The Parieur retrieved a book from his bag and handed it to Drágoslav. The cover featured horses, elephants, and all kinds of odd creatures, swordsmen, spearmen, archers, and arrows flying all over in what looked like a war.

"Don't judge the book by its cover." The Parieur watched the expression on Drágoslav's face. "Our story ahead begins after the last chapter. I added the details in the back and had it rebound. But do read the whole thing."

The Parieur pulled a piece of paper from his bag. "This is the key to decrypting it. It'll answer most of your questions." He paused and stared into Drágoslav's eyes. "After reading the book, if you think I'm who I am, then ask your men to contact me."

The door opened. A guard walked in. "It's twenty minutes."

"I'll wait for them," the Parieur said. "And the answer to the question that you've longed to ask all your life is—" The Parieur stared into Drágoslav's eyes. "—BROTHER!"

CHAPTER
17

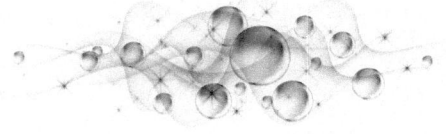

The Flying Dog

Coffeyville, Kansas, USA
Darren's Story — A few years before the abduction

'Welcome to Coffeyville,' read a signboard on the roadside as Darren Swanson and his father entered the town through Highway 169, driving their Dodge Ram. The speed limit plunged from sixty-five to forty miles per hour, and Darren's father let go of the gas pedal, aware of this trap.

After driving a few more miles, they had to come to a complete stop as the red lights of the railway crossing flashed and the gate arms came down.

"Goddammit!" screamed Darren's father. He was a muscular fellow, about a foot and a half shorter than Darren, with big, grumpy eyes and short white hair.

In fifteen minutes, a rail engine crossed the road, followed by a long line of oil tankers.

"Can't these refinery asses find another time to send this shit? They've got to do it right at lunchtime when people are driving all around town."

The red lights stopped flashing, arms rose, and traffic slowly moved ahead. They passed a few streets. Darren's father pulled over in front of his regular liquor store.

Exiting the truck, he spat his Copenhagen and replenished his mouth with more fresh tobacco.

"Wait in the car," he ordered Darren. A few minutes later, he walked out with a twelve-pack.

"It was only last night that you passed out," Darren complained. "I had to carry you to your room." He hated his father's excessive drinking.

"I earn my living, boy. I can do what I want with it. Don't ever question me again." He started the car and backed up. "As if your mother were not enough, she also taught it to you."

Darren's face reddened with anger. He loved his mother. She was the most important person in his life. But he kept quiet.

They returned to the road, crossed the city boundary, and turned left on a small dirt road. *'Swanson Family Farm'* read an iron gateway arch as they entered their property.

Coffeyville, a small town in the American countryside of southeast Kansas, was split between Kansas and Oklahoma. It was sparsely populated, and everyone knew everyone. Many large farms and ranches surrounded the city, one of which was the Swanson family farm.

It was a Sunny day in the middle of May. Temperatures were back in the upper eighties after a freezing winter that lasted well into April. Bugs, insects, flies, and all types of tiny creatures launched their yearly spring attack on the households. People responded by arming themselves with plungers filled with insecticides and pesticides. Pollen was in the air, and lawnmowers were on the grass. Backyards were planted with young floral plants, and the nights glittered with the timely blinks of the magical firefly buttocks.

The Dodge Ram came to a halt near the front porch. It was an old, two-story house, off-white with a gray, weathered roof. It had a big living area with heavy wooden furniture, a beautiful golden chandelier, and an antique grandfather clock. Floral wallpaper decorated the inner walls of the rooms. The kitchen was enormous and separate from the dining area.

"I'm hungry," Darren's father declared, which was usually Darren's line.

As they both entered the house, Darren's mother greeted them with a warm smile. She was a plump woman, about the same height as her husband, with a round face, small nose, and curly, shoulder-length hair.

"Didn't you hear? I said I'm hungry. What's for dinner?"

"Ch—Chicken, fried ch—chicken with mashed potatoes and corn on the cob," Mrs. Swanson stammered.

Mr. Swanson opened the refrigerator and placed the twelve-pack inside. He withdrew a bottle from the box, twisted the crown with his fingers, and gulped the pint in one go.

"What're we waiting for," he said. "Bring the damn food."

Darren clenched his fist.

Mrs. Swanson hurried inside, brought the hot food, and placed it on the dining table. Darren ate his regular serving, two whole chickens worth of chicken-fried chicken. Right from birth, Darren was a big kid. He was a big baby, and as he grew up, he was the tallest student in his class. He ate a lot but never became obese. His mother was a stay-at-home mom, while his father earned his living by farming and raising cattle.

Since birth, Darren had lived on the Swanson family ranch. In high school, Darren was on the football team because of his size, although he seldom showed up for practice. Sometimes, he had to tone it down for the safety of the other kids and play gently. Though he barely liked football, he continued playing it, hoping to get a scholarship to get into a university. He was not much into academics; he just wanted to get away from his hometown, especially from his dad. Other than excessive drinking, one of the main reasons he disliked his father was because of the way he treated his mother.

"What're you looking at? Go move the hay bales from the truck into the barn," his father ordered as he opened himself a fifth beer.

Darren banged his hands on the table. It jumped into the air, launching food, dishes, and utensils everywhere. He had controlled his temper for too long.

"How do you put up with him?" The nostrils on his big nose flared as his face went red. His fingers still formed fists, solid as a hammer.

"You're still under my roof. Think before you speak, boy, or I'll kick your ass out," his father shouted.

"Let it go, Darry," his mother replied. Her nervous eyes looked into Darren's angry ones. She knew Darren's temper. Once, Darren was so angry with his father that he almost hit him. His mother had come between them back then and slapped Darren instead. "In our family, sons don't hit their fathers," she had said. "Remember, if you hit him, it'll mean you have hit me." Since then, he had always walked out when angry at his father.

Darren pushed his chair back as he stood up. "You've got to stand up for yourself," he said and stormed into the kitchen. His mother came after him.

"I know he is not the best, but he has never let us go hungry," she said softly.

"That's all you care about?" he said, tossing his dish in the kitchen sink. "I've never seen him treat you well." He turned his head to face her.

"Let it go, baby." Her shaky hands patted his back.

Darren rushed to the front door and slammed it behind him. The entire house shivered under its force. He stormed toward the barn, picked up an axe, went into the woods, and rammed it into the thickest trunk he could find. The tree broke into two pieces with his single blow.

One by one, his rage devoured the entire patch of vegetation around him.

"AAAAAHH!" he shouted toward the sky. "I want to get out of here."

Darren was desperate to leave his home and live on his own. He wanted to see the world. Deep within, he felt that he was destined for something more, something other than living on this farm, something big. He didn't know what it was. His heart yearned for this missing unknown.

Their dog came running toward him, begging for attention. Darren shook his head and smiled. "Where have you been, you little monster?" He stroked the dog's belly. His temper was like a high striker puck, quick to shoot up and fast to come down. Their dog usually did this job. He loved him.

Darren walked back toward the barn and made room for new hay. The Dodge Ram towed an extended portion that carried eight big hay bales. Round and cylindrical, each weighed several thousand pounds. A person would need a forklift, tractor, or equipment to move such a heavy load from the truck. Darren, however, was a different beast. He climbed, picked up a hay bale above his head with his bare hands, jumped back onto the ground, and carried it to the barn. He repeated this routine for the remaining hay bales one by one.

While he did so, an unusual phenomenon took shape. Floating midair around him were several bubble-like objects. Through them appeared scenes of an otherworldly landscape. There were mountains, caves, and waterfalls. They were unlike anything he had ever seen before.

The next minute, something shocking and terrifying unfolded in front of him. Defying all the rules of the season, out of nowhere, on a clear and sunny day, without a drop of rain for miles and miles, a tall, slender, and powerful funnel touched the ground.

The tornado accelerated toward him, destroying everything in its path. Darren darted toward the tornado shelter beside the house. The winds were close.

When he had almost made it to the shelter, the dog barked and cried. It was at the edge; the tornado was about to swallow it.

Darren stopped, turned back, and bolted toward the dog. He dived and caught the dog as it became airborne. Now, he was in the line of fire of the menacing twister.

It engulfed him. The noise and impact of the winds were intense. He could feel the pressure. He hugged the dog tightly to his chest, between his two muscular arms.

His feet were still on the ground. To his surprise, his strength was enough to withstand the pull.

He tried to open his eyes. No debris swirled inside. It was only dust obscuring the thing hidden within. To his shock, a gigantic humanoid figure was inside. It appeared as if the twister originated from it and was driven by its force.

Darren resisted the pull with all his might. The speed and power of the twister increased, but it could not lift Darren. In a few seconds, he was ejected.

The next moment, just like that, the twister vanished. But right before it disappeared, two big, blood-red, menacing eyes gazed at Darren from inside the storm.

And he knew they were there for him.

CHAPTER 18

Palais de Chaillot

Paris, France

The Parieur exited La Santé satisfied.

That went as planned. Now, I just have to wait for them.

He pulled out his smartphone, opened the maps app, and searched for directions to Tour Montparnasse. A twenty-minute walk.

On his way toward the tower, he came across Cimetière du Montparnasse. Although he had no particular interest in the cemetery, fascinated by its gravestones, decorative columns, obelisks, and statues, he decided to pass through it.

The cemetery was created in the nineteenth century from several small farms and was the final resting place for many of France's famous personalities. The street Rue Émile Richard dissected the cemetery into two portions, one big, one small. The place was a major tourist attraction and served as a quiet and peaceful park for neighborhood residents.

The Parieur entered the smaller section of the cemetery and moved on to the bigger section, crossing Rue Émile Richard. A few feet from the entrance, on his right, four men frantically dug a grave under a big tree. They looked suspicious. A familiar tattoo was on the exposed arm of one of the diggers. It had a skull with two crossed bones inside a big O.

The digger noticed the Parieur and pulled his sleeves to cover the tattoo. The Parieur ignored him and walked toward the exit. In a few minutes, he reached the entrance of Tour Montparnasse.

A tall skyscraper built in the late seventies on top of the Montparnasse— Bienvenüe Metro station, the tower had fifty-nine floors with a restaurant on the fifty-sixth and an observation deck on the terrace. The remaining area was office space. The observation deck had tower viewers with coin slots to zoom into Paris's landmarks. Beside each of these viewers was an exhibit with pictures of attractions in that particular direction, along with their descriptions. The terrace could act as a helipad for helicopter landings with minimal preparation.

The view from the observation deck was hawk-eyed. It covered a radius of forty kilometers on a bright and Sunny day. One could spot the Eiffel Tower in all its glory, the hill of Montmartre with the white dome of Sacré-Cœur Basilica atop, the golden dome of Les Invalides, the Notre-Dame Cathedral, the Louvre Museum—home of Mona Lisa—and many other famous delights of Paris. In addition, Cimetière du Montparnasse and the La Santé prison were easily visible to the naked eye. This was precisely what the Parieur was interested in.

He entered the building and walked toward the ticket counter.

"*Bonjour, Combien de billets?*" greeted the attendant, asking him how many tickets.

"One ticket for the terrace observation deck, please."

"That will be twenty-six Euros."

He handed her the cash. Seconds later, she threw the ticket through the semicircular opening in the glass. "The elevator is on your left."

He proceeded toward the elevator and stood at the end of a queue. The elevator door opened. He boarded.

After a few minutes, the door opened again, and the fifty-sixth-floor lobby greeted him. It had a fine dining restaurant, hosting several neatly dressed people savoring dinner, soaking in the views of the beautiful Parisian skyline.

From the lobby, he took the stairs to the terrace. Wasting no time, the Parieur went toward the side opposite the Eiffel Tower, retrieved his telescope from the bag, and focused it on the ground.

The view was that of La Santé. This time, he got a better view of the prison as he was at a height. The satellite views of several online websites had blurred the prison.

Moving his telescope slowly, one by one, he observed all the buildings and wings inside the prison in detail. Every now and then, he took notes and sketched on his notepad.

After the prison, he surveyed the terrace. He took pictures of the assembly used to lower the glass walls along the perimeter for helicopter landings.

When he was done, he moved his view toward the cemetery. He saw the same gravediggers from earlier.

An idea sparked in his mind. He pulled out his notebook and scribbled *Gravediggers*.

His phone beeped. A text notification from an unrecognized phone number popped up on the lock screen.

It read, *Palais de Chaillot, 10:00 PM*

⧸⧹

The Parieur exited the tower and found an empty seat in a nearby restaurant facing the street. The arrangement was customary in Parisian cafés and restaurants where the tables were at the boundary of the premises, and the chairs were arranged overlooking the street. It was an ideal arrangement for people-watching.

After ordering an onion soup and a pâté en croute, he went over his notes again. Halfway into his dinner, he tapped on his phone. It was seven-thirty.

Will they show up on time? His left leg shook nervously. *They'd contacted soon. It's only been a few hours.*

He took a sip from his bottle of sparkling water. *How will they recognize me?*

A souvenir seller stared at him from across the street. He ignored him.

Why did they choose such a crowded place for our meeting? Palais de Chaillot? He sighed.

Palais de Chaillot was one of the most famous places in Paris. It presented excellent views of the Eiffel Tower. Many high-end fashion shoots, wedding albums, and selfies were snapped here. Countless people proposed to their sweethearts at this romantic, picture-perfect place. Thousands of tourists flocked to this spot every day, whether cold, hot, or wet. The ambiance was worth it. The place was packed after Sundown, especially at the end of every hour when the entire tower glittered with thousands of lights for five minutes. It was spectacular, and visitors were overwhelmed by the display. Couples kissed, people posed for trick shots, while some absorbed the magnificent sight with a glass of champagne. This was also when everyone would have their eyes fixed in awe toward the tower, and pickpockets would take the field.

"Taxi!" the Parieur shouted after finishing his dinner. A cab reading Taxi Parisien with a green light on top pulled over on his side. "Bonjour, Palais de Chaillot."

The driver started the ride, and the green light on top changed to amber, indicating occupied. The taxi navigated through traffic, crossing the intricate maze of narrow and wide streets that were the city's trademark. The streets were filled with cafes, restaurants, flower & gift shops, salons, and designer stores. Every few minutes, there was a tourist attraction. With such a rich history, the city was full of them. After about twenty minutes, the cab came to a halt. The Parieur exited. He took a few steps, and there it was. The enormous Eiffel Tower in all its glory.

He tapped his phone again. Nine-thirty.

It was a late sundown, and the golden lights on the tower were lit up. In thirty minutes, the tower would sparkle for the first time today. In thirty minutes, he would meet Drágoslàv's men.

He walked in the direction of the tower. The entire platform was full of cheering tourists. There were giggles and laughter everywhere. He could hear many different languages. Many had their camera phones out. A few had professional cameras. Flashes clicked ubiquitously.

As the Parieur walked toward the tower, souvenir sellers came buzzing toward him every few steps, trying to sell miniature replicas and keychains of the Eiffel Tower. There were so many that he felt like a nest of bees was chasing him.

"Get lost," he shouted at one, moved toward the side, and sat on the wall looking at the tower. He could see the cars and cabs crossing the bridge across the Seine at its base. He soaked in the view of the river cruises ending their night tours, the restaurants along the banks, and the water fountains lit up across the entire length of the garden.

As the time drew close, anxiety overtook him. *Any minute now.*

A group of teenagers counted down. "Ten, nine, eight—"

Several things happened at the same time: the Eiffel Tower sparkled from top to bottom, people stood up in amazement, eyes fixed on the tower, and thieves looked for targets.

It was ten, the time of his appointment. The Parieur looked around, but no one looked like from the mafia. In all this cacophony, a souvenir seller approached him. He was the same one from across the café where he had dinner.

"I don't want anything," the Parieur shouted before the souvenir seller opened his mouth.

"Are you here for La Santé?" the souvenir seller asked.

The Parieur's eyebrows rose in surprise. He wasn't expecting to hear this from the souvenir seller. "Yes," he replied.

"Show me some identification?"

The Parieur fetched his wallet and handed him his ID. It read,

Dr. Lucas Sánchez

Chief Scientist - Computational and Systems Biology

National Medical Research Laboratory

After comparing his face against the picture, followed by a quick examination with a UV flashlight, the souvenir seller reached for one of the replicas of the Eiffel Tower in his possession.

"Now, hold on, this won't hurt much."

Seconds later, there was a prick on the Parieur's neck, and slowly, he felt like someone was pushing him into a wheelchair.

His body collapsed onto the chair, his vision blurred, and finally, he closed his eyes.

CHAPTER 19

The Great Gambler

Las Vegas, Nevada, USA
Months before Sánchez went into a coma

Although they were near their kids after moving to Las Vegas and everything seemed perfect, every now and then, Mrs. Sánchez got an awkward vibe from her husband. Sometimes, he would behave unlike his usual geeky, calm, and cautious self. She wondered what it was.

It must be because of the move here; he is out of his comfort zone from Boston.

One Friday, after a stressful day at work, Sánchez was exhausted. He locked his lab, dragged himself out of the building, and started his Toyota Prius. As he was about to push the gas pedal to head home, several giant floating bubbles appeared around him. The next minute, a sudden pull took hold of his senses, a pull he could not explain, a pull he could not resist.

Like an addict, he was compelled to follow this desire. He had not felt anything like this before. Sánchez continued driving where this impulse commanded him to go. It was in the opposite direction from his house.

What's happening to me? Where am I going?

He realized he was headed toward the Las Vegas Strip. The intensity of light increased. The hybrid zoomed fifteen miles above the speed limit. He soon found himself within the glamor of the dazzling casinos.

Sánchez parked his car, went to his bank, and stood in line at the counter. Plush, white sofas, indoor plants, and calm music from overhead speakers filled the bank lobby. A teller called him from behind the glass partition of the counter. A pair of black-framed glasses sat on her slender nose. She had long, dark hair. A subtle maroon lipstick covered her wide lips.

"How can I help you?" she asked, looking at him with a wide smile.

"I need to withdraw some cash," he replied, his right leg shaking nervously.

"How much?"

"Fifty."

"You could have withdrawn fifty dollars from the ATM, sir."

"I need to withdraw fifty thousand dollars," he said. "From my savings account," he added. He stopped shaking his leg. Smiled.

"Oh, okay." The teller's face looked surprised. But she didn't make much of it.

After inserting his card into the reader and signing a few forms, Sánchez left the bank with fifty grand in cash. His urge was so strong that he didn't care if Martha got a message about this withdrawal on her phone.

I must be going mad. But- but it feels so right.

He had never gambled before. But the pull for gambling grew stronger by the minute.

In front of him stood the MGM Grand Casino. With great hesitation and an equal amount of determination, he entered the building.

Why do I feel like taking a big risk? Why do I feel an urge to gamble this cash?

It was like he had two personalities, one forcing him to go home, one dragging him deeper inside.

The casino was majestic. The ceiling was high with beautiful chandeliers and running neon lights that changed color every few feet. The patterned carpet with geometric shapes of pink, yellow, red, green, and blue seemed to go on forever under rows of slot machines, lounge chairs, roulette, blackjack and craps tables, and other gambling stations. One section had several rows of seating like that in cinemas, facing lines of wall-mounted screens that showed sports and race books. Bar counters were in every area, with bartenders spinning bottles and jars, mixing cocktails, and filling jugs from taps.

Sánchez went to the cashier's window at the entrance and exchanged his cash for chips.

Where am I supposed to go? He decided to walk for a bit, still unable to find the mass of this intense gravity. He observed the surroundings and felt intimidated. People played various kinds of slot machines. Lion's Share read one display. Beside it was a *Star Wars machine,* followed by *The Big Bang Theory*. Enter cash, pull the lever, and await his luck.

He walked past a roulette table where a croupier spun the wheel and threw the ball. Seconds later, the ball landed on a number, and the winners raised their glasses with joy.

What am I doing? I should go back.

"What would you like to drink, sir?" a waitress asked.

"Thank you, but I don't want anything."

"It's on the house, sir. Try this shot. It's terrific."

Just refuse. Her job is to get people buzzed, kill inhibitions, and give a false sense of confidence.

"Just try one, sir; trust me, it's unbelievable."

Alright, let's get it over with.

He gulped two shots, one after another. They kicked in quickly.

What shall I play? How do I do it?

The roulette, the slot machines, the card tables, nothing felt right.

After searching for a few minutes, he finally found it. The gamble he wanted to play. The craps table.

People placed bets and threw dice around it. A provocatively dressed blonde stood beside a gentleman wearing a polished tuxedo. He had a neatly trimmed beard. Beside him was an old fat man wearing shorts, a t-shirt, and a baseball hat. Next to this man were four young ladies wearing matching gowns. Pink sashes hung from their shoulders. One in the front had '*Bride To Be*' written over her sash, while the other three had '*Bridesmaid.*'

The man in the tuxedo placed the highest bet and picked the pair of dice. He handed them to the beautiful blonde next to him. She kissed his cheek, then the dice, and threw them on the table. They rejoiced when the dice rested. They won their bet. The four young girls screamed in despair. The fat man did not react.

That's it! This is what called me here, the game of dice.

The Craps table was his black hole. There was something about the dice that had captured his senses.

Without wasting any time, he went to the table. "I'd like to bet all of these on twelve." He placed all his chips in this game, all fifty grand worth.

People around the table were flabbergasted.

"I have the biggest bet; I'll throw the dice."

No one argued.

Sánchez held the dice inside his palms.

No sooner did he do so than confidence rushed through his nerves like an electric current. A surge of energy coursed through his muscles. He felt invincible. The dice in his hands were his babies.

When all bets were placed, the croupier asked him to throw. Instead of kissing the pair of dice, he raised them to his forehead, closed his eyes, and uttered words he did not know before.

Next second, he launched them flying into the table, and, to everyone's disbelief, the dice rolled in his favor.

He had won and won big!

◈

Hours after Sánchez's first triumph at the craps table, the phone at his residence rang. Mrs. Sánchez answered, "Hello?"

"This is Officer Aguilar with LVMPD," came the reply. "Your husband is in custody."

"What? But why?"

"We'll discuss the details once you come here and pick him."

Mrs. Sánchez rushed to the station where Sánchez was held.

"Why was he arrested? He is a respectable scientist with the government, for God's sake."

"Ma'am, this respected scientist won a lot of money today," the officer said. He pointed at a bag stashed with one-hundred-dollar bills. "The casinos could not understand how he won so much and restrained him from entering. Yet, your husband tried to break in. We had no option but to arrest him."

Mrs. Sánchez looked from the loaded bag to her husband. He looked more satisfied than he had ever looked in his life. Inside his palms were the pair of dice that had won him his fortune.

He was the great gambler, the master of dice.

CHAPTER 20

The Clouded Leopard

Hunan Province, China

Liang's Story — A few years before the abduction

Droplets of water trickled rhythmically from the moss-covered terracotta roof tiles atop Liang Li's house as the misty air relinquished its moisture. It had been a week since the sun showed its face. The house was in a small village at the feet of the enigmatic mountains of Zhangjiajie National Forest. The beautiful lakes, dense trees, and perpetual fog created a mystic aura.

"Liang, get up," his mother shouted. She was in the middle of kneading the dough to make noodles. "Help your *baba* carry water."

When she was done, the dough was placed aside to rest, and she moved on to cut vegetables. "You know the rice won't grow without water. He needs all the help to carry it from the river."

"We have levees around our farm to hold the water from rain," Liang said with half a yawn as he stretched his arms in the air from the bamboo-framed bed.

It was a small house with a single room serving as the kitchen, living and bedroom. Girthy wooden pillars held the frame and terracotta roof overhead, and below the animal skin rugs, the floor was made of wooden planks. A small bathroom and toilet were outside the house.

"Don't I know that?" Liang's mother stood up, her hands on her hips. "Owner of the lowest farm opened them in the night once again to direct the water to his holding. That fool; there's none on ours as a result."

It was a small farm with many cascading terraces. Wearing a conical bamboo hat, Liang's father carried the buckets tied to the ends of a long stick on his shoulders. It was strenuous. Every now and then, Liang helped him with the work.

"Just yesterday, I helped *baba* plow the farm. You know how hard it is to drag them using shoulders?" Liang got out of bed and rubbed his left eye with the side of his index finger.

"I know very well. I did it before you were born," she said. "You're a big boy now. Remember, no rice means we sleep hungry."

Liang drooped his shoulders, grunted.

The village had no school, hospital, or doctor. A fourteen-something Liang traveled more than five kilometers daily, each way on foot, to the neighboring village to attend school. He was brilliant but hated sitting inside a classroom.

"I visited your school yesterday," Mrs. Li said. "You were not in the classroom, and your *baba* said you were not on the farm."

"I was in the library, Mama. The school is boring, I already know what they teach," Liang said. He went to the bathroom to brush his teeth.

"You know better than the teacher now, huh?" Mrs. Li followed him and hit him on the shoulder.

"Yes, ask me anything."

Liang often left school and spent hours reading books in the village library. During his brief stay here, a doctor fell in love with the village and created a makeshift library. It was decent and had books on science, history, geography, and English. Though young, Liang was sharp. He could self-learn and understand complex concepts. One by one, Liang finished the books.

On days when Liang was not at the library, he wandered in the valley picking fruits using his slingshot, catching fish, and hunting rabbits. Every time he went on these excursions, he made sure he knew his way back and was close to the village. He never ventured into the dense part of the forest.

"Don't act too smart, go help your *baba*," Mrs. Li said after Liang finished brushing his teeth.

"Uhhh, I'm going to fix this for good." Liang clenched his fists and went inside the house. He stuffed a book he had read the previous night into his cloth sling back and stormed out. When he reached the farm, instead of helping his father, he spent the entire morning gathering ropes, tree branches, buckets, and other similar materials.

"What are you doing?" his father asked. "I need help carrying water, not collecting trash."

"Trust me, *Ba*. This will make your life, and most importantly, my life, easier." Liang wiped the sweat on his forehead with the back of his left hand.

When he found what he was looking for, he started building. It took a good part of the morning. With tree branches, ropes, hand-fashioned pulleys, and pedals, he assembled a conveyor.

"Well, what do you think?" Liang asked his father with a wide smile. His left palm extended in the direction of the conveyor as if presenting something extraordinary.

"About what? What the hell is it?" Mr. Li came close, his eyes narrow in confusion.

"Here, I'll show you. Sit on this and push these pedals." Liang patted on a makeshift seat as he spoke.

His father followed the instructions. A series of small buckets tied to a rope moved toward their farm and carried water upstairs from the stream running at the base of the hill. It was ingenious.

"Amazing." Liang's father's face lit up.

"I can build more," Liang replied excitedly.

"Like what?" his father asked, still in awe of his son's creation.

"Help me find two broken bicycles, and I'll show you."

Days later, his father found a broken tricycle in the village junkyard.

"That's the best I found. See if you can make use of it," Mr. Li said, dragging the handle of the broken trike.

"I reckon it's better than two bicycles for what I want to make." Liang rubbed his two palms in excitement, looking at it.

In a few hours, Liang fixed the tires, fashioned a makeshift plow, and fastened it to the tricycle.

"Try it," Liang said. A wide smile occupied his face, like the one he had when he created the conveyor.

His father moved it through the farm. It took strength and hard work, but it was easier than digging sticks. "Excellent," he said.

"Now, can you tell Ma to stop forcing me to come here?" Liang chortled with both his fists on his waist

CR&O

Several days passed. Liang was wandering into the woods, skipping school yet again, when he spotted a rabbit in a nearby bush.

He pulled out a slingshot from his bag and aimed. The first shot missed; the rabbit darted. Liang chased it, trying to keep pace. After a while, the rabbit stopped and grazed again.

Liang hid, reloaded the slingshot, aimed, and *Satackkk*! It hit the target and knocked the rabbit down.

No sooner did Liang walk to claim his prize than the sounds of something sprinting in the bushes alerted him. Faster and faster it went.

When Liang was done reloading the slingshot, there was a loud *Roar*! A leopard jumped in front of him. Not any, but a clouded leopard- rare anywhere. The black market paid handsomely for its body parts. The claws, teeth, and skin were sold as decoration, while bones and teeth were used to prepare traditional Chinese medicine.

Liang bolted. He didn't think about where he was going. He wanted to put as many steps between the leopard and him as possible.

In what seemed like an hour of running, Liang was exhausted. His muscles screamed in pain. He stopped at the banks of a river, fashioned a small cup from the leaves of a nearby tree, and scooped some water.

As he drank, something spectacular transpired. Giant, floating, bubble-like objects appeared around him. Soon after, sounds emanated from the depths of the bushes.

What is it? Wait a minute, it's music. But here, in the forest? Oh, it is so beautiful, so soothing, and so different.

The music was faint, as if coming from far away.

Liang lost his trail while following the music. Deeper and deeper, he went into the forest. The music grew louder with each step.

Suddenly, there were loud cries, as if those of an animal. Liang froze.

The next second, two big arms got hold of him. He found himself surrounded by a few men. Poachers.

In front of Liang were the bodies of clouded leopards.

"We have to kill him," said one of the poachers. "The punishment for poaching is severe; it's on the government's list of most endangered. We will go to prison."

"But he is from our village," another said.

"Exactly, he knows who we are. We've got to get rid of him."

"No, no, I promise I won't tell anyone." Liang knelt, pleading with both hands.

The leader of the gang ignored him. "Very well, kill him," he said. "But first, finish the job we came here for."

They tied Liang to a nearby tree and butchered the dead cats. They had killed four, the most in several years. A jackpot. Finding the cats these days was becoming impossible as their numbers dwindled.

Several minutes later, the poachers finished and turned their focus back to Liang.

"Are you sure? Do you really want to kill our village boy?" one of the men asked.

"There is no other option," the leader said.

Silence.

"Proceed," he ordered.

One of them wiped his blood-soaked Dao used on the cats minutes ago, and placed it on Liang's neck.

"Please don't kill me. I won't tell anyone, I swear. Please, please, please—"

They laughed.

Liang's heart raced.

The poacher with the Dao looked at the leader, waiting for his command. Liang closed his eyes.

There was a pause.

Just when the Dao was about to slit Liang's throat, hundreds of twigs flew through the air. Like sharp needles, they pierced the poachers' bodies.

The criminals howled.

In the next moment, several humanoid figures emerged from the bushes. Their bodies were made of branches, leaves, and twigs. Their faces, however, were fleshy. It looked as if a human face was encapsulated inside a humanoid tree with limbs. Rope-like branches shot from their hands and tied the poachers to the trees nearby. The pressure slowly increased, and their bodies were crushed by the force.

Liang was dumbfounded, scared. "I didn't do it, I swear. They were going to kill me."

The figures nodded.

"Who are you?" he asked.

"You will know when the time is right," a soft, calm, and clear voice spoke. It sounded like a human.

Silence. A gust of wind hit Liang's face.

The next moment, they slowly retreated.

"Xièxiè," Liang shouted as he saw them disappear behind the bushes.

Liang hurried back to the village and told everyone about the creatures. No one believed him. He kept going to the forest every day, looking for them everywhere. He found nothing.

Many years later, Liang still couldn't fathom who saved him that night.

CHAPTER 21

The Meeting

Paris, France

Sánchez slowly opened his eyes and found himself on an old couch inside a big room. It had one rusted metal door on the wall opposite the couch, one window boarded with ply on each side, and several dirty, flickering tubelights held inside rusted fixtures suspended from a brick ceiling. The paint on the walls blistered and cracked, with flakes peeling off everywhere. A small wooden coffee table of withered wood occupied the space in front of the couch. Several chairs randomly sat here and there while dirty bundles of rugs, cardboard boxes, and folded metal cots lay haphazardly near the wall behind the couch. An old wooden cabinet with glass panels stood behind a counter on the left wall. Bottles of whiskey, vodka, cognac, and other liquors lined its shelf along with glasses of all kinds.

A huge face stared at him from the far end. It had long hair and prominent eyebrows. Next to the owner of this face were two well-built bodyguards.

"I am Gustáv, Drágoslav's most trusted," the owner of the face said in a thick Ukrainian accent, "can't be too careful these days, especially after cops captured Drággy. We had to make sure you not here to trick us. We scanned your body and belongings for GPS trackers."

"I—I understand." Gustáv's face appeared like a ringing tuning fork. Trace amounts of the tranquilizer were still in his body.

"In fact, I was skeptical, but Drággy insisted," Gustáv continued. "However, I have a question for you, and whether I trust you depends on your answer."

Many years back, when Gustáv and Drágoslav were young, they had almost died at sea on their way to Western Europe from Odessa. But someone saved them. That someone prophesied to them that a man would come in the future to save them again. He revealed to them a question that they should ask this person.

Gustáv and Drágoslav had waited to ask someone this question for a long, long time. It was a very bizarre question indeed. They didn't understand its meaning or its answer. But they knew they had to ask it.

"I will be happy to answer all your questions." Sánchez knew the question that was coming. He knew its answer.

With a big sigh, Gustáv spoke. "Who are you to the blind whose gaze can make one's body as strong as the strongest thing in the world?"

Sánchez smiled. His heart was filled with joy on hearing this question. It was the same question, the answer to which he had told Drágoslav before leaving La Santé.

"I want to emphasize again that whether we trust you with breaking out Drággy and let you live depends on your answer." Gustáv had waited to ask this question to someone for many years, more, to hear its answer.

"My answer is—Brother!"

Gustáv's eyes widened. He laughed. "Oh. Oh, so it's real. You're real. I thought you would never come. I thought it was a dream. We were so young when it happened."

Gustáv rushed toward Sánchez and embraced him like a brother.

"Some in my team are still suspicious of you; for all they know, you could be an undercover cop. But I'm convinced now. I know, you are whom Drággy and I were waiting for. Sorry, I brought you like this, Dr. Sánchez."

"It's fine. I'd have done the same thing."

Excitement filled the room. It was as if they had met a long-lost comrade from the battlefield. Gustáv's face was filled with pride.

Everything was true after all. What happened in the past was real, not a hallucination, a real person who saved us, Gustáv thought. *As prophesied, Dr. Sánchez came to show the way.*

Gustav beamed like a child receiving their favorite Christmas present. He poured two glasses of the most expensive cognac and handed one to Sánchez. "So, tell me everything about what it's all about; what Drággy and I supposed to do."

"Sorry, but I can't tell that in front of everyone. I'd rather wait till the master is out. For now, let's plan how we'll disappear after we break the master out of La Santé."

"Master? You call Drággy master?" Gustáv raised his eyebrows.

"Yes, and you should too. He's much more than the drug lord he is, much more than just your friend. He is royalty. You will understand in time."

It was a while before anyone spoke.

"Well, as you said, first things first. We tried to get him out twice and failed. Prison security is very tight. Bribing does not work either." Gustáv talked hastily. "And, even if you break him out of La Santé all by yourself, you would need my entire team's help in making Drággy disappear. So, tell me, how exactly do you plan to break him out?"

Sánchez stood up, walked toward the bar, and poured himself another glass of cognac.

"Calm down, Gustáv," he said. Holding the glass in his right hand, he placed his left hand on Gustáv's shoulder. "Let's take it slow. Tell me your plan to take him out of the city, and I'll explain how I plan to break him out. But only to you, no one else should know. Not even people you trust. Is that clear?"

"Yes."

"Now, tell me your plan. But first, send your men out. I will only talk to you."

Gustáv gestured, and his men rushed outside, closing the door behind them.

It took a long time for Gustáv and Sánchez to exchange their plans.

"Gustáv, after listening to your plan, I thought of an improvisation. After I had visited the terrace earlier, I thought about how it could be incorporated. Now, it's clear," Sánchez said. "On my way from the prison to the tower, I noticed men belonging to your mafia in the cemetery, they had the tattoo."

"Yes, it's our way of moving drugs through the city. Sorry, but I can't share the details with you right now."

"That's all right. But perhaps we can use them?"

Gustáv considered for a minute. "How?"

Sánchez's elaboration went on for a few minutes.

"You and your men execute your part of the plan, and I'll execute mine. However, I've one more requirement."

"No problem, whatever you need."

"I need to bring in a few of my packages, and I need them delivered to our final rendezvous." Sánchez went to Gustáv and handed him an envelope. "Can you get it done?"

Gustáv opened the envelope and went through its contents. Surprise showed on his face, followed by confusion. Before he could ask, Sánchez spoke, "Trust me, it's all for the master and our plan."

Gustáv nodded. "It'll be done."

"One of my comrades will accompany the packages. She will explain to your men exactly how they need to be handled."

"Whatever you need will be arranged," Gustáv said with a serious face.

"Remember," Sanchez said, "no one should know of our La Santé mission besides us, not even the people where these packages will go."

CHAPTER 22

Drágosláv Baranski

Odessa, Ukraine
Many years back

Ice-cold air gushed in as Mr. Baranski entered the warehouse through its weathered wooden door.

Mr. Baranski was a tall man of strong build and a prominent walrus mustache. He wore an elegant black suit underneath a long winter coat with an ushanka hat.

"Good evening, son," he said, looking toward a boy who was busy arranging boxes.

"Evening, Father," came the reply.

The warehouse was small, but its location was perfect for Baranski's operation. Minutes away from the port of Odessa, it was where he and his men prepared and held the consignments that shipped across Europe. Baranski was the leader of the Odessa mafia. Named after the city of the same name in Ukraine, the mob was infamous for prostitution, extortion, and kidnapping, to name a few of the many crimes they had their hands in.

"Consignment was on time?" Baranski asked. "Any issues with product or delivery?"

"No, Father, everything good. The new supplier gives me no reason so far to be disappointed." The boy stopped arranging the boxes, came around, and stood in front with his hands behind his back like an obedient student answering questions from his teacher.

"And you've everything for onward journey?" Baranski's head turned to look around the warehouse as if doing an inspection.

"Yes, Father, the arrangement's done. I'm finishing a few last things."

"*Duzhe dobre*, Grigori, your work always perfect." Baranski's stern expression vanished. His big mouth broke into a wide smile.

The most critical arm of the mafia's business was drugs. Baranski worked very hard over several years to build his network. It spanned all the way from South Asia to Western Europe. Narcotics came from as far as Afghanistan through several secret routes and were transported to the mafia's headquarters in Odessa, from where they were distributed through the mafia's network to cities and towns across Europe.

"We must be on our game every time, Grigori. The mafia needs discipline, order." Baranski's smile was replaced by a rigid expression. "People from all of Europe are on our payroll. Some work directly for us, some work for local government. Port Authority officers, law enforcement agents, local gangsters, and politicians are armed and gloved by our organization. I make sure they're happy and pay them handsomely. But I also show no mercy for disobedience and treachery."

Behind Mr. Baranski stood a young boy. He pulled the boy forward. "That's how mafia runs. You both should learn that."

The three of them stared at each other in silence.

"Say hello to your elder brother, Drágosláv."

"Hello, brother," Drágosláv said, staring at Grigori.

Grigori did not speak. He avoided looking at Drágosláv.

"Grigori, you'll say hello to your younger brother." Baranski's eyes bulged as he looked at Grigori.

"Hello," Grigori said, looking toward the roof.

"Hello, brother, and look toward him when you say it," Baranski raised his voice.

"Hello, brother," Grigori said, his face filled with contempt.

"That's more like it." Baranski nodded.

Baranski kept his two sons, Grigori and Drágoslàv, by his side so they could learn all the tricks of the trade. His only weakness was that his sons resented each other. Grigori, his elder son, was born of his first wife. Drágoslàv, on the other hand, was born of his second wife. He loved both of them equally and wanted them to get along. Given his stern demeanor, the kids pretended to play well before him. In reality, though, fueled by their mothers' disdain for each other, they kept their hatred alive.

Grigori was the smart one. He ensured he stayed in his father's good books and did not give him a chance to complain. His father trusted him so much that he got many essential and dangerous assignments, even at twenty. Drágoslàv, on the other hand, was three years younger than Grigori and handled things with force and intimidation. He stood tall, robust, and powerful.

Grigori never accepted Drágoslàv as a younger brother and heir apparent to half of the mafia empire. He, however, understood very early that while his father was alive, he could not get rid of Drágoslàv. Thus, he purposely created trouble for Drágoslàv, kept him away from operations, and tried to sabotage his assignments. Grigori wanted it all for himself.

"Grigori, you have done this for quite some time," Baranski said. "I think it's time to take Drágoslàv with you."

"But father—" Grigori spoke.

Baranski cut him off midway. "It's an excellent opportunity to introduce him to people that work for us on these routes. He has done small things till now. I think it's time to teach him real business."

Grigori stared at Drágoslàv's face, his face red in anger. Drágoslàv smirked.

"Zrozumilo?"

Silence. Behind his back, Grigori's fingers made a fist.

"Is that clear, Grigori?" Baranski's hoarse voice echoed through the warehouse.

"Yes, Father." Grigori nodded.

"And I better not hear of trouble from both."

"Yes, Father," this time, both the boys answered in unison.

Before Baranski walked in, Grigori made preparations to take a big consignment of heroin to Barcelona. For the past three years, his father had entrusted him with handling operations in Europe. Grigori made sure the product reached their customers on time and that they were satisfied.

"When do you sail, Grigori?" Baranski walked toward Grigori and put an arm around him. Drágosláv followed.

"Tomorrow night," Grigori answered as the three of them walked side by side to another area of the warehouse.

"Very well," Baranski said as he picked up packet filled with a white powder. "Drágosláv, be ready tomorrow. I want you to listen to your elder brother at all times. He knows how it's done, and you should obey him at all costs. *Zrozumiv?*"

Drágosláv did not reply.

"Do you understand?" Baranski tossed the packet back into a box, turned to face Drágosláv.

"Y- yes, Father," Drágosláv stammered.

"Very good. Now stay here and help your brother."

"But, Father—" Drágosláv came close and placed a hand on Baranski's right arm.

"Yes?"

"Can I take Gustáv with me, please?" Gustáv was Drágosláv's best friend. They seldom stayed apart. Gustáv's father also worked for Baranski and was among his most trusted.

"All right." Baranski nodded. "But only if his father agrees, and remember, I better hear nothing about any mischief. You two create problems wherever you go."

"Thank you, Father." Drágosláv sniggered, looking at Grigori.

"Good." Baranski walked out, giving the chilled air another chance to barge into the room.

CRUE

The next morning, while Grigori was loading the boat, Drágosláv and Gustáv hatched a plan. They stood on a balcony overlooking the black sea. The sun had risen high into the sky on a cold, cloudless day. Seagulls chirped around, flying here and there in search of food.

"Grigori will boss over us for the entire trip." Drágosláv screwed his face as he rested his arms on the wrought iron railing of the balcony. "I don't know how I'm going to survive it."

"Be patient, Drággy. Your time will come." Gustáv came next to Drágosláv, patted his shoulder. "Your father trusts him; he likes him very much."

"Yes, that's what I hate the most. Father thinks of him as his heir apparent."

"You've got to make sure that you get most out of this trip, show your father what you're worth."

"But Grigori will never let me; he'll not let me learn anything. He's smart." Drágosláv slammed his fist on the railing.

A cold breeze hit his face as he stared endlessly toward the horizon.

"I have an idea!" Gustáv pushed Drágosláv's arm from the railing to make him turn away from the sea and face him.

"What?" Drágosláv tilted his head as he faced Gustáv, his eyes lazy.

"How about we drug him and his whole crew, then toss them into the sea?" Gustáv suggested.

"Father will kill us both." Drágosláv held Gustáv by the shoulders and shook him as if bringing him to his senses.

"It's the sea; accidents happen. You know what I mean, Draggy?"

"I don't know." Drágosláv turned back toward the sea, pondering over the idea.

"Draggy, If you don't kill him, some day, he will kill you."

Drágosláv nodded, his eyes still gazing at the rhythmic rocking of the waves.

"Then what are you waiting for? Let's do it." Gustáv slammed his palm on the railing.

"But it's not easy. How would we do it?"

"Food?" Gustáv asked.

"But father's men stock the pantry; they are among his trusted. It'll be difficult to mix anything beforehand. Besides, it'll be cold. Everyone will be in the cabin instead of the deck. That will make it impossible to slip something in while we sail." Drágosláv shook his head.

"You don't worry, leave that to me." Gustáv smiled

Later that night, all of them reached the dock. Grigori had the narcotic consignments loaded and hidden in the boat well before Drágosláv and Gustáv showed up. He did not want Drágosláv to learn anything.

At precisely midnight, they left the port. The sky was clear and filled with dazzling starlight. The sea was calm, calling for a smooth sail. The breeze, however, was ice-cold.

They had sailed for under an hour and were almost at the edge of Ukrainian waters when a boat with searchlights appeared on the horizon. It was the coastguard. They communicated on the radio with the captain. "Stop boat. I repeat, stop boat immediately."

Grigori was surprised. This never happened. The coastguards were paid handsomely for their non-interference. When the guards reached the boat, they boarded onto the deck. Grigori and all his men exited the cabin and went onto the deck.

"You better have good reason for this," he said on seeing the officer.

"Mr. Baranski, I—I didn't know it is you, sir. I—I'm so sorry. We got a tip," he replied.

"And what was the tip? That I'm carrying drugs?" he said intimidatingly. "Like we've done for past several decades?"

"I'm so sorry, sir. The tip was that terrorists were entering the country. So, we couldn't take it lightly. I'm so sorry for inconvenience, sir, I'll leave immediately."

The officer apologized several times and left without further delay.

Grigori stormed back inside the cabin. "Do you understand what's at stake here? It is business, not your foolish child's play," he shouted at Drágosláv, his face red with anger. "I know you did it. Father will know, I'll damn make sure that he does."

Drágosláv and Gustáv, however, did what they had planned to do. They got their window of opportunity in the cabin alone. The food was compromised. After venting his anger at the two for several minutes, Grigori opened a bottle of vodka, poured himself a glass. The others fetched some of it as well. The bottle was empty in no time.

"I want some too," Drágosláv said.

"Not after this, not at all."

"I don't need your permission."

He walked toward the cabinet and opened the only bottle of scotch. Though everyone in his family was fond of vodka, Drágosláv loved whiskey. He started drinking at a very early age.

He poured two glasses on the rocks and took the bottle with him. He handed one glass to Gustáv, and they both gulped it down in no time. He again poured for both.

Grigori did nothing but stare. After two glasses, both were disoriented, unable to move their arms and legs. Their vision became blurred. They screamed, but no sound came out.

"Thought you would outsmart me, you d'yavol? I had guessed that you would spike our food. Have you seen any of us touch the food?" Grigori smirked. "Just understand one thing, I'm smarter than you. I'll always be one step ahead of you, no matter how good a plan you come up with. "

In minutes, there was darkness in front of their eyes. Grigori and the crew lifted them up, carried them to the deck, and, without any hesitation, launched them into the freezing water. "Enjoy the cold water, 'Brother'."

⳩

The ice-cold water brought sensation back into their bodies, but Drágosláv and Gustáv still couldn't move their limbs. They sank lower and lower into the deep, dark abyss. The air in their lungs plummeted. They tried hard, but nothing worked. There was nothing they could do to come to the surface.

Drágosláv saw giant floating bubbles around him inside the water. Light beamed from inside.

When he was about to give up, a jet stream touched their backs. There was enormous pressure and speed. It pushed them toward the surface.

Surely enough, in no time, there was air they could breathe. They were above the surface.

Two hands belonging to something held them. They carried them toward the land.

Their visions were still blurred from the drugs. They could not really make out who or what it was.

After some time, they reached a tiny island. Their savior lifted them, brought them to the shore, and placed them on the sand. It turned its back on them and receded into the water.

When Drágosláv rubbed his eyes, and his vision cleared for a moment, he was sure he saw a pair of scaly hands and legs with translucent webs between the fingers and toes, like those of amphibians. But in the next second, the hands and feet looked normal, and before he could look at their savior's face, his vision blurred again.

"Wait!" Drágosláv shouted, rubbing his eyes frantically. "Who are you?"

No one replied.

They saw the unfocused outline of their savior's humanoid figure walking back toward the water.

Gusts of ice-cold wind made a whooping sound as it went past them. They shivered.

"Why did you save us?" Drágosláv shouted, his teeth chattering from the cold.

Still silence. But this time, it seemed like the blurred outline stopped and turned to face them.

A few minutes later came the reply. "It's our duty."

"Duty?" Drágosláv took a few steps toward the figure. Gustáv followed. "Yes."

"I don't understand. Did Father send you?" Drágosláv asked.

"Father? Whose father?" the figure asked, still standing at the same spot.

"My father." Drágosláv took a few more steps toward him.

The next gust of wind was fast and loud.

The figure came close. "You don't know, but you are special men—both of you." He looked into their eyes, but their own couldn't focus on his.

"Special? How?" Drágosláv rubbed his eyes some more, hoping to fix them, see the figure clearly. No luck.

"I can't tell how, but you are," the voice replied. There was a sense of urgency in it. "I can't stay much longer."

"Why not?" Drágosláv asked

"All I can say right now is that our prophecy is fulfilled."

"Prophecy?" Drágosláv and Gustáv shouted in unison.

"Yes, prophecy. Thousands of years ago, our ancestors prophesied about two men drowning in a foreign sea. They told us that it's our duty to save them."

"But how did you know we are the two men in your prophecy? Thousands of people would've drowned in this sea," Gustáv asked.

"I did not know."

"Then?"

"This sea is foreign to us; it was only recently that we could come here. I saved everyone who drowned in this sea ever since I came here, over months," the voice answered. "The details of the prophecy were lost; we only knew to save the drowning when we encountered a foreign sea. But—"

"But what?" Drágosláv asked almost automatically, coming closer to the figure.

"Every time I'd bring the rescued to shore, they died."

Drágosláv and Gustáv were astounded.

"That's why I did not look at you."

"If this sea is foreign to you, where did you come from?" Gustáv asked.

The creature ignored the question. "You two are the first ones who survived, and now that you have, I have a message for you."

"Message?" Drágosláv and Gustáv asked together.

"Yes, a message," the creature replied, waiting for their attention.

"One day, a man will come seeking you. It'll be when one of you is in trouble. He'll explain everything, who you really are, what all this is supposed to mean, what you're meant to do. You just have to wait for him."

"But how do we know it is him?" Drágosláv asked.

"Ask him this question," the creature said, looking at Drágosláv. "Who are you to the blind whose gaze makes one's body as strong as the strongest thing in the world?"

"What does it mean?" Drágosláv's face looked puzzled.

"I don't have time to explain that." The creature looked back toward the water.

"And what should be the answer?" Drágosláv asked

The creature turned back to face them, took a deep pause and spoke. "Brother."

CHAPTER 23

The Half Brother

Paris, France

Back in the room where Gustáv brought Sánchez, they looked at each other in silence. Gustáv had narrated his and Drágosláv's story about their savior at the sea to Sánchez.

"Do you know who or what that creature was?" Gustáv asked. "Did it meet you, too?"

"Nothing like that happened to me," Sánchez replied. "It's intriguing."

"Then how do you know the answer?"

"It was revealed to me. Long story; will talk about it when the master is with us. But coming back, tell me, what happened after that? Where's Grigori?"

"You want to talk about Grigori?"

Sánchez nodded. "Seems like he will make it hard for us if he finds out about my plan."

Gustáv sighed. "That's one reason we decided to give you a chance. You're on no one's radar in our network."

"Go on, tell me more about Grigori."

"Uncle Baranski divided the business and gave Drággy and Grigori respective territories to operate. He kept an eye on both. Then Grigori's mother passed away, and taking advantage of the situation, Drággy's mother secured most important sections of business for us. Grigori did best with what he had, but the heart of business was with us."

Gustáv smiled. "In a few years, uncle Baranski died, and all hell broke loose. Our two sections of the mafia fought against each other. Draggy and I learned with age, made sure we held our territories. The business, however, suffered. Rivals of the Odessa mafia gained because of it."

"Then?"

"Then Grigori proposed truce. Drággy did not agree at first, but I convinced him. But that d'yavol was just waiting for the right time. He slowly built his network of law enforcement officers inside our territories, placed moles under our noses. One day, he got a tip about Drággy, and he passed the information to his sources. I was away then, in Afghanistan, when they captured Drággy in Paris." Gustáv's face burned with anger. "That son of a bitch, if I can only find him."

He stamped his fist on a desk. "I made several attempts to break Drággy out, but all futile. Grigori on the other hand took advantage and seized more of our territory, there were attempts on my life, too. He knows Drágosláv is trapped, La Santé is a very secure prison."

"He is mistaken, my friend," Sánchez replied. "He is not aware that fate has its own plan. He does not know I'm here now." Sánchez gulped his drink in one go and slammed the glass on the counter. "I'm going to break the master out, and I'm going to guide him in wars to come."

He came close, held Gustáv by the shoulders. "This is just the beginning."

CHAPTER 24

The Boot Camp

Manaus, State of Amazonas, Brazil

Diego's Story — A few years before the abduction

At the end of an exhausting day on the soccer field, the team, comprised of teenagers, recuperated on the turf as their coach gave them feedback.

"Boys and girls," the coach spoke in a thick Brazilian accent, "you worked very hard this week. I know the conditions are extreme here in the Amazon, and it puts a lot of strain on the body as well as the mind. You must have realized this past week that when you come out of your home environment, especially into these difficult ones, things that were easy before now need more effort and attention."

Tired from practice, their shoulders drooped like half-dead tree branches. Nonetheless, they listened. They loved their coach.

"You'll realize that the shots, the free kicks, the things that seemed comfortable until now are no longer easy. The natural instincts that work in your home conditions now fail." The coach's eyes met with each one. "Remember, there will come a time when your style of play will betray you, however good it is. That's when you've to think differently, improvise, devise a plan, work together, and rise above the hardships." They had all struggled today, even Diego, their star player.

"He's so cute," Paola whispered as she stared at Diego. "I've never seen a boy that handsome."

"Aren't you with Carlos?" Ericka asked.

"Yes. But I can't stop looking at that one. Oooh, I just want to—"

"Get in line," Ericka interrupted. "The entire girls' team is after him."

"Well then, I'd better hurry."

Diego caught Paola's eye. She winked. He winked back. The flirting continued for a few minutes.

"You must practice in the harshest of conditions, improve your game, improve your fitness," the coach continued. "You all have impressed us with your dedication and hard work this week. Good job and keep it up." He paused. "As a reward, Assistant Coach George and I have decided to give you a day's break."

The half-dead tree branches came to life. They cheered.

"That's not all. We have a little surprise for you. We planned an excursion for you in the Amazon Rainforest."

The students jumped, clapping and dancing.

"*Obrigadão!*" Diego thanked them.

"*De nada!* Are you enjoying the camp?" the coach asked.

"*Sim treinador*, I learned so much this week. I'm so glad we have you. You're the best."

ⱷ

The next morning, they took a bus from their hotel to the port. It was about an hour's drive. When they reached it, the cruise ship was waiting for them. As everyone got off the bus carrying backpacks, cameras, and hats, the coaching staff counted them.

"Here's what we're going to do. We'll assign each of you a buddy, and you're responsible for knowing where your buddy is, all the time, until we return. If you can't find your assigned buddy, you'll immediately come to me. Understood?"

"*Sim, Senhor,*" they shouted in unison.

Diego was paired with Paola. She giggled, looking toward Ericka.

A few minutes later, they all boarded a double-decker ship.

Wasting no time, the kids raced to the top deck, where the captain welcomed them with a wide smile.

"As some of you might already know, the Amazon River is one of the largest rivers in the world. The city of Manaus is surrounded by several wonders of this region, one of which is the meeting of waters," the captain explained in an American accent. "Now, what's so interesting about it?"

No one spoke.

"Well, this is where two upstream tributaries of Amazon—Rio Negro, and Rio Solimões meet, but don't mix. They run side by side for miles and miles. You know why?" he asked a boy who looked puzzled.

"That's because these two rivers have different temperatures, densities, and a whole bunch of other properties. These features keep them from mixing."

"So, are we going there?" Carlos raised his hand.

"Of course. In fact, that is the first destination on our itinerary."

They sailed for several minutes before reaching the spot. The two rivers looked distinct; Rio Negro was a dark shade of black, while Rio Solimões looked muddy. The two shades indeed ran together, yet also separate, like twin babies in a mother's womb. As others watched this scenic beauty, Diego and Paola sneaked to the lower deck.

"Hey, Carlos, your girl's getting too familiar with that new boy Diego," Ricardo warned. "Lower deck."

"That swine, I'll–" Carlos charged toward the stairs, but Ricardo stopped him.

"Easy, Carlos, the treinador loves him. Wait for the right moment."

"Our next destination is an Island. For that, we'll board these skiffs," the captain interrupted their conversation, pointing at the approaching skiffs.

They disembarked and, using the skiffs, went to an island.

"Who has seen a dolphin before?"

Several hands went up.

"And who wants to swim with them?"

"Me! Me! Me!"

"Great. Then jump!"

They dove on the word jump. The dolphins approached them and played along. A few threw toy balls in the water; the dolphins fetched them. Diego and Paola climbed back on the pier and fed them, laughing and flirting all along. Carlos stared menacingly, grinding his fists.

"All of you, that's enough; we must visit other places. Out of the water in one minute," the coach ordered.

They boarded the skiffs, which took them into the interiors of the forest with narrow water lanes covered by dense trees. Rain drizzled. After a while, the guides anchored the skiffs, and they all jumped onto a hiking trail.

"Everyone, put on your ponchos," the captain said. "We'll hike on this trail for quite a while. We'll see many wild animals, some found only here, so keep your cameras ready."

"Keep in mind, you must keep track of your assigned buddy," the coach reiterated.

They marched into the forest. The trail twisted and turned, with branches and plants often obstructing their path. Rain dripped endlessly, making everything wet and muddy. Animal calls echoed everywhere.

"Stay away from my girl," Carlos came beside Diego and whispered into his ear.

"But she is assigned to me."

"Don't be too smart, I've watched you since we boarded."

"Leave us alone, Carlos." Paola pulled Diego toward her.

Carlos grunted. He looked for the coach. He was far away. Carlos turned toward Ricardo and nodded.

Ricardo held Diego from behind.

Carlos punched Diego in the face. "Next time, if I see you with my girl." Carlos punched again.

"You assholes." Paola kicked Ricardo.

He fell, releasing Diego from his grip.

"Diego, run!" Paola shouted.

Diego stood firm.

"He's too strong for you. Run!"

Diego ran.

Carlos chased.

They went off-trail.

After a lot of running, Carlos lost track.

Diego was alone. Dark, gnarled branches of broad trees intertwined above him, sometimes coming as close as his head. Their thick roots ran in and out of the earth, accompanied by thick bushes, plants with enormous leaves, and ferns.

Diego heard the sound of movement coming from the bushes. His eyes scanned the area slowly.

"Paola? Treinador?" he shouted. "Guys, anyone there?"

No reply. Sweat broke on his forehead, ran down his neck. There was fear in his eyes.

Several monkeys passed overhead, hanging and jumping through the branches.

He tried to trace his steps back.

No luck. He swallowed, wiped his forehead with the back of his hand.

He proceeded onto what he thought was the correct path.

The next second, he heard a creeping sound. Something was following him.

His head moved frantically, looking for the source of that sound. His body trembled in fear. He walked gently, looking here and there as tiny droplets of rain fell from above, mixing with his sweat.

A few steps later, not paying attention, his head bumped into a tree branch. It knocked him to the ground. Pain soared through his head. Dizzy and nauseous, he looked around.

Floating bubbles appeared in every direction. Their boundaries shone red, orange, and black, like the edges of a half-burned piece of paper.

No sooner did he compose himself than he heard slithering. He stood up. Mist filled the area. Something circled near his feet. The next second, it advanced upward. Another second later, it was all over his body, coiling him tight in its grip.

He tried to focus his eyes as much as he could. To his horror, a blurred vision of what looked like a humongous snakehead stared at him.

Anaconda? he thought.

This thing, however, seemed a little different. His hazy vision prevented him from perceiving the monstrosity of what was about to devour him. The snakehead looked intently into Diego's eyes as if trying to inspect something. It engulfed Diego's body.

Diego knew it was going to kill him, crush him. "Socorro!" he shouted. "Help!"

Diego closed his eyes, submitting to the inevitable. He expected the crushing and squeezing to tighten. He expected excruciating pain.

To his surprise, however, nothing happened. The crushing stopped.

Maybe it will swallow me whole. Diego opened his eyes to see the world one last time.

The snakehead opened its mouth and, like a thirsty vampire, dug its fangs into Diego's neck.

The next second, something horrible spread from the bite and sank deep inside, like a plague taking over.

He lost all hope. It was changing him in ways he could not understand.

The trees around him shook. Birds and monkeys around him called.

Surprisingly, the grip around Diego's body loosened. The monster had let go of him. It retreated and disappeared into the thick depths of the rainforest. The mist vanished with it.

Diego's vision became clear. He found himself surrounded by vultures. One by one, they landed on nearby branches. The vultures looked at him and made their calls.

Diego stared at his body. Surprisingly, he could still move.

In the next second, though, terror gripped him. He realized what was happening. The color was spreading over his body, and his arm was turning a dark shade of violet.

The vultures called louder as if venting out their fear and desperation.

The thumping in Diego's chest grew louder. To his astonishment, he realized he could think more clearly than before.

A hidden instinct came to the surface. He followed his intuition, looked for something. He did not know what it was; all he knew was to find it.

He staggered into the forest. The venom made it challenging to move. The vultures followed.

After a few minutes, he saw a seedling glowing in the bushes. The surrounding plants and shrubs had curled away from it. It looked out of place, unique.

Diego limped toward it as fast as he could, but didn't uproot it. His intuition told him what to do.

He brought his palms together, touched the glowing tip of the seedling, and uttered a few words he had never known.

A bright luminescent thread emerged from it and glided inside his closed palms.

He opened them, dragged the thread through the air onto the site of the bite. The thread appeared tied to the wound and drew the dark violet color out from Diego.

As the whole process unfolded, Diego's body healed. In a few minutes, the seedling sucked the venom out.

The next moment, Diego closed his eyes, inhaled the misty rainforest air, and collapsed onto the drenched ground.

CHAPTER 25

Mission La Santé

Paris, France

Two days after he met with Gustáv, Sánchez was once again on top of the Montparnasse tower. This time, however, there was nobody else on the terrace. Gustáv had arranged it by buying off the tower staff. The manager scheduled a repair job for the terrace glass, closed the downstairs ticket window, barricaded the entrance, and placed a *'Personnel Autorisé Seulement'* sign, indicating entry reserved only for authorized personnel. The employees, though, had no idea what was about to take place.

The sun dipped into the distant horizon. Dusk colors subdued the blue canvas of the clear sky. Slowly, the city landscape glowed with street and building lights.

Sánchez had his pets with him this time. He opened the metal cages and ushered them out. The birds looked magnificent. They stood on the floor like obedient students, as if at attention.

Sánchez removed the matchbox-sized electronic devices from their ankles, positioned them on both the birds' heads, and pressed a tiny button. Small needle-shaped arms protruded from the devices and covered their brains. The electrodes adhered tightly to the eagles' heads and secured the devices during flight. No sooner did this happen than their pupils dilated. The eagles looked possessed. Two more arms protruded from the gadgets and pierced the wing muscles on both sides.

Sánchez pulled out his tablet and typed in a few commands.

The birds' actions complied.

Drones were common these days, with countless aviation laws against flying them, and had acquired much attention near sensitive areas, especially prisons. In recent times, during the dark hours, some inmates at La Santé and their minions outside used this avenue to move contraband in and out of prison. The prison installed its own local radar for this. It detected drones, and accordingly, guards intercepted them before they reached the inmates. Birds were organic, thus did not register with the same signature on the radar as the drones did and were, therefore, disregarded.

Sánchez fastened two more devices to the eagles' ankles. They were encased in deceptive packaging, making them look like mini energy drink bottles.

Energy drinks. Huh. Sánchez smirked. *The customs officer bought the lie so easily. Fool.*

Each device was capable of carrying out a massive explosion. Made from a newly developed non-metallic, non-nitrate substance, the explosives were tiny. They could not be detected through X-rays, sniffer dogs, or security screens at the most high-tech airports, so that CIA agents and assassins on their missions abroad could carry them without detection. Still a prototype; they were not yet released to field agents. But Sánchez got hold of them through his friend Jaime, a CIA agent with whom he collaborated for a joint top-secret project between the NMRL and the CIA.

"God bless Jamie," Sánchez murmured. "Still can't believe he gave them to me."

Sánchez assembled his equipment.

The eagles glided toward La Santé in no time.

The Parieur had a good view of the prison from his position. He navigated the birds toward his target with precision and monitored their flight through his telescope. Their headgear made the birds obey his commands. Sánchez possessed their brains, controlled their reflexes.

After a few minutes' flight, the eagles landed under a bush beside the prison wall at two separate locations. No sooner did they touch down than Sánchez typed in a few commands on the tablet, and the ankle attachments holding the explosives detached from the birds and fell to the ground.

"Come in Erysichthon," Sánchez radioed Gustáv.

"Go ahead for Erysichthon," Gustáv replied.

"Birds are home. I repeat, birds are home."

"10-4. Diamond is at the desired location. I confirm, Diamond is at the desired location."

"Roger that, stand your ground." Sánchez typed some more commands into his tablet, and the birds flew out of the prison.

The next second, he spoke into the radio. "Fireworks in five, four, three, two, one."

BOOM! BOOM! Came two loud explosions almost simultaneously.

The intensity was colossal. Several walls of La Santé blasted off. It went dark. The guards were shocked. They ran haywire like ants on the loss of their mound.

Fire spread here and there. Smoke and dust filled the air. The air became unbreathable. Chaos spread like wildfire. Inmates ran in all directions. Some overpowered the guards and took their weapons.

The second bird's blast disabled the sirens and radio communication. Sánchez could see the destruction from his vantage.

"Your turn. Move in, get the Diamond."

Gustáv and his men rushed inside the prison through the blown-up wall, wearing respirators and night vision goggles. They were armed with automatic weapons. The company shot every guard that came in their path.

"Anyone have eyes on the Diamond?" Sánchez radioed.

"Negative," came several replies.

They searched for several minutes. With smoke all around and dust on the inmates' faces, it was a difficult task.

"I have the Diamond," Gustáv radioed. "I repeat, I have the Diamond."

Drágosláv's face was covered in dust. His hair was in disarray. Gustáv placed a mask on Drágosláv's face. He breathed hard. Next, Gustáv gave Drágosláv a radio.

"Diamond, are you good? Can you walk?" Sánchez asked.

"Yes, I'm fine," Drágosláv replied on the radio.

"Put on what Gustáv gives you. Now, let's go. "

It took Drágosláv a few minutes to get ready.

"Diamond ready to go," Gustáv radioed. "Seeking approval for exit."

"Copy that. Standby," Sánchez replied. He peeked into his telescope and radioed again. "Black elephants are in place. I confirm, black elephants are in place. Are the three Gems ready?"

"Gem one ready," came a reply.

"Gem two ready," came the second.

"Gem three also ready."

"All right, Erysichthon, please resume control." Sánchez keyed into the radio. "See you soon."

"Everyone," Gustáv spoke into the radio, "we'll exit on the count of three. One, two, three."

On three, three men with identical masks and prison uniform—the gems—walked out from the smoke cloud. Three black SUVs of the same make and model—the black elephants—waited at different spots around the prison.

The company escorted the three uniformed prisoners to the SUVs. Each took off in a different direction, making it impossible to track and decide which one ferried Drágosláv.

Several minutes later, La Santé's backup communication system came to life.

"*Trois SUV, suivez les trois SUV noirs,*" the jailor broadcasted on the police radio channel.

"*D'autres détenus s"enfuient, que faisons-nous à leur sujet?*" one officer asked what to do about the inmates which escaped on foot.

"*Ils n'iront pas loin. Concentrez-vous sur les VUS, nous ne pouvons pas perdre Drágosláv,*" came the reply. The chief ordered to leave them and follow the SUVs. Drágosláv was too important.

The police cars tailed the SUVs. Choppers chased from above.

The escape was superbly coordinated. The timing was precise.

Finally, after three long chases, the cops forced the three SUVs to halt. They were at three separate spots far away from La Santé, outside the limits of Paris.

"*Placez vos mains sur votre tête et sortez lentement du véhicule*," a cop ordered via megaphone. He was commanding the passengers in SUV at the first location to get out.

As they exited the vehicle, the cop scrutinized each one of them in detail, especially the one wearing a prison uniform.

"*Drágoslàv n'est pas là. Je répète, Drágoslàv n'est pas là.*" The cop keyed on the radio.

"*Drágoslàv n'est pas là non plus.*" An officer at the second location radioed after examining his captives.

"*Pas de Drágoslàv ici aussi.*" The officer at the last location radioed.

None of them had Drágoslàv.

CHAPTER 25

Continued-

Following the two explosions at La Santé, inside the smoke cloud, Drágoslav undressed his prison uniform, took a few deep breaths from the respirator, and placed a wig on his head. The three decoys walked out while Drágoslav and Gustáv stayed.

"Here, put this on." Gustáv handed him a full-body suit. "It'll make sure we don't show up on the thermal cameras. They won't be able to trace where we went."

The SUVs left with the decoys. Gustáv and Drágoslav escaped. It was Sánchez's plan; only Gustáv knew about it.

"This way, Drággy, across the street."

They crossed the road. Smoke and dust filled it, like inside the prison.

"Our men, the gravediggers that move our drugs," Gustáv said, lifting the manhole cover on the sidewalk. "They dug up small tunnels from Cimetière du Montparnasse and connected them to underground sewage system, Dr. Sánchez's idea. He recognized our men even before our meeting."

"Do you believe him?" Drágoslàv asked.

"Don't you? Drággy, he gave the right answer. Exactly what that creature had told us so many years ago."

Silence. They stared at each other.

"Drággy." Gustáv held his shoulders. "We had been waiting for this man since that day, you remember?" He looked into his eyes. "He is real. He is here now."

Drágoslàv nodded.

"This manhole is our entry point, an underground shortcut to tower." Gustáv threw the heavy iron cover aside and extended his right arm toward the manhole. "After you. Jump."

The underground sewage system and the dug-up tunnels led Drágoslàv straight to the Montparnasse tower. A small, operated trolley sped things up. They exited the sewage system by opening the cover on the sidewalk next to the tower, went inside, and boarded the reserved elevator to the terrace. The antennas and glass assembly on the terrace's periphery were already lowered.

Sánchez spotted Drágoslàv. He rushed toward him.

"Welcome back, master." Sánchez beamed.

"What next, Dr. Sánchez?"

His question was answered by a loud chopping sound and strong winds. A helicopter with France 24 NEWS written across its body descended onto the terrace.

"Our helicopter, pretending to cover the prison break."

"You're a genius, Dr. Sánchez." Drágoslàv held him by the shoulders.

They hugged.

Dr. Sánchez extended his arm toward the helicopter. "Come now, master. Your new life awaits you."

Drágoslàv stared at the beautiful skyline, closed his eyes, and breathed deeply. "Freedom."

The three of them beamed like teenagers about to go on a rollercoaster.

Within minutes, the chopper took off and disappeared into the night sky.

CHAPTER
26

Initiation

Kenya-Tanzania Border
Ojore's Story — A few years before the abduction

The departing sun cast a mesmerizing spell on the African landscape. The sky was brushed with silhouettes of birds returning to their nests in the backdrop of yellow grass and umbrella-like acacia trees.

Along the Bángá settlements, herdsmen directed cattle toward the enkang, a circular fence surrounding the village. Made from branches with sharp ends pointing outward, the enkang protected cattle and people from the nocturnal attacks of lions, hyenas, and cheetahs.

The Bángá people were a semi-nomadic tribe that roamed parts of northern Tanzania and southern Kenya alongside the African Great Lakes. They were herdsmen who grazed cattle and fierce warriors who protected them from predators and other tribes. Cattle were currency in these villages, where the diet consisted of meat, milk, and sometimes animal blood. Weddings involved an exchange of cattle. So did the settlement of disputes.

"This our homes. We call them Inkajijiks," Saboré—one of the tribesmen—explained to a visitor in broken English. "They is made from grass and tree branches. We use cow dung and mud to bind them."

The Bángá wore red clothes, had body piercings with stretched earlobes, and donned traditional jewelry made from beads. In their society, older men made all the important decisions. Though they were tough and loved their simple nomadic lifestyle, they welcomed people from outside with open arms as long as they did not interfere with tribal traditions.

Today, the village was hosting a safari expedition mainly consisting of Western tourists and a few Kenyans.

"Come, you dance with us when you visit our tribe," Saboré urged the visitors to join the dance performance by tribespeople. The visitors danced to their ancestral music.

There was clapping, jumping, singing, and hooting. Cheers and happy faces shone all around.

After the celebrations, the tribeswomen served food.

"This our traditional food, all made from wild and nearby ingredients. We don't go supermarkets." Saboré chuckled.

The guests enjoyed every bit of it and bought loads of jewelry as souvenirs. It was a perfect day.

Night took the village, and it was time for goodbyes.

"It was wonderful spending the day with you," an American lady told a tribeswoman. "I will come back and visit you wherever you are camped next time." A translator explained to the tribeswoman what the guest said. She smiled and shook her hand.

A few minutes later, the visitors boarded their safari jeeps and left for their cabins.

There was one person, though, who stayed behind.

"Stranger, yoa' people leave. You no supposed to be here afta sun is going," Saboré said. "Visitors no allowed to spend the night. Village rules."

"I want to speak to your tribe chief," the stranger replied.

Saboré was puzzled. He wondered what the visitor had in mind. Nonetheless, he walked toward a distant Inkajijik, entered the hut, and returned several minutes later.

"Chief says he see you. This way." He pulled the stranger by the shoulder. "You should talk in respect."

They entered the chief's Inkajijik. It was bigger and taller than the others. An oil lamp illuminated the hut. The floor was cured with cattle dung and decorated with white paint. In the corner was a log seat on which sat the chief. A lion's skin was placed on the floor before the seat.

"I kill this lion when I was child," the chief said, watching the stranger's gaze upon the lionhead. "They no allow hunt lion no more," he continued in broken English. "That's 'ow a Bángá become man in old days."

The stranger stood silent.

"Sit." The chief pointed toward a nearby log stool. "What your name?"

"Ojoré," the stranger replied.

"Why you no leave with others?"

"I want to live with you—in the tribe."

The Bángá present in the hut looked at each other in surprise. Silence. The chief stood up. He walked toward Ojoré. Looked him in the eye. "Why you say this?"

"I visited your village many years back as a child. The simplicity, the bare necessities, and the connection with the land, I loved it all."

"You from here? Kenya? Tanzania?"

"Kenya. Nairobi, to be precise."

The chief walked around Ojoré, listening intently. There was silence for a while.

"The world outside is corrupt, plastic, crazy. I'm fed up with that lifestyle. Tired of pretending to be who I'm not. Tired of living a superficial life." The frustration in Ojoré's voice was visible on his face. "I've had enough. I want to live a basic life, a simple life, be one with nature, be one with myself."

"So, you want to be one of us?"

"Yes."

The chief stared into Ojoré's eyes for a long time.

He walked back toward his seat as if in deep thought. "For city people, it no easy to be Bángá people. No comfortable."

"I know, I've given it thought. I'm ready to do whatever it takes to be one of you."

The chief closed his eyes. Sighed. "But you follow our rules strictly, no excuses, no questions, no- no dis- disobedience."

"As you say, Stamhoof."

"Very good." The chief nodded. "Saboré, take visitor to empty Inkajijik."

"Yoa initiation start tomorrow," he told Ojoré and gestured them to leave. They all left the hut.

Saboré directed Ojoré toward an empty one. "This your hut tonight."

"What about tomorrow?"

"You no live in village tomorrow."

"Why? The chief said I can live here."

"For yoa initiation, you live out of village, in wild."

Fear and excitement gripped Ojoré at the same time. "What do I have to do in the initiation?"

"Village give you goat. Then you go out of village, stay alone for one moon cycle."

"And then?"

"If you come back alive with goat, you one of us. There will be ceremony of celebration, then you called Bángá warrior."

Ojoré stood silent.

"Understand?"

Ojoré nodded.

Saboré left the hut. Ojoré unfolded an impala skin placed in the corner and lay down.

Tomorrow is a big day, he thought. I have to begin my quest, my journey to discover myself. I have to detach from my past to forget my pain.

This is my pilgrimage.

He closed his eyes and thought of what made him do this. His mind filled up with memories of the many painful episodes. He remembered feeling different in school, the feeling of not belonging there. He recalled how he accepted his feelings, his orientation, and what he wanted. But that was not acceptable to anyone; not to his friends, not his family, certainly not to his deeply religious, old-fashioned, and conservative Catholic father.

He remembered when he mustered courage and told the truth to his parents.

What are you talking about? Are you a fool? It is a sin. Do you have no fear of the Lord? His father's response rang through his head.

He remembered how his father took him to a long list of doctors on discovering this. How the doctors made him take medicine, pretending to cure him of the so-called disease he had. How the drugs drove him crazy. They made him vomit all the time. When the drugs did not work, he remembered them performing shock treatment, causing pain, which made him pull his hair.

He remembered how, on his mother's pleading, his father moved him to a monastery where they made him a brother, confined to a room with the bible and Jesus. He remembered the enslavement, the helplessness, how they watched his every move.

Why am I like this? Why do these feelings not go away? Why am I a sinner? He kept on asking himself, and an equally tortured man pinned to the crucifix above the altar.

Look what they did to me, son, he heard the man on the crucifix reply.

Ojoré remembered how one day he could take it no more and ran away. He sold all the gold he wore. The Bángá were the only people that came to his mind. He came here and how he now lay inside this hut.

Tears rolled down his cheek. He thought of all the things that happened to him out of no fault of his own, just because he was born this way. He tried hard to let go of his past and fell asleep trying.

The roar of a lion woke him up in the morning. He rubbed his eyes and found Saboré standing in front.

"It's time, come out."

Ojoré stood up, rubbed his eyes, and put on his clothes. They both exited the hut.

"You new to wild, so I going to teach basic thing to survive. Most important, 'ow to use rungu."

Saboré pulled out two club-shaped weapons. "This are rungu," he said and handed one to Ojoré. There were two targets made from dried grass in front of them. "Aim center."

Ojoré pulled his arm back, aimed, and launched the rungu. His aim was nowhere near the center.

"Try harder," Saboré ordered.

Again, it missed.

Ojoré was determined. He tried and tried and tried. Giving up was not in his nature. It went on for hours and hours, but Ojoré kept on going.

No luck.

"Try again."

Ojoré picked up the rungu and kept going at it. Again and again, he aimed. Again and again, he missed.

After many unsuccessful attempts at the target, he closed his eyes and sighed.

A vision of an eye came to his mind. His mind focused on the eye. It felt as if it had happened before. He aimed for the target once again and launched. This time, the rungu hit the center.

After that shot, it was as if he had known it for ages. His every shot made dead center.

Saboré was amazed.

Satisfied, they went to the assembly area. The entire tribe was waiting for him. A village elder took him inside a hut and made him sit on a log stool. Another came and shaved Ojoré's head. After that, a white paste was applied to his face and head. They gave him red clothes, sandals, and bracelets.

A few minutes later, he walked out of the hut wearing the traditional attire. The village priest blessed him and handed him a rungu and a spear. The chief gave him the goat, which he was supposed to protect.

Music played. They sang, jumped, and danced. A few elders escorted Ojoré out of the village.

He was on his own now. An ordinary villager in pursuit of becoming a warrior.

CRSO

Ojoré spent his first morning thinking about where he should spend the night. He lacked the experience and wisdom he would have gained if he had grown up with the Bángá. Saboré had given him some guidance, but the wilderness still overwhelmed him.

After walking the scorching African terrain for a long while, he devised a plan.

All I have to do is gather enough grass, wood, and thorny stuff to build a shelter and barricade it. He decided to replicate what the Bángá did in their village, but on a smaller scale.

Keeping a wary eye on his goat, he spent the entire afternoon gathering materials. Cutting tree branches, uprooting grass, and finding dung exhausted him. However, working without any breaks, he accomplished his objective. He erected a hut around a tree and built a thorny, pointy barricade to protect it. The village ladies had packed him enough food for the first two days to make it easy for him. Saboré sneaked in a few matchboxes in case he needed a fire and couldn't start one alone.

"Remember, fire best weapon if you attacked by lion pride," Saboré had advised. "But don't worry, because of poachers, they stay away from human. They rarely come near you."

Ojoré tied his goat to the tree and placed some grass as feed. He climbed the tree with his food, unpacked it, and ate, looking at the enchanting sight of the sun diving down into the distant tangerine horizon. The magical colors, beautiful landscape, and quietness soothed his body. He could feel himself become one with nature. He could feel his soul healing.

A spectacular night followed the picturesque sunset. As this part of the wilderness was blessed with a lack of light, he could see the sky filled with billions of stars, as if bathed in tiny diamonds. The arm of the Milky Way appeared mesmerizing. There were shooting stars almost every minute. The day's labor took its toll. He descended, went inside his hut, and fell asleep without trying.

Early morning the next day, Ojoré was out of food. He decided to hunt an antelope.

That should last at least a few days.

He and his goat left the comfort of their hut in search of prey.

I have to find water. That's the best chance to find it.

They walked for hours and hours but found nothing. The goat bleated. It resisted Ojoré's pull.

Ojoré decided to take a break. He spotted a tree. The shadow it cast on the searing ground looked inviting. Luckily, he discovered it was also very close to a river. He tied the goat, sat down to catch his breath.

No sooner did his buttocks kiss the ground than there were loud sounds of stamping. He climbed the tree and scanned the place. A herd of antelopes leaped toward him. He jumped down, picked up his goat, tied its limbs together, and fastened it on his back. The two of them climbed again.

As the herd came closer and closer, like a predator, Ojoré concentrated. Soon, he realized he was not the only one. A deafening roar echoed from nowhere, and a lioness jumped out from the yellow grass. She had her eyes on the weakling. The antelope tried to evade her attack, but she was relentless. The antelope was no match. It fell prey. She dragged the carcass into a bush, and when she was about to devour her prize, a clan of hyenas approached.

Although big, the lioness was no match for the hyenas' planning, team-work, and cunning. She fought hard and chased a few of them away. For a moment, the hyenas dispersed, but only to attack again. They wouldn't let go of easy meat.

Ojoré saw his chance. He mustered all his courage and tried to get hold of the hunted antelope. It was difficult.

The struggle between the lioness and the hyenas blocked his access.

After trying and trying, he found an opening.

Wasting no time, he grabbed the antelope, carved a leg with his spear-head, and retreated. The lioness and hyenas were busy fighting.

Or that was what it seemed.

Ojoré was almost at the tree when he found himself staring into multi-ple pairs of eyes.

The hyenas had returned after getting rid of the big cat. They stared at him, poised for attack.

With all his strength, he broke into a sprint. At that same instant, the hyenas charged.

He launched his rungu. It hit the target, put one down. The spear took care of the second. The third, however, took a long jump and knocked him down.

Ojoré hit the ground hard, his head dizzy. The next second, the hyena pounced.

He gathered his senses in time, held its neck with his two hands to keep it from biting. The other hyenas circled.

The hyena's paw made a cut in his arm through which blood oozed.

He panted. His vision became hazy. His grip became loose. He turned his head sideways, still holding the neck, the jaws biting millimeters away from it.

When his body was about to give up, bubble-like objects appeared floating nearby.

In the next moment, a dazzling beam of light shot out from them toward him.

A few seconds later, he opened his eyes. The hyenas had retreated. He looked for the thing that caused the hyenas to run.

Is there a bigger predator? Has the lioness returned with her clan?

To his amazement, a feminine figure emerged from the river. The animals and beasts ran away from wherever the figure went.

Her whole body was illuminated with a radium-like glow. Her skin dazzled as if embedded with tiny jewels. She had a flawless, curvy body with beautiful, silky, knee-length hair. She wore clothes that looked mesmerizing. There was something magical about them. It seemed as if water was woven into fabric.

As she approached him, her presence filled the entire area with misty vapors of fragrance. The scent was bewitching, unlike anything he had smelled before. Unearthly.

She approached Ojoré.

As the mist droplets pecked his body, Ojoré relaxed.

Walking into a slow catwalk, she carried the dress elegantly. To complement her appearance, she wore a smile that instantly energized Ojoré. His arms slowly gained back their strength.

The magnitude of her beauty increased as she came closer. Her eyes stared into his. They hypnotized him. Healed him. There was no struggle, no hyena, no pain.

She tore a piece from her misty dress and tied it around Ojoré's wounded arm. It healed right away.

The next minute, she retreated toward the bubbles and disappeared.

ᘯᘯ

At the end of the moon cycle, Ojoré returned to the Bángá village. His goat was alive and healthy. No predator dared to come close to him after the incident.

Deep, long bruises covered his body, and each step he took sapped his already depleted strength.

On his return, the villagers celebrated with a loud cheer. They carried him on their shoulders and rejoiced. He went straight to the chief's hut.

"Welcome, you one of us now, a Bángá warrior," the chief greeted him with delight.

He breathed a heavy breath and closed his eyes.

Alas, he was free, happy, and content!

The only thing that troubled him was recurring dreams of that misty lady.

CHAPTER 27

Flamenco

Barcelona, Spain

The sun was yet to down, but light already found it difficult to reach the labyrinthine streets of Barri Gòtic.

A bus halted, and excited tourists disembarked. "All right, everyone, gather over here, please. Ma'am, ma'am, over here, please," a tour guide holding an extendible stick said.

A small, yellow triangular flag with the travel agency's name extended from the top of the stick.

"Welcome to Barri Gòtic or the Gothic Quarter, as they say in English," the guide spoke slowly and clearly. The tourists huddled around him. "It's one of the oldest neighborhoods of Barcelona, surrounded by La Rambla, Via Laietana, Ronda de Sant Pere, and the Mediterranean Sea. It's full of ancient medieval-aged buildings, some dating as far back as the Roman era, and as you can see around us, it's very popular."

Many of the meandering streets of Barri Gòtic opened into small squares where several artists performed mini-acts. The low light, cobblestoned streets, and stony walls gave it a dungeon-like, haunting ambiance. A majority of its restaurants and lounges resembled cells of an ancient castle prison.

"If anyone is interested in flamenco, Palau Dalmases over here,"—the guide pointed toward a tiny mansion to his right—"has an excellent performance at a reasonable price."

Built in the seventeenth century, Palau had a massive gate at the entrance with a small door carved in it for people to walk through. It was lit with candles and oil lamps to give it an old, yesteryear effect. Complementing the lighting were the courtyard, spiral columns, floral plants, and stony walls, which made it look exceptionally medieval. Several antique-looking seats were arranged in front of a small makeshift stage on the covered side of the courtyard.

"What's flamenco?" a tourist asked.

"Flamenco is a traditional Spanish folk art, a performing art consisting of singing, passionate dancing, intense clapping, and guitar. If you've not seen it before, I highly recommend it."

"Thirty euros will buy you a seat to the live performance along with a complimentary glass of sangria," a man guarding the Palau Dalmases' door shouted in a Catalan accent. "Only a few seats left for the next show. It'll start in fifteen minutes. Come, have a peek."

The tickets were gone in minutes. Visitors were impressed by the elegant ambiance of the place. It was mystic.

The guests were courted inside on entry, and the guard closed the door. When the spectators were in the middle of getting their complimentary drinks from the bar counter and seating themselves, the stage lights came to life. The announcers spoke into the microphone in a thick Catalan accent.

"*Señoras y Señores*, welcome to tonight's live performance of the traditional dance form called flamenco. I request you to please take your seats as soon as possible and remain seated. The show is about to start in a few minutes."

The lights on the seating side dimmed. The audience hastily occupied their seats, holding the complimentary drinks.

When everyone settled, four men and a lady marched from behind the audience. They took the stage. One of the four men sat on a chair holding a guitar while the other two sat on Cajóns beside him. The last man and the lady remained standing.

The standing man donned a white long-sleeve shirt. A red tie and a black waistcoat enhanced its elegance. The lady wore a magnificent traje-de-flamenca—a traditional flamenco dress. The vibrant, red-colored traje-de-flamenca was long, extending almost to her shoes. It fitted tightly to her curvy hips but flared out as it spanned toward her ankles. The flare was made of ruffles. It gave the dress a shaky, swirly, dazzling look.

"Wows" and "Ooohs" were murmured as she walked across the stage. A spectator whistled.

The performer played the guitar with a traditional flamenco rhythm. Seconds later, the one next to him sang with a deep voice as if in grave pain and wanted to tell the whole world about it. The one next to the singer played the Cajón, which he sat on. The others clapped along.

As the music became more and more intense, the lady danced. She twisted, turned, and moved her body in the most remarkable manner, stamping her feet along with it in a way similar to tap dancing. Her eyes narrowed as if focused on something, unblinking. She didn't smile. Her lips pressed. Finishing her fabulous dance, she moved and stood to the side while the man beside her came in front. He matched her every subtle move, dancing with equal vigor and grace.

It was thirty minutes into the performance. On the other side of the Palau, near the door, the owner, Miguel, enjoyed his sangria. The door guard entered and whispered into his ear, "A few men are here to see you. I told them we are busy, that we have a live performance going on," his voice shook as he spoke, "but, they got angry and threatened me. Here, they gave me this note."

Miguel opened the folded paper.

"*D is here,*" it read. "*Make arrangements now.*"

Miguel panicked. He rushed toward the announcer, whispered in his ear.

Concluding the first part of their fantastic display, the two dancers went inside to change their costumes. The remaining members continued the performance by playing some exquisite music.

Right when the two dancers were about to return on stage, a loud, unbearable ringing filled the Palau. The performance stopped.

"Ladies and gentlemen, it's the fire alarm. Please evacuate from the premises onto the street," the announcer spoke into the microphone. "Please be calm as you exit. We apologize for this unfortunate circumstance and the sudden cancellation of the show."

Everyone, including the dancers, evacuated. As they were in the middle of stepping out, four men entered the premises. They went straight into the room on the far, secluded side of the courtyard.

"Off-duty firefighters," Miguel told one guest as he paused before exiting. "They are usually in the area. It's most probably a false alarm, but we can't continue the performance as per regulations. Don't worry, you will get your money back. I apologize for the inconvenience."

A few minutes later, all guests, most of whom were grumpy and disappointed, left the premises. The doors closed. The next show's details on the blackboard outside were wiped out, and a *Next Show Canceled* notice was put up.

Making sure all his orders were properly followed, Miguel hurried inside. The four men sat around a table. The room was big, with textured slate floors of a yellowish hue. A round wrought-iron chandelier holding flickering electric candles along its circumference hung from the dark-brown wooden ceiling that rested on stone arches rising from limestone pillars. The walls were made of beige limestone bricks with only one window opposite the wrought iron door. The window had a grille on the outside with designs of flowers. Besides the wooden table and chairs, the room had several antique upholstered armchairs and a settee.

Miguel went straight to the master, knelt, and held his hand.

"Master D—D—Drágosláv, w—welcome, S—Señor. S—So happy to see you after such a long time," he said.

Drágosláv said nothing.

"If I knew that you were on your way here, I would have made pr—r proper arrangements, *Señor*."

"Wanted to surprise you, Miguel," Gustáv said. He took the chair beside Drágosláv.

"No one told me you two were coming here. I saw the news of your escape on TV."

"Didn't want information to leak on where we were going." Gustáv smiled.

"Anything you need from me, Master, anything *Señor* Gustáv?"

"Yes. We need to stay here for a few days, and then we will leave," Drágosláv spoke this time.

"Where are you going, Master?"

"That's none of your business, Miguel. Just be ready to make arrangements for whatever we need," Gustáv shouted.

"Yes, of course."

Miguel hesitated. "But there is one thing, Master. There is a problem."

"What?" asked Drágosláv.

Miguel stood up. "Since you went to prison, Grigori's gang has been attacking us. As you know, all of our assets were focused in the north, to get you out and- and..." Miguel paused as if afraid to speak the next sentence. "We have lost the port to them. A few officers on their payroll control the entire port."

"Miguel, Miguel, Miguel. I might've been locked up in the prison, but I've my ways to get all the information I need. Especially if it's about my enemies," Drágosláv replied. "That's why we didn't go to the port directly, we came to this busy part of town, to evade detection. Anyways, we will deal with that later. I have other pressing matters for now." Drágosláv paused for a few seconds.

"All of you, leave me, Gustáv, and Dr. Sánchez alone. We need to discuss an important matter."

They obeyed.

"Just a minute," Sánchez interrupted. "Gustáv, can you please confirm if my packages were delivered here?"

Gustáv turned toward Miguel.

"Sí, we received the packages two nights ago, *Señor*," Miguel replied. "They're in the basement."

He cleared his throat. "To be honest, I was shocked to get them. I didn't expect you caballeros to be here in person to collect them, least of all Master Drágosláv."

"Aren't you happy we are here, Miguel?"

"Of course, *Señor* Gustáv. I'm delighted to have you here. It's just that if I knew, I would have made proper arrangements."

"I trust you'll take care of us just fine, Miguel," Drágosláv said.

"Whatever you need, Master. Whatever you need," Miguel said with a wide smile. His white teeth flickered from the dancing lights of the candles overhead.

"Very well, Miguel. Thank you very much for your help." Sánchez stood from his chair and shook Miguel's hand. "Before you leave, though, are you handling my packages precisely the way Alexis asked?"

Miguel looked puzzled. He had not met this stranger before. "*Señor*, you are?"

"He's one of us. He is the one who broke Drággy out." Gustáv rose from his chair, stood beside Sánchez with an arm on his shoulder.

"Very well, sir, welcome to Barcelona." Miguel showed his teeth again with a bow.

"So, you're handling the packages precisely the way Alexis asked?"

"Sí, *Señor*. Alexis Birdwhistle arrived with the packages and instructed us on how to handle them." Miguel nodded. "We followed her instructions."

"Excellent! You have done a tremendous job, *Señor* Miguel." Gustáv patted Miguel's back.

Miguel made a slight bow and left the room.

CHAPTER 28

The Common Bond

Back in the basement, the mood was ecstatic. Although the five hostages still couldn't move, their voices showed their enthusiasm.

"I was a kid when I ran into those creatures in the forest, told my mother, but she wouldn't believe me." Liang's voice was excited. "I roamed the forest countless times looking for those creatures, but it was futile. As days passed, I convinced myself it was a dream. I almost forgot about the incident."

"Well, they saved you from the poachers, unlike the creature that attacked me," Diego said. "I almost died that day if not for the sapling."

"How did you know about that sapling? The Amazon is filled with plants and trees. How did you know that it would heal you?"

"I just knew it; don't know how. My intuition guided me toward it."

They pondered in silence.

"Like Liang, I, too, thought I'd imagined it," Darren said. "How would a person get inside an effing' tornado and come out gosh-darn alive?"

"I'm strong, but I didn't believe I was strong enough to pull something like that off."

"That's extraordinary, and that's why they've restrained you with more chains than us. They know about your strength," Aarno said.

Ojoré raised his head. "Nobody in the Bángá village believed me either. I told myself that the lady who came from the water and saved me was a hallucination. But I kept on having dreams about her. Even now, I was woken up by the same dream."

"I, too, dream about the darn tornado all the time."

The others nodded.

"Aarno, unlike us, you're the only one who went into a different world instead of someone coming into ours. What was it like?"

"It was unlike anything I'd experienced. It was just amazing. Gold everywhere for miles and miles. Breathtaking."

"I'm wondering if the creatures we all encountered came from the same world," Diego said. "Maybe from the same place where Aarno went."

"Yes, and the bubbles—the bubbles are windows into that world," Aarno spoke with energy. "We all saw those bubbles. I fell into one and entered that world of gold."

Silence hung curiously in the room.

"Whatever it is," Liang said, "this is the thing that ties us all. These paranormal, these extraordinary incidents that happened in our past. I believe these incidents are why they've taken us hostage."

CHAPTER 29

Where Are the Five Men?

Barcelona, Spain

Miguel turned around, walked out, and shut the door behind him. Gustáv, Drágoslàv, and Sánchez were the room's only occupants.

Before the doors closed, Gustáv repeated, "We don't want to be disturbed at any cost. I'll call you when we're done."

Sánchez turned to Drágoslàv. "Well, Master, where do we begin?"

Drágoslàv pondered. There was so much to talk about, so much to tell, so much to ask. Finally, he decided to start by talking about himself. "This is my family business. I took it from my half-brother," he said, concentrating on the ceiling, "but—" he paused, his tone hesitant "—now it looks like I have to leave it for good." He took a few steps toward Sánchez. "I knew there was something else waiting for me, something that is bigger than anything I'd done before."

His eyes widened, chest swelled. "When you said this to me in jail, though it resonated, I was skeptical. But when you asked me that question, it all came back. It sounded perfect. I was convinced. I had almost forgotten that incident and the question. That answer."

"Brother," he whispered.

Drágosláv stared at Sánchez intently, waiting for his comments. Sánchez stood silent.

"The book you gave me—" he slowly walked around the room as he talked "—explained a lot of things. Although it seems bizarre, I for some reason believe it. It feels real. I understand who I am supposed to be. I know what needs to be done in the end, but I don't understand how we'll find them and what we'll do after that?" He paused again for a while, expecting a reply from Sánchez.

None came. After a few seconds of silence, he spoke again, "And the biggest question is, what's the purpose of it all?"

Sánchez was still silent as if waiting for Drágosláv to vent his anxiety, his doubts.

"It's like finding a needle in a haystack. Were you given any more information, some kind of clue? Any tools?" he asked impatiently. "How do we find those five men? Are those packages you inquired about with Miguel some kind of tools to help us find those men?"

Drágosláv kept on asking more and more questions. All of them were about those five particular men. "Where are they from? Do they know who they are and what they are supposed to do? What are their names?"

Like a patient teacher, Sánchez waited for Drágosláv to ask all the questions on his mind. When Drágosláv finished, he spoke, "Firstly, I think I must start by calling you, Your Majesty," he said. "From now on, I'll serve, and you'll lead. My life's sole purpose is to guide you and counsel you as I did in those ages." Sánchez turned around, took a deep breath, and spoke again. "To answer your question, I do know their names, Your Majesty."

He looked into Drágosláv's eyes. "Ojoré, Aarno, Liang, Darren, and Diego are the five men we seek. Secondly, the packages are not tools. They're more than that."

Drágosláv's face lit up like a child's in a candy store. "What then?" he asked

Sánchez remained silent for a few more seconds, staring at Drágosláv as if waiting for him to concentrate on what he was about to say. "The men we're looking for, the men you've been asking me about, the men that hold the key to everything that will happen," he paused, building up the eagerness in Drágosláv further. "The men themselves are my packages, Your Majesty. And—"

"And? And what?" Drágosláv asked, unable to contain himself any longer.

"—and they are in the basement of this building as we speak."

CHAPTER 30

Archaeologist's Adventure

Mumbai, India

A few years before the five men's abduction

Platforms appeared on either side of the windows of bogie B1 as the Nagpur-Mumbai Duronto Express approached the CST station in South Mumbai. Before the train had come to a halt, the occupant of berth twenty-eight gathered her luggage and waited at the coach doors to disembark. She had visited the city of dreams quite a while ago.

"Saira, Saira," Anwesha—Saira's friend—screamed from a distance, waving her hands. "Over here."

Saira jumped from the train before the motion ceased, ran toward Anwesha, and embraced her tightly. "Anwesha, my darling. It's been so long."

Anwesha stepped back and looked at Saira from head to toe. "Bro, you look so thin. Dieting?"

"No, bro, just my research. Have spent a lot of time on site lately, excavating near Nagpur."

"Is it so? How many dinosaur bones have you found?"

"Duffer, paleontologists work on dinosaurs. I am an archaeologist."

"Big difference, both dig, don't they?" Anwesha pulled out the handle of Saira's bag and rolled.

Saira put her arm around Anwesha's shoulder. "You need to take a break from the prison of computer, code, and caffeine, my software engineer friend. There are other professions too." She smiled.

They walked from the platform toward the exit through the bustling atrium of the terminus. "Are you sayin' you gave up chai?"

"Are you insane? Who gives up chai? It just sounded good to say. Computer, code, and caffeine."

Anwesha hit her on the right shoulder.

"Ouch." Saira rubbed her shoulder. Screwing her face, she pushed Anwesha on the side. They laughed.

"Remind me what you are studying?" Anwesha asked as they resumed walking.

"I work in the Department of Ancient History, Culture, and Archaeology." She said with a proud voice, sure eyes and a straight back.

Anwesha mocked with her tongue out. "Boring!"

"Seriously, bro?" Saira rolled her eyes with her hands on her hips.

"Okay, okay, please explain what you study, Your Grace?" Anwesha bowed and flapped her right hand three times before Saira.

"Well, I study ancient Indian texts, documents, various prevalent and long-gone social customs, and myths, and try to correlate with what we find in archaeological excavations. Sometimes, it's the other way round, where we excavate is determined by what we have read or heard." She stopped before explaining further. "You don't care about any of it, do you?" She raised an eyebrow.

"What? Sorry, I dozed off."

"You devil!" Saira squeezed her jokingly by the neck.

Anwesha chuckled.

"How long will it take to get to your flat?"

"I advise using the bathroom. Mumbai traffic is terrible. My place is in Bandra. It'll be a while."

They boarded their Olá cab from the station to Anwesha's flat. As the taxi took off, Saira gazed at the glorious CST station building with its Victorian-Gothic-Indian blend architecture. "It's amazing," she said.

"It is, isn't it?"

The cab moved through lanes big and small with autorickshaws, cars, bikes, and people in its path, navigating the complexities of undocumented, untold, and unsaid traffic rules.

"We have only three days to have fun. What do you want to do tomorrow?"

"Let me finish the work I came for, then we can think about fun. I must visit the Archaeological Survey of India Museum and meet the curator. After that, I'm all yours."

"Great, I have planned something for tomorrow evening."

"Tell me."

"Well, I have some news. There's this guy at work."

"Guy? What? Why haven't I heard about him before?"

"Well, I don't know where it's gonna go."

Saira raised her eyebrow.

"Well, we have worked in the same team, spending late hours on a project. A week ago, he asked me out. I told him my bestie is coming from my hometown, and I'll only meet him with you. So, he has invited his friend too. It'll be like a double date. Although for you, it'll be a blind date."

"I'm not going on a blind date with a random guy."

"You can dump him if you don't like him and find someone else. Please? For me? I like this guy. He's kind of cute."

"Fine, but only for you, bro. You owe me one."

☙

The following day, Saira visited the ASI office to meet the curator. The building had a colonial-era British architecture style with arched windows, towering facades, and massive courtyards. It was white both inside and out, with a red terracotta tiled roof and polished mahogany doors.

Saira went through a long and high hallway with wrought iron chandeliers and a spiral staircase before reaching the curator's office on the first floor.

She knocked at the door. "Hello, Dr. Pradhan, I am Saira Solanki. We talked over the phone."

"Yes, yes, Saira. Please come in," Dr. Pradhan answered. He removed his bronze-framed glasses and let it hang on the retainer around his neck. A wide smile spread around his square face. The salt-and-pepper hair on his head and mustache reflected his experience.

Dr. Pradhan sat behind a polished teakwood desk on an old mesh chair. His office had a tall ceiling with slate floors and expansive windows. Several bookcases and cabinets lined the walls, holding old editions of rare manuscripts and broken artifacts.

"So, where have you been excavating these days?" He asked.

"Mostly central India, around Nagpur."

"What about you, sir?"

"Where else would I go? Nálandá and the areas along that belt."

"Isn't that already well-studied?"

"That's the general consensus among many, but the tools and technology available now have changed by leaps and bounds. We found a lot of hidden chambers outside the university ruins and also in various nearby regions."

"Fascinating."

"Well, same with you, I must say. Just by what you told me over the phone, I'm excited to see what you have uncovered."

She retrieved a big envelope from her backpack along with some stone artifacts.

"These are the pictures and stenciled copies of all the written scripts carved into the stone walls of the excavated compound." She laid them all on the long desk. "Sanskrit text in Devanagari script."

She paused for a second. "And these are the 3D prints we discussed over the phone."

"Excellent." Dr. Pradhan's face lit up like a child holding a popsicle. "Saira, give me some time. I need to review these in detail. I'll get back to you when I have finished my analysis."

"Thank you, Dr. Pradhan. I will wait eagerly for your take on it." Saira left the envelope and 3D prints on the table. A few minutes later, she walked out of the ASI office with a wide smile.

Her phone rang. "Bro, where are you? I texted you so many times."

"Sorry, I got busy. I didn't look at the phone. What's up?"

"It's five, and we must be there at seven; when are we gonna go to the beauty parlor? I need to get my hair done."

"I'm on my way. There's a lot of traffic. Be patient. They'll wait for some time, no biggy."

With the parlor, selecting the outfits, cab, and start-stop traffic, they were a full hour late. This time, they boarded Mumbai's local red double-decker BEST bus. Saira took the stairs to the top deck. It was empty. She went straight to the first row.

The view through the front windows directly above the driver was exciting. As the bus entered the Lower Parel area, Saira was mesmerized by the modern high-rises on either side of the road. Sounds of honking cars hit her ears. Boutiques of famous designers, luxury car dealerships, shopping malls, hotels, cafes, and restaurants lit the streets in various colors.

Saira and Anwesha were the only passengers on the upper deck for quite a while. At the next stop, two men boarded the bus and went upstairs. One took the seat right behind them while the other sat on the one beside them, in an adjacent row.

They ogled at the girls shamelessly, sometimes at their breasts, other times at their exposed legs.

"What're you looking at, pervert?" Anwesha shouted at one.

"Aren't you fiery?" The one beside them licked his lips. "Nice dress, and those legs of yours—" He blew her a kiss.

Anwesha stood up, her face red with anger. Saira pulled her down, whispered in her ear. "It took us a couple hours to get ready and look pretty; why ruin the effort for these fools?" She smiled calmly. "Especially when you have others at your disposal."

The bus had slowed down because of traffic.

"What do you mean? These guys must be taught a lesson."

"I agree, but why do it ourselves when we can have others do it for us. A wise girl knows when to fight and when to get others to fight for her."

She winked and pointed at a group of guys smoking at a pawnshop near the sidewalk.

"Show me."

Saira peeked out of the window. "HELP! Hello, sirs, please help! These guys are troubling us," she shouted. The traffic had almost halted the bus.

Two more men boarded the bus and joined them from the lower deck. The four rushed upstairs.

"You troubling these women?"

"N- no." The two troublemakers stood up. Their faces were sweating.

"They're lying." Anwesha came forward. "They were ogling at us. That one,"—she pointed at the one beside her—"he spoke of my legs."

The one who had commented received several slaps. The other attempted to run but fumbled and received more. More people came upstairs and punished the two. Finally, the two were deboarded and handed to the cops.

"Let me look at you," Saira inspected Anwesha. "See, you look like you just stepped out of the parlor,"—she blew on her nails—"and the two goons learned their lesson."

Anwesha pushed Saira's shoulders. They laughed, rolling on the seats.

In fifteen minutes, their stop came, and they exited on the opposite side of the road from their venue. The bus stop was surrounded by high-rises with glass facades and shiny lights. Some buildings changed color from blue to purple, to red, to orange, and yellow. Between them were small open areas with small ponds, fountains and flower beds full of pink roses, white jasmines, and scarlet hibiscuses.

Anwesha's date waited for her outside the club on the sidewalk. It was the only two-story structure on the street, covered with dark glass and neon signs of red, yellow, purple, and pink.

"There he is." Anwesha giggled, pointing her hands toward her date standing on the opposite side of the road.

"Oh, cute," Saira replied.

"Isn't he?" Anwesha blushed.

"What's his name again?"

"Om."

"Nice. I don't see anyone with him. Where's my date?" Saira asked, her eyes scanning everyone standing on the sidewalk.

"Dunno. Let's see," Anwesha said and held Saira by her arm.

They crossed the road in a hurry.

"What took you so long?" Om hugged Anwesha.

"Long story!" Anwesha said, catching her breath.

"You look fabulous." Om stepped back to look at her.

"I know." Anwesha winked. "By the way, this is Saira, my best friend." "Saira, this is Om."

Om smiled a wide smile. "Heard so much about you, Saira." They shook hands.

"Where's your friend?" Anwesha asked Om. She looked around to see if anyone was approaching them.

"I'm really, really sorry." Om shook his head as he apologized. "But he left. He thought you both stood us up. It's been more than an hour." His face showed his awkwardness.

"I'm really sorry, Saira. I really tried to convince him to stay." He leaned toward Saira.

Anwesha's face fell.

"Don't worry about it. I'll find someone inside." Saira patted Anwesha's shoulder as she talked to Om. "The important thing is that you stayed. I expect nothing less for my best friend."

Om beamed.

"Alright. It's been a hell of a day. Let's get inside, I need a drink."

Om and Anwesha walked toward the entrance holding hands. The three lined up at the door, where a bouncer examined them and wrapped bands around their wrists after the payment of a cover charge. "Enjoy."

The room was dark with lights of purple, red, blue, and white. Accented booths and tables were arranged in a semicircular fashion in front of the central dance floor. On either side of the floor were two bar counters, the tops of which glowed pearly white, lit from underneath. Several bartenders mixed cocktails behind them. In front of the dance floor was the stage where a DJ mixed pop music. Several patrons grooved to it under the flashing and flickering laser beams.

"Over here, this looks good." They descended into a cozy booth with a bucket of ice holding a bottle of sparkling wine on the table. The server opened the bottle with a pop and poured three glasses.

"So, tell me. What happened? What took you guys so long?"

Anwesha and Saira narrated their whole ordeal on the bus.

"Those buggers. Why didn't you call me?"

"Don't worry, girls can handle their own shit these days." Anwesha winked at Saira. "Actually, Saira handled it."

"It was nothing. I just shouted and asked for help."

The glasses emptied in no time and were topped off immediately.

"Dance? Let's go."

"You both go; I will wait here for a while."

"C'mon, Saira."

"Seriously. Don't worry about me. Go on." She pushed Anwesha and Om out of the booth.

The music changed. She watched them begin awkwardly, but they got comfortable with each other in a few songs. Her gaze moved to a handsome man looking at her. His silky black hair was styled with shiny gel, while his sharp jawline was covered with a neatly trimmed beard. He wore an off-white, button-down shirt over blue denim, complemented by a pair of cool white sneakers.

As their eyes met, he raised his glass. She raised hers.

The next minute, he walked toward her.

"Are you a book at the library?" he asked, leaning on the side of the booth.

"I'm sorry?" Saira's face showed her confusion.

"Are you a book at the library? Cause I can't stop checking you out," the man said, staring into Saira's eyes.

Saira laughed uncontrollably. "Did you just make that up, or have you tried that before?" Saira asked, still trying to control her laughter.

"Well, I have an app for that," the man replied with a smile that showed his perfect white teeth.

"Perhaps I should be hit on by the one who wrote that app." Saira giggled.

"No points for honesty?" The man took the seat opposite her.

"Fine, I'll give you that."

"Rohan." He extended his hand.

"Saira," she replied, shaking his hand.

"So, what are you doing all alone?" Rohan asked, still holding her hand in his.

"I'm not alone. I have friends here." She pointed at Anwesha and Om.

"They seem busy," he said, looking at Anwesha and Om making out.

"They do, don't they?" Saira grinned.

Rohan stood up without letting go of her hand, gently pulling, "C'mon, let's go dancing."

She followed him through the cluster of bodies to find a corner. He placed his hands on her waist and pulled her close.

"Easy now," she said and smiled. He winked.

They danced for a while, song after song, getting closer with each beat.

"So, where are you going after this?" he asked.

"To my friend's flat, I guess," Saira replied, her slender waist moving to the beats.

Rohan came close and spoke into her left ear. "How about you come with me? We can check out an awesome place?"

"Don't get your hopes high, mister. You're not gonna get lucky tonight." She stopped moving and laughed heartily, patting him on the cheek. "C'mon, I like this song." She pulled him and danced again.

As the song ended, Saira finished her drink and placed it on the nearby pub table shared by a couple. "Sorry, may I?"

They nodded.

"I'll be back from the girls' room," she said in Rohan's ear.

"I'll get us some drinks. What do you want?

"Get me a Manhattan."

He nodded as they parted. Saira borrowed Anwesha from Om and went to the girls' room.

"Looks like you both got quite comfortable with each other," Saira said, raising her eyebrows.

"Just went with the flow." Anwesha blushed. "Looks like you found someone. He's hot."

"Isn't he? And his dancing moves just draw you in."

They giggled.

"So, what's the plan for the night? Are you going to go with him?"

"Nooo! I don't do one-night stands. Are you planning to go to Om's place?"

"I don't want to rush things." Anwesha hesitated.

'Wise decision." Saira nodded. "Alright, let's get back."

Saira stood by the pub table, waiting for Rohan and her drink. "You guys enjoying?" she asked the couple with whom they shared the pub table.

"Yeah, what about you two?" the woman asked.

"Incredible. Is that a Manhattan you are having?" she asked the guy. He nodded. "I'm getting one too." She smiled. "Thought of it looking at your drink."

"It's nice." He raised his glass.

Rohan appeared holding two glasses. "Man, there's a crowd there." He handed Saira her drink. "There you are, one Manhattan for the lady." He smiled.

"Fabulous. Thanks." Saira kissed him on the cheek.

"Cheers!" Rohan raised his glass. She raised hers, took a sip, and placed it on the table.

"Let's go." She took his hand. "Let's get back to the dance floor."

"Let's finish our drinks first. I need a buzz. Bottoms up?"

They finished their drinks in one go and rushed to the dance floor.

The DJ behind the glass on the stage increased the tempo of songs that she mixed, raising the decibels in the room with it. The people on the dance floor and their outfits flickered in the shiny laser lights that flashed from the ceiling. Glasses rose in the air as people danced, holding them, some spilling droplets on the floor or onto others.

On the opposite side of the dance floor, separated by countless bodies, Anwesha waited for Om in the booth.

"Where were you?" He placed two drinks on the table. "I've been searching for you for the last fifteen minutes." He looked worried.

"I ran into a friend from college on my way from the ladies' room. Why?"

"Where's Saira?" Om asked, his face nervous.

"We parted at the restroom. What's the matter?" Anwesha asked

"The guy she was with—" Om swallowed.

"What about him?"

"I- I saw him spike her drink," he stammered as he spoke.

"Are you sure?" Anwesha's face tensed.

Om pulled out his cell phone and showed her the video he had recorded.

"Shit, shit, shit. Why didn't you stop her?" She covered her face with her palms.

"I tried to find her, but there's so much crowd. I lost them." Om looked all around the club as he spoke.

"Oh, my God, oh, my God, we've got to find her. C'mon, let's go." Anwesha marched out of the booth, pulling Om by his arm.

"Call her first."

Anwesha called Saira's phone. No answer. They looked for Saira all through the nightclub. She was missing.

"What do we do?" Anwesha's eyes were moist. She wiped a tear with her hand.

"Let's go to the police." Om placed an arm around her.

The next second, they both rushed out. Anwesha jumped over a wasted guy on the floor on their way to the exit.

Outside the nightclub, in a car, Saira rested her head on Rohan's shoulder. Someone else was driving the vehicle.

"Where's her phone?" The driver turned his head toward the back seat and asked Rohan. His right hand moved the steering wheel as he spoke.

"I tossed it outside the nightclub," Rohan replied.

"Good."

The car made a noisy turn.

"Hey, take it easy, you don't want people to notice?" Rohan shouted.

"Sorry." The driver looked through the rearview mirror. "Let's take her in the car."

"Patience. Let's not take the risk. We'll take her to the room. I'll go first, then you can have your turn," Rohan replied, looking at the driver's eyes in the rearview mirror.

"Remember, I pay for your clothes, cover charge, drinks, and everything else—" The driver turned to face Rohan again.

"Don't worry, you will get your turn." Rohan patted the back of the driver's seat, nudging to look ahead.

"Wake up." Rohan slapped Saira as she fell from one side to another.

After several minutes, the car came to a stop. The driver scanned the area. "All clear." He signaled Rohan with a thumbs-up.

Rohan exited the car. They both put a shoulder around Saira, walked her to a room on the ground floor of a deserted building, and latched the door.

It looked like a storeroom with construction material cluttered all around. There were no windows. One bright tubelight was fixed on the wall opposite the door. There was dust everywhere.

They laid her on top of a shabby bed.

"Go out, keep watch," Rohan told the driver. He obeyed.

As Rohan placed his left hand on Saira's thigh and his right on Saira's breast, out of nowhere, his cheek shook with a slap so powerful that his whole face shook.

"You nasty piece of shit—" Saira stood up, sturdy as a statue.

She knocked him to the floor with a jump-front kick. "I saw you spike my drink, you asshole. Fortunately, I chose Manhattan by looking at the couple next to us in the club. When you got me the drink, I placed it on the table and swapped with him."

"So you- so you—"

"I was acting all along."

Rohan stood up and knocked on the door. The driver entered.

"Never mind that, you are ours now."

She smiled a wide smile.

The two men looked puzzled.

"I'm not yours," she spoke calmly. "It's the other way around, you dimwits." She flicked back the strands of hair on her face. "You both are mine."

With that, she launched herself onto them.

ॐ

A couple of hours later, someone knocked on Anwesha's door. She opened it to find her friend standing there.

"Saira. Where have you been? We called you, looked for you everywhere, and went to the cops. Traced your phone. That guy at the club spiked your drink."

"I know. I taught them a lesson they'll never forget. He and his friend are in the hospital."

"How? Why did you take the risk, Saira? You could have been—"

"Anwesha, honey." Saira sat down, unbuckling her high heels as she spoke. "Sometimes, a girl stays back and lets others fight her battles. But there are times when a girl must fight her own fights. Tonight was that time."

CHAPTER 31

The Scientist's Project

Barcelona, Spain

"They're here? They're here? The five are in the basement? Now?" Drágosláv shouted at the top of his voice. "I can't believe it! You're a genius, Dr. Sánchez." The animation in his voice was uncontainable. 'I can't wait to see them. I want to meet them right now."

"I perfectly understand your enthusiasm, Your Majesty. But I urge your patience for a little while longer. They're not going anywhere. Let's discuss some important issues first," Sánchez reasoned. "At the moment, our focus must be on our plan ahead. I'm sure you've got a lot of questions for me. I've many questions for you as well."

"But—" Drágosláv countered.

Sánchez cut him short. "Trust me, Your Majesty, I won't keep you from them for long."

"I trust you. But tell me, what about the people on our side? Have you found them all?"

"Some of them, yes." Sánchez paused. "Search is on for others."

As he finished his reply, Sánchez's mind drifted away.

I am glad Alexis is back, Sánchez thought. *Foolish rebels. They thought Alexis was helping their cause.*

Alexis Birdwhistle, one of the first ones Sánchez found on their side, was an anchor at the BBC. She helped the Scottish rebels in their London mission. Her aim, however, was different from theirs. She was there on Sánchez's behalf for the crown, for the Black Prince's Ruby.

If only she had succeeded in the mission, secured that ruby.

"Where are the ones on our side that you found? Where are they from?"

"They're from all over the world, Your Majesty. One by one, I found them, explained who they are, and their purpose in what is to unfold. I couldn't have abducted the five men, arranged all this by myself. They did a lot of it. Alexis Birdwhistle, whom Miguel mentioned, who is here in the building, was one of the first I found. She did a lot of the work. For you, though, I had to do it myself. You are too precious."

Sánchez paused. *Where's the ruby?* The thought came back to him. *Who must have taken it?*

"What about my most important comrade from those days? You found him?"

"No, my lord, but I'll have my best look for him."

Is the ruby with its owner? Is he back? Is The Ghost back? Will he side with us like the last time?

Like a splinter in the skin, the failure of the London mission still bothered Sánchez. From the time he roused from the coma, it was the only thing that had not worked according to his plan.

"We should search for him. Isn't he very important?" Drágosláv shook his head.

"Indeed, my lord, we're looking for him everywhere. It's only a matter of time now. But we must handle the five men first."

"Handle? What do you mean?"

"I'll come to that in a minute. I understand that you've other pressing matters right now, something with your half-brother that we must take care of right away?"

Drágosláv did not answer. The information, the questions, everything was too much to comprehend.

Knock! Knock! Knock! Someone knocked on the door.

"Miguel!" Gustáv shouted. "We told you not to disturb." He walked to the door in frustration. When he opened it, a tall woman of medium build with straight, shoulder-long, dark hair, square face, and deep-blue eyes smiled at him.

"Hello. I am Alexis." She spoke in a thick British accent. "Miguel informed me that Dr. Sánchez is here."

"Ms. Alexis." Gustáv smiled a wide smile. "Yes, yes, please come in. Dr. Sánchez just told us about you."

Alexis entered. The door closed behind her. Sánchez rushed toward her and embraced her.

"I—I'm sorry, I let you down," Alexis said, her voice shaking with guilt. "I couldn't retrieve the Black Prince's Ruby."

"It's all right. We can't win all our battles." Sánchez looked in Alexis' eyes. "Besides, we wanted it only to make sure that its owner comes to our side. It seems, since he has not come to us yet, he has chosen the other side." He clenched his fist.

"What of Castello, Laine, Doug, and the others?" Sánchez asked. "They did a fantastic job abducting the five men for us. Where are they now?"

"I've asked them to stay put at their locations and wait for my instructions," Alexis replied. "I wasn't sure of our meeting place, so I thought it's best if they stayed where they were."

"Yes, let's keep them on standby. We'll call them when we need them." Sánchez nodded. "Anyways, come this way, Alexis." Sánchez pulled Alexis by the arm, walked her toward Drágosláv. "This is the man I told you about. This is the master. This is, His Majesty, Mr. Drágosláv."

Alexis' eyes lit up. She looked in awe. "I can't believe it! I have been dreaming of meeting you, Your Majesty, since the day Dr. Sánchez talked about you." She extended her right hand."

Drágosláv held it with both his hands. "You did a great job helping Dr Sánchez, bringing the five men here." He patted Alexis on the shoulder.

"Anything, anything for you, Master. I will do anything for you all."

Drágosláv nodded with a smile. "Very well."

"Alexis, there is that one important person I had talked about. We haven't found him yet," Sánchez said. "Put all your efforts into finding him. We want him on our side before the owner of the ruby finds him."

"As you command. I will get on it right away." Alexis nodded. She turned toward Drágosláv. "Let me take your leave, Your Majesty. Words cannot describe how happy I am to have finally met you."

Drágosláv shook Alexis' hand once more. Alexis left the room and closed the door behind her.

Drágosláv sighed, walked to the cabinet at the far end of the room, opened it, and withdrew a bottle of twenty-four-year-old single malt. "Scotch always been my favorite, although everyone in my family likes vodka." He smiled. "Ice?"

Sánchez nodded. "I like it neat."

Drágosláv transferred three cubes of ice into one glass. "Dr. Sánchez, I can smuggle anything in and out of Barcelona; it won't be a problem to leave from here. We can disappear and go to our planned destination." He handed the glass with ice to Sánchez. He picked the other two glasses and passed one to Gustáv.

"I chose this place precisely for that reason, my lord. Gustáv's suggestion."

"But right now, to do that, we have to take care of the problem that happened last night during our prison break." Drágosláv's face went red.

"I understand. I did not foresee it either, my lord."

"I have to take back the port from Grigori. Once the port is ours, I've good friends and partners all over the world. We can go anywhere."

"I understand that you want to settle scores, set things in order before we venture on our journey. Perhaps I can offer some insights into this."

"Yes, I trust your guidance, the way you planned my prison break." Drágosláv quaffed his scotch in one go, then poured himself another. "But before that, I don't know anything about you, Dr. Sánchez. Tell me everything: who you are, and most importantly, how you found me and the five men?"

"Of course, Your Majesty."

Sánchez paused. He gazed at a dark corner of the room. "A few years back, I was just an ordinary scientist, living an uneventful life. Gosh, that feels like another life, my former self. Can't believe that person was me." He sighed. "But like you, I soon realized that something was not in place, something was out there waiting for me, something I was waiting my whole life. But I couldn't find it." Sánchez finished his drink, walked to the bar, and poured himself another. He took a sip and continued, "In the hope of satisfying this emptiness and on my friend's relentless cajoling, I took a job in Las Vegas, and I must tell you, it has turned out to be exceptionally significant for us. It has fit in perfectly with our mission." Sánchez's chest protruded, his face smug.

"How?" Drágosláv asked.

"The place I work at is called the National Medical Research Laboratory, NMRL for short," Sánchez explained. "The Nevada government shows that it funds this institute by collecting new taxes from the casinos and uses them for cutting-edge work in the field of medical research. But the truth is something else."

"What's that? What's really done there?"

"Well, it's another arm of the CIA. It is twinned with the secret weapons development program. We work in collaboration with the National Security Agency and the CIA. Their moles are inside NGOs, non-profits, charities, hospitals, and pathological laboratories all around the world. Any agency that deals with people, their bodily fluids, biometrics, identity information, etc., has people on their payroll." Sánchez took a big sip from his ice-cold peg of scotch. The warmth of the alcohol glided down his esophagus.

"I don't understand, what's the purpose of all that? How does that help CIA?"

"My lord, the sister agencies of the CIA are scattered all around the world. They collect data from people with or without their knowledge. Blood samples, voice samples, facial features, iris scans, walking patterns, handwriting, absolutely anything they can lay their hands on. It's done while they're at a clinic, a pathological lab, at blood donation camps, through vaccination drives, or at any such place. They send this material to their covert local cells. Some countries already have these systems, and the CIA simply hacks into those ready-made mines," Sánchez explained. "These cells send the data to us in Las Vegas. This is where my job comes in; I was heading a group that was building a massive database of DNA, biometric, and identity data of the entire Earth's population. Well, practically speaking, as many people as we can phish. It's a very ambitious project. I was responsible for designing and maintaining this database. It's enormous, grows every second."

"Oh, my God!" Drágosláv went silent for a minute, realizing the scale of this operation.

"What is the difference between this and what they already have at the CIA?" Gustáv asked.

"Excellent question, Gustáv. The intention is to build a mammoth resource capable of identifying every human, not only in the United States but also on the entire planet, and their location. You can't imagine how much money is being spent on it," Sánchez replied. "It's still a work in progress, not fully functional. Only a few others and I have access to it right now. For security and confidentiality, only my biometrics can access the database."

"And how did you use it to locate our five hostages?" Gustáv asked again

"That's the sixty-four-thousand-dollar question, isn't it?" Sánchez said. "Remember, I didn't use it only to find the hostages."

"Then?"

"How do you think I found you two?"

Drágosláv and Gustáv's face tensed.

"Relax, it ended up great for us, didn't it? Aren't you glad I found you both?"

They nodded reluctantly.

"Besides, only I have access to it right now. I have locked it up for others, so no one tracks us," Sánchez reassured them.

The air was still awkward.

"Anyways," Sánchez continued, "so this database is just one part. Its other complementary part is the gargantuan network of online surveillance that we command. This enables us to hack into countless phones, computers, CCTV cameras, TV sets, smart speakers, thermostats, home security systems, and all kinds of smart devices."

"And how did it help us?" Drágosláv asked.

"I was coming to that. If you remember, I wrote this in the book that I gave to you in prison," Sánchez answered. "When I was in a coma at the hospital, the great truth that we know now was revealed to me. The DNA markers of the five men and many others, including you two, were part of that revelation. Once I had this information, I used the database to cross-reference their names and all available data and located them using our surveillance tools."

Sánchez paused for this to sink in, then continued, "But our friend, whom you mentioned earlier, has still not turned up on the database. That's why we're unable to find him."

"We must find him. He's very important." Drágosláv looked into Sánchez's eyes as he spoke.

"Don't worry, we will. In time, we definitely will." Sánchez held Drágosláv's hand and patted on it. "But if we don't, I've a Plan B as well."

"Plan B?" Drágosláv's right eyebrow rose in curiosity.

"Yes, my lord, plan B." Sánchez's face filled with pride as he spoke. "And it's already in motion." Sánchez came close, whispered the plan in Drágosláv's ears. "We have someone just as capable as our unfound friend."

"What? Who is this person?"

"You've not met him yet. I will introduce him to you in a few days, and I assure you, he can more than fill in for our friend if needed."

"Excellent!" Drágosláv cheered. "What now? What is our next move?" Drágosláv asked impatiently.

Sánchez walked toward the cabinet a second time, withdrew a few ice cubes, poured a generous amount of scotch from the bottle, and raised his glass. "Now, my lord, let's go and meet the five men."

CHAPTER 32

The Ghost's Mission

Somewhere

The White Ghost closed his eyes. The Black Prince's Ruby, his ruby, had not only revived his sick, frail body but also restored his long-lost abilities. He was once again young, strong, alive.

This is my chance for redemption.

"Aaahhh." He clenched his fists.

No one has suffered like me.

Tears rolled down his cheeks. He ran his fingers over the rejuvenated skin to wipe them.

It felt as if it would never end.

The fingers moved to the forehead and felt the embedded ruby, where it had been millennia ago, where it belonged.

But now it's over. The Almighty left a way out for me.

It was time, time for his mission, time to realize the purpose for which he had lived all these millennia, time for him to play his part in the events that had exploded when he woke up from that long slumber, right when Sánchez came out of a coma. Though separated by thousands of miles, his resurrection was a result of Sánchez's rebirth from the long slumber at the hospital in Las Vegas. His part was crucial. So much depended on what he had to do. He was not nervous, though. He had experienced it back in the day. His London escapade was a few days ago, but he knew he couldn't spare time relaxing before the next task.

Things worked against me while I was occupied with getting back my gem. I'm already behind. He grimaced.

With the powers of his ruby, he had seen Sánchez, his team, and the people they had captured.

But I had to do it, I had to take the red gem back. Without the gem, I could not have known where the men were. He nodded to his thoughts.

Never mind that. All is not lost. He held his hands behind his back. *I'm not on their side this time. I'll deal with him and his men later.*

He walked toward the mouth of the cave and stared outside. A gentle breeze went through the trees, making the leaves sway.

I have to begin what I've planned. I have to go after the most important one first. I have to find him before they do. Yes, that's what I'll do.

He turned around to face the cave and concentrated on the wall ahead. White rays shot from the ruby, projecting that important person from his thoughts on the stone. The person's town, his street, his house, everything displayed on the wall one by one.

He knew the next mission couldn't wait. He knew he had to start collecting his people.

The ghost walked out of the cave, closed his eyes, and concentrated. This time, the rays of light that shot out were red. They spread three hundred and sixty degrees, forming a circular pattern midair. It seemed as if the light was burning a hole in the vastness ahead. The next moment, a circular floating bubble appeared. Its boundaries shone red, orange, and black, like the edges of a half-burned paper.

The White Ghost opened his eyes, walked toward the bubble, and disappeared inside.

CHAPTER 33

The Next Step

Barcelona, Spain

Drágosláv had his questions answered. The reality was overwhelming. Sánchez did his best to explain everything, the grand story, the truth that bound them all.

"I've never been so excited in my life, Dr. Sánchez." Drágosláv beamed. But instead of marching to the basement to meet the five men, as he so desired, he waited on Sánchez's suggestion. The fact that the five men were under his control in the basement, secured with chains, indisposed by drugs, and surrounded by armed guards, calmed his anxiety.

"I like your plan, Dr. Sánchez. I must find a way to work everything out to implement it."

"Of course, my lord."

"And I need time to convince my people to join our quest."

"I understand."

"Now, if you'll excuse me, let me talk business with Gustáv to wrap things up." He turned toward Gustáv, who listened patiently all along, trying to process all the information Sánchez had revealed. "Why didn't you tell me that we lost the port?"

"I didn't know about it either, Drággy. It happened while we were planning your rescue mission. Besides, getting you to a safe house was our priority."

A painting of a torero wearing red traje-de-luces and facing a charging bull hung on the wall beside Drágosláv. He stared at it, deep in thought.

"Cigar?" Gustáv asked nervously, breaking the silence.

"Hmm."

Gustáv rushed outside and returned a few minutes later with an expensive cigar case. He held it open for Drágosláv.

Drágosláv lifted one and placed it on his nostrils. "Crisp and fresh," he said as he inhaled its aroma. "Oh, I missed it in prison." He placed it back in Gustáv's hand.

Gustáv at once made a guillotine cut at its end, handed it back, and held the lighter up for him. Drágosláv lit it up and took a deep drag. He closed his eyes and exhaled from his mouth, satiated.

"Grigori might have the port, but he can't move his product beyond the port without making a deal with me. My men will make things impossible for him, so I'm sure he wants to strike a deal."

Drágosláv took another drag and let it out. "I thought we had a understanding, had clear division of territories." The pitch of Drágosláv's voice increased steadily. "I should've destroyed him." He fetched an ashtray and pressed the cigar's tip hard into its base, thinking of Grigori. "He made a terrible mistake." It made a *sizzz* sound as it went out.

"I want to destroy him." He looked directly at Gustáv. "Let's plan an attack."

"I urge your patience, my lord, you just broke out of prison," Sánchez said. "Sometimes it's wise to do nothing until things clear out; sometimes it's good to wait until the time's right."

"So, you say I do nothing to that *svoloch*? Even after what he did to me?"

"There is one thing you can do, my lord. You can compromise; talk to him."

"Are you insane, Dr. Sánchez? Do you want me to look weak?"

"Of course not. It'll be just for the time being while we sort things out."

Drágosláv's eyes followed the smoke trail from the cigar's doused tip as it glided toward the flickering tubelight above. It was not in his nature to stay unavenged.

"*Dobre*," he said after a long silence. "I trust you, Dr. Sánchez. That's why I'll do it. Gustáv, fix a meeting with Grigori. Let's see what he says. Dr. Sánchez, let's devise a plan meanwhile."

"I already thought of something, my lord." He grinned. "Why not use the five men?"

CHAPTER 34

Face to Face

Barcelona, Spain

The basement door opened. The man wearing a white coat entered the room again.

Holding a briefcase, he walked toward Darren.

Darren's limbs were motionless. He was only able to move and turn his head. The man placed a tray on a tall side table and pulled out a big syringe. He fetched a vial of clear liquid, pierced the needle, and loaded the syringe by pulling the plunger. Lifting the syringe, he gave a few taps on its side to make the air bubbles rise at the top and discharged them by pushing the plunger a little. A few drops oozed.

"What are you doing to me?" Darren screamed. "No, don't touch me. I warn ya—"

"I'm only doing what I'm told, sir. I sincerely apologize."

"You'll pay for this, I swear. I'll damn make sure of that."

Ignoring further cries from Darren, the man inserted the needle in Darren's left thigh and pushed the plunger. He repeated the same procedure for the other leg. Once this was done, he disconnected the IV fluid hanging on the stand beside the bed from Darren's arm.

"You better run when I get out of these." Darren pointed his eyes toward the chains on his body.

"I'm really sorry. I've no other option."

Ojoré was next. This time, the man prepared a small injection for Ojoré's two legs.

"I heard your story. I apologize for eavesdropping," he said to Ojoré in a low voice. "I heard how your father treated you." He pierced Ojoré's left thigh with the needle. "I know how it feels."

Ojoré did not reply.

He rubbed a piece of cotton at the point of injection as he retrieved the needle. "I underwent the same ordeal with my family when I was young," he said. "Actually, it was worse."

"You—?" Ojoré asked, but was interrupted.

"I should not talk to you. I'm under strict orders to just do the job; sorry." The man scurried to the next person.

"Wait. Please," Ojoré shouted.

The man ignored him. There was a ring on the man's finger.

One by one, they were injected with the clear liquid, and all their arms were disconnected from the IV bags. The man waited for a few minutes, after which he lifted a small hammer and, one by one, tapped their knees to verify the lack of reflex action. Once done, the man picked up the tray and walked toward the door.

"WAIT," Ojoré shouted once again. "What is going on? At least tell us what you did to us."

"You'll find out in about ten minutes," he replied and left the room.

Ten minutes passed.

They looked at each other, expecting something to happen. Their anxiety increased with time. They waited some more.

In the next minute, Diego felt the sensation in his arms slowly come back. "I can move." He lifted his right arm. The others tried to move their arms as well.

"I can move them too." Ojoré waved.

"Me too," Aarno cheered.

Excitement filled the room.

"No, wait, everything below my waist is still numb."

"Aaaah," Darren screamed. "What trick are they playing on us?" He slammed his hands on the bed. It shuddered. "Why make only our upper body move?"

No answer came.

For the first time, the five men properly saw each other's faces. They looked as similar as the five fingers on a palm. Aarno had ash blonde hair, a small nose, a round face, and blue eyes. Shoulder-length blonde hair formed a ponytail on Darren's head above a broad face with prominent cheekbones and a sharp jawline. Dense, tiny curls of dark hair on Ojoré's head were short, with almond-shaped eyes on an elongated face with a prominent nose and lips. The skin on Liang's face was smooth, with ear-length black hair, shiny, and silky. Diego was the most attractive, with dark hair, a pale complexion, a small forehead, a narrow nose, large eyes, and a neat beard.

In a few minutes, the answer to Darren's question presented itself. Five helpers rushed into the room carrying small bedside tables. They increased the incline on their beds by rotating a lever on the foot side and placing the table in front of its occupant. After doing so, all of them left the room and, minutes later, returned with dishes topped with plate covers. The helpers placed the plates on each bedside table and lifted the plate covers simultaneously.

"Mmm," Darren inhaled deeply, his temper vanishing.

The aroma mesmerized the five men's deprived senses. They were served their favorite dishes. Wine glasses were placed on the side for each, except Aarno.

They know about my sobriety, he thought.

The helpers poured their glasses with a twenty-year-old Tempranillo red. The captives were starving and, without hesitation, dug in. The portions vanished in minutes. Glasses were replenished as soon as their bases touched the bedside tables. None of them remembered how long ago they tasted food. The alcohol kicked in. Panic and frustration were replaced by calm.

No sooner did they all begin to drift into their happy place than the door opened again, and three bodies rushed inside.

"Hello everyone," Drágosláv displayed a broad smile. "I hope you enjoyed the meal."

Gustáv and Sánchez stood on either side behind him in silence, arms folded.

Drágosláv looked solid with his muscular body and intimidating persona. His commanding voice complemented his personality. He was a foot short of Darren, the only hostage undaunted by him.

"What the heck do you want from us?" Darren shouted at the top of his voice. "Why are you holding us?"

"Relax, my friend." He walked toward Darren and patted his right ankle. "Take it easy. We're not going to harm you—as long as you cooperate with us."

"How long are you going to keep us here?"

"That depends on how fast you can get the job done." Drágosláv turned to answer Aarno.

"Job? What job?"

"Well, we need your help in acquiring something." Drágosláv moved from Darren to Diego. "It is of great interest to us."

"And why would we help you?" Ojoré asked.

"Excellent question." Drágosláv stretched his palm toward Gustáv, who quickly passed him an iPad.

Drágosláv unlocked the iPad and handed it over to Ojoré. The visual on it was that of his mother. They had held her in a small room. There were a few more captives with her.

Along with the five men, Sánchez had also arranged the abduction of their loved ones. He knew the five men wouldn't be easy to tame. He made sure he had leverage.

"You bastard! How dare you!!!"

The other four looked at Ojoré, wondering what he saw in the iPad.

One by one, Drágosláv passed the tablet to each of them. Liang saw his girlfriend, Aarno, his brother, Darren, his mother and Diego his coach. The captives looked pale, terrified. Blood rushed through Darren's veins, his nostrils flared out, and he jerked violently to free himself.

"Yaahhhhh!" he shrieked. However, with his body immobile from the waist down, leaving only his arms active but loosely chained, it did not work.

Drágosláv waited for the commotion to subside. "Don't worry. They're all well taken care of. You are all brilliant people. I'm sure I don't have to emphasize that as long as you cooperate with me, no harm comes to anyone."

The room echoed with silence. The five men stared at each other, desperate for a way out.

Sánchez still stood behind Drágosláv, maintaining a low profile. Although he orchestrated this all, he behaved only like a sidekick.

His eyes met those of Liang.

"But why us?" Liang kept looking at him. There was sadness in his voice.

"Well, I'm sure all of you know this in your heart, know that you are not ordinary." Drágosláv walked around each one of them slowly.

The five men exchanged glances; they had already figured that part out. They knew what connected them. One by one, they had shared their past encounters, encounters that involved magical creatures and floating bubble-like objects.

"All of you know that there's something special about each of you." Drágosláv paused for a moment. "Why do you think we restrained you in this fashion?" He walked back and stood beside Sánchez so they could see him clearly. "We want to use your unique abilities in our ultimate mission."

"Mission? What mission?" Liang asked almost instantaneously. He stared at Sánchez again.

"Well, don't you worry about that right now. You'll know everything about it when the time comes. For now, I have urgent business needs that I want to use you all for. Let's see how you fare with not-so-special situations first."

"How do we know that after we help you, you will hold your side of the deal?" Aarno stared into Drágosláv's eyes.

"Who said we are making a deal?" Drágosláv replied with a cunning smile on his face, looking straight back into Aarno's. "I guess the only option you have right now is that to trust me, don't you?"

CHAPTER 35

Vengeance

Kashmir Valley, India

After the enormous flood that left hundreds dead, Jhelum retreated within its banks, docile as a lamb. While life was slowly returning to normal, the scars it left behind, with uprooted trees, leveled power poles, washed-out roads, and missing traffic lights, were visible for tens of kilometers. Silt, mud, twigs, leaves, and debris overwhelmed the streets. The wrath of its currents destroyed countless homes, sparing only a few. Among the lucky ones to survive was the house of Mr. and Mrs. Iqbal.

The house had quintessential old Kashmiri architecture consisting of wooden structures decorated with intricate carvings running over its columns and ceiling. A traditional Kashmiri rug lay in the living room with designs of flowers and leaves. Airy curtains covered the windows, the panels of which were carved with exquisite interwoven wooden screens. Rays of the morning sun flooded through them and lit the rooms marvelously.

The house had a balcony that displayed the beautiful Himalayan range spanning the horizon in all its grandeur. The fresh breeze, lovely people, houseboats, snowcapped mountains, sapphire blue lakes, kingfishers, bulbuls, and cabbage butterflies, everything made the valley, as they called it, a paradise on earth.

"Begum, can you please get me some kahwah before I leave for the market?" Mr. Iqbal asked. He was loading a fresh lot of vegetables onto his shikara—a small Kashmiri boat resembling a Venetian gondola. Mr. Iqbal earned his living by selling vegetables at the morning market on the lake.

"Of course, give me a minute," Mrs. Iqbal shouted from inside the kitchen.

Exactly a minute later, she rushed outside, holding two earthen cups filled with the saffron-flavored chai. They enjoyed it in silence, gazing at the first light of dawn, peeking through the serene mountains, listening to the calls of early birds.

The Iqbals were kind, helpful, and pure-hearted people of faith. They lived a modest life in the remote parts of the valley along the banks of the Jhelum. Their love for each other could not be explained in words. Much to their sadness, they were unable to have children of their own. It left a big hole in their lives.

Some years back, however, this missing hole in their lives was filled. They were blessed with the company of a child, and although this was all they ever wanted, how it happened left them somber every time the memory resurfaced. Their story was one of the many tales of Kashmiris who were torn between the constant struggle between India and Pakistan. If one could imagine heaven and hell in a single place, life in Kashmir was such.

Even today, Iqbal could remember his conversation with his neighbor, Mr. Kachru, several years ago. It felt as if it happened yesterday.

"At least go back for a few months. It's not safe for you here," a worried Iqbal had said. 'We'll take care of your house. Don't you trust us?"

"Don't be silly. We trust you with our lives. You're not just our neighbor, you are family," Kachru replied.

"Then listen to me this time, brother; I beg you."

"This is our land, our ancestral home. Someone has to stand up to them." Kachru rose from his chair. "It took us more than a decade to come back. God knows how long it'll take if we leave this time."

"You know how it is for the Hindu community these days in the valley. We're worried about your safety. If not for yourself, think of Aroon. He's so little."

"No. We won't run away. We will stand up to them this time."

"Why are you so stubborn? Why don't you just listen to me? Things are getting bad. People have already died in villages not very far from here."

Kachru moved his chair opposite Iqbal's, sat down, and held his hand in his own.

"Our fathers were friends before us. We've been friends since we were born. You know better than any what happened to our community, don't you?" He stared at those hands as he spoke. "You know how the terrorists forced us Kashmiri Hindus into exile inside our own country. You remember those days of militancy when there was genocide of our people across the Kashmir Valley. We had to leave our homes, businesses, and belongings and live as refugees in different parts of India. I had to leave my best friend, my brother," he said, patting Iqbal's hand.

"You are my best brother, too. I cried for days when you left, but—"

Kachru cut him off. "I was a little boy then, had to go with my parents, but I never felt at home wherever we went. I always dreamed of returning here someday, to the place where I belonged, to our ancestral home. My heart longed for it." He stood up and walked toward the parapet of the wooden balcony, staring as the sun set into the mountains.

"When the current government took charge in Delhi, scrapped Article 370 of the constitution, and announced the program for resettlement of Pundits into the valley with protection, my joy knew no bounds. It was my opportunity to return home."

He turned back to face Iqbal again. "It took me many years of hardships to come back. I'm not going anywhere now. Like I said, we have to stand up to these terrorists."

"I understand it all, my friend, but I'm extremely worried about you after what I hear on the news. Militancy has returned to the valley after this resettlement program. The Pakistani Army doesn't like it. Their terrorists don't like it."

"It'll be all right, my friend, trust me. The Indian Army is already adding boots, I'm sure things won't be like last time. We just have to ride it out."

A few days later, a group of militants did what Iqbal feared the most.

Mr. and Mrs. Kachru and their whole extended family were gunned down in their own house.

"We could've saved them. I warned him. If only he'd listened to me. What will we do now?" Iqbal wailed.

The Iqbals were devastated. The wooden wall of their neighbor's house was porous like a sieve, with bullets from the terrorists' guns. Blood trickled through them. The only thing that survived the attack was their son, Aroon. It happened when he was at school.

"He's our son now. I'll take care of him; we owe it to them," Mrs. Iqbal said.

Since that day, the Iqbals took care of Aroon. They shielded him from terrorists. They raised him as their own and loved him with all their heart. Aroon was fond of them, too. He was a well-behaved kid and caused no problems for the Iqbals. Rather, he helped them and brought the missing joy into their lives.

"I understand it now. Allah did not bless us with a child for a reason," Mrs. Iqbal said as she ran her fingers through Aroon's hair while he slept with his head in her lap. "He is all I ever wished for. Look at him. He is perfect."

Aroon was a robust kid. He never fell sick. The Iqbals never had to take him to a doctor the entire time he lived with them.

Many years had passed since the death of his parents. Aroon was now in his twenties.

"I wish the Kachrus were alive to see what a handsome, gentle young man he has grown into," Mrs. Iqbal said as she put down her cup of kahwah.

"I wish it, too," Mr. Iqbal said. He handed her his finished cup. "The situation in the valley is not bad either; there is less militancy, and the army's footprint is on the decline."

"Government's effort to earn back goodwill, I guess,"

"Schools, hospitals, and government offices are working normally, tourism is back in the valley. If only they had listened and left this place for a short while."

"We can't undo the horrors of the past," she said, looking into his eyes. "Let's make the most of what we have."

"Hmm. Anyway, I should hurry. The market is about to open."

Mr. Iqbal untied his shikara and pulled his paddle.

In recent times, wealthy products from a rising economy in other parts of India brought with them lots of disposable cash to spend. Kashmir was sought after and regarded as better than the Swiss Alps. Things looked better than the dark times of the past, but the valley was not completely free from terror.

"Be safe. Don't forget it's election season. There was an attack a few weeks ago, not far from our village. A small group of militants crossed the line of control, they say to undermine the polls," Mrs. Iqbal reminded her husband. "They don't want the elections to go smoothly."

"That was a minor attack; they can't prevent everything, but it's still better than what it used to be."

"Yes, but I fear the army numbers will go back up again. They want successful elections. The cycle of violence can start once more."

Mr. Iqbal nodded.

ॐ

A few days before the election

"Are you sure?" Inspector Khan, who was charged with the area's security, asked.

"Yes, Sahib, we know they're hiding in the area," Iqbal replied, referring to the terrorists hiding in the house of their next-door neighbors. "My poor neighbors, Sahib, they're not bad, but what can they do when men storm into their house with guns?"

"Then why are you here to reveal this? Don't you sympathize with their cause?"

"We're poor people, Sahib; we're fed up with this never-ending conflict between the two countries. After all these many decades, we don't care who controls Kashmir. We just want to live a normal life. We don't want to be jailed as traitors."

"We'll arrest them, or if it comes to it, kill them. But we'll need your help."

"We're poor people, Sahib. We have a son. We don't seek any trouble. I came here because I thought it was the right thing to do."

"It's not enough, my friend." Khan placed his hand on Iqbal's shoulder. "We can't prevent them from causing mayhem if you don't help us."

Iqbal closed his eyes. He slid his palms over his face.

"You want your neighbor to get out of this, don't you?"

With eyes still shut, Iqbal inhaled deeply. *I can't leave them alone in this.* He swallowed. *We are like family. I have to help them.*

He exhaled, opened his eyes, and spoke. "Okay, Sahib, what help do you need from me?"

"Couple of my officers will stay in your house as guests. Can you arrange that?"

Iqbal sat silent for a few seconds. "As long as you promise that our neighbor and my son will be safe, I will help." There was hesitation in his voice.

"I promise. We'll make sure of it."

Iqbal considered for a few seconds. "One more thing, Khan Sahib."

"Yes?"

"Please make sure our identities are never revealed to anyone. We don't want a revenge attack."

"Don't worry, I give you my word."

☙❧

Khan's team killed the militants and foiled the attacks on several election booths that summer. Many months passed. Thanks to Iqbal, the elections were not only held without incidents, but there was also a record turnout.

With troubles behind, today was a beautiful day in the valley. Spring announced its arrival with a wonderful sight. Acres and acres of gardens dazzled with bright colors of blooming flowers. It looked as if a rainbow descended from the sky and painted the earth. Locals were busy picking the right flowers for the market. There were roses, tulips, lilies, orchids, and various colorful flora. Along with them, apples, a specialty of the area, were being handpicked and packaged to cater to the rest of the world. The everyday market on water, where vendors on small shikara boats sold their produce, was filled with the sounds of paddling and shouts of bargaining.

"Cabbage, crisp and fresh, picked minutes ago," Iqbal shouted. His entire shikara was filled with fresh and vibrant veggies.

Freshly melted ice water gushed down the rivers while cheerful tourists flocked down the streets. Couples cruised on romantic shikaras fitted with roofs and beautiful cushions. With the steersman rowing the boat for them from the rear, they savored sips of champagne, soaking in the majestic landscape of snow-clad peaks.

Aroon returned home after helping Mr. Iqbal sell vegetables at the morning market. He changed from his kurta-pajamas into neatly ironed trousers and a shirt. He combed his hair and wore his only tie.

"I'm leaving, Ammi," he said to Mrs. Iqbal.

"First, eat something. Do not leave the house on an empty belly."

She forcefully fed him a generous amount of Kashmiri pulao and yogurt raita, along with some Kahwa. She also packed some snacks for the road.

"Ammi, it's Srinagar, only a few hours away. I'm not going halfway across the country," Aroon protested.

"Don't argue. It's for when you're hungry. I don't want you eating outside food."

Aroon packed his bag with the food and his folder. He had an interview in the nearby city of Srinagar. The opportunity was Aroon's dream job. He prepared for the interview for weeks. Mr. Iqbal made sure that he completed his education. Aroon contributed by working part-time to take the load off his shoulders.

"May Allah bring you good fortune," Mrs. Iqbal said, kissing him on the forehead. "May he bless you with everything you desire."

Aroon went to the side of the house that had pictures of his late parents and joined his hands in a Namaste for prayer. Beside them were pictures of Hindu deities. He prayed to them as well.

Aroon left the house and walked toward the bus stop. The bus for Srinagar was on time and parked in its usual spot, ready to depart. Aroon boarded it and found an empty seat in the bouncy last row. From the window seat, he saw two kids of seven or eight begging on the street. Their upper body was devoid of clothes, making their skeleton-thin torso visible. Their rib cages protruded from the chest as if there was no skin. Helplessness trickled from their faces.

Aroon's heart sank. A teardrop oozed from his left eye and ran along his cheek. He snorted, then swallowed.

"Hey, come here, have my food," he said, handing them his Kashmiri pulao that Mrs. Iqbal had packed for him. "Here's some money. Sorry, I don't have much. Take care of yourself."

The pulao was devoured in seconds. He knew they had not eaten in days. When they were done, they kept staring at Aroon as if expecting something more.

"What is it? I gave you all I had."

The children cried like never before.

Aroon got off the bus. "What is it? You can tell me."

"Sahib, our mother—" said one and sobbed uncontrollably.

"She is very sick," the other said. "No one is ready to help us. They say they don't have time for people like us who live on the streets. We've been asking for help since yesterday."

"Our father is dead,"—the first one composed himself—"our mother is a daily wage laborer. We have nothing to eat, nothing to take care of her."

The bus driver honked, indicating imminent departure. Aroon looked from the bus door to the hopeful eyes of the kids. He closed his own and sighed deeply. After a long pause, he unbuttoned his collar, loosened the tie, and said, "Take me to her."

The bus honked a second time. The next minute, Aroon saw it depart in front of his eyes.

With it, went the job he so dearly desired.

⚬৪৹

Aroon spent several hours at the government hospital helping the two boys. Before taking their mother to the hospital, he went to the ATM and withdrew what he had in his account. He spent the money arranging an ambulance and buying clothes and supplies for the kids. Although he lost his chance, he was happy his sacrifice did not go in vain.

"It's typhoid. She'll get better in a few weeks," the doctor said. "Good that you brought her here. A day later, and things would've been out of our hands."

"Shukriya," the elder kid said. "We would've lost our mother if you had not helped us. Allah sent you like an angel for us."

Aroon smiled. "Glad I could help, but I must go now. I'll check on you in a few days."

He left the hospital and called Mr. and Mrs. Iqbal to share what happened, but neither picked up.

Why don't they pick up in the first few rings? They're always far from their phones when I call.

Aroon paced toward home. It was only a few minutes away. As he approached the house, two men rushed past him.

"Hey! Look where you're going," he shouted as they almost knocked him down on their way back. Both their faces were covered in shawls, with only their eyes exposed. They gave a kick to their motorbike and sped away.

Something is wrong.

Aroon bolted inside and was horrified by what he saw. Both Mr. and Mrs. Iqbal were lying in a pool of red, their throats slit. On the wall behind their bodies was a text written in blood.

'*Gaddaar*' it read, calling them traitors. A message to make clear the repercussions of working against the terrorists.

"Ammi. Abbu," Aroon shouted. It was déjà vu for him. All the memories of losing his parents crept back into his life.

"No, no, please, no. This can't happen," he cried. A deluge of tears ran from his eyes.

The next minute, anger spread through his entire body. He clenched his fist, stormed out of the house carrying an Indian machete, a sword-like tool with a billhook at the end.

"I need your motorcycle," he said to Amir, his neighbor, who ran toward the house upon hearing his cries. "They killed Ammi, they killed Abbu."

"Oh, my God, no," the neighbor screamed.

"I have to avenge them."

"Don't be stupid. They're dangerous people. Terrorists."

"Don't stop me. I'll not let it go unpunished this time."

"No, I won't let you go. I can't let you run into doom and not do anything." Amir held his arm tightly.

"I'm going, even if it means I've to fight you." Aroon shook his arm in a jerk.

Amir stared into Aroon's eyes. "I'm coming with you then."

"No, I can't put you in danger. Just tell me which way they went."

Amir looked eastward. Aroon kick-started the motorcycle, pushed Amir away, and chased the trail.

On the way, he passed a chai stall. He knew the owner and shouted at him. "Chcha, did you see two men on a motorcycle? Which way did they go?"

"The men with covered faces, black shawls?" the chai seller asked.

"Yes."

"That way." The owner pointed to the left side of the fork on the road.

Aroon rode as fast as he could, out of the village, into the mountains, onto a dirt road.

After frantically searching for close to an hour, he found the same motorbike abandoned on the side. Footprints originated from the bike leading into the mountains. He, too, left his bike on the side and entered the dense coniferous terrain. He kept running, climbing, gaining more elevation with every step. The air became cold and thin. The area was secluded.

After a long climb, a makeshift camp came into sight. There were two men there. They wore the same shawls. This time, however, they did not cover their faces.

Aroon drew his machete, charged.

They saw him coming. One of them drew a knife while the other raised a handgun.

Aroon launched his machete in the air toward the gunman. It left his hand like a bullet, hitting the forehead.

The gunman crumbled onto the ground and breathed his last.

Aroon was surprised at his skills, which he knew nothing of before. The other militant stormed toward him, attacked with his knife.

In a flash of a second, Aroon's left hand came forward, blocked the attack. The assailant was no match for Aroon's strength and agility.

Am I really doing this? Aroon couldn't believe it. *How?*

The next second, Aroon moved sideways, went behind the terrorist, took his knife, and slid it past his neck. Red sprinkled all over the fresh green grass.

Aroon held him until the blood stopped squirting, after which he let go. The body hit the ground hard.

How did I do that? How did I get so good at fighting? All those moves, those skills? He questioned his abilities, staring at the fallen bodies ahead of him. He had never fought before.

Aroon exhaled heavily. He had had his vengeance.

But it did not pacify him. He wanted the grief to go away, the pain to subside.

"Aaaaaah—" he shouted toward the sky.

Weak and overwhelmed, Aroon collapsed onto the ground. As the life blood dripped out from the bodies of his parents back in his village, his soul slowly trickled out from his. He cried and tried to take the feeling out of him by shouting it out toward the mountains.

"Aaaaah—" he shouted again.

The mountains returned it as an echo.

Right at that moment, something moved nearby.

He looked around.

A bright light flashed into his eyes, blinding his retinas. He closed his eyes momentarily, then squinted, trying to see what was happening. The light seemed to emerge from a bubble floating mid-air.

The light advanced closer and closer toward him. It emanated from the forehead of a very tall figure.

Within seconds, it was in front of him, staring right into his eyes.

Aroon was unable to move. He stared back at the tall figure. The light coming out of his forehead had subsided.

The figure was easily the tallest person Aroon had ever seen. His eyes twinkled red as blood, his hair silky like silver strands, his skin glowing like radium. Warmth oozed from him. Aroon could feel his strength, his grandeur, his brilliance.

The figure wore long white robe-like clothes. They looked primordial. Although his body was covered, Aroon could see his toned, muscular torso as the wind flapped the fabric around it. A large ruby was embedded on his forehead as if it were part of his body.

The hypnotic eyes of the tall figure stared into his as if scanning his entire brain.

After a few minutes of observing in silence, the White Ghost spoke. "Don't worry, I'm not here to harm you."

The ruby on his forehead shone like fire. He waited to gain Aroon's full attention. The ghost spoke again in a precise and clear manner. "Tell me, my friend, are you ready to begin your new life? The life you're meant to lead?"

CHAPTER 36

The First Task

Barcelona, Spain

D arren trumpeted like a wild elephant. He shook his body with all the strength he could marshal, but only half his body obeyed. The bed still moved with him.

Drágosláv turned toward Gustáv and nodded. Gustáv rushed outside.

Minutes later, he returned with the same man who was in charge of drug delivery—the man in the white coat. The man prepared another vial like he did before the dinner and raced toward Darren's bed.

He hesitated, stood waiting, ready to inject.

"Don't you dare," Darren shouted. "Don't you freakin' dare."

"Fetch his mother." Drágosláv's face was a furious red.

Gustáv darted toward the door and vanished behind it. In a few minutes, he escorted Darren's mom inside.

The sight of his mother pacified Darren. His movements slowed.

"Oh, Darren. What have they done to you, my baby?" She ran toward him and threw her arms around him. "Who are these people? Where are we? Why have they taken us?"

Drágoslàv smiled a broad smile. "I so miss motherly love. I am sure you don't want any harm to come to your mother, do you?" He looked at Darren's mother. "Don't worry, ma'am, we'll keep everyone safe and sound as long as your son and his friends cooperate with us."

"Mom, are you alright? Did they hurt you?" Darren asked softly.

"I'm alright. I'm worried about you."

Darren clenched his fists. He wanted to crush Drágoslàv's head. "Your time will come." He looked into Drágoslàv's eyes. "You're messing with the wrong guy here."

"I look forward to that day, Mr. Swanson." Drágoslàv turned to face the others. "Now, anyone else needs more motivation?"

Blood boiled in their veins like hot lava. But no one replied.

"I will take your silence as agreement to cooperate."

Gustàv ushered Darren's mother out of the room.

Still holding the syringe, the man in the white coat looked into Darren's eyes. He placed his hand over his arm for a second. "Sorry, mate," he whispered. With a push, the contents of the syringe flowed into Darren's arm. "They forced me into doing this. I don't like to do this to you." Before stepping back, he fastened the IV tube to the catheter.

"Now that we're on the same page, let's get to business," Drágoslàv interrupted. "Before we begin, let me give you some background."

"Drugs. That's my main business. I am the biggest producer, procurer, and distributor of these products in Europe," he said with his chin up. "My family is the most important player in this business for decades. We're running this network since three generations. Nobody dares to go against us." The muscles around his mouth curled on one side to display a smile as he walked around the room. "But we've had a setback recently while I was captured by Interpol in France. I was betrayed."

"My half-brother," he shouted, looking at the plywood-covered windows. "He challenged my authority, that scoundrel." His nostrils flared, lips pressed hard. "We had mutually agreed territories. He had Eastern Europe, some parts of Asia, while I got Western Europe."

He turned around to face them. "Anyways, coming straight to the point, he has taken over a critical stronghold of my business, and you all are going to help me retake it from him."

Drágosláv waited for questions. None came.

"My associate, Gustáv here," he tilted his head toward Gustáv, who was standing beside him on the right, "has arranged a meeting between him and me to reach a compromise. But I'm in no mood for a freaking compromise. This business is mine, and only mine." He clenched his fist, slammed it onto the stony wall. It chipped at the point of impact.

Darren noticed. Drágosláv was strong as well.

"So, how do you expect us to help you?" Liang asked.

"By killing him."

"But why us? You've run this business for so many years. I'm sure you have many able men to take care of this?"

"You're right. My people can indeed take the fight back to him. He has the upper hand, so it'll take time. But we can do it. However, since we all have to work together in our next, more important mission, we thought, why not use your supposed abilities? Have you all get your feet wet?"

"And what's this next more important mission after we help you with your brother?" Diego's arms were crossed.

"Half-brother," Drágosláv corrected. "And I told you, you'll know when the time is right."

"Where is this meeting?" Aarno asked.

"Now we're talking." Drágosláv clapped once. "Port of Barcelona."

"Barcelona? We're in Barcelona?!" As a football player, Diego held this pace in special regard.

"Oh, I forget, you people don't know that. Ah, silly me."

"Wouldn't the port be full of customs and security officers?" Liang's analytical mind ran at full RPMs.

"Smart thinking! Indeed, it will be, and mind you, they'll be heavily armed."

"Then how are we supposed to hold up against all that gun power?"

Drágosláv walked toward Liang, went behind the bed, and patted his back. "I'm impressed by your way of thinking, Mr. Li. Your ability to move over shock and confusion of your situation and think about the task at hand, it's very good."

He came to the front and extended his arms to hold Liang's shoulders. "I'm sure you are smart enough to guess that customs and security officers let us run our business as long as they get their cut. It does not matter who pays it. They'll just facilitate this meeting at the port. They have more to lose if there's a gang war. They'll make sure both parties are unarmed."

"Then how do you plan to kill your stepbrother and his men? How do you intend to do it without any weapons?"

"Ohh, there will be weapons," Drágosláv smirked.

"You, my dear gentlemen. You are the best weapons I got! And if you are who we think, we won't need anything else."

CHAPTER 37

The Warrior

Kashmir Valley, India

A roon drowned in the hypnotic eyes of the White Ghost.

Am I going mad? Am I hallucinating?

He rubbed his eyes several times and examined what stood in front.

Is my grief showing me things that are not real?

Fear dripped as sweat from the side of Aroon's forehead. He had not seen anyone, or rather anything, like him.

After all, he said something about my next life.

"I'm not the Grim Reaper if that's what you're wondering." The tall figure seemed to read his thoughts. "And you're not dead. On the contrary, you're more alive than ever."

How did he know what I was thinking? Aroon was dumbfounded.

"Who are you?"

"Hmm, let's see. I have many names. Some call me the White Ghost, some call me the Ancient Spirit, some call me the Cursed One," he replied. "It has been so long since I lived with my people, so many centuries, it seems like I've forgotten my name from that era after all." The Ghost scanned Aroon with his ruby. "Never mind, I don't want to use my name from those times anymore."

"What do you want from me?"

"I don't want anything from you, my friend. I'm only here to find you and serve you in the war."

"War? War? What war?" Aroon's face looked puzzled. *Is he insane? I'm no soldier, just a normal person.*

"Oh, no, no, no, no," The Ghost said. "Don't judge yourself that way. You are a warrior; one of the finest the world has ever seen." Once again, the White Ghost had read his thoughts.

"I've never fought in my entire life; today was my first."

"And how did you manage to do what you just did, don't you wonder? Where did you get that courage, that skill?" He paused. "Trust me, you are a warrior. You haven't realized it yet."

"No, I'm not a warrior. Even if I am, I won't fight. I've lost my family. I've had enough of this violence, enough of bloodshed."

"You're wise not to choose war,"—the figure smiled—"but war is an evil beast, Master Aroon, with a mind of its own. It took me thousands of years to realize that. It chooses its fighters whether they like it or not."

He looked at Aroon intently. "A war is coming again." The White Ghost came closer to Aroon. "It is not a war of nations as they stand on earth now. Nor is it a war of this age. It is a war of ages long gone, of ages to come. It's a war of worlds—worlds you have not perceived yet." He placed his finger on Aroon's chest. "And you, my friend, won't be able to keep out of it."

Silence.

Aroon was stupefied. He could not understand what age, of what worlds, the White Ghost spoke.

"Let me do my duty. Let me show you who you really are. Let me tell you what the purpose of your life is," the White Ghost continued.

He lifted Aroon by the shoulders and stood face to face.

A cold breeze gushed through the woods. The White Ghost's presence, however, spread its warmth around Aroon. The Ghost held Aroon's hands, closed his own eyes. "Please close your eyes, my friend."

Aroon obeyed.

No sooner did Aroon close his eyes than rays of blue light emanated from the ruby on The Ghost's forehead. The light slowly circled Aroon's head. Their bodies shook, and the light engulfed them as if tying them in a bond.

Aroon's brain filled with visions, visions the White Ghost showed him. Visions that looked familiar, but he couldn't fathom. The light flooded the entire surroundings. The breeze transformed into a strong wind that circled them. There were visions of a war, millions of soldiers, horses, swords, spears, maces, chariots, blood for miles and miles; the land was soaked in it. He saw faces, faces of kings and commanders, of magical creatures. Finally, the vision settled on a man. His entire body, including armor and helmet, shone like dazzling gold. When he used his weapon, the ground quivered, and the sky thundered.

It was unworldly, overpowering. Aroon could not comprehend it. His brain was about to go supernova with the information.

After several overwhelming minutes, it stopped. The wind died. The light was sucked back into the ruby.

The White Ghost opened his eyes. "Did you see the warrior, my friend?"

"Yes." Aroon's eyes were still closed.

"Think about his face, think about his grace, above all, think about his ruthless power."

"Who is he?" Aroon opened his eyes.

"The cycle of time is the most powerful force in the universe." The Ghost stared into Aroon's eyes. "That warrior you saw in the vision, my friend, he is not only your past but your future. You are him; he is you. The time has come for you to take your rightful place—"

"—and as the Almighty has foretold, finally, after all these millennia of this cursed life, you are my redemption!"

CHAPTER 38

The Conundrum

Barcelona, Spain

How do we get out of this situation? It was the only thing on everyone's mind.

"During the meeting with his half-brother, that's the time," Diego suggested. "That's our best chance to escape."

"But how will we free our families? They'll still hold them here when we're out at the port." Liang sighed.

"That's true."

They pondered over it.

"Then we must do it either while leaving for the meeting or when we return. Only during that time, they will take these IVs off," Aarno said. "Only then will we be able to walk and move our arms."

"I think, while leaving for the mission. Yes, that's the best time," Liang suggested. "We don't even know what we'll face there at the port, what condition we'll return in."

"Yes, he wants us to kill his half-brother. We don't know how that will play out," Ojoré chimed in. "But they will expect something like this from us, won't they? They know we will try to escape."

"Yes, they're not that dumb. Why do you think they've gone out of their way in making it so hard for us to move?" Darren added. "Drágosláv ain't no fool."

"I don't think it's Drágosláv's plan," Liang said.

There is something about that guy Sánchez. His face tells that he knows more than he lets out. Sánchez's face was stuck in Liang's mind. *He stands in silence as if he's just Drágosláv deputy, but every now and then, Drágosláv glances at him as if checking something. Yes, he definitely is something.* Liang thought.

"Did you guys observe the man standing behind him? Liang asked. "Didn't he seem intriguing?"

Ojoré nodded. "I noticed him, too."

"Right. Can't put a finger on it," Darren said. "But there was something about him."

"Whether it's his plan or not, I know one thing: Drágosláv would make sure no one created any problems." Liang scratched his forehead with his eyes closed.

"Then what do you suggest, *amigo*?" Diego asked.

"That man in the white coat," Darren replied.

"The man who helps them keep us like this?" Aarno asked

"Yes." Darren nodded.

"But what makes you think he will help us?"

"When I made that attempt to free myself earlier, and they brought my mom to strong-arm me into being docile—"

"Yes. Then?"

"When I let him inject the vial into me, he apologized, said they are blackmailing him into doing this, he does not want to do it."

They stared at Darren.

"They have held him, too?" Aarno asked.

"I don't know; he did not say. That's what we have to find out."

"I don't think we have anything to offer him in return," Liang said.

"He talked to me as well, said that he overheard me telling you guys about my past, that he experienced the same thing with family while growing up," Ojoré added. "If he indeed is being blackmailed as he said, maybe we need to connect with him on a personal level. I don't think he is a bad person. Maybe he will help us somehow."

CHAPTER 39

Drágosláv's Plan

Barcelona, Spain

A few sundowns later, Drágosláv and his men were back in the basement. "Hello again," he greeted loudly. Gustáv followed him along with a few helpers.

None greeted back.

Aarno came straight to the point. "When do you need us to take back the port?"

"That's exactly what we're here for." Drágosláv turned his gaze lazily toward Aarno. "But, before we discuss the plan, I thought, why don't we have a good dinner together. Get on the right note." He smiled a wide smile. "After all, we need teamwork."

The helpers brought in several folding tables and chairs and arranged them in the space between the two rows of beds on each side to make a long dinner table. There were more chairs than there were people in the room.

"If you're wondering if someone is joining us, I say yes," Drágosláv cheered. He walked toward Ojoré and patted him on his back. "I'm not your enemy, it's just the situation." He walked from Ojoré to Darren. "So, I extended the invitation to your families and friends that we have here, to get everyone in good spirits before our task."

The helpers arranged plates and silverware onto the tables.

"Gustáv, will you please bring our guests here?"

Minutes later, Mrs. Odinga, Ojoré's mother, Roberto, Diego's coach, Aarvo, Aarno's youngest brother, Sun, Liang's girlfriend, and Mrs. Swanson, Darren's mom entered the room. No sooner did they see the five men, than they all ran toward them. The scene was full of hugs, embraces, kisses, tears. There was a sense of relief.

Along with them was the man in the white coat. On Drágosláv's command, he once again performed the same procedure to make only the upper body of the five men mobile. The helpers placed the bedside tables and arranged plates on them.

"Why don't you all take your seats?" Drágosláv interrupted.

Not a leg moved.

"Ladies and gentlemen, please," he raised his voice a little.

This time, they listened and sat on their seats.

The helpers served wine first.

"I also arranged for entertainment."

The flamenco dancer, who performed upstairs in the courtyard but was out of work because of Drágosláv, appeared inside the room along with her team. With elbows raised, she took her stance beside her partner while the singer and musicians took their seats behind. The music started, and she performed an elegant dance. The sound of tapping feet filled the room. Her body moved like a gentle breeze, flaring the white traje-de-flamenca with it.

After many courses, complemented by enchanting acts by the dancers, the dinner was over. Drágosláv went to the front and spoke once again.

"I'm sorry, but that was it. Now, let's return our guests to their rooms so that we can return to business."

All the hostages left the room reluctantly. Others left the room, too, with only Drágosláv, Gustáv, and Sánchez staying behind.

"Gustáv, make arrangements."

Without wasting any time, Gustáv went outside. In a few minutes, a few helpers brought several electronic tablets. They handed the master device to Drágosláv. The remaining tablets were given to everyone else. Drágosláv unlocked his master device and, through it, launched the maps app on everyone else. The map zoomed into the satellite image of Barcelona and further narrowed down on the Port de Barcelona.

"Gentlemen, this is where the meeting will take place. That's the entrance, everyone will pass the heavy security area there," he continued scrolling to the top-view of a medium-sized building. "Here they will make sure all of us are unarmed."

"What kind of security is it?" Liang asked.

"Good question, Mr. Liang. Usual airport security, metal detectors, X-ray machines, and they will also pat down each of us."

"They will ensure no party carries any weapons," Gustáv added. Sánchez remained silent as before.

"*Desculpe, Senhor*, but how do you expect us to kill them?"

Drágosláv looked at Sánchez, then replied. "We have our ways, be assured, Senhor Diego. We'll get weapons to you."

"I've not used a gun before," Liang declared.

"You won't have to. You'll get weapons you are meant to use."

"What does that mean?"

"You'll know when the time is right. Moving on, I, Aarno, Liang, Darren, and Diego will pass through the security area. My stepbrother and his men will do the same. After that, port officials will escort everyone to the meeting area."

"What about me?" Ojoré asked.

Drágosláv scrolled sideways to zoom in on a place called Castell de Montjuïc. Located on a hill opposite the port, it was a castle with unobstructed views of the port. It was a popular attraction among tourists. Lots of people visited this place. A cable car at the base of the hill connected to it.

"Mr. Odinga, you will accompany Gustáv on this hill, doing your part from there."

"And what is that?"

"You will aim our enemies with a sniper."

Ojoré looked at the scale on the map. "Are you insane? That distance is massive. I bet even the most experienced shooters won't be able to make that shot. How do you expect me to shoot the target from that far? I have never used a sniper gun before. "

"Trust me, if you are who you should be, you will not miss that target."

"But—"

Drágosláv cut Ojoré short. "You're backup option. I expect these four to finish them off before we need your assistance."

"How are you so sure that the port officers will not let your stepbrother and his men carry weapons?" Liang stared intently. "What if, after we all go in without any weapons, defenseless, they all come in heavily armed, and finish us off? How can you trust the port officers? They won't have any allegiance to either party."

"Smart thinking. That's what I'm looking for, that's what I expected from you, Mr. Li." Drágosláv looked at Sánchez, nodded as if thanking him for finding Liang. "We took care of that already. Family members of officers will stay here at this place while we are at the port. We'll release them only when we return safely."

Drágosláv waited for more questions, and when none came, he continued. "Moving on, we'll not go by usual means of transport, at least not until we have the port back, given that all of Europe is looking for me."

"Then how will we get there?"

"Only you will go by ordinary means of transport. We, on other hand, will use tunnels."

"Tunnels?" Aarno thought he had misheard it.

"Yes, tunnels. Few people know this, but there's a secret and vast network of ancient tunnels under Barcelona. That's how we move our product from port. It can take you almost anywhere in the city."

The five men glanced at each other. No one spoke.

Drágosláv waited for more questions.

Darren, who was silent all this time, spoke. "You did not tell us when this damn mission would take place."

Drágosláv looked from Gustáv to Sánchez, then back to his five captives. "Tomorrow. Midnight."

CHAPTER 40

The Next Destination

Kashmir Valley, India

A roon's soul, slowly trickling, gushed back into his body. His grief evanesced as if nothing had happened, as if he had not existed before this moment. The vision that The Ghost showed eclipsed the memory of his foster parents' murder. Everything happened so fast. Moments ago, Aroon was a small-towner who had lost two of his most beloved people. Although he didn't understand everything, he felt energized, determined, and poised.

"We must leave now," The Ghost said.

"But—"

"I will answer all your questions, but not now." The Ghost looked around. The majestic snow peaks peeked defiantly through the trees.

I wonder if they would have discovered it, is it too risky? The Ghost concentrated. *I can handle it, but him? He is too fragile right now.*

"Where are we going?"

"It's very dangerous for you, the path we will take to go there," The Ghost answered, preoccupied partly with his previous thought.

"But where is it?"

"It's far, deep inside the jungle, many miles from here."

"And how will we go there?"

The White Ghost ignored the question. He sank back into his thoughts and concentrated hard. "I should probably not take the chance. It's too risky," he murmured. "But the access has just opened, maybe no one has noticed it yet."

"What's too risky? What access?"

"The route I'm contemplating for our journey back to my jungle."

"Jungle?"

The Ghost once again ignored Aroon.

I guess there's no other option. After all, I've used this route to find Aroon. Until now, I had no problems using it. On the contrary, it had made things easy.

"Come with me." The Ghost brought forth his left arm. "Hold it tight and make sure that you're always connected to some part of my body. You must hold my arm. Never let go of your grip."

"All right. I will do as you say." Aroon wiped his sweaty hands on the side of his thighs.

"Very well." The Ghost nodded and closed his eyes. "Are you ready?"

Aroon's face showed his nervousness. He swallowed and replied, "Yes, I'm ready."

Once again, The Ghost used the powers of his ruby. This time, a beam of white light shot from it. With their hands connected, Aroon could see everything The Ghost could see. The surrounding landscape of the never-ending mountains and trees around them was filled with transparent, bubble-like objects. They floated midair. It appeared as if they were windows into another world. They were dark.

"What are they?" Aroon's eyes were full of wonder.

"You'll experience it in a minute."

They both walked toward a bubble. Aroon continued to hold on to the White Ghost's arm.

"Go ahead, get inside."

Aroon moved forward and inserted his right hand into it. Nothing happened.

"Go all the way inside, with only one arm stretching out and in contact with my arm."

Aroon obeyed. He sighed, closed his eyes, and pushed his body through it. Only his left hand was touching The Ghost.

The experience was unparalleled. He felt that his body passed under an ice-cold waterfall. Pain soared as though thousands of needles had pierced his flesh. However, once he crossed the interface, there was no pricking. It was replaced by a sense of momentum as if his entire body was being pulled inside. When this feeling subsided, he opened his eyes and found nothing but darkness. He could not see a thing. He panicked. He tried pulling the White Ghost's arm, but realized he was losing his grip. To his horror, there was a jerk, and he lost contact.

The Ghost had asked me to never lose contact. What would happen now?

Right at that exact moment, his body squeezed. The next second, he had the same feeling of passing under an ice-cold waterfall, excruciating pain, and *swoop*! He was ejected from the bubble.

Aroon opened his eyes and found himself on the other side of the bubble, standing a few meters away. The White Ghost remained where he stood.

"What was that?" Aroon screwed his face. "Why did you jerk your hand?"

"I wanted you to see how it works." The Ghost replied with calm eyes.

"What works?" Aroon's hands stretched out, his palms pointing toward The Ghost.

The White Ghost took a step toward Aroon. "The Confluence."

"Confluence?" Wrinkles showed on Aroon's forehead as his eyebrows came together.

"You will understand it all when you see more of it. When you see and believe who you really are. We'll be in there briefly, only to use a shortcut to the jungle."

"Umm—" Aroon rubbed his forehead with his hands. He could not understand anything The Ghost told or showed him.

A cold breeze swept across the tall trunks, sweeping along fragments of broken pinecones and needles on the ground. A small stream of freshly melted ice gushed in the distance. They had walked away from the two dead terrorists.

The Ghost drew close. "What did you experience, my friend?"

Aroon told him about the pain, the cold, the pull, and the push. "But I didn't see anything. It was completely dark." His eyes grew wide as he explained.

"Exactly, that's how it's supposed to be." The White Ghost leaned and placed a hand on Aroon's shoulder.

"How is it supposed to be? I don't understand." Aroon shook his head.

"All dark,"

"But why?"

"Because those lands are always dark. Besides, you're not yet ready. You're still in the nascent stages."

"I don't understand, I am confused." Aroon sighed.

"The interface you saw was the boundary between this world and another."

Aroon's heart pounded at full speed. Once again, he could not make out if this was real or if he had gone mad because of his grief.

"The bubbles you saw, it's only recently that I've been able to conjure them. You could see and stay inside it only because you held my arm." The Ghost waited for this to sink into Aroon's brain. After a few seconds, he continued, "When I let go of your hand, you were ejected immediately. You stay there on your own only when you have attained the necessary powers or if it happens organically, without the help of any gem, on its own."

Aroon's brain worked at double the speed to process this information. "Sorry, I do not understand how it works." He looked up. Glimpses of the clear blue sky were obscured by the canopy of coniferous trees.

"You will in time. For now, we've got to go."

"A while ago, you murmured it's dangerous, didn't you?" Aroon looked at The Ghost. "If that is so, why are we going there?"

"That's because it'll get us to my jungle faster without ordinary people spotting me."

Aroon had many more questions, but noticing the urgency in The Ghost's voice, he decided not to ask. "What now?"

"Now we go home to my jungle, my cave."

The Ghost signaled him to hold his arm again. Aroon held it tight, and the bubbles became visible to him once again. They both walked toward it. This time, however, The Ghost took charge.

"On the count of three."

"One, two, three."

On three, both crossed the boundary and disappeared.

CHAPTER 41

Man in The White Coat

Barcelona, Spain

B arri Gòtic was quiet tonight. Most bars and restaurants were closed. After finishing sumptuous meals in the peculiar cellar-like restaurants, a few remaining visitors were already on their way out. Performers at corners and squares were wrapping up their bags. It was not yet midnight, but the quarter was deserted.

Palau Dalmases had not seen any audience for its nightly Flamenco for several days. At the moment, it was home to Drágosláv and his men. Right in the middle of Barri Gòtic, this place was a perfect cover for them to stay in the city while the Interpol searched for them all over the continent.

Several feet below the premises of the Palau Dalmases in its basement were Ojoré, Aarno, Darren, Liang, and Diego, trying desperately to find a way out of it. Unfortunately for them, they couldn't leave. On the contrary, they were not even in a state to move their limbs. Even if they could move, their loved ones were kept as hostages by Drágosláv and his men.

Sometime after midnight, which was in a few hours, they were supposed to help Drágosláv execute his plan. The plan was to kill Drágosláv's half-brother, Grigori, who had broken the truce with him while he was in prison and took over a crucial part of their drug business. All the details were explained to the five men. They knew they had little time to free themselves and their families. In a few hours, Drágosláv would get them ready for his meeting, and they would lose any chance they might have to escape. They knew he would make sure that they could not make a move to abscond during his offensive on Grigori.

The door opened. The man wearing the white coat walked inside. Like on previous occasions, he had a small hammer in his hand. He walked straight toward Ojoré and tapped the hammer on his knee. He did not make eye contact with any of the men and kept his head low. On confirming there was no reflex action, he tapped the other knee. Ojoré looked at Darren, who signaled that he should start the conversation.

"What's your name, sir?" Ojoré tilted his head to look at the man's eyes.

No answer.

"Sir?" Ojoré smiled.

"Matthew." Still no eye contact.

"Are you married, Matthew?"

Matthew's eyes dampened. He quickly tried to hide his tears.

"I'm sorry. I didn't mean to hurt you. What's the matter?" Ojoré turned toward the other four for a help. He didn't want to upset Matthew. None could help.

Matthew did not reply. Ojoré decided to wait.

On seeing Matthew compose himself, he continued. "What did you mean the other day when you said that you went through the same thing as me?" Ojoré calmed his voice some more.

There was only the slow chirping of the two ceiling fans for a while. The stone walls of the basement echoed the sounds. The air smelled musty.

Finally, Matthew decided to speak. "Your story, you told the other day," he said in his thick Australian accent, "it reminded me of the miserable days of my life, mate. I generally don't talk about it, but hearing someone go through a somewhat similar ordeal, I couldn't control myself." He stopped at the footboard of Ojoré's cot and placed his right hand on the metal frame, facing away from Ojoré.

"It's all right. You can share your story with us."

Mathew remained silent, recollecting his memories.

"I shouldn't." His voice shook.

"It's all right, Matthew, we are here to listen," Ojoré said in a reassuring tone.

He sighed. Turned to face Ojoré. "I shouldn't." His nervous eyes showed his struggle.

"Please." Ojoré looked into Matthew's eyes. They stared at each other under the flickering of the tubelights.

Matthew came close to Ojoré, closed his eyes, sighed, and spoke.

"Mine was an extremely conservative Christian family." He placed the hammer on the bedside. "We lived in a small town in Australia." He snorted. "In those days, the society was not very accepting of blokes like us."

Ojoré and the others listened without creating any distractions, their eyes focused on Matthew.

"My parents soon realized my sexual orientation, and like your father, they too decided to control it. They pulled me out of middle school and homeschooled me. When I showed no 'improvement' in their eyes, they sent me to live in a church that claimed to cure kids of these mental illnesses."

"I know how these places are. I went through the same things." Ojoré pressed his lips as he spoke.

"They kept me hungry, made me pray ten times a day, and like you, they gave me shock treatment." Matthew stared toward a corner of the room. "But that was not the end of it. The pastor over there did unspeakable things to me." He clenched his fist. "It's to drive the devil out of my body he would say. When I told my parents about the molestation, the church told them that I was making things up to get out of this place and that I had no fear of the Lord."

Ojoré's face reddened like hot iron. He exhaled heavily. He could relate to this story, to Matthew's helplessness, to the torture, to the frustration.

"I attempted suicide several times but did not succeed. One day, there was a chance, and I escaped. I ran like I had never run before. After a few days, I somehow managed to land in an orphanage in Melbourne, where

I told them a different name. A kind and generous couple adopted me. I grew up happy in their care. They helped me go to medical college, where I met my spouse. He was a Spaniard. We decided to move to Barcelona and live here until—"

"Until what?" Ojoré asked impatiently

"Until I lost him."

"Why? How?" Ojoré felt genuinely sorry for Matthew. *This is not right. Why do people like us suffer so much?*

"I can understand how it would have felt to lose the love of your life after so much suffering," he told Matthew. "Love is the best medicine to cure all the wounds of the past."

"My spouse's father worked for Drágosláv. He changed his allegiance and joined Drágosláv's half-brother, Grigori. So, to set an example, Drágosláv killed my husband."

"Despite this, you are freakin' working for them?" Darren asked, his voice a little loud.

Liang shook his head gently, looking at Darren, signaling him to keep quiet.

"I'm sorry. I shouldn't have said that," Darren apologized.

"No worries." Matthew swallowed. "Before they killed him, my husband and I adopted a child. Among your family members is also my boy, Travis, held hostage by Drágosláv. That's why I'm doing this, without protest. He's the only hope in my life."

"We're so sorry for what you're going through, Matthew," Aarno said.

Matthew did not say anything else. He moved from Ojoré to Darren.

Matthew hesitated.

"Go on. Don't worry, I understand your situation."

Matthew completed his routine procedure of tapping with a hammer. "I obey them. I have to do these things to you to keep my child safe. I'm really sorry, I don't want to do this, I wish I could help." He moved from Darren to Liang.

"You can still help us," Liang said.

"But they will hurt Travis. I can't go against them."

"I have a plan. It'll allow you to help us, and they'll not punish you for it."

"How?"

"Let's say, by mistake, you make the air puncture in the IV bag at a low point. That'll allow the fluid to drip down and not enter Darren's body. You can say that Darren scared you, and that's why you made the mistake. They've seen you get scared around Darren yesterday, so they'll believe you. Then Darren will regain his movement and free himself. You've seen his strength, haven't you? Do you doubt he can free himself?"

"No, but what about the others?"

"So you doubt I can free the others?"

"Not at all. But—but, what if they find out? They will torture my boy."

"They won't find out, and to save you, we'll take you as our hostage along with someone else to show that we consider you one of them," Liang reasoned.

Matthew did not speak. He ran the plan in his head. "But what about your family and Travis?" he asked Liang. "They will still be hostages."

"That's one more thing you need to help us with. Where are they kept?"

"In the rooms at the far corner of the premises, right near the tunnel entrance."

"That works perfectly; we can rescue them and escape from the tunnels."

"But this room is on the other side of the premises. You'll have to cross several buildings and the courtyard. The security is tight, men with guns all over."

"We'll figure something out; you just help us by making us regain our movements and come near the tunnel entrance when you hear the commotion."

"What about Travis after we get out?"

"Once we get out, I'll call my family in Finland. They'll collect him, they know of a safe place that no one knows about," Aarno said. "Kind of a family safe house."

"They will find us again. Didn't they find you and your family from five different continents?"

"Well, we didn't know about them then. We didn't try to hide. This time, we do. We'll be watchful and stealthy," Liang added.

"Will you please help us, sir?" Aarno asked. "I beg you."

Matthew stood silent, tapping the hammer in his palm.

"Please, you are our family's and your boy's only hope," Diego pleaded.

Still no reply.

"Please, Matthew." Ojoré looked into his eyes.

Matthew shook his head. "I can't let those murderers have their way. I will help you."

He quickly replaced the IVs of the five men with a new bag. "This should flush the effect of the previous drug." He injected a vial of additional liquid into each of them. "This should speed it up." He spilled some fluid on Darren's side to make it look like his IV bag had leaked.

"How long will it take before we get back our movement?"

"Thirty minutes to one hour. This is the best I can do for you right now. I'll wait near the tunnel entrance for you."

"Thank you, I can't thank you enough." Ojoré felt a sense of connection with him. A bond.

Matthew walked toward Ojoré and held his hand. "I'll keep this door unlocked." He walked toward the door, held the handle, and turned to face them. "You better save my boy."

CHAPTER 42

Half Brother's Plan

Barcelona, Spain

Forty-five minutes passed. Darren's neurons fired, and his limbs once again felt their existence. The effect of the drugs was waning. Darren was first among the five captives who were able to move their body, though barely. He felt exhausted. But he knew this was their only chance. He gripped the chains that anchored him to the wall behind his bed, rotated his wrists around them, and yanked forward. The wall exploded as if cardboard. They waited to check if anyone outside had heard it. The thick plywood on the windows and the stone walls, and the ceiling prevented the sounds from leaking above. Darren did the same to rip apart the chains around his legs. The metal was no match for his strength. It gave in without a fight. Effortless. He pulled apart the iron cuffs as easily and got out of bed.

Unlike chains, though, the dizziness was stubborn. It took him a few steps to regain balance. He fought hard with the residual drugs in his veins and walked toward Ojoré. Once again, he tore apart the chains that re-strained Ojoré's body. Aarno was next.

"I'm not sure about us four, but I totally get why they had you drugged and chained," Ojoré said.

One by one, the chains fell to the ground. They were free.

As they tried to walk, like Darren, their motor skills deceived them, making it hard to stand.

"Slap me," Darren told Ojoré.

"What?!"

"Slap me. That'll get some adrenaline going."

Smack!

Darren shook his head hard. "Again."

Ojoré repeated.

Darren lapped around the room, jumping and squatting. Blood raced through his veins. He was ready. Others followed his suit and slapped each other. Aarno worked on his biceps by lifting the bed. Ojoré high-jumped around. Liang and Diego did pushups.

"I feel better," Aarno said.

"Now what?" Diego finished his hundredth pushup.

Liang fetched the map of the premises that Matthew had sketched for them. "We're here. We have to go all the way on the opposite side of the property." He moved his finger from one corner to the other.

"We'll sneak out one by one," Aarno said. "I'll go first, then you three. Darren, you should go last; you're the most visible. We'll indicate to you when it's safe to pass across."

"But what if we run into an obstacle or something else that needs strength?" Liang reasoned. "We'll need Darren in that case."

"Good point. How about you go third, Darren?"

"I don't care. I just want to get out of this freakin' room."

"Let's not waste time. We must hurry." Ojoré stared at the door.

Aarno brought forth his hand. Diego placed his on top. The others followed suit.

"We can do this," Aarno said, "and together we will."

"Together," they repeated.

A few minutes later, Aarno pushed open the heavy iron door. Matthew left it unlocked as promised.

Through the narrow slit-like opening, he peeped. A dimly lit hallway. Guards approached from the far end. Aarno shut it. He placed his ear on the inner lintels. The footsteps faded.

Aarno peeped again. This time, it was clear. Aarno came out of the room, walked forward, and scanned the hallway. Satisfied, he moved his arm back and forth around the elbow with an open palm, signaling all clear. The others followed.

In a few minutes, they reached the end. The hallway opened into a large hall. Cupboards, chairs, tables, and coat hangers lay stacked haphazardly.

"There must be a stairway somewhere," Liang whispered.

They dispersed.

"Here," Darren shouted.

"Shhhh." Aarno placed his index finger on his lips. "You want to get us caught?"

"There's one here too," Ojoré whispered

"One more here," Diego called from the other side.

Liang unfolded the map. "That one." He pointed to the one next to Ojoré.

Aarno rushed in front. Before he could descend, a guard appeared in front. He looked at them, puzzled.

Before the guard could lift his gun or shout, Darren stormed toward the guard, snatched the weapon with ease. He went behind the guard, covered his mouth, hesitated for a second, and twisted the neck.

The body collapsed on the floor.

Darren sighed a deep sigh. It was his first time killing a person. He felt weird. He didn't know why he didn't feel guilty. It was as if something was returning to him from a past he couldn't remember. Darren lifted the body, shoved it inside a cupboard.

Aarno looked down the stairway. It was clear. He descended. Others followed. The stairs lead them to a courtyard.

Aarno glanced out from the edge of the stairs. "I see four guards. They have guns."

Five backs lined the wall beside him. They paused. "We have to wait," Ojoré whispered.

"We can't wait here for long. Someone will catch us," Liang replied. "We need to sneak out one by one."

"But that will expose us." Ojoré shook his head.

Liang looked up the stairway, then at the courtyard, his face intense. "There's no other way," he said.

Silence.

"I'll go first." Aarno took a step ahead with determined eyes. "Liang, you follow me," he said in a commanding voice.

Liang nodded.

"Darren, you next. Then you two." Aarno pointed his index finger at Darren, then at Ojoré and Diego.

The three heads bobbed.

"If I need Darren, I'll make this sign. Darren, you should come instead of Liang." He made a cross with his two index fingers to demonstrate the sign.

Darren nodded.

Aarno turned. He glanced down the edge of the wall toward the court-yard. It formed a rectangle surrounded by four hallways with wide stone columns. Flickering light from gas lamps illuminated the area. A water fountain occupied its center.

Aarno took a deep breath and bolted. He hid behind the closest column. Panting from the sprint, he scanned the entire area for guards. There were none. He moved to the next column. Gave all clear.

Liang took his place. He unfolded the map once more, looked at it, then at his surroundings.

One by one, they all came out and hid behind the columns.

Aarno stared at Liang, waiting for directions.

"We need to cross the courtyard," Liang whispered. He pointed at the hallway on the opposite side. "That door."

Aarno looked at the perpendicular hallways on either side. They were fenced.

"We have to cross via the courtyard." Liang looked at him. "No other way."

"Damn, it's too risky. What if guards are watching from above? We'll be a freakin' shooting practice." Darren scowled.

"Do you see any other option?"

Aarno shook his head. "Damn with it. I'll run to the other side when I see an opportunity. Just like we did now, one by one, you guys follow. But we must be quick. Timing is everything."

Liang nodded. He whispered the information to Darren, who passed it on to the other two.

Aarno readied himself and looked for guards. Two were in the second-floor hallway. They were chatting with their backs toward the courtyard. Like a mouse, Aarno broke into a sprint. He landed behind the pillar on the other side of the courtyard. Liang followed, took the next pillar.

It was Darren's turn. He ran as fast as he could. Halfway on his way toward the other side, suddenly, out of nowhere, a bullet zoomed past him. It narrowly missed his head and collided with an Iron door behind him. The impact rang like a bell.

Darren looked upward. His eyes met one of the guards. They, too, looked puzzled. The shock was because they found Darren in the courtyard, and they heard the gunshot hit the door. They had not fired it. Also, there was no sound of the shot until it struck the door. This meant the shooter had silencers.

Darren ran toward the other side. He took cover behind a column, extended his palm toward Diego and Liang, signaling them to stop. One of the patrolling guards sounded the siren. The next second, a deluge of bullets came from above.

Drágoslav, Gustáv, Sánchez came rushing down. They stood beside a window. "You're right, Dr. Sánchez. Grigori, that *predatel*!" Drágoslav crushed his knuckles. "He didn't wait for the meeting. I didn't think of it, but you did. You rightly guessed that he would attack first." He punched the wall. "I should've seen this coming. He has done it in the past on the boat we took from Odessa."

Grigori's men took care of the guards on the upper level. More climbed from outside and joined them. They shot below from their vantage.

"Thanks to you, Dr. Sánchez, we're ready for him." Drágoslav turned toward Gustáv. "Bring me that bastard."

Gustáv donned his bulletproof vest, grabbed his gun, fastened his hard hat, and disappeared. Next second, he charged into the courtyard, joined his men who hid at each level, expecting Grigori.

Bullets zoomed in all directions. One of Grigori's men shot toward Diego and Ojoré. They were stuck on the other side of the courtyard.

"Stay there," Aarno shouted. He looked around for a weapon. An antique piece of art with two spears crossed behind a shield hung on the next pillar.

Aarno sprinted, retrieved one. He pulled his hand backward, took his aim at the shooter, and launched. It went bullet speed. The next moment, the spear pierced the shooter's chest. His body fell into the courtyard.

"Yes!" Aarno cheered. He retrieved the second spear and shield.

Drágosláv curled his lips into a wicked smile. "It indeed is a weapon made for him, just like the javelin." He wanted to see this. He wanted to see what these five men were capable of, but at the same time, he felt nervous.

"I told you, Your Majesty. Trust me, we have the right people."

One of Drágosláv's men aimed at Ojoré. "You fool," Drágosláv screamed. "I want them alive. No one shoots at them. Kill that bastard Grigori. Kill his men instead."

The five men were trapped, split on either side of the courtyard. A steady torrent of bullets passed between them. Diego and Ojoré were desperate to get on the other side. Impossible. Grigori's men shot from the upper floor and the roof. Drágosláv's men countered from below.

One of Grigori's men got hit. The body fell next to Ojoré. He carefully slid out, collected a handgun.

Ojoré peered from the edge of the column. A bullet missed him by a whisker. Crossing to the other side was risky. He stared at Darren helplessly. Darren stared back. "You all go, don't wait for me. Save my mother." Ojoré told them.

Darren looked at the others.

"We're not leaving them behind," Aarno shouted. "We said together, remember?"

Darren turned, searched for a heavy object he could use as a shield. Nothing.

"How about the door?" Liang shouted, pointing toward the iron door that took the first bullet. It was only a few feet away from Darren.

Amidst the firing, Darren ran toward it using the cover of the columns. He opened the door, entered the room. The next second, the door blasted outward. Darren quickly picked it up with its large handle. He held it like a shield covering his body and ran to the other side. It was solid.

Everyone looked in awe at Darren's display of strength. The bullets hit the iron door but did not harm it. It was too thick for them to penetrate.

"I'll make two rounds; the door won't cover three of us," Darren told Diego and Ojoré.

"That'll cover us against bullets coming from Grigori's men, but what about Drágosláv?"

"Drágosláv wants us alive. I heard him tell his men not to fire at us. Quickly, who wants to go first?"

"Diego, you go. I'll provide cover fire from here." Ojoré showed them the gun he had retrieved from the fallen man.

Darren lifted the door. Diego slid behind. They both rushed toward the other side. The firing was relentless.

Ojoré peeped from behind the column. He took five shots toward the roof. Seconds later, five bodies fell to the floor. All of them had single bullet holes between the eyes. His aim was flawless.

Drágosláv smiled, looking at Sánchez once again, and nodded. Sánchez smiled back.

"I'm convinced about them all." Drágosláv nodded enthusiastically.

"This is not even the beginning, my lord," Sánchez smirked.

After crossing Diego to the other side, Darren ran back toward Ojoré. "Come on, let's go." Darren had to shout to be heard.

"Make sure you take us through the pile of those bodies. I want to collect their guns." Ojoré pointed toward the bodies lying haphazardly on the floor of the courtyard. Darren looked at them, nodded.

Amid incoming bullets, they crossed the courtyard, collecting several handguns on the way. Shards of stone, bricks, metal, wood, and glass splintered from walls, ceilings, columns, stairs, lamps, chandeliers, and furniture and flew in all directions as bullets struck them. Dust hung thick in the air.

"Which way is the tunnel?" Darren asked, crossing the courtyard. Sweat dripped from his head as he looked frantically from one side to the other.

Liang closed his eyes. He screwed his face recollecting the map in his head. "That way. Let's go," he shouted.

"Don't let them leave. Follow them," Drágosláv shouted from the other side, his right hand pointing toward the five men. "Shoot them on their legs or arms, if necessary. But be careful!"

The five entered an archway, took the stairs leading below. It opened into a narrow passage that sloped downward and was lined with rows of sconces on both sides, lighting up its length. The walls were made of stone, and the floor was slate. Small wooden doors came every few feet, opening into storerooms.

Drágosláv's men followed. Some were already present where the five were headed.

Ojoré distributed the guns. They followed the map toward the tunnel entrance amid fire from Drágosláv's men. Hiding behind openings for the small doors, the five returned fire. Most of them missed their targets. But not Ojoré. He aimed precisely, took only a few shots. They proved fatal every time.

After several minutes, they reached their destination through a stone archway. It was a big circular underground chamber with wide stone columns. Along its circumference were several small wrought iron doors that opened into small rooms that held their loved ones. They must have been tens of feet below ground.

On the opposite side of the archway was a big iron gate that opened into a tunnel connected to the vast, secret Barcelona tunnel network. Matthew was hiding next to a door when they arrived. He joined them.

One by one, Darren flung open the doors with his hands. The hostages looked stupefied.

"Hurry, we got to get out of here," Matthew said. "Follow me."

"*No tan rápido,*" one of Drágosláv's men shouted. "Master ordered not to shoot you, but we can kill these people." He pointed toward the hostages. He and the others took cover behind a column, pointed their guns toward the hostages.

Darren lifted an iron door like a shield, quickly came in front. He tried to cover as many people as he could.

"Everyone, go back inside the room," Aarno shouted.

Bang! Bang! Bang! The firing resumed. Shards and dust were flung everywhere.

Ojoré killed several. Others missed their targets, wasted bullets.

Aboveground, the battle between Drágoslàv's and Grigori's men intensified.

Near the tunnel entrance, after what seemed like a long while, the five, as well as Drágoslàv's men, were out of bullets. They attacked each other with whatever they could find. Liang and Diego retrieved daggers from the corpses of dead guards. They stood with their backs touching each other.

Drágoslàv's men surrounded them. They attacked with their own daggers.

Liang and Diego worked as one unit. They jumped, bent, supported, and rotated around each other in synchrony. Their blades moved through the air like a circular power saw, making deep cuts into flesh that came in their path. The attackers were no match for their speed and agility.

At the same time, Aarno fought with the second spear that he withdrew from the courtyard. Darren, on the other side, demolished the attackers with his bare hands, lifting, throwing, and crushing them against the wall.

While these four fought, Ojoré and Matthew escorted the hostages toward the tunnel. "Move," Ojoré shouted. "Faster."

One by one, Mrs. Odinga, Mrs. Swanson, Sun, Aarvo, Roberto, and Matthew's son, Travis, entered the tunnel.

"Let's go. Everyone is out."

They slowly retreated toward the tunnel entrance. Matthew held the gate open.

Suddenly, Drágoslàv and Sánchez appeared. They aimed their guns. "Don't even try. I have the weapons, I have the bullets, and I have the men. I know you are out of them," Drágoslàv shouted. "Trust me, you don't want to take any chances. You don't want your loved ones as casualties, do you?"

They were beaten. They had to obey Drágoslàv.

"Now, be good. Drop whatever weapons you have."

One by one, they dropped their arms.

Sánchez walked toward them, collected the arms. When he reached Liang and was about to collect the dagger, several things happened at the same time. Liang, in lightning speed, picked up his dagger. He held it to

Sánchez's throat. In retaliation, Drágoslāv took a shot at Sun. She moved swiftly, exposing Ojoré standing behind her. Matthew, who stood next to Ojoré, pushed him out of the line of fire. The bullet missed Ojoré by a whisker but hit Matthew instead, a little above the waist.

"Maathewwwww!" Ojoré screamed.

The next second, Darren placed the heavy door between Drágoslāv and them. "Everyone, keep low."

Matthew fell into Ojoré's arms. Travis ran toward him. "Everything will be all right. You are going to be all right."

Matthew breathed fast. His body went heavy.

"Stay with me, Matthew. Stay with me. I'm here." Ojoré patted Matthew's cheeks.

"Drágoslāv, we have Dr. Sánchez," Aarno shouted. "We know you care about him. We know you regard him as important. Let us go, and no one gets hurt."

"Aaaaahhh," Drágoslāv screamed. He emptied his handgun at the ceiling. The echoes rang through the hallways. He paused, looking at the five. Next, he looked at Sánchez. Sánchez gave a nod.

"Okay, okay," he said. "No one shoots," Drágoslāv commanded his men. "Let them go."

Ojoré lifted Matthew by the shoulders. "Try to stand. You can do it."

"The bullet was headed toward me. Matthew sacrificed himself," Ojoré murmured. Blood soaked his clothes, and guilt filled his mind.

The five men, Matthew, and all the hostages rushed inside the tunnel. The iron door slowly retreated with them. On reaching the tunnel gate, Darren let go of the door and grabbed the gate instead. He swung the gate closed and locked it from the outside. Next minute, they sped into the depths of the labyrinthine tunnels.

"Let them go. Let's go back to help Gustáv. Let's finish Grigori for good," Drágoslāv said. "We found them once. We'll find them again."

CHAPTER 43

The Apes' Treatment

Somewhere

The sun was not above the horizon, but hints of its rays reached the ground, lighting up the wilderness on its way. With dark and light, pre-dawn was spellbound. Fog engulfed the landscape and lingered at the base of trees. The jungle was filled with sounds of tigers, monkeys, leopards, and bears waking up on the Sun's command.

As time passed, dawn marched with sunshine, slowly reclaiming the land. Droplets of dew clung to threads of spiderwebs spun between trees. The rays fought with the dense trees and tall grass to kiss the ground. The lush green vista spanned miles and miles across.

She chose her target; there was a lot to choose from, prey in this part of the world was plentiful. Her gaze pinned, she observed its every movement. The prey—a spotted deer—was happy eating leaves with other members of its herd.

She made no sound. With gentle steps, steady head, eyes locked only on one thing, the tigress advanced, placing its paws one after another.

When the time was right, she charged, covering a vast distance with each leap. The deer tried its best to evade her, but was no match. Using her momentum and razor-sharp claws, she knocked it down.

Kicking and screaming, the deer struggled. The job was almost done.

When she was ready to pierce the neck, a bubble-like object appeared in front. The tigress immediately let go of her catch. It sped away and disappeared into the nearest bush. The tigress' gaze was fixed on the giant bubble as if expecting something to come out. The object pulled all the fog around it, making it invisible.

Wasting no time, the tigress opened its mouth wide and roared toward the sky. It spread far and wide.

A few minutes later, big cats of her kind filled the surroundings. They encircled the area, perhaps to keep anyone from coming near it. Who would dare to go past? They accepted commands from only one. He had lived here for ages. He knew not just them, but also their long-gone ancestors. It had been his home for centuries, his refuge in those testing times.

The White Ghost emerged from the bubble-like object with Aroon in his arms. Aroon was unconscious. Blood oozed from their scarred bodies.

As The Ghost rushed toward the trees, branches untangled automatically, forming an archway, unraveling the path toward his cave. He entered, placed Aroon on the stone bed, and tore his shirt to examine his upper body. Dissatisfied, he pulled away his pants and examined again. There it was. Two tiny dots were imprinted on his left leg. He lifted Aroon's eyelids. They were a dark shade of purple. Aroon's body was turning the same shade as if succumbing to an infection.

I should not have taken that route; I should've let him come by the ordinary means.

The Ghost looked at his own body. The armor under his robes had taken the impact for him. It was covered with elongated, needle-shaped thorns.

But I have used that route so many times. No one ever used it. It was hidden. How did they know?

He removed the armor and placed it on the stone table.

Do they know of the confluence's opening? Or is it a coincidence?

Aroon changed color by the minute.

I have to hurry; otherwise, it will get worse.

The Ghost dashed out of the cave and made a loud sound. It was not human, more like a monkey call.

No sooner did he do so than his calls were replied to with a cacophony of sounds. *HOOP, HOOP, HOOP, HOOP...*

Branches moved. Trees shook. Tigers roared.

Hanging from branch to branch, a large tribe of monkeys moved along the trees and landed at the mouth of the cave.

"The enemy bit my guest," he told them. "The poison is spreading."

The Alpha monkey came forward and accompanied The Ghost inside.

The Ghost pointed his index finger at Aroon's leg. "Please do something."

The Alpha jumped toward Aroon and took a good look at the purple dots. He immediately hopped outside.

Hoop, Hoop, he called the others.

More monkeys joined him inside.

Hoop, Haap, Haap, Hoop, they exchanged calls as if discussing further course of action.

A few minutes later, the congregation broke. One after another, they all lined up in front of Aroon's body. The first monkey placed his mouth on the purple dots, sucked, and spat a dark purple liquid out on the floor. Once it finished, the next monkey took his place.

As this process continued, Aroon's body lost its purple shade. The infection receded. They did this till all the purple was spat out, and Aroon's body was back to its original wheatish color.

The Ghost came closer to Aroon. Rays beamed out from his ruby and scanned the length of Aroon's body like an X-ray. He nodded toward the Alpha monkeys. They cheered. Hearing their calls, the cats roared in celebration.

Aroon opened his eyes to this loud mix of sounds. He looked at The Ghost, then at the animals around him. He moved back, scared, confused, and hit the stony wall behind. "Where am I?"

"You are in my cave," the White Ghost replied. "Fear not. Everything is all right. You're safe now."

Aroon stared at the alpha monkey.

"Relax, none here will harm you."

Aroon looked around. Formed in rock and stone, the cave was spotless and covered with animal fur. The animals had allowed The Ghost to retrieve the fur from their dead ones and use it in his cave. "What happened? Who were those?" Aroon remembered the struggle inside the bubble.

His question was interrupted.

THUD! THUD! THUD!

One by one, the monkeys collapsed onto the floor.

CHAPTER
44

After the Escape

Barcelona, Spain

"Hello?" answered a voice as it picked up the phone. Aarno heard the sadness in it.

"Hello, Father, it's me, Aarno," Aarno spoke into the phone, which he had borrowed from a passerby on the street.

He stood in a dimly lit side street, far from the rest of the escapees. They had decided to divide the party into four smaller groups and spread across town to make it difficult to track. They chose high-traffic areas to blend in with the tourists.

"It's Aarno! It's Aarno!" Aarno's dad told the other occupants of his room. "Oh, son! Are you all right? Where are you? Is Aarvo with you? We are all so worried." He spoke fast and breathless. "I looked for you everywhere. I put fliers and missing person advertisements all across Finland."

"Yes, Aarvo is with me. I don't have time to explain everything, Father," Aarno replied impatiently. "I'm in trouble. Someone kidnapped us and a whole bunch of other people."

"Kidnapped? How? Why? You both all right? Where are you?" The shock on Mr. Heikkinen's face was evident in his voice.

"Don't worry, we managed to escape. We're doing good for now. But they are looking for us; the danger is not yet over. I need your help."

"But no one contacted us for ransom," his father's voice softened.

"It's not about ransom, Father," he said, looking nervously at his surroundings for Drágosláv or his gang members. "They want something else."

"What do they want then?

"I can't explain now." Aarno closed his eyes and sighed. "But can you help us?"

Cars, buses, and motorbikes zoomed ahead on the main street, adding background noise to their conversation.

"Anything, anything, my son."

Aarno opened his eyes. The phone's owner looked impatiently at him. Aarno turned away from him. "I'm in Barcelona. We need to get out of here."

"Don't worry. I'll come get you both myself. I will call the captain to ready our jet."

"It's not just Aarvo and I, other people must be rescued too. They all have helped me. I can't leave them."

"I'll make arrangements. I'll take care of it. You, your brother, be safe and wait for my call." The urgency in his father's voice told Aarno that his father was already getting ready to make some calls.

"I don't have any number right now for you to call, but I will call you again in about 30 minutes."

"Son, take care and be safe. I love you."

Aarno could not remember the last time his dad had said that to him. He turned to face the phone's owner, who was walking toward him. He gestured a five with his palm, requesting five more minutes on the phone.

"Father, one last thing, can you arrange for a surgeon?"

"Surgeon?" Aarno's father shouted. "Are you hurt? Is your brother hurt?"

"We both are fine," Aarno replied in a calm voice to pacify his father's concern, "but the guy who saved us, helped us escape, got shot. We need a surgeon to operate on him."

"Okay. I'll wait for your call."

Several hours had passed since their escape from Palau Dalmases. The escapees had managed to stay underground so far, but it was difficult. Aarno's dad arranged for them to get out of Barcelona as promised. He asked one of his closest business associates for help. Using his political contacts, the associate made arrangements for a big luxury yacht and ways to smuggle it out through the port of Barcelona. The port officials were on the payroll of many organizations. The politicians, though, had the last word.

The yacht arrived. It was a herculean task to regroup and load everyone onto the vessel, especially a bleeding Matthew, but it went through without any problems. Everyone made it onto the yacht. The five men, along with their rescued family and friends, were on their way sailing into the Mediterranean Sea.

"I assume we're heading directly to Finland, sir?" the captain asked.

"No, I don't think we should go to Finland," Liang interrupted. "They'll expect us to go to one of the places we consider safe."

"Sí, they know a lot about us," Diego agreed.

Aarno nodded. "All right, captain, let's sail in the opposite direction. Let's go south."

The yacht was a high-end luxury model. There was a makeshift operation room along with a surgeon that Aarno's father's associate had arranged for them. No sooner did they embark on the vessel than Matthew was taken into the surgery room. The procedure lasted hours. Despite their exhaustion, they waited outside for updates.

Ojoré's heart was heavy. His guilt grew by the second. *All I wish is for Matthew to come out of this all right.*

After several hours, the surgeon walked out.

"Is he all right? Will he make it?" Ojoré asked desperately.

"Yes, he is fortunate. The bullet did not hit any major organs. But..."

"But what?"

"I'm not going to lie; he lost a lot of blood."

"I can give blood. We all can."

"Well, as it turns out, his blood is the rarest."

They all stared at each other.

"But luckily again, I'm told that the owner of this boat has the same blood group as Matthew. Because it's so rare and difficult to find if there's an emergency, they keep it stocked, just in case. We'll start blood transfusion immediately, he should be out of danger, and gain consciousness in a few hours."

Father's associate must be an important person, Aarno thought. *What kind of business is he in to have medical equipment on board?*

"Thank you, doctor." Aarno shook his hand.

"Yes, thank you, thank you very, very much, doctor." Ojoré followed.

He turned around and looked at the others. They were relieved.

"Matthew helped us, risked his life for us. We owe him our freedom."

"Yes, I'm so glad he's safe."

They nodded.

"So, what now?" Liang stood with his arms folded.

"I guess once we go to a safe port, we go our separate paths," Darren replied.

"Are you insane?" Liang said. "These guys know where we live. They tracked us down somehow; they won't let go of us so easily. We have to stick together."

"You're right," Aarno concurred. "We must find out what they're after, what they need from us."

"And how the hell do we find that out?" Darren banged his fist on the counter.

"Sánchez." Liang displayed a confident face. "He's the key to all our questions."

"Then what the hell are we waiting for?"

CHAPTER 45

Let's Begin

Mediterranean Sea

Ocean breeze caressed their faces and soothed their bodies as they stood on the yacht's upper deck. The vessel took them hundreds of miles from Barcelona, deep into the Mediterranean Sea. Calm. Their exhaustion disappeared. Their fatigue vanished.

After many days of fluid injections, the sumptuous meal prepared by the yacht's chef enticed their taste buds. With a full belly, Darren was the happiest. "Aarno, thanks a lot, man." He shook Aarno's hand. "With the escape, running around everywhere, and tension, I never got the chance to thank you for what you've done for us and still doing."

"Yes, can't thank you enough, Aarno." Ojoré shook Aarno's hand too.

"The way you lead us out from there—" Darren patted his back, and Aarno shook with the force. The others nodded.

"C'mon, guys, it was not just me. Darren, we couldn't have come out of there without your strength or your aim, Ojoré. Liang, your ideas always help us, and Diego, your sharpness. We all did it."

"But arranging that place to hide after the escape and now this yacht—"

"It's all my father. None of it is because of me."

"But still," Diego chimed in, "we owe you for this."

"Guys, we're all in this together. Let's not get into all this, I'm sure we will have a reason someday to thank one another for one thing or another." Aarno smiled at them and patted each one on the arm. "Now, let's not waste time and see where Sánchez is."

They all went downstairs. Sánchez was locked up in the bottommost cabin of the yacht, handcuffed to the bed. One crewmember was tasked with patrolling him.

"Open his handcuffs," Aarno ordered the crewmember as they all rushed into the room.

"Yes, sir."

As the handcuffs came off, Sánchez brushed his wrists and sat on the edge of the bed. The small cabin made it difficult for them to fit in, but somehow, they managed. Diego and Ojoré took a corner and stood in silence with folded arms. Two small oval windows presented views of the endless water outside. The side table, chair, and walls were lined with polished wood trim, while the floor was covered with a maroon carpet. Bulkhead lights mounted on the walls lit the room in a warm yellow.

Aarno was about to open his mouth, but Darren cut him down and shot a let-me-handle-this look. Aarno stopped.

"Listen carefully." Darren came face to face with Sánchez, staring directly into his eyes. "We'll ask you questions only once, and you better answer them with utmost honesty."

"What if I don't?"

"We'll find your family, and we—" Liang said.

But Sánchez interrupted. "I no longer have a family; they are my past. I'm a new man now, my mission is my only purpose. Go ahead, do whatever you want with them."

Silence. The room rose up and down as a few strong waves hit the yacht. They moved their bodies to balance themselves.

When things calmed, Liang asked. "So, what's your mission?"

Sánchez smiled. "Again, why should I tell you?"

At that instant, Darren grabbed Sánchez, pulled his arms backward from his torso.

Pain surged through Sánchez's body. "Aaaaaa," he screamed.

"I'm not even trying yet," Darren whispered in Sánchez's ears. "You've seen my strength, but you haven't seen my rage." Darren smiled a devious smile. "I don't know what your mission is, but my mission is payback."

"Please stop it, please. I'll tell you. What do you want to know?" Sánchez screamed.

"Easy, Darren." Aarno placed a hand on Darren's back.

"Aarno, you know he deserves this," Darren said, still holding on to Sánchez.

"I do, but please let him go." Aarno's eyes were stern.

Darren released Sánchez's arms reluctantly.

"Why did Drágosláv kidnap us?" Liang asked, staring into Sánchez's eyes.

"You know that; we told you. You are special; all of you." Sánchez looked from one to another as he spoke.

Unsatisfied with the reply, Darren pulled the arms back again. "Tell us something we don't know then."

Sánchez screwed his face in agony. "Okay, okay, but release me, please. It's a long story. It'll take hours for me to explain."

"You better not play with us. I'll skin you like a chicken with my bare hands." Darren's face went red.

"I promise; just stop, please stop the pain." Sweat ran down Sánchez's neck.

On Aarno's insistence, Darren released him.

Sánchez coughed hard. With a short breath, he composed himself and reoccupied the edge of the bed. "It'll take a long time to explain," he said, wiping the sweat on his face and neck. "You'll need a lot of patience and concentration to understand. Are you ready for that?"

The five looked at each other.

Nodded in unison.

CRISES

The yacht was huge, and so was the upper deck. It had several sofa-type seats, a bar, and a hot tub on the top deck. Sánchez was moved from his room and handcuffed to the edge of the bar counter. They all took the plush seats.

"Seriously? You think I can escape from here, in the middle of this freaking sea? Do you have any idea how many miles I'll have to swim? Do you really think I can survive that?"

"Like I said, I want payback. It's for what you did to us." Darren took his clothes off and descended into the hot tub. His weight caused the water to rise to the rim.

It was indeed a good idea by Liang to move outside where they held Sánchez. The room was too small for all of them.

"Before I begin, would you please extend me the courtesy of a drink?" Sánchez looked at Aarno. "It'll make it easier to start."

Aarno nodded at the bartender.

"Get me whichever most expensive single malt you have. On the rocks, please."

"Anything for you, sirs?" the bartender asked, looking at the five. One by one, they all ordered their drinks. Aarno ordered a Red Bull. He decided to stay sober. Minutes later, the bartender returned with all their drinks.

"Please leave us alone. I'll call you if I need you. Tell the others not to disturb," Aarno said after the last drink was served.

"To the beginning of our new lives." Sánchez raised his own glass.

No one responded. They all gulped their drinks.

The burn of the liquor slowly cascaded down their chest and into their bellies. Their heads got lighter. Tiny hints of bronze and gold appeared in the night sky. The sunlight subdued the darkness and the mercurial waters beneath. The water displayed its usual deep blue. It was the best scene they had seen in months.

"That's enough, let's get back to it."

"Alright, big man," Sánchez took a big sip from his scotch. "But, before I begin, make sure you listen very carefully. The knowledge of what I'm about to tell you is wealth in its most precious form, more precious than anything in this world." He took another sip.

"Sometimes it'll feel overwhelming, other times confusing, and a few times it'll even feel absurd. It'll feel as if it does not make sense or as if there's no logic. But trust me, it all makes sense in the end."

They stared at him like deer.

"One more thing, absorb it as it is, without prejudice." He looked at them again. No one said anything. They were losing patience. Sánchez took a big pause.

Realizing there was no way out, he closed his eyes and wondered where to begin. The reality, the truth, the weight, the unworldliness of the reason was so grand and enormous that he found himself overwhelmed.

He breathed a deep sigh, inhaled a vast amount of air, and readied himself to begin the mother story. "Let's begin."

CHAPTER 46

Are They All Right?

Somewhere

"What's happening to them?" Aroon's joints ached, muscles stiffened, and his throat dried as he asked that question. Pain soared through his head. It felt like a hangover from a night of heavy drinking. Sweat ran down his forehead. His heart pounded like a steam engine.

In front of him, the monkeys collapsed like pieces of a domino.

Poor animals, they sucked the venom from my body, and now suffering because of that. What if they die? I don't want them to die.

"Are they dead?" he asked.

"No," replied The Ghost, "they're not dead. They are unconscious."

He lifted the Alpha monkey's eyelids. The eyes lacked the purple of the venom.

"The venom does not have the same effect on them as it has on us. Their bodies are immune to the poison, but it causes pain; sometimes they pass out."

"But they will be all right, won't they?"

"Yes. They'll be all right."

"When will they wake up?"

"It'll take a few hours for their bodies to digest the venom. It's dangerous indeed. You would have died or worse, had they not sucked it out from your wound."

"Worse? Worse? What's worse than dying?"

The Ghost turned and smiled at Aroon. "There are worse evils than death, my friend. Just hope that we don't come to see them."

Outside the cave, tigers continued to roar. Aroon slid to the edge of the stone bed, placed his feet on the ground, and stood up. His body swayed from one side to another. He panted.

"What's going on? Will they attack us again?"

"Don't worry, we're safe. They can't come here, at least not for quite a while."

"Aaah!" Aroon's pain was unrelenting. "What's happening to me?"

"Sit down. You must rest." The Ghost held his shoulders and pushed him down. "Here, drink this, you'll feel better."

The White Ghost walked outside and let out a roar. The tigers obeyed and dispersed to guard their respective territories. When The Ghost returned, Aroon, who tried to stand again, gave up and reclined on the bed, resting his back on the hard wall.

"I don't understand. I could not see anything in there. What happened?"

"We were attacked by the—" The Ghost said but stopped mid-sentence.

"By the what?"

No reply.

I wonder how they knew about our presence, The Ghost thought.

"I was using it precisely for that reason," he murmured.

"What reason? Who were they?" The decibels in Aroon's voice increased.

"Oh. Umm, they? They're the denizens of the Shiny City, the city of innumerable riches."

"What happened to me over there?"

The Ghost ignored it and murmured again, "But how did they get there? Do they know about the confluence already?"

It's still in the nascent stage. Even I have to use my gem. No one used that route till now. Was it mere chance?

"What happened to me?" Aroon shouted.

"You? Right. You were attacked by them, bitten, to be more precise. One of them got hold of you while others attacked me." The Ghost paused for a few seconds, staring at his armor pierced with the needle-shaped thorns. "Their bite, their bite is very dangerous. The venom spreads to the entire body."

"And then you die?"

"If you're fortunate, you die, but if you're not, then—"

"Then what?"

"It gets worse."

"What can be worse than death?" Aroon asked a second time.

"A cursed life. You would've turned into them, but only partly, half human, half them." The ghost picked up his armor, inspected it for damage, and placed it on the side.

Half human-half them? Cursed life? Aroon's eyes widened in horror. *What have I gotten myself into?*

"If the monkeys had not sucked it out of me, I would have—?"

"Yes," The Ghost replied before Aroon could finish, "and then, you would've lost your identity, like a mutant, neither here nor there. You would've done their bidding."

"But won't the monkeys turn into them? Won't they force the monkeys?"

"No. As I said, the venom does not affect the apes in the same way as it affects us."

"But it will still have some effect on them, more than being unconscious, right?"

"Of course. It would have paralyzed a monkey or caused pain severe enough to drive it insane, but only if one had sucked the poison. So, you see, the creatures are not dumb; they know more than we give them credit. They all shared the poison, precisely sucking the right amount one by one."

How can I ever thank them?

"The time will come sooner than you think."

Aroon stood up again, but fell back on the stone bed immediately. He gathered his strength, stood up once more, waited a few seconds, and walked toward the armor on the side. Needle-shaped thorns protruded from it.

He ran his hand through the ends. "What are these?"

"One of their weapons." The Ghost plucked one out. "They shoot these at their enemy, You have to be careful while fighting them, the tips of these thorns are dangerous. Too many of these can paralyze."

The Ghost stared at his armor. "Luckily for me, my armor took the blow."

Aroon plucked a thorn. It was bone colored with black tips. After observing, he threw it away.

"What are we going to do now? What's our plan?"

"Our plan, my friend, is to continue our mission."

"Mission?"

The White Ghost used his gem's power and projected a vision onto the cave's ceiling. A building appeared. It was made of stones and had carvings on all sides that looked primeval.

"This is where we have to go."

"For what?"

"You know now what you're up against. You've experienced the dangers that lie in those worlds. What you saw was just the tip of the iceberg. This place is where you'll find your weapons. "

"Weapons?"

"I told you, the war is coming. And—"

"And what?"

"—and you have to arm yourself before the other side does."

CHAPTER
47

The Maiden's Ring

Mediterranean Sea

Five faces stared at Sánchez like a lender at his unpaying debtor. Not an eye blinked. Sánchez gulped a mouthful from his glass and deliberated on the silence for a few more seconds. Diego's left leg shook restlessly. Ojoré paced the deck.

"What the heck are you waiting for?" Darren shouted.

Sánchez's glass rested beside him on the deck floor with a *thud*. The expensive single malt was infused with melted ice. Aqueous and organic layers in the glass danced with each other like a couple performing salsa.

"It's a story from the old ages," Sánchez began, "of times forgotten." His eyes focused on the sky. "It started with her, the maiden. She lived deep inside the jungle near the banks of a river in her father's hermitage." He closed his eyes as if recalling times past. "Her beauty was mesmerizing. Her thick black hair fashioned into a long braid, her ocean-deep eyes, her wheatish complexion, her silk-soft skin, her fragrance, and every other detail about her made her irresistible."

Sánchez opened his eyes and brought the glass to eye level, observing the golden and clear strands mix and mingle. "She was unaware of the effect she had on others. After all, she had not met many people from outside. The jungle and hermitage were her home. It kept her insulated from the world outside and its complexities. She was gentle, humble, pleasant, and soft-spoken."

Sánchez continued, "Her father found her as a baby left inside a floating basket on the banks of the river that flowed by his hermitage. What a cherubic infant she was. He picked her up at once, embraced her, and took her inside. There, he raised her as his own and loved her with all his heart. Little did he know that she was not an ordinary child. She was born out of the union between a magical nymph and a famous sage. The sage was resolute, wise, and powerful. The nymph was commanded by the Noble Beings themselves to seduce him. He was in the final stages of his mission to obtain weapons that could destroy the Noble Beings. The Ignoble Beings were his masters.

"It was an easy job. The nymph broke his concentration. Her beauty was such that the sage abandoned his mission and became obsessed. His dedication perished against the sweet nectar of her fragrant and curvy body.

"Their passion gave birth to a girl child. After childbirth, the nymph left him and returned to her magical abode, for she did not belong there. It was just a task for her. It was time for her to get back to the world where she dwelt.

"Her absence drove the sage mad. He searched for her everywhere but could not find her. The child reminded him of the nymph, for she had her mother's uncanny resemblance. He tucked her in a basket and left her in the river."

"What's this to do with us?" Darren shouted. "You trying to fool us by telling us whatever comes to your mind?"

"I am not fooling you, I promise," Sánchez replied. "It'll make sense in the end, just listen. I'll tell you everything you need to know. I told you it would not make sense initially. But for you to understand it, I have to tell you everything."

The five men stared at each other. Although the story made no sense and didn't seem to have any connection to their abduction, something about it pulled them in, like a string from a fishing rod.

After eye contact with others, Aarno nodded. "Go on, what happened next?"

Sánchez swallowed. "Well, one day, when her father was away, the maiden went to the river to fetch water. She submerged her crock into the running stream, filled it up, and placed it on the side by her waist. On her way back, as she followed the familiar footpath, out of nowhere, armored men surrounded her. They had swords, shields, and spears. Her crock fell and shattered into a thousand pieces. She sobbed. She was not used to people ganging up like that.

"Retreat," came a voice from behind the men. A young, handsome man sitting on a pearl white horse emerged from the bushes.

"Kneel before the king," shouted one.

She obeyed without question. Her body trembled in fear.

"Please, rise," the king said. "Something as beautiful as you should have nothing to fear about, my lady." He smiled a wide smile. "I was hunting with my crew. We did not mean to intrude, my lady. Please forgive us."

"The entire jungle is yours, Y- Y- Your Majesty," she stammered. "And I'm no lady. I am just a simple girl."

Her father had told her about the king and the royal family.

Her beauty, her gentle voice enchanted the king. Her simplicity, her charm struck him. "Where do you live?" he asked.

"In my father's hermitage, my lord. Over there."

"I'm sorry about the crock. Is there anything I could do to make up for it?"

"You need not worry, my lord. I'll make another one."

Their eyes met. There was silence. He smiled. She returned the smile.

"It's getting dark, I must go back." The maiden bowed and retreated.

They went their separate ways but couldn't stop thinking about each other. The memory of her kept him awake all night. Miles away, she could not stop thinking about his charisma.

The following day, the king couldn't resist the temptation, returned, and so it went on. Their courtship continued for several weeks, and they fell in love.

"I want to marry you."

"My King- but you- you. I don't know what to say."

"A yes, perhaps."

Silence.

"You'll have to ask my father, ask my hand in marriage, I mean."

"So it's a yes?"

She blushed.

"When will your father return?"

"In a few weeks."

"Oh." The king sighed, his face dismayed.

"What is it?"

"There's unrest in the West. Soon, I will go far to meet the lord of that province. It can be months before I return. I'm afraid I can't wait until your father returns." He held her hands, kissed her cheeks, and looked into her eyes. "Let's get married now," the king proposed.

"But my father is not here. Besides, who will be the witness?"

"The trees can be our witnesses," he suggested. "The Sylvan Beings do it this way, don't they?"

"Father says so, but I haven't met any of the Sylvan Beings."

"Don't you trust me, my love?"

"With my life, my lord."

Their mutual attraction was tantalizing. They got married the same evening.

The trees in the hermitage and her cattle bore witness to their wedding. For two days, they made passionate love to each other as husband and wife. After the honeymoon, the king left on his expedition to the West. Before leaving, though, he gave his royal ring to her.

"Something to remember me by."

Her eyes unleashed the tears.

Days went by like they always do when a person is longing for another.

"Lady, I told you umpteen times the king is not in the city," the palace guard yelled.

"But he said he will return from the West in a few months."

"He told you? He told you? Guys, she says the king told her he'll be back in a few weeks."

The guards laughed. "Who are you? His wife?" The laughter continued.

"Yes. I am his wife. We married in the hermitage; the trees bore witness."

"The trees bore witness, she says, the trees, my friends." The mocking broke like a plague.

"Listen, lady, you have to stop coming here and stop making up stories. Whoever's it is, it's not the king's," the guard said, looking at her pregnant belly, laughing some more.

"Besides, the unrest in the West has turned into a rebellion. The king has more important matters right now. No one knows how long it'll take for him to return."

Crestfallen, she returned to the hermitage. A few months later, she gave birth to their son. It took several years for the king to defeat the rebellion. Then, one day, the maiden's father came running into the house.

"The king has returned, he's back. But—"

"But what?" she asked.

"They say he is bruised and frail. The battles have taken a toll, affected his memory somehow."

"He will remember me. I am his wife." Without wasting time, she rushed to the palace.

"You say you are my wife, woman. Yet I don't remember you. You have witnesses, someone who was there during our wedding?" the king asked.

"Yes, my lord, the trees."

"The trees, the trees, you say!"

The court broke into a guffaw.

"You have other proof, my lady? Unfortunately, the trees cannot speak, can they?"

"Don't you remember me, my beloved?"

She had searched for the royal ring. But it was lost.

"I'm sorry, but I don't remember you. How can I accept you without proof? It can be my enemies' plot for all we know."

She wiped her tears. "I swear," she said, looking at the nobility present in the court, shaking her head.

The next second, she composed herself. A determined expression took her face. "I will never step another foot in this palace again." She turned and stared into the king's eyes. "Even if you come begging."

oჳ80

Years passed like they do when one is raising a child. The maiden's son grew up to be a handsome man. Like his father, he had charisma, strength, and skill.

Maybe it was the son's luck or the maiden's, but the ring was found.

"I won't set foot in the court that humiliated me. If you want to see your father, I won't stop you. Take the ring with you."

No sooner did the king see the ring than all the memories resurfaced.

"No, no, no! What sin have I committed?" he screamed.

He immediately rushed to her. "Please forgive me, my beloved. My brain deceived me. Please come with me and take your rightful place as queen. I beg you."

"That'll be unfair to your present wife, the rightful queen and mother of your children."

"My firstborn will be my successor," the king declared.

"That'll not change a thing for me. I'm withdrawing from the world and dedicating my life to the Almighty. If you desire, take our son with you," she said.

It was the king's turn to suffer. This time, though, he was not going to part from her. He passed the kingdom into the hands of their son and joined her.

Sánchez looked at the others. They looked tired but still curious.

"What happened next? The king's other wife and kids did not complain?" Liang asked

"They did, even fought. There were coups, but the king was adamant. Besides, in no time, the maiden's son won over everyone's hearts in the court. His mother passed the nymph's and sage's blood to him. He had the looks, the brains, and the dedication. On the other hand, the maiden and the king lived for many years in each other's company, away from the kingdom before death did them part."

"And what happened to their son?" Ojoré asked.

"Their son became one of the greatest kings who ruled the land. He established and ruled an empire that stretched for thousands of miles. His was an ideal reign, it's said."

"What was his name?" Aarno asked.

"The maiden's name was Shakoontalá, the king was called Dooshyant, and their son was called Emperor Bharat."

"It's like a fairytale," Diego said.

Liang stood up, lingered along the deck rails, and peered into the distant ocean. "It's fascinating."

Darren stared at the sky from the Jacuzzi. "Shakoontalá," he murmured.

"It's complex," Aarno said. "Noble Beings, Ignoble Beings, Sylvan Beings, there are so many things in the story."

"I have not even scratched the surface of this story yet," Sánchez smirked. "You have no idea how complex it's about to get."

CHAPTER 48

The Arabian Mansion

Mediterranean Sea

A arno heard footsteps approaching the deck and stood up. An attendant was rushing up the stairs. "I told you not to disturb us."

"I'm sorry, sir," the attendant replied, "but it's urgent. The doctor wants you in the operating theater immediately."

"Why? What's the matter?"

"I'm not sure. He told me to get you immediately."

"Darren," Aarno said looking at Sánchez. "You wait. Keep an eye on him."

The remaining four hurried downstairs. Ojoré was in the front.

"Doctor, is everything all right? Is Matthew okay?" he asked before Aarno could speak.

"We need more blood," the doctor said, removing his facemask.

"But you said you have enough blood."

The refrigerator broke. Only one bottle survived. I'm sorry, but we need blood right away. I'm afraid he won't make it otherwise."

"What blood type do you need?"

"B, Rh Null, it's very rare. We should immediately call for emergency help and go to the nearest port. But—"

"But what?"

"But we might still be late."

This can't happen. There must be a way. He can't die like this. God, please help.

"Anyone have that blood type?" Aarno looked around.

Silence.

Ojoré went to the bedside and held Matthew's hand. "Don't worry, we'll not let you die."

"I'll go check with others. Maybe someone has the same type." He ran outside.

He went to each and every room. Friends, family, crew, anyone he could find. Unfortunately, no one had a blood type that matched. Downhearted, he rushed to the upper deck.

"What is your blood type?" Ojoré panted as he asked.

"A positive," replied Darren.

"We need blood for Matthew. They're out of it, a very rare type." Ojoré's face fell. He walked up to the rails, rested his hands on them, and stared at the deep blue sea. The rising and falling waves reflected light as the sun shone on them from above.

"What's his blood type?" Sánchez's voice came from behind.

Ojoré ignored, closed his eyes. "He is critical, I don't know what to do." A tear rolled down his cheek.

Darren stood up, went beside him, and placed an arm around him.

"What's his blood type?" Sánchez asked again.

"B Rh Null."

Sánchez laughed. Ojoré and Darren turned around. "What're you laughing at?" Darren's nostrils flared as he asked.

"Well, it's his lucky day. I have the same blood type. Let's go." Sánchez grinned.

Sánchez was uncuffed and rushed downstairs.

The surgeon escorted him inside and asked him to lie down on the bed beside Matthew. Next second, he rubbed a piece of alcohol-infused cotton on Sánchez's arm, inserted the needle, and started the blood transfusion.

The wait was nervous.

After a few tense hours, the doctor returned. "There's good news, he is stable, the blood saved his life."

"Will he be all right?"

"Let's all pray."

They came out of the room and onto the aft deck. Aarno stayed behind to talk with the doctor.

No one spoke for a while.

Darren and Ojoré stood by the rails, looking at the yacht's wake beneath.

"I just hope he'll make it through this." Ojoré stared at the hypnotic patterns of the wake.

Darren placed a hand around his shoulder. "Don't worry, he'll be all right. Despite having the rarest blood types, we found a match on the yacht, didn't we? It's not his time yet."

"Darren." Ojoré smiled at Darren. "From outside, you seem very strong and menacing. Some would even call you arrogant. But now that I know you better, I can see you have a soft heart."

"Well, most times I am all right, ain't I? It's when people mess with me that I get angry."

They laughed a hearty laugh.

Diego and Liang stood by the taffrails beside the door on the other side of the deck. Diego's face looked as if longing for something.

"Missing home?" Liang's back rested on the rails.

"Missing football. Haven't gone without being on the field for this long since I was six. God knows when we will get out of this, when I will get to play again."

Liang nodded. "It is so weird. A few weeks back, we didn't know of each other's existence, but now, look at us. Who would have thought I would be here, on this yacht, with four strangers from different corners of the world? Fleeing from danger."

"We are strangers, but it doesn't feel like it, does it? When we were fighting back there during the escape, our synchrony, our timing, was effortless. It's not easy to develop that trust, that connection. Trust me, I have played football all my life. It takes months to years of playing together to get that in teammates."

"That's true. I could read you pretty well in there. It didn't feel like I was fighting for the first time with you. It felt like we had teamed up before."

Aarno came to join them.

"Why did you stay back?" Liang asked

"Just wanted to ask the doctor about Sánchez," Aarno said

"Yeah, let's take that freaking s.o.b back?" Darren raised his hand.

"They withdrew a lot of blood from him, as much as they could. The doc says he's weak and should rest."

"He'll be fine." Darren patted Aarno's upper arm. "Let's go get him," he said to the others.

"Easy, Darren, he's not going anywhere. Besides, we all need some rest as well." Aarno looked at the others. "Alright, folks, let's rest while we can."

⚜

Lack of motion woke Aarno. He grabbed his pants from the nearby chair, pulled them above his boxers, slid his feet into the slippers, and darted toward the deck. The yacht was docked. Ojoré, Darren, Diego, and Liang were also on the deck. The captain was on the level below, giving instructions to his crew.

"Captain, captain," Aarno shouted. "Where are we?"

"We're at Jeddah, sir."

"Saudi Arabia?"

He nodded. "Your father called and asked me to make a stop here."

No sooner did they anchor than a tall man wearing a thawb and keffiyeh walked inside. He ascended to their deck and came toward Aarno.

"Hello and welcome to Jeddah, Mr. Heikkinen. My name is Abdullah. I work for your father's friend."

"Is this his yacht?" Aarno asked.

"Yes. Your father is here too. He is waiting for you."

In a few minutes, they disembarked and followed Abdullah. A fleet of Rolls-Royces took them to a mansion along the coast. It was colossal. The rooms were spectacular. Rugs with designs of flowers and leaves covered the floor, while pure silk curtains—handcrafted to perfection—enhanced the décor of the chamber. The mansion was filled with Middle Eastern antiques. A large brass ewer stood in the corner of every single room, while beautiful glass chandeliers hung from the ceilings above. The mesmerizing fragrance of attar promulgated from the linen into the air.

"My boys, oh my boys, are you all right?" Aarno's dad rushed into the room. He hugged Aarno and Aarvo tightly. "I was so worried. Tell me, tell me, are you both all right?"

"We're fine, Father," Aarno replied.

"Who are these people that kidnapped you? What do they want?"

"We don't know. The person who kidnapped us is the leader of the Odessa Mafia, a large drug cartel. We're working on getting that information."

"Thank God you got out. You can't imagine how miserable I was." He hugged the two brothers again.

His father wanted to ask more questions but decided against it. "We'll go home. Figure this out."

"Father, I know you want us to return home, especially after all this, but I am sorry. I can't come with you. Take Aarvo with you. I have to stay to figure this out, know the reason behind our abduction."

"But we've connections in Finland. You'll be safe there."

"They're dangerous people, Father; they'll find a way to get to us. The best way to be safe is to find out why they are after us and then take action." Aarno looked into his father's eyes.

"I suggest you not return home for some time as well. They're not just after me, they'll take anyone I care about. Please listen to me, Father."

Mr. Heikkinen shook his head, not ready to accept.

"Father, he's right. He needs to do this," Aarvo spoke.

"All right, we can stay here. This is my friend's place. We can stay here as long as we want."

"It's best if we don't stay anywhere for long, Father. You both stay here and relocate in a few days. Meanwhile, my companions and I will leave. I hope your friend will let us borrow his yacht for some more time."

"But, my son–"

"You have to let me go."

Aarno's father stayed motionless.

"We need the yacht, Father."

Mr. Heikkinen took his time to nod his approval.

"Of course, anything you need, my son. I'll let him know. He's abroad on some business at the moment, but it won't be a problem."

"Thank you, Father. Now, if you excuse me, I have to go check on my friends. I'll be back soon."

CRISO

The five men met where Matthew was moved. He was conscious.

"How do you feel, Matthew?" Ojoré occupied Matthew's bedside and took his hand.

"Not bad, a little weak though."

"Thanks for saving my girlfriend." Liang shook his hand. "I can't thank you enough."

"I'm sure you would've done the same thing, mate." Matthew smiled.

"Your son's safe now." Aarno came forward. "He's here. He'll be moved to a safe place shortly."

"Thank you, thank you very much, Mr. Heikkinen. I don't know how I'll repay you."

"Call me Aarno, and about repayment, you already have my friend, you already have."

Everyone except Ojoré left the room. He kissed Matthew on the forehead.

"Thanks for everything. We're waiting for you to get well soon," he said, looking into Matthew's eyes.

CHAPTER 49

Benign Murders

Jeddah, Saudi Arabia

Matthew's recovery relieved them, especially Ojoré.
"The captain said he'll be ready to sail early morning," Aarno told the others.

"Let's not waste any time. I want to get over it. Where's Sánchez? I want to hear rest of the damn story." Darren scowled.

They made a beeline for the room where Sánchez was held. Darren and Ojoré escorted him out onto the terrace.

"Easy, easy, I'm complying, ain't I? No need to rough me up like that." Sánchez freed his hands from Darren and moved toward Ojoré. Ojoré handcuffed him to the door.

"Not again, my wrists are sore from these."

"These are just handcuffs. You freakin' covered us with chains, forgot that? If I had my way, you would be in those same chains. Thank your luck these four are here to save your ass from me." Darren was in Sánchez's face, his lips pressed in anger.

"Let it go, Darren, come let's sit," Aarno said.

Darren retreated.

The view from the terrace was majestic. The sun was on its way out. A neatly landscaped lawn with several palm trees stretched from the mansion to the beach. Gentle waves kissed the sandy beach like a lover caressing his lady.

They took seats. A man brought out a few hookahs made of stained glass with a ceramic top to hold the tobacco and a protruding stem on the side connected to a pipe. At the end of the pipe was a nozzle to suck the vapor.

"With compliments, enjoy," he said and left.

Darren was the first to grab the pipe. He inhaled a long drag and coughed his lungs out.

"It's very strong." He coughed some more.

They laughed a hearty laugh.

The pipe moved from one hand to another. Nicotine calmed their nerves.

As they settled down, Darren came straight to the point. "What happened next? What happened to Bharat?"

"Good, so you remember what I said." Sánchez smiled. "But first, won't you offer some to me?" He pointed at the hookah. "Just to get me started."

Ojoré moved his hookah toward Sánchez. "There. Now begin."

Sánchez sucked hard, exhaled, smoke.

"So, Emperor Bharat, son of the maiden and the king, ruled his empire justly. His subjects loved him. He had several queens and fathered many sons. His empire was filled with abundance, and justice was served without prejudice; the ideal reign, they say, was only second to King Rám, who preceded him thousands of years ago. With many children, everyone wondered who Emperor Bharat would choose as his heir. In his eyes, though, none was worthy.

"Royal blood is not enough; only a deserving person should be king, and that could be anyone," Emperor Bharat told his court one day.

After his marriage to his youngest queen, the Noble Beings–the Dévs—presented Bharat with a boy named Vitáth. Bharat adopted him as his own. As Vitáth grew up, Bharat became very fond of him.

"All the qualities I desire in my successor, Vitáth has them all," Bharat told his council of ministers. "I want Vitáth to take over the reins after I am gone. He will be my heir."

"But, Your Majesty, the laws of succession don't allow a commoner or adopted son to take the throne," his prime minister reasoned.

Bharat struggled with the dilemma of succession for several months. It was then that his youngest queen told him a secret, a secret she held dear to her heart. Only the Dévs knew about it. They had orchestrated it.

"My King, I need to tell you something," she said.

"What is it, my Queen?"

"I beg your pardon for not revealing this to you sooner."

"Speak freely, without fear."

"Vitáth was born to me before marriage, and according to the laws of lineage, Vitáth is eligible for the throne."

Bharat's heart split between anger and joy, but eventually, Bharat's love for Vitáth won, and he named him the successor.

"So, let me guess, he and Vitáth were killed by his own children in a coup," Darren said lazily, his face looking unimpressed.

"Nothing about this story is that predictable, big guy." Sánchez smiled at Darren. "Emperor Bharat was so revered and loved by his children that they all believed in his words and obeyed without question."

"Then?" Liang's curiosity showed on his face.

"Well, like his father, Bharat gave up his kingdom and retreated into the mountains for spirituality. It was a custom in those times, at least in those lands, to let go of one's earthly possessions and make way for the next generation to take responsibility.

"Vitáth ruled the empire as fairly as his father, upholding the same values. Vitáth's descendant Hustee was another famous emperor in his line. Hustee built a grand capital for his vast empire. Named after him, it was called Hustinápoori.

"Hustinápoori was a magnificent city, full of wealth, riches, and all the comforts of the world. Drenched in marble, silk, and gold, the royal palace was like none ever built. Beautiful gardens with magical fountains bloomed throughout the palace. There was plenty for everyone."

Sánchez closed his eyes as if imagining the entire city. His nostrils exhaled the nicotine-infused vapor.

Beneath the terrace in the lawn, sprinklers popped out. A breeze from the Arabian Sea hit their faces. As the sun disappeared, lights sprang to life. Sermons for evening prayer emanated from the loudspeaker installed on the minaret of a distant mosque. The prominent silhouette of the minaret, its crescent moon on top, along the backdrop of the Arabian Sea, was breathtaking.

"For ease of administration, Hustee divided the empire into several smaller territories," Sánchez continued. "All the chancellors of these territories answered to the Emperor in Hustinápoori."

"After a generation, Emperor Hustee's grandson Kuru occupied the throne. Kuru's reign was challenged by countless rebellions. The empire fragmented, with chancellors breaking away and declaring themselves kings of their territories. They say Kuru's deputy plotted against him and encouraged the chancellors to rebel.

"In response, Emperor Kuru cleared a vast piece of land around Hustinápoori and converted it into a battleground to fight anyone who challenged to take over the capital. This land was called Kurukshetra.

"Kuru fought many wars in Kurukshetra and defeated all his enemies. Many good soldiers, generals, and kings lost their lives there. Innumerable stories of valor, friendship, sorrow, and joy come from this land. Legend has it that whosoever died in Kurukshetra fighting bravely went directly to Swarg—home of the Dévs."

Uhoo, Uhoo, Uhoo. The narration was interrupted as Sánchez coughed.

Darren walked toward him, snatched the pipe. "Ain't no need for you to smoke."

Uhoo, Uhoo, Uhoo.

"Go on," Darren ordered. "Now."

"Fine." Sánchez coughed some more. "Jesus." He gulped down the water beside him to help his throat. He sighed a long sigh.

"Emperor Kuru passed the empire to his son Prateep, who was a pragmatist. He knew that the kings who broke off from the empire had grown in strength, and it was not wise to fight them. He understood that they could join hands to take over his empire. Through diplomatic missions and marriages, he carefully made alliances with some of the weaker kingdoms. He helped them become strong. After some turmoil and brief wars amongst themselves, there was a truce. Prateep had saved his empire from disintegrating further. He still ruled Hustinápoori.

"Prateep's son Shántanu maintained the status quo. There were no new wars. All the broken-off kingdoms and the empire lived in peace. There were marriages among the royal families of the many separated kingdoms and the empire."

"Now it gets very important, so listen carefully." Sánchez stood up.

"Where do you think you're going? I still can't think of any connection between us and this story."

"I'll tell you. Have some patience, country boy. Maybe you'll figure it out yourself if you use that brain instead of the muscle."

"Let him complete, Darren," Aarno said, "in the end, you can have your way if this turns out to be bullshit."

"Your damn right I'll have my way!"

Silence.

Liang scribbled in a notebook that he got from the captain. As Sánchez narrated, he mapped the lineage.

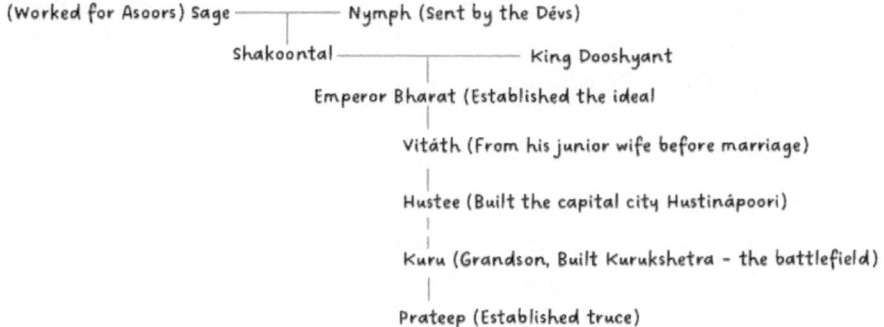

"Moving forward—" Sánchez hastily got back on track to avoid Darren's wrath. "—one afternoon, Emperor Shántanu was taking a stroll along the banks of Gungá—the holiest of rivers. After carving mountains, valleys, and rocks for hundreds of miles with its powerful currents, the river donned a calm character in this kingdom.

"The day was hot. Shántanu paused to catch his breath. He splashed the cold, soothing water on his face, and when he raised his head, a beautiful lady emerged from the depths of the gentle waters. She slowly catwalked in his direction.

"To Shántanu, it appeared as if she walked on water in slow motion. Her perfectly curved body was draped in a fabulous dress, which looked as though water droplets were woven together to make up its fabric. Mist oozed from it and cooled the surroundings. As she came closer, a mesmerizing fragrance filled the air. It was nothing like Shántanu had ever smelled before. It was out of this world. Shántanu was spellbound."

Ojoré stood up. The same thing had happened to him. He dreamed of it night after night. His heart soared. *Is it her? The one I met in Africa. The one who saved me from the hyenas?*

"I think I have met her," he said.

The other four knew this. Ojoré had told them his story during their captivity in Barcelona.

"You have? That's intriguing. Where did you meet her?"

Liang shook his head sideways, looking at Ojoré.

Ojoré understood. He went silent.

"Doesn't matter," Darren intervened. "Get back to the story."

"So now, do you believe I'm not making this up?" Sánchez looked at Aarno. "Don't you believe there's a connection between this story and you?" He moved his gaze toward Ojoré.

No reply.

"Really?" He stared into each of their eyes. "Right then." He seized the pipe from Ojoré, sucked deep from its mouth, and exhaled toward the sky. "Shántanu looked into her eyes as she approached him. They were a hypnotic deep blue, capable of drowning the best swimmers within its mesmerizing depths."

"Who are you, beautiful lady?" he asked

"I'm Gungá, my lord." Her voice was melodious, like a nightingale's song.

"Where did you come from? I've not seen you here before."

"I have always been here, my lord. Always." There was a pause between "My Lord" and "always" that emphasized it.

"Gungá was no ordinary woman," Sánchez continued. "Like Shakoontalá's mother, she was an Upsará—nymph of the river that gave her the name, and like Shakoontalá's mother, Gungá was sent by the Dévs."

"Dévs, Dévs, Dévs—and who were the others you mentioned?" Liang asked

"Asoors–the Ignoble Beings."

"Seems like the Dévs and the Asoors influence much of what happens in this story."

"Indeed. Dévs and Asoors are each other's nemesis. The Dévs live in a place called Swarg, while the Asoors are dwellers of Narck. There are other groups as well. Gundharvs—the Sylvan Beings—treelike celestial musicians and warriors, Yakshs—keepers of the golden lands, then there are Rákshass—masters of the wind, barbaric nonetheless, and Nágs—serpent lords, dreaded for their venom. If I delve into these beings, we'll have to wait weeks before you find out how this relates to you."

The five were on their feet. Sánchez's revelation about the Gundharvs, Yakshs, Rákshass, Nágs, and Upsarás shook them. They huddled together.

"This is it. Sánchez's story is finally connecting to our pasts," Aarno whispered. "I had accidentally entered the golden lands of the Yakshs after the death of my mother. Darren, the tornado you survived in Kansas was driven by a Rákshass. Ojoré, you were saved from the hyena in Kenya by an Upsará. Diego, you were bitten by a Nágs in the Amazon rainforest, and Liang, you were saved from the poachers by the Gundharvs."

"Why are you all standing? Is there something you all want to tell me?" Sánchez interrupted.

No one spoke.

"Don't be shy. Ask."

The silence continued for several minutes. They all stared at each other.

Finally, Aarno spoke, "We don't want to break the momentum. Continue where you stopped."

"I can almost read the questions on your minds from your faces. I have answers to all. Go ahead, ask."

"No need," Darren said. "Continue your story."

"Did you all realize something just now? A connection between you and this story?"

"None of your freaking business, tell the rest of your damn story."

Looking at Darren's menacing face, Sánchez decided not to push. "Fine." He shrugged. "If that's what you want." He took a sip from his glass of water, gargled, and spat it out. "So, Shántanu stared at Gungá uninhibited, admiring each and every part of her divine body. Enchanted.

Out of nowhere, the words parted his lips. "Marry me."

It was déjà vu', like Dooshyant and Shakoontalá again. However, the fate of this relationship was different.

"But, my lord—"

"You will be my queen; I'll give you all the pleasures of this world."

Gungá considered for a while. "I don't want the pleasures of this world, my lord. I dwell in Swarg. I have them all."

"Then what is it that you desire, my lady? I'll do anything for you. Anything. Please marry me."

"Are you sure?"

"I've never been surer of anything in my life, my beautiful lady."

She paused again. "I'll marry you only on one condition."

"What is it?"

"If I marry you, you will not question what I do or stop me from what I do. No matter how bizarre or cruel it may seem. You will never question me. You will trust me and my decisions."

Shántanu was so infatuated by her beauty and charm that he said, "I will not question you ever. I promise."

"If you break your promise, I will leave you immediately and never return. Agreed?"

"I will not break my promise, no matter what. I give you my word."

"Then, I accept your proposal. I will marry you."

"As strange as it sounds, they got married the next day. Months passed in bliss, as they often do when people are in love. Gungá made Emperor Shántanu very happy. Joy spread through the empire like spring through a valley."

"Your Majesty, congratulations, it's a boy!" the queen's maid announced.

"It's the best news I've heard in my entire life!" The king removed a gold ring from his index finger and handed it to the maid. "Your reward."

"Thank you, thank you, Your Majesty." She dismissed herself.

"Minister! Minister! Distribute sweets in every house of Hustinápoori, arrange for celebrations, put on the fireworks."

There were celebrations across the empire, the likes of which had never been seen before. Kings from far away sent their gifts. Gungá retained her mesmerizing beauty hours after childbirth. After all, she was an Upsará.

"Just when I think I can't love you more, my queen, you prove me wrong. My love for you can only grow stronger."

"I'm sorry, my lord, but even though he is ours, our own flesh and blood, he's not ours to keep."

"My queen, I understand it was stressful. Childbirth is exhausting."

"It's not what you think, my lord. I'm not out of my mind." Gungá cut him off immediately. "I completely understand what I am saying, and if I may remind you, you gave me your word. You promised you'd never question me. Now, unless you want to lose me, you will choose your next words wisely."

Shántanu did not dare to question her further.

The next day, Gungá took the baby to her river, gently placed him into the water, and, with teary eyes, drowned him.

The realm was shocked.

Shántanu was horrified. He mourned alone. Still, he kept his promise.

☙❧

Six months later, everything returned to normal, and to everyone's relief, Gungá was with child again.

"Minister, minister!" Shántanu's heart was filled with joy again.

But this child, too, met the same fate as Shántanu's firstborn.

Why is she doing this? Oh, God. Shántanu was miserable.

But I still love her; I don't want her to go. I can't break the promise.

On the streets, there were rumors.

"I think she is demented," said one.

"But who would question the Emperor?" asked the other.

This continued till Gungá ruthlessly drowned seven newborn babies in front of their father. Now, people cursed her openly.

"She's a witch, I tell you," a guard said.

"I think she's insane. His majesty should put her in the dungeons and find a new queen," said the other.

Shántanu himself questioned his love for her. *I won't let her kill any more of my children.*

So, when the eighth child was born, he stopped her on the way to the river.

"Wait! You're an evil woman, a witch. I know I promised to never question you, but I can't see any more of my innocent babies killed. Why are you doing this? Tell me. Tell me, for god's sake!" He shouted. "I will not let you kill this one. I forbid you!"

Tears trickled from Gungá's eyes.

"I was and I am only doing my duty, my lord. On your command, I will not hurt this baby. But, as you have broken your promise, I will leave you now."

The next few seconds went in silence.

"I will return this son of yours when he is ready and worthy to take the throne. But your interruption has cast dark clouds of misfortune on his and the entire empire's fate. You and your descendants will regret this in time."

"But, but, wait—" Shántanu realized he still loved her a lot. He ran toward her.

Her eyes were unfazed. "Farewell, my lord. Our journey together ends here," she said with a stern face.

Sánchez paused. They all looked at him.

"So, why did she kill her babies?" Liang asked almost instantly, his face showing his struggle with Gungá's deeds. He moved in his seat.

Sánchez made smoke rings in the air from the vapor he sucked from the pipe. They floated toward the dark sky and dispersed quickly as the sea breeze hit them. Stars twinkled here and there as night took hold, their numbers increasing with every passing minute. The gentle breeze on the terrace had cooled a bit, and the sound of the waves grew louder along with their height.

"Well, as I said, Gungá was no ordinary woman," Sánchez replied. "Like Shakoontalá's mother, she was an Upsará."

"Upsará?" Liang asked.

"Yes, Upsará, a water nymph. Like the one Ojoré said he met." Sánchez winked at Ojoré. "She descended from Swarg to further a cause."

"What cause?"

"Isn't this a cracking story?" Sánchez smiled.

"Once there were eight Vásus—the Celestial Beings. They lived in the heavens with the Dévs. One day, the Vásus broke a terrible rule set by the Dévs and were therefore cursed to live one mortal life on earth. Terrified of their mortal life, they all pleaded with Gungá to descend on earth with them as their mother and kill them as soon as they were born so that they could once again live their lives as their previous selves. Seven of them managed to get back. The last one, though, the one that Gungá did not drown, as you will see in the story ahead, had to live a terrible life."

"Did Gungá return Shántanu his son?" Ojoré asked.

"Yes. After sixteen years, when he completed his education with the greatest teachers of the era, she returned him to his father."

Before they could ask any further questions, an attendant entered the terrace.

"Mr. Heikkinen, the captain says he's ready for you to sail."

It was early morning. They were so immersed in the story that they lost track of time.

"Tell him we'll be there in a few minutes."

Aarno turned to the others. "Gentlemen, I hate to break, but we must keep moving. I want to be one step ahead of Drágosláv this time. Let's continue this on the yacht."

CHAPTER 50

The Expedition

Nagpur, India

Saira scanned the passengers one after another as they exited through the arrivals gate of the Nagpur Airport and made their way toward the passenger pick.

"Dr. Pradhan,"—she waved at a middle-aged man dragging a small duffle bag on its wheels—"this way."

"Saira, so nice to meet you again." Dr. Pradhan smiled widely. He shuffled his bag into his left hand and extended his right.

"I'm so glad you decided to come. Welcome to Orange City." Saira shook his hand.

'It's quite chilly out here." Dr. Pradhan shivered a bit. "I didn't expect it to be this cold."

"Winter mornings are generally like this," Saira said, rubbing her palms.

"As a Mumbaikar, I'm not used to the cold that much." He smiled and rubbed his.

"Don't worry, it'll warm up in a few hours."

The two walked toward the parking lot, navigating amongst cops, carts, cabs, and the crowd.

"Very well, so, what's our plan for today?" Dr. Pradhan asked as they stopped near a Mahindra Thar with the Archaeological Survey of India seal on its doors and a lion emblem on the bonnet.

"I've planned quite an exhausting day for us, as you will return tomorrow," Saira said. She opened the trunk, took Pradhan's bag, and stowed it inside. "But before that, let's have some breakfast. I hope you're hungry."

"I'm starving."

Exiting the airport, they drove south for a few minutes on NH-44 before stopping at a small roadside eatery opposite the VCA cricket stadium.

"I hope you eat spicy." Saira smiled as she pulled over at the curb.

"Bring it on." He winked.

"Two pohas and chai," Saira ordered as they took a table beside a window. Minutes later, a server brought two bowls of cooked flattened rice tempered with turmeric, mustard seeds, onions, and cilantro. After placing them on the table, he poured a red and spicy broth of sprouted black chickpeas, garlic, ginger, and tomatoes.

Uhoo, Uhoo, Uhoo. Dr. Pradhan coughed after the first bite. "That's quite spicy. Delicious, but spicy."

"Squeeze some lemon. It'll cut down the heat."

"I no longer feel the cold, though. It's good that way."

"It's a local delicacy." She dug into the poha uninterrupted and asked for more.

"So, tell me more about the site we are headed to." Dr. Pradhan finished his poha and took a sip from his short, cutting glass of chai.

"So, the pictures and the 3D models I left with you in Mumbai were all discovered at this site." She blew over her chai before sipping. "It's deep inside the Tadoba-Andhari National Park." She took another sip. "As you might know, the national park is quite famous as a Tiger habitat. Once, I went on a safari with a few friends, and this site somehow just pulled me in. I can't explain how, but I was driven to the place. It was rubble beneath dense bushes, but I knew something was there. So, I requested permits from the forest department and began the excavations."

"That's quite amazing? You seem to have a knack for places like these, Saira."

"I don't think so. I had never felt like this on any other site before, but this is something else. I always feel connected when I am there."

"Interesting. Anyway, so how would we access the place today? I heard the permits are gone months in advance."

"Ohh, we don't have to worry about that. ASI has special access now. A few rangers will accompany us while we work at the site, keeping an eye around for wild cats. We have cordoned the site perimeter with a wired fence, so that gives us some protection."

"What are we waiting for, then? Let's go. I'm quite excited."

In two and a half hours, they were at the gate of the Tadoba-Andhari National Park. Two rangers boarded the back seat of the Thar, and the party left for their destination. After a well-defined dirt track, they ventured off-road. For a while, the woods were dense, with tall trees and foliage all around. They spotted a sloth bear on their way, followed by a troop of monkeys jumping from branch to branch. In a while, the woods opened into a small meadow surrounded by tall and thick vegetation.

"There's our site." Saira pointed at the center of the meadow where a fence of wire and pipes appeared. They unloaded their excavation instruments and tools from the vehicle and entered the fence. A big cavity in the ground led into a vast chamber beneath.

Saira and Dr. Pradhan descended into the chamber. The rangers lowered the instruments and tools from above. Both of them fastened a headlamp on their foreheads and examined.

"Take me to the wall in your photographs." Dr. Pradhan pulled the pictures from his bag.

"Over here." She pointed to the far end from where they stood.

On reaching the wall, they lit the area with additional lamps.

"Fascinating." He gazed with wide eyes.

Dr. Pradhan looked at the script on the wall, murmured what he read.

"Treasures from times long forgotten are not yet lost o seekers from the past. They wait patiently for their true owners at places hidden from all. Prove your worth if you wish to reunite with them, for they can only be won by their true masters as in the days long lost."

"Intriguing indeed." He leaned to take a closer look. "Show me the miniature carvings you built the 3D models from."

Saira walked him toward another corner.

"Unbelievable." His eyes did not flinch for a second.

"They are some kind of monuments, temples to be precise, five in total. Very well preserved."

"I can see." He ran his hands over the miniature temples sculpted in stone on the ground.

The temples had five distinct designs. Some had tall and slender vimanas, while some had short and plump ones. They all had shikars and mandapams, but only a couple had gopurams. Different animals were carved at the bases of each temple, along with wheels as if drawing them forward. The first temple had carvings of a giant water buffalo with long, curvy horns. Next to it was a temple with carvings of gazelles. The third had an elephant with seven trunks and four tusks carved into its base, while the remaining two had galloping stallions.

"We carefully analyzed each one, but none are replicas of existing temples in the country or elsewhere abroad," Saira added.

Dr. Pradhan carefully observed each one of them. "I'm sorry, but your 3D prints had some details missing."

"Yes, we have a very old scanner. That's why I wanted you to visit the site in person."

Dr. Pradhan's eyes lit up as he finished his observation. "What a coincidence! I found drawings of similar temples carved into a wall at our recently discovered chamber at Nálandá as well. But they are two-dimensional carvings, unlike these." He retrieved another set of photographs from his bag. "But there was no text, like on that wall." He handed them to Saira. "Take a look."

She moved her eyes from the photographs to the miniature temples. "I think they match quite well. See the outlines, the pillars, the sanctum sanctorum here and here."

They spent hours noting and comparing every detail of the carved drawings to the sculptures.

"This is incredible, Saira! Based on your pictures and mine, I also looked into these in detail and tried to find if there are any in the country or abroad resembling the drawings, but found none that match."

"We are at a dead end, Dr. Pradhan. My advisor told me you are the only one who might decipher this and point us in the right direction."

"Well, I think it's time to collaborate. We have active sites in Nálandá, and I feel we might find some more clues there."

Saira and Dr. Pradhan drove toward the jungle exit with a sense of achievement. Saira worked on this for several months, and now, at least, she had some breakthroughs. On their way back, they spotted a Tigress and three cubs.

"People spend days and weeks spotting a tiger in the wild here, Dr. Pradhan. You spotted one on your first trip."

Dr. Pradhan smiled widely. "Guess we're going to find good things ahead, Saira. I hope we do."

CHAPTER 51

Dévine Intervention

Jeddah, Saudi Arabia

"Take care of the others, Father," Aarno shouted. He walked up the ramp toward the yacht. "And yourself, too."

"Keep me updated on your whereabouts, son," his father shouted back. The ramp lifted.

"Captain, are we prepared?" Aarno asked. "It might be a long sail."

"It's loaded with as many supplies and fuel as it could hold, sir."

"Do we have enough blood of each type? Is the refrigeration working? I don't want to be in that situation again."

"I checked it myself, sir. We have backups this time."

They boarded the yacht with lots of clothes, considering each kind of weather- rain, snow, heat-and were prepared for everything. However, they didn't know where they should go.

"We'll sail until we know where to go," Aarno suggested. No one had a better plan.

"Aarno, we don't want to head back to the Mediterranean Sea, we can't go where they expect us to go. How about we go south, toward the Arabian Sea?" Liang asked.

"But the pirates; is it safe?" Aarno asked the captain.

"The yacht's owner is well known in this part of the world; I'm assured no one will dare hijack us," the captain replied.

The host and crew have been very helpful till now. I should trust their advice, Aarno thought.

There was no other choice; they had escaped from the north. Drágosláv could still be there.

Everyone moved their luggage into their respective cabins, napped, and assembled back onto the top deck. The sun rose into the sky and shone brightly over the calm waters of the Red Sea. Like before, the bartender made all of them drinks and left.

"Let's continue." Aarno looked at Sánchez, who was once again handcuffed to the bar.

"What happened next, to Shántanu, to his son?" Liang asked. The story ran in his head like a playlist on a loop.

Sánchez savored his single malt and resumed from where he had left.

"Shántanu waited for the time when Gungá would return with their son. He hoped to somehow convince her to stay back.

When Gungá returned with Dévavrut—their son, she spoke, "Vows and oaths are sacred, my lord. A commitment not just to a person but to the divine. One has to accept the full consequences of breaking them. You have broken yours. For that reason, I can't live with you. I have done my duty in raising our son. It's now your turn to make him your own."

Shántanu had no choice but to let her go. It broke his heart, but a part of him was consoled to have his only son back in his life. He spent time with Dévavrut, teaching him everything he knew: administration, politics, compassion, and many other things from his experience as the ruler of an empire that one day he envisioned Dévavrut would inherit.

There was one thing missing, though. A queen.

"Your Majesty," his deputy bowed as he spoke, "if I may humbly present my advice, which I gave you some years back when Her Grace left the palace."

"I know what you're going to say," the king said. "You want me to marry again."

"You are the strength, the authority of our empire, my King. But a queen is the heart. The empire needs a queen."

Shántanu loved Gungá immensely. He was sure she would stay when she returned. Now, the hope he had for the past sixteen years was gone.

"Your Majesty, I urge you to please reconsider my counsel."

"He's right, Father," Dévavrut said. "You should marry again. Mother will not return."

But Shántanu could not feel love for anyone else.

Months passed, and his misery continued.

Then one day, like a déjà vu, in a manner similar to Gungá, Shántanu met a beautiful woman. It was the same spot where he had met Gungá. Though there was nothing magical about her and she did not possess the same divine aura, there was something that reminded him of Gungá. Like in the past, he fell for her.

"What's your name, beautiful lady?"

"Satyavati," she said, and added, "my lord," when she looked at the royal jewelry.

"Marry me," he proposed to her at that very instant, like he had done to Gungá.

"My lord, I beg your pardon, but I don't understand."

"I want you to marry me and be my queen."

"Your Majesty, forgive me. I don't know what to say. Besides, I can't accept your proposal without my father's permission. You will have to ask my hand in marriage."

"Very well then, take me to him."

Shántanu and Dévavrut accompanied her to the village on a river island. Although an ordinary fisherman, Satyavati's father was ambitious for his daughter. "My Lord, I give you my permission, but—" he paused and swallowed,"—but forgive me, I have one condition."

"What is it?" Shántanu asked.

Dévavrut stood beside him.

"I need a promise from you that the children born out of this union will inherit the throne of your empire."

Shántanu was dumbstruck.

Dévavrut was the crown prince. Strong, intelligent, and unbeatable at warfare. People loved him, enemies feared him, and allies respected him.

Your interruption has cast dark clouds of misfortune on his and the entire empire's fate, and you and your descendants will regret this in time, Shántanu remembered Gungá's words.

"But I already have an heir." Shántanu pulled Dévavrut forward. "He's the crown prince."

"I don't know about that. My condition is final."

Silence seized the room.

Shántanu shook his head.

Finally, Dévavrut spoke. "I renounce my right to the throne."

"No. No, my son, you will not do that." Shántanu stood up to leave.

"I am meant to do this, Father. I feel it's my destiny."

"That's a noble gesture, Your Grace," Satyavati's father addressed Dévavrut, "but what about the children you have? Won't they claim their right to the throne, fight with my grandchildren?"

"I will never marry. I will never father a child. I will be celibate till I die. I take this vow."

Shántanu was beyond sad. But he couldn't stop Dévavrut.

People were shocked. The commoners and elites felt sorry for Dévavrut together. In time, they idolized him. His stature and respect touched new bounds.

Sánchez paused. His throat dried. He coughed. "Can I have a refill?"

Darren grunted.

"Please." He coughed some more.

Aarno walked toward the bar, filled up his glass. The yacht cruised near the Yemeni peninsula.

"What happened then?" Liang asked.

"Well, Shántanu and Satyavati married and had two sons," Sánchez continued. "The elder was named Chitrángad, and the younger was Vichitraveer."

"Who followed Shántanu to the throne?"

"Vichitraveer; Chitrángad died young. Accident, it is said," Sánchez replied and waited for more questions.

None came.

"Before we proceed, I have to point out the peculiar laws of succession in this empire," he continued. "According to them, all children born by a woman, irrespective of their biological fathers, belonged to her legally married husband. Even if they were born before the marriage or out of adultery."

"Wow." Liang gasped. "Really? That's quite contrary to the history of the dynasties I have read about. Any child born out of wedlock was considered a bastard."

"Yes, that's quite different from what I've read in history, too." Aarno nodded. "Why would a king accept anyone else's child?"

"History and stories of this time are different." Sánchez smiled. "One has to set aside the prism of what we know and keep an open mind. Take it as it is. This rule is instrumental in the story that will unfold."

The five men pondered. The complexities of this tale were overwhelming.

"So, in the end, Satyavati's father did manage to change the fate of his bloodline, secure the throne for them?" Liang asked.

"In a way," Sánchez replied, "but it did not happen the way he would have liked. The truth about his relationship with Satyavati was different."

"What do you mean?" Ojoré asked. "He was not her father?"

"If you mean her biological father, then no, he wasn't. Satyavati was the daughter of another beautiful Upsará and a Rishi." Sánchez paused. "I know, it gets repetitive and weirder." He smiled. "But that's how it is."

"As is evident, the Upsarás play a crucial part in shaping the story. Perhaps that was the reason Shántanu was attracted to Satyavati in the first place. She was, in a way, similar to Gungá; although not an Upsará like her, she was a child born of an Upsará. Satyavati's parents didn't keep her. She was born neither of love nor marriage, but lust. Another one of the Dévs' schemes. Her fisherman foster father found and raised her."

"What happened to Dévavrut?" Liang knew what he wanted to ask.

"He served as interim head of the house, mentor to Vichitraveer. Vichitraveer was incompetent. It's said that he was so much of a loser that when it was time for him to compete for a bride, it was Dévavrut who won over three brides for him."

"Compete? Won brides?"

"Well, well, well. The things I assume you already know. Anyways, yes. Kings with daughters of marriageable age held contests, inviting eligible kings and princes from various kingdoms to participate. It involved tests of skill, intelligence, and courage. Whoever won the contest could take the king's daughters in marriage."

"That's sexist, isn't it? What about the bride, what she wants?" Ojoré said.

"Well, that's how things were. The bride, though, got to veto out any participant she did not like. She also got to choose the contest and its rules. But it had to be before the contestants were chosen. She had to accept the winner from her selected participants."

Ojoré shook his head.

"So, moving ahead, Dévavrut was the fiercest warrior there was. Vastly skilled. He won all three contests and took all three of the king's daughters with him for Vichitraveer. The eldest of the sisters, Umbá, was in love with another man, a commoner. She could not veto anyone because of pressure from her father, but she asked for an incredibly difficult contest. She thought no one would win. To her dismay, Dévavrut won them all. She pleaded with Dévavrut and Vichitraveer to let her go. Out of compassion, they did. But the love of her life did not accept her back, for another man had won her. She came back to Hustinápoori but was not accepted back by Vichitraveer. Finally, she gave up and committed suicide.

Umbá's sisters, Umbiká and Umbáliká, married Vichitraveer without protest but soon discovered that he had no interest in them and could not father children. They went to Satyavati with the news.

"I pray you, please visit Umbiká and Umbáliká's bed chambers and give me my heirs. My father and I release you from your vow. Please, please, it's your duty," Satyavati said to Dévavrut.

"I can't do that. I'm a man of my word, even for a woman who asked me to take the vow and is releasing me from it. I can't repeat the mistake my father made by breaking his vow. It forced my mother, Gungá, to leave him. Sorry, but my vow is unbreakable."

A wicked twist of fate it was.

Desperate to have an heir, Satyavati tracked down her firstborn, Vyás, and asked him to father her children with her royal daughters-in-law.

"Firstborn? Vyás?" Liang asked.

"Yes, Vyás. This tale has many layers that one must peel gently."

Sánchez swallowed, then continued, "Many years before Satyavati met Shántanu, a renowned and influential Rishi visited her village.

"I offer you a boon," he said when he met her. "You can be the queen and grand queen mother of emperors in the future. But—"

"But what, my lord?" she asked. Her eyes sparkled with excitement.

"For the past several years, I lived deep in the mountains, meditating. Since returning to civilization, you are the most beautiful woman I have seen. I am attracted to you and want to make love to you."

"Pardon me, my lord. You are a Rishi—an ascetic, and Rishis don't raise families. The purpose of your life is spirituality. You will go to the mountains again, leaving me alone. No one will marry me."

"That's why I offer you the boon. With my ascetic powers, I will restore your physical virginity. Your body will emanate fragrance that kings will find irresistible."

She agreed.

Out of their union was born a son named Vyás. She gave him away to a childless couple, and as promised by the Rishi, became a virgin again. Her body gained a peculiar fragrance that turned heads wherever she went. There was already news on the streets about the emperor looking for a queen. Deciding to make the most of her boon, she orchestrated a meeting with Shántanu in which it appeared as if he found her, and you know how things went from there," Sánchez finished. He took a sip.

As the sun went overhead, seagulls rested on the calm waters of the Arabian Sea. A few glided above the top deck, catching whatever pieces of snack Darren threw upward.

"Oye, stop it," Ojoré shouted. "It's not good for them."

Darren stopped. "Phoo." He sighed. "This story's like a maze, dude. It's so difficult to keep track of who married whom, the Upsarás, the Rishis, the kings, the children."

"Fetch me a paper and pen. I'll draw it for you," Sánchez replied.

"No need. I'm doing it already. Let's continue," Liang said. He absorbed the story like a sponge.

"All right. So, after all these years, Vyás finally met his mother and accepted her request. From his union with Umbiká, a son called Dhritaráshtra was born. Unluckily, he was blind. Umbáliká also bore him a son. They named him Pándu."

Dhritaráshtra married Gándhári, while Pándu took two wives-Koonti and Mádri. As the elder, Dhritaráshtra was supposed to be the next emperor, but there were strict rules of succession. Because of his disability, he could not succeed to the throne unless he was the only heir.

Pándu thus got the throne, but he had his own troubles."

"Trouble?" Darren was curious.

"He could not father children. A few years after his marriages, a Rishi cursed him that if he ever made love to his wives from then on, he would die that same instant."

"Then? The line stopped?" Liang asked impatiently.

"Not at all. This time, there was divine intervention to further the royal lineage. No Upsará, nothing of that sort."

"But the line was already broken, wasn't it?" Diego said.

"Not according to the rules of succession," Sánchez smirked. "As I mentioned, all children born to the wives belonged to the legally married husband. Thus, the line continued."

"What do you mean by divine intervention?" Liang asked.

"Aahaa! Isn't it funny how history repeats itself, especially over hundreds or thousands of years?" Sánchez peered into their eyes one by one as he said these words. "Again and again."

He paused.

"Like Satyavati and Shakoontalá before her, Koonti was special too."

"Special? Don't tell me she was an Upsará or a child of an Upsará or she got a boon like Satyavati?"

"Last." Sánchez nodded. "Like Satyavati, she received a boon from a powerful Rishi, but this boon was different."

"Different? How?"

"This time, the boon involved the Dévs themselves."

"Dévs?"

"Yes, Dévs. Koonti was given a boon that if she bedded with the Rishi, she could summon any of the Dévs and compel them to father children with her, and—" Sánchez paused for a second.

"And what?" Liang was unable to contain his excitement.

"—and the children born of these Dévs would have extraordinary powers,"

The story got bizarre by the minute. It sounded like a fairytale. They didn't know why, but however weird it got, there was familiarity.

"Tell us about the children."

"Hmm. Let me tell you about Dhritaráshtra's children first. It is said that Dhritaráshtra made up for Pándu's impotency. He took many junior wives, perhaps to compensate for the loss of the throne to his younger brother. He fathered one hundred sons and one daughter. The eldest of them was Dooryodhan. Next to him was Doosshásan and then followed the remaining ninety-eight. His only daughter was named Doosshalá."

"Pándu had only five sons. The first three were from Koonti, and the last two were from Mádri, born similarly from the Dévs using Koonti's boon."

"Koonti had the boon, but how did Mádri have two sons?" Liang's questions were always ready.

"Pándu asked Koonti to share the boon with Mádri, which she did."

"Then?" Darren asked.

The more Sánchez told them, the more excited they got.

"Eldest of the five of Pándu's sons was Yudhishtir, born out of the union of Koonti with the Dév Yamá, lord of righteousness. He's the one who decides which soul would go to Swarg and which would go to Narck. Yamá, it's said, is impartial and always truthful. He exercises his duty without prejudice. He's considered the epitome of justice," Sánchez said. "Yudhishtir had a similar personality. Truthful, idealistic, compassionate."

"The second son was Bheem, from the all-powerful Váyu–god of wind. Bheem was formidable. Like a hurricane, he could uproot trees with his bare hands; a herd of elephants was no match for him. His appetite was enormous."

Sánchez gulped the last sip from the melted ice infused with the single malt and continued. The seagulls sat on the railings, anticipating food.

Darren ignored.

"The third son was Arjun, from Indra—the king of Dévs—elite, charismatic, magnetic. Arjun had great skills. Like Indra, he had a magnetic personality. The poster child of the Pándavs."

"Pándavs?" Liang asked

"The sons of Pándu. That's what the five were called."

"What about the last two of the Pándavs?"

"As I said, the last two were born of the second wife, Mádri. They were conceived from the twin Dévs—Ashwini twins. One was Sahadév, and the other was Nakul." Sánchez completed the sentence hastily and took a deep breath. "I need a refill before we go further."

Aarno fetched his glass again, filled it with several ice cubes, and poured the single malt. Too excited by the story, he wanted to hear what came next.

"Alcohol has been the best drink since eternity." Sánchez gulped it down.

"The sons of Dhritaráshtra, what were they called?" Liang asked.

"Kauravs."

"Pándavs and Kauravs," Liang murmured.

"What were the qualities of the last two Pándavs?"

"Let me recap the qualities of all five one by one," Sánchez said as the scotch seeped into his veins. Sánchez sounded like a preacher commanded to tell this story to everyone he could find.

Alcohol makes people tell things voluntarily, without having to force, Aarno thought.

"As I said, the eldest Yudhishtir was righteous, truthful, and compassionate. He was the master of the spear. No one could beat him in a spear duel," Sánchez said. "Bheem was the expert in mace combat and everything to do with strength. Arjun, the jewel of the pack, was one of the best in archery and aiming."

Although he felt nostalgic telling them the story, disdain filled Sánchez's face as he described each one of them.

"Nakul, the first of the twins, was gifted with looks, the most handsome man ever. Women fell for him, a master of sword warfare, an expert in Ayurvèd—the knowledge of herbal medicine. His half-twin, Sahadév, on the other hand, was knowledgeable and smart. He, too, was skilled in swordsmanship."

"What about the elder brother's children? What was his name again?" Darren asked.

"Dhritaráshtra," Liang answered before Sánchez could speak.

"All this alcohol and liquid—" Sánchez screwed up his face. "—I need a break."

"Yes, I need to take a piss." Darren stood up.

"Alright, if that's the consensus, let's take a break before we proceed," Aarno declared.

Liang scribbled everything he heard. His memory was flawless.

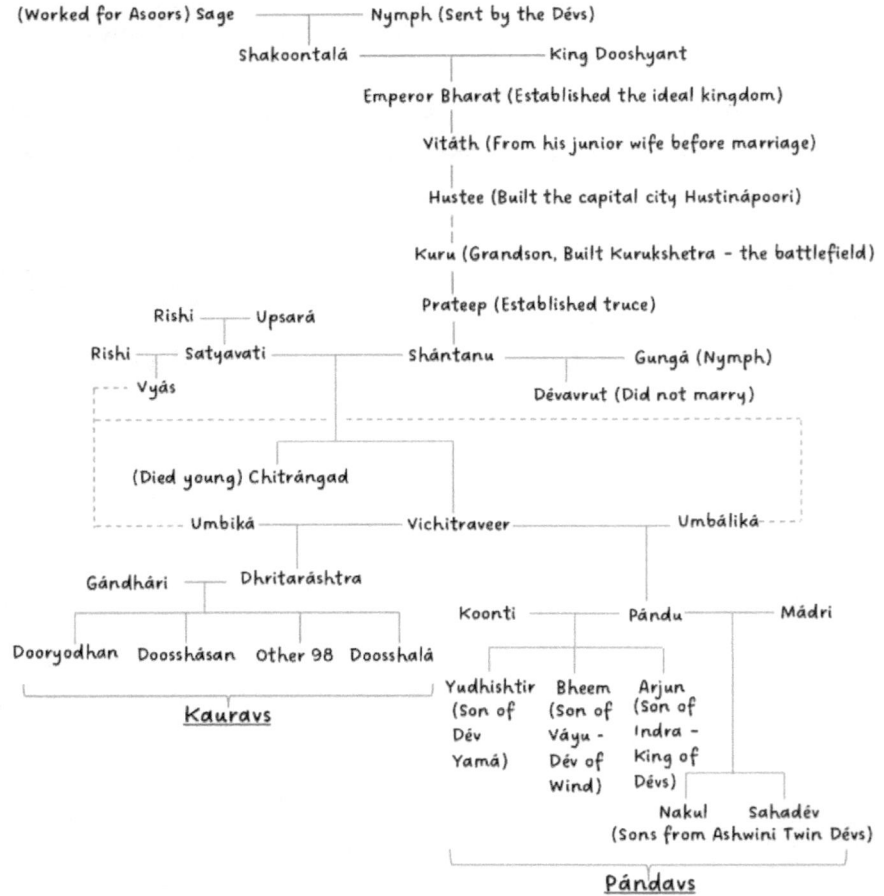

(Worked for Asoors) Sage ———————— Nymph (Sent by the Dévs)

Shakoontalá ———————————— King Dooshyant

Emperor Bharat (Established the ideal kingdom)

Vitáth (From his junior wife before marriage)

Hustee (Built the capital city Hustinápoori)

Kuru (Grandson, Built Kurukshetra - the battlefield)

Prateep (Established truce)

Rishi ———— Upsará

Rishi ———— Satyavati ———————— Shántanu ———————————— Gungá (Nymph)

Vyás   Dévavrut (Did not marry)

(Died young) Chitrángad

Umbiká ———————— Vichitraveer ———————— Umbáliká

Gándhári ——— Dhritaráshtra   Koonti ———— Pándu ———— Mádri

Dooryodhan Dooshásan Other 98 Doosshalá

Yudhishtir   Bheem   Arjun
(Son of   (Son of   (Son of
Dév   Váyu -   Indra -
Yamá)   Dév of   King of
            Wind)   Dévs)

Kauravs

Nakul   Sahadév
(Sons from Ashwini Twin Dévs)

Pándavs

CHAPTER 52

The Lost University

Patna, India

"You excited?" Dr. Pradhan turned around and buckled his belt in the front seat beside the driver.

"Beyond excited," Saira said, buckling hers on the second row of the Tata Safari after loading their bags, survey instruments, scanners, and other excavation gear in the trunk and atop the SUV carrier.

It had been eight months since their last meeting in Nagpur, where they had studied the miniature temples.

"I have waited for this gear for months. Finally, we got it. And now I have you to help me as well." Dr. Pradhan's upbeat mood was visible on his face.

"Didn't you have help before?"

"Oh no, those interns were no good. Very lazy, I must say. I had to let them go and hire some local laborers to help me out. We still have them, but nothing like an additional set of professional eyes."

"Agreed," Saira said, turning the wrapper of a Chikki—a bar made from nuts and jaggery—and handing another to Dr. Pradhan.

"Thanks." He undid his wrapper, too. "So, did you and your team find any more sites or items apart from the ones we visited in the Tadoba - Andhari National Park?"

"Well, I also had to wait for the geophysical survey gear for quite a while. When we got it, we searched extensively and found a few more chambers around the one we visited, but they were all empty. No other sites either. We surveyed the entire park and the small towns surrounding it, but nothing was found."

Dr. Pradhan nodded. "I'm excited about this visit. Your findings might give us more insights, some clues for further excavations."

"I hope the same."

Their ride lasted two and a half hours.

"This is the newly built ASI guesthouse. Building on the right is the Nálandá Museum."

"Where are the University ruins?"

"Across the street."

"Oh, that's quite convenient."

"Yup, they built this building recently. Anyways, let's do this. Let's get our rooms, place our luggage, freshen up, and then I can show you around."

"Sounds good."

Saira retrieved her belongings from the SUV. The guesthouse staff unloaded their scientific instruments—a ground-penetrating radar, magnetometer, SONAR, and conductivity meter—from the trunk and atop the carrier.

After about half an hour, they entered the ancient ruins. It was Saira's first time. Walking around broken gateways, crumbling walls, and scattered pieces of rocks, they reached the main complex.

"Remains of the monasteries that once existed." Dr. Pradhan wiped his glasses with a handkerchief. "These used to be the lecture halls."

Saira gazed at the intricate carvings on the walls, which still stood high, and sculptures that once belonged to a grand building. In a few steps, they came across remnants of a library.

"It's said that this library once housed around nine million manuscripts." Dr. Pradhan gazed at the tall columns and wide rows of shelves.

"It makes me wonder how it must have been in those days, among scholars and monks from around the world, surrounded by so much knowledge and wisdom." Saira gaped at the surroundings. "It's a shame that most of it is lost." She placed her right hand on one of the walls and closed her eyes.

"Well, that's why we both are here, isn't it? Resurrect as much as we can of that lost knowledge."

"Indeed." She opened her eyes and looked ahead. "So, where's the new chamber you discovered?"

"Way on the other side. There, outside the premises of the university ruins. This way."

They walked for a while before reaching the new site.

"Alright, be careful, the opening is quite narrow. They still haven't opened it all, so it's more like a cave."

They fastened their headlamps and turned them on before entering the cavity. A few hand-held lamps were also lit up, illuminating the chamber. Dr. Pradhan went straight to the carved illustration.

"They do look the same. Like the sculptures near Nagpur."

"But that's all I got. There's nothing else. No pottery, no tools, no artifacts, no other relics."

Saira stood with her hands on her waist, absorbing everything before her eyes.

"Well, looks like, starting tomorrow, we've got quite a lot of work to do."

CHAPTER 53

The Prodigy

Near Yemeni Peninsula

The yacht sailed across the Gulf of Aden toward the Arabian Sea. In days past, merchants from the Middle East and Europe made long voyages, braving these testing waters on their way to India. There were no engines and propellers then. Nonetheless, the weather of this region assisted their endeavors—trade, tourism, education, and diplomacy.

At the onset of monsoon, merchants entered the Arabian Sea on ships with expansive sails hanging from tall masts. The advancing monsoon, though creating rough seas, generated strong winds to propel them toward the Indian coasts. A few months later, when they returned home with ships full of cinnamon, black peppers, cardamoms, herbal medicines, cotton, and other items, the retreating monsoon pushed winds in the opposite direction, shepherding them back toward the Red Sea. The Himālayas induced this weather, their prominence making the climate stable, and mankind learned to use it to their advantage.

The monsoon calmed the subcontinent scorched by the Indian summer, turning landscapes across the country into beautiful retreats. Rain brought life, happiness, and festivals, some of which were millennia old and continue today.

Aarno breathed the crisp air. "Let's get back to it."

They had mustered again on the top deck. Darren opted out of the hot tub and descended onto a beanbag. The bartender poured drinks. Alcohol made Sánchez more than willing to start narrating. He commenced without the usual arm-twisting from Darren.

"Pándu was confident that his eldest son would succeed him to the throne," he began, "but the truth that his sons were not his flesh and blood constantly bothered him. The thought ate him from inside. Depression took hold of him. He lost interest in running the empire."

"One day, he renounced the throne, left Hustinápoori, and went into the wilds. His two wives-Mádri & Koonti, and five children-Yudhishtir, Arjun, Bheem, Nakul & Sahadév, accompanied him. Dévavrut and Vidur, meanwhile, tried to govern."

"But chaos followed. They sent dignitaries to beg Pándu for his return. When he refused, the court's nobles, scholars, and sages suggested that his elder brother Dhritaráshtra, who had been ignored the first time because of his blindness, should take the throne. No one else besides Dévavrut, who was still adamant not to break his vow, was eligible."

"He can be the interim ruler until Pándu decides to return or his sons come of age," the elders advised Dévavrut.

He agreed.

Dhritaráshtra ran the empire with help from his half-brother Vidur—born out of the union of Vyás with a palace maid. Vidur, Pándu, and Dhritaráshtra shared the same biological father, Vyás, but only Pándu and Dhritaráshtra's mothers were the legal wives. Therefore, Vidur was not allowed to assume the throne," Sánchez explained.

He sighed, lifted his wrists, and rang his handcuffs together. "Can you please get me out of these? Where am I gonna run?"

"No," Darren shouted before anyone could speak. "I freakin' don't have to remind you what you did to us, do I?"

Sánchez looked toward Aarno hopefully.

"Don't look toward him, you jackass. I said no; that better be enough for you, understood?"

Sánchez looked at Aarno again. Aarno shrugged.

Disappointed, Sánchez shook his head. "It was worth a shot. You all kinda listen to Aarno. He seems like your leader."

"That doesn't change a thing for you, even if he's. You ain't getting out of them handcuffs."

"Okay, okay."

Sánchez continued, "Several months passed. One day, Pándu saw Mádri bathing under a waterfall. The volcano of pent-up lust inside him was uncontainable."

If you ever make love to your wives, you will die, Pándu remembered the Rishi's curse. But the lava within was ready to explode from his manhood. He ignored the curse, took her in his arms, and kissed like he had never kissed before.

That same instant, as warned by the Rishi, he collapsed on the floor. Feeling guilty for her husband's death, Mádri committed suicide, leaving her two sons in their senior wife Koonti's custody.

After their demise, Koonti and the five sons of Pándu were by themselves. They had no option but to return to Hustinápoori."

Sánchez cleared his throat. "Here, the story becomes more complicated," he continued. "Koonti, children, the royal family, the entire city mourned for Pándu."

"Time, though, healed the wounds."

"Soon after Koonti's return, the sons of Pándu, along with the Kaurav children, went to Gurukul-the royal school. There, under guru Droanáchárya-a world-renowned and sought-after teacher- they learned the art of warfare, science, religion, righteous conduct, and administration. Droanáchárya was the husband of Kripi, the girl child among the twins that Emperor Shántanu had adopted to fill the emotional void when Gungá had parted with him. More commonly called Droan, he was the master of weapons, warfare, and combat skills. He taught the royal children everything he knew. His services were reserved only for the royals, and he refused to teach anyone else, even if they possessed extraordinary talent."

Sánchez's face lit up. *Fools, they know nothing,* he thought. *They think I am their hostage, that they are safe, that I can't escape.* He smiled a deceitful smile. *They don't know who works for me.*

He sighed deeply.

"Once, a commoner named Eklavya, came to Droan," Sánchez continued. "He was an immensely talented boy and was determined to learn from him."

"My lord, will you please accept me as your pupil?" Eklavya pleaded. "You are one of the best teachers in the world." He held his palms together. "I admire you with all my heart. I promise I will work with utmost dedication. I promise I will never let you down."

Droan scanned him from head to toe. "I don't teach commoners, boy, no matter how determined or talented you are," Droan replied. "You should stick to your father's profession. My services are only for the royals."

Eklavya was heartbroken. Nonetheless, he didn't give up. He sneaked and spied from the bushes when Droan taught the Royals. He erected a dummy effigy of Droan made from hay and practiced what he observed from the bushes. Through trial and error, determination, and God-gifted talent, Eklavya mastered the art of archery. His aim made the target every single time. He performed magical things with his bow and arrow.

Inside the Gurukul and the entire empire, Arjun was considered the greatest archer. He was the best student Droan had ever taught. Arjun impressed Droan with his focus, dedication, and determination, so much so that out of fondness, Droan taught him the unique secrets of archery, warfare, and weapons that he had reserved only for his son Ushvatthámá. They both, though, were unaware of Eklavya, the self-taught prodigy who followed them like a shadow.

One day, Droan took Arjun on a field trip toward the countryside, where they met Eklavya.

"Guru Droan," Eklavya beamed with excitement. "You can't imagine how delighted I am to see you here. Please permit me to display what I have learned, my lord."

Droan nodded.

Eklavya performed magnificent feats with his bow and arrows, some of which he had developed himself. Even Arjun did not know how to do such things. He displayed his genius and mastery at archery.

Arjun's face fumed with jealousy. "You promised to make me the world's best archer," he protested. "He's clearly better than me. Are you still committed to the royal family, Guru Droan, or has your interest waned?"

"Who is your guru, boy?" Droan asked Eklavya.

"You, sir."

"What? But I never taught you?" Droan furrowed his brow, narrowed his eyes. He was puzzled.

"You taught me only in spirit, my lord," Eklavya answered. "I taught myself by drawing inspiration from your effigy and learned through distant observations when you taught the princes."

Arjun breathed heavily in anger. His eyes were a shade of red. Unable to satisfy an insecure prince, Droan did the cruelest thing.

"You used me as your inspiration, pretended to be my student, did you not?" Droan asked Eklavya.

Eklavya nodded.

"You spied on my school, learned things that were not meant for you, stole my teachings, did you not?"

"Yes."

"Very well, then I believe you owe me gurudakshiná. Won't you agree?"

"Whatever you ask of me, my Guru," Eklavya replied.

"What's gurudakshiná?" Liang interrupted. His hand paused from scribbling.

"It was a one-time fee that a guru charged his disciple. The rule was that the guru could ask his students anything he desired, but only once. After the student paid this debt, he owed the guru nothing," Sánchez answered. "Although Eklavya did not directly interact with Droan, he still considered him his guru, and there was no greater mark for a student than to obey his teacher."

Taking advantage of this rule, Droan asked, "Which is your arrow hand?"

"Right, sir," Eklavya answered obediently. He wanted to impress Droan. He expected that the guru would accept him in his Gurukul.

"I want the thumb of your right hand, as gurudakshiná," Droan commanded.

Arjun was dumbfounded, and so was Eklavya. All his hope washed away like lines drawn in the sand.

Nonetheless, such was his dedication that he pulled out a knife, severed the thumb from his right hand, and handed it to Droan. "Here it is, my guru."

"There." Droan tossed the thumb at Arjun. "Now you're the greatest archer in the world."

The five men's faces were a sight to see.

"Just like that? Like that? Really? He didn't question?" Ojoré was unsettled.

"No, not a bit. As I said, it was a custom never to question your guru."

They stared at each other, feeling guilty, although they didn't know why.

"Monarchy took advantage of the poor for so long," Darren spat on the deck. "I hate the royal families everywhere, don't know why people make so much fuss even when a royal poops in England. Fools. Like it's gonna reduce their taxes."

"What happened then?" Ojoré asked, ignoring Darren's comment. To him, the story of Eklavya seemed intriguing. He felt sympathetic toward Eklavya.

"What can happen? Eklavya could not shoot an arrow ever again. Arjun's insecurity was pacified in this cruel manner."

It seemed unfair, but no one said anything. They still processed Droan's callousness. The uncomfortable part took time to digest. But they sat silent.

"Many years passed," Sánchez continued. "The royal children were nearing the end of their formal education. At the conclusion of their stay at Gurukul, a graduation exhibition was organized."

People from far and wide came to witness the extravaganza. Kings, nobles, ambassadors; the who's who of the land. One by one, all the princes presented their skills. Only Arjun was left to perform.

Droan kept his best for last.

Arjun enchanted the audience with his archery. The speed, the magic of his arrows captivated the arena. Cheers and claps filled the stadium. "Arjun, Arjun, Arjun," echoed everywhere.

When he was about to wrap up, another young man emerged from the crowd with a bow in his left hand and a quiver on his back. He was about the same age as the other princes, maybe a couple years older.

"Karn," he told his name. "I can do feats trickier than this with my eyes closed," he challenged Arjun, to everyone's disbelief.

So began a contest between them, with Karn not only repeating each and every skill that Arjun displayed but even outperforming him. The audience could not believe it. Droan was surprised. Arjun was jealous and angry.

"He should be punished. Despite being a commoner, he challenges and dishonors a prince! How dare he take up a bow against a royal?"

"Guru Droanáchárya," Dooryodhan intervened. "He's a great talent. One shouldn't be punished for talent, no matter their birth. I'd be honored if I were defeated by such a great display of genius," he said, looking at Arjun.

The rift that brewed between the sons of Dhritaráshtra and Pándu inside the Gurukul was on display to the public. Dooryodhan was aware that one day or the other, his father would have to pass on the kingdom to Yudhishtir, the eldest son of Pándu. He despised the thought and wanted the throne for himself.

Karn amazed everyone in the stadium. In their hearts, they rooted for the underdog commoner. No one, though, knew that he was not of common birth at all. A charioteer adopted him after finding him at his doorstep, but the truth was that he was the firstborn of Koonti and, thus, the most deserving of the throne.

This was a secret that Koonti revealed to no one.

When she first received the boon that helped her conceive children from the Dévs, out of curiosity, she tested it by invoking the Surya Dév—the sun god, asking him to father a son with her. The boon came true, and so was Karn. Unmarried and scared, Koonti left the baby on the steps of a house."

"But if you remember the rule I told you before," Sánchez said, "he was the eldest Pándav, even though he was born outside wedlock."

"Like Arjun, Karn was dedicated, persistent," Sánchez continued, "and the reason he outperformed Arjun was not because he was older, but because of his teacher. Karn was taught by Parshurám, the most famous guru there. Parshurám taught many famous personalities of the era. The royal teacher Droan himself and patriarch Dévavrut were his students."

"Parshurám was so impressed by Karn's humility, kindness, and dedication that he gifted him his dearest weapon, the famous bow Vijayá."

"What was so special about the bow?" Ojoré's curiosity showed up on his face.

"Are you bow-curious?" Sánchez winked.

"Answer the fuckin' question." Darren scowled.

"Aahem," Sánchez coughed.

"It's said that it was one of the most powerful bows in the world. At times, it surpassed Arjun's bow-the great Gándeev. Arjun acquired the Gándeev much later, while Karn received Vijayá much earlier. Legend has it that whenever an arrow was launched from Vijayá, flashes as bright as lightning, and sounds that rivaled the loudest thunderstorms emanated from it. He kept it hidden from the world to use on a greater occasion."

"What happened then?" Liang asked.

"Dooryodhan waited for someone to challenge his opinion of Karn. None dared. Having his father on the throne helped.

"From now on, he's my friend, and his enemies are my enemies," Dooryodhan declared.

It was not openly discussed, but there were murmurs on the streets about the episode. This event had deepened the ridge of antagonism between the Pándavs and Kauravs. Sensing further deterioration in relations and to avoid possible confrontations, Uncle Vidur suggested building a new Royal palace for the Pándavs. The suggestion was well taken, and a new grand palace was planned near Hustinápoori.

Recognizing an opportunity to eliminate competition, Kauravs bribed the architect and asked him to fill the walls with combustible materials to burn the Pándavs alive. Uncle Vidur got wind of it and confronted the architect.

"Carve out a tunnel below the new palace and disappear from Hustinápoori forever. In return, you will skip the death penalty for treason," he said. The architect obeyed and fled the capital for good.

Vidur told the Pándavs about this coup. "Use the tunnel when the palace is set on fire and get as far from the city as possible. Leave your clothes and jewelry. I'll arrange for six bodies to make it look like it was you all."

"But why should we run? It's our right! We'll confront the Kauravs."

"There will be civil war, the empire will suffer, and split. Besides, you're not powerful enough to match the Kauravs. You must forge alliances with other kingdoms to challenge them," Vidur reasoned.

"For now, just play along, lay low, pretend to be dead for some time. It will only serve you well. Build alliances with other kingdoms that hate the Kauravs while you are underground."

When the Pándavs moved into the new palace, as planned by the Kauravs, it was set ablaze. No sooner did the fire start than the Pándavs escaped into the wild using the tunnel."

"What happened then? Did they come back?" Darren asked. His eyes widened in excitement.

"Yes. They spent many months in the jungle, roamed like commoners, and visited tiny villages and towns. Their journey was filled with strange experiences and adventures.

During their time away, they thought carefully about Vidur's advice. "Make alliances," he had said.

The opportunity appeared sooner than they had anticipated. They discovered that Drupad, king of Pánchál—the kingdom through which they were passing, had organized a competition to find a suitable match for his daughter, Draupadi. They realized that if one of them won the contest and married the princess, they would form an alliance through marriage. Drupad, a famous king with a large army and several friends, would back them against any aggression from the Kauravs.

Kings and princes from far and wide came to participate in the event. Dooryodhan and Karn were present too. Although Dooryodhan was allowed, Karn was barred from taking part as society considered him a commoner.

The Pándavs went there in disguise and without any challenge from Karn, Arjun won the archery competition with ease. In fact, he was the only one who hit the target, which seemed impossible. Draupadi wed Arjun, but upon Koonti's condition, she had to marry all of them."

"Just one wife for all five?" Darren was beyond surprised.

"Yes, they all shared Draupadi."

It was uncomfortable for them to digest.

"I told you, the story will sound Bizarre," Sánchez said. "Koonti's condition was calculated. Draupadi's beauty was flawless. Koonti didn't want a rift among the Pándav brothers because of a woman. So, she insisted on this condition."

No one spoke. They pondered on Draupadi's polyandry.

"Then?" Darren broke the silence.

"Then they all returned to Hustinápoori along with Draupadi. People in Hustinápoori had accepted their death and moved on, but to everyone's amazement and Dooryodhan's disappointment, they returned.

This time, though, they were not weak. Their wife, Draupadi, and her father were with them.

"A separate palace won't work this time," Uncle Vidur reasoned. " Any harm to the Pándavs would result in immediate war with the army of Drupad. I think it's time to split the empire, build another capital for them."

Dhritaráshtra had no option this time. He divided the entire empire. Yudhishtir, as the eldest, was made the king of the other half with the newly created capital called Indraprasth. Pándavs chose their architect this time.

Two factions arose: the Kaurav camp, comprising the sons of Dhritaráshtra and all kingdoms who supported them, and the Pándav camp, made up of the five Pándav brothers, Drupad, and all kingdoms that sided with them. Karn, although being the eldest son of Koonti and thus, according to law, a Pándav, was in the Kaurav camp.

Dhritaráshtra still presided over Hustinápoori, but Dooryodhan slowly gained power and ran the show. The desire to kill the Pándavs and take the other half of the empire burned within him like wildfire. Along with Karn on his side were his brothers and his maternal uncle, Shakooni.

Vidur, Dévavrut, and Droan stayed neutral in this struggle between the two royal factions, but it was only a matter of time before they, too, had to pick a side."

CHAPTER 54

Pásá

Near Yemeni Peninsula

Dévs, Asoors, Upsarás, Emperor Bharat's family tree, right up to the Pándavs and Kauravs, it was overwhelming.

They struggled to keep up with who was who and who did what. Liang was the only one who grasped it, jotting notes on the paper.

"What happened next?" he asked Sánchez.

Sánchez swallowed. "Things settled down for a while after the empire was divided. The Pándavs built Indraprasth—a grand capital city for their empire. But it was the calm before the storm."

"Not even a year, and the new city dwarfed Hustinápoori in grandeur. Dooryodhan was jealous. One day, he invited the Pándavs to Hustinápoori.

"Now that we have our own kingdoms, let's bury our differences. How about we try our luck at Pásá," he cajoled. "It's said that beginner's luck is always with the new king."

"Pásá is a game of dice," Sánchez explained. He smiled a wicked smile.

"Yudhishtir agreed and played on behalf of the Pándavs. Shakooni—Dooryodhan's maternal uncle, played for the Kauravs. Shakooni had mastery in Pásá. He had special powers to make the dice fall the way he desired, while Yudhishtir had a habit of betting grand. It was a recipe designed for ruination.

Shakooni let Yudhishtir win for the first several games to boost his confidence. The court maids served generous amounts of mead to all five brothers. As the game progressed, Yudhishtir lost his bets consistently and followed up with an even bigger one to reclaim his loss. The maids continued their part. His brothers advised him against playing further, but he didn't listen.

After an embarrassing hour, Shakooni let Yudhishtir win a small bet. Dooryodhan followed this with an offer to give back Yudhishtir everything he had lost in previous games, provided he won the next, but if he lost, the Pándavs would lose everything they had, themselves and their wife."

"Even Draupadi?" Darren demanded.

"Yes, even her, and—to everyone's disbelief—Yudhishtir agreed."

"Then what?" Darren asked impatiently. "What happened next?"

"Well, he lost. The Pándavs were left with nothing, reduced to being slaves."

"Goddamit, I can't believe he was such a fool?"

"Passions make men lose their brains, my friend. No matter how great they are."

"Then what happened?" Aarno asked

"After much humiliation of the Pándavs, the elders intervened. Dooryodhan, though, would not let go of his win. Vidur and Dévavrut tried hard to make him see sense, but he did not budge. They had to settle for a thirteen-year-long exile for the Pándavs as Dooryodhan's win."

"And the Pándavs agreed?" Diego asked.

"Yes, they did. They had no choice." Sánchez paused. "There was one more condition about the exile, though. They must be unseen by the Kauravs during the thirteenth year, else,"

"Else, what?"

"Else another thirteen-year exile would ensue upon them."

Darren shook his head.

"They were also required to leave all their royal possessions and live as a commoner."

"So, the Pándavs did go into exile?" Diego was unable to come to terms. "For real?"

Sánchez nodded. "One had to honor their words, especially the royals."

"What happened then?" Liang asked as he scribbled.

"As agreed, the Pándavs spent thirteen long years in exile, into the wild."

"What did they do during their exile?"

"For the first twelve years, they visited holy places, jungles, hermitages of great Rishis, and mysterious spots. During this journey, they gathered celestial weapons and fulfilled prophecies that they were destined to fulfill. It'll take me days to tell the details."

"Were they discovered during the thirteenth year?" Liang asked again.

"They played it well. They knew Dooryodhan would make his life's mission to find them during the thirteenth year. They lived in disguise in the nearby kingdom as servants, never communicating amongst themselves in front of others. Kauravs used all their resources to find them but failed."

"They returned?" Ojoré was on his feet.

"Yes." Sánchez sensed the excitement in each one of them.

"Then? They got their palace, their kingdom back?" Darren asked.

Sánchez smiled. "What do you think?"

"I bet Dooryodhan refused."

Sánchez winked.

"Kryshná himself went to convince Dooryodhan to do what was right and give Pándavs their kingdom. He tried to reason with him and asked the other elders to make him understand how important it was to have peace. Dooryodhan, though, was unwilling to compromise."

"Kryshná?" Liang asked. He had read about him at a monastery in China. His monk friends had told him divine stories of the dark-skinned extraordinaire.

"Yes, Lord Kryshná," Sánchez said.

"Your stubborn attitude and unreasonable stance will result in an unprecedented war," Kryshná said. "Millions will die, and for what? Just to satisfy your ego?"

But Dooryodhan did not budge. On the contrary, he wanted a war and control of the whole empire. Shakooni encouraged him and supported his decision. He, too, wanted this war.

"Then?" Diego asked impatiently.

"After all options of persuading Dooryodhan were exhausted, Kryshná declared war on behalf of the Pándavs."

"The war was inevitable." Liang stopped writing. "I could guess it right from the birth of the princes of the two sides. It was obvious that a conflict was slowly festering."

"What happened then?" Diego asked

"Well, as expected, a war of catastrophic proportions began between the Pándavs and Kauravs, a war of unimaginable scale."

"But didn't they want to avoid war?" Liang asked.

"Yes, the Pándavs did not desire war, but they had had enough."

"When your back hits the wall, the only way you can go is forward." Darren stared at Liang.

"They knew it wouldn't be settled until there was war." Sánchez ignored Darren. "They wanted their right; they wanted Dharma to prevail."

"Dharma?"

"Yes, Dharma-the state of balance, righteousness, universal harmony. It was the most important thing to them."

"Hmmm, what happened then? What did the elders do?"

"Well, this time, the elders had to take sides. Droan, Dévavrut had to fight on behalf of the Kauravs. Their duty was to serve the original throne of Hustinápoori.

Soon after the official declaration by Kryshná, both sides formed alliances. The Hustinápoori throne had more influence than the new Pándav kingdom of Indraprasth. The odds were in favor of Dooryodhan. Droan, Dévavrut, and Kripa - the most powerful warriors of the era, whose stories were famous all over the empire, were on his side. This made many kingdoms side with the Kauravs. Shakooni personally went with Dooryodhan to convince them. Kings that believed in the rule of Dharma sided with the Pándavs."

"Tell us more about the war, how it happened," Aarno said

"I bet Bheem took care of the lot with his power," Darren added.

"Here's how the war went." Sánchez ignored Darren.

"Warriors from kingdoms on the Kaurav side were organized into eleven battalions. The Pándavs had only seven battalions on their side. Each battalion comprised precisely twenty-one thousand, eight hundred and seventy chariot-riding soldiers, an equal number of elephant riders. Sixty-five thousand, six hundred and ten horse riders, and one hundred and nine thousand, three hundred and fifty foot soldiers. Their science of war dictated these exact numbers, the combined number in the war being greater than four million, it's said.

Each battalion had a commander who led and directed it. Along with other kings supporting the Kauravs, Droan- the royal teacher, Kripa— Droan's brother-in-law, Ushvatthámá—Droan's son, Karn, and Shakooni were made commanders of the battalions. Dooryodhan asked the patriarch Dévavrut, considered invincible in war, to lead his entire army.

Karn, who had personal differences and ego issues with Dévavrut, declared that he wouldn't participate in the war as long as Dévavrut commanded the armies. Dooryodhan tried to convince him, but he did not budge.

On the Pándav side, Draupadi's twin brother Dhrishtadyumna was made the leader. Bheem and other supporting kings were made the commanders of the Pándav battalions. The other four Pándavs, along with their companies, decided to fight wherever there were more losses or if a high-value Kaurav target was in sight.

The soldiers followed their respective leaders by identifying their particular flags.

On the Pándav side, Bheem's flag was a ferocious lion, while Yudhishtir's flag had a crescent moon. Arjun's flag had a majestic ape; Sahadév had a swan, while Nakul's had an antelope.

On the Kaurav side, Ushvatthámá's flag was a lion's tail with golden rays emanating from it. Dévavrut had trees with stars on his flag; Karn had an elephant, while a hooded snake occupied Dooryodhan's flag.

The war broke with the sound of conch shells.

Kurukshetra—the battlefield built by their ancestor, emperor Kuru-spanned over hundreds of miles."

Sánchez closed his eyes as if picturing it.

"The war lasted for eighteen days."

"At that time, nobody knew that those eighteen days would change the world forever."

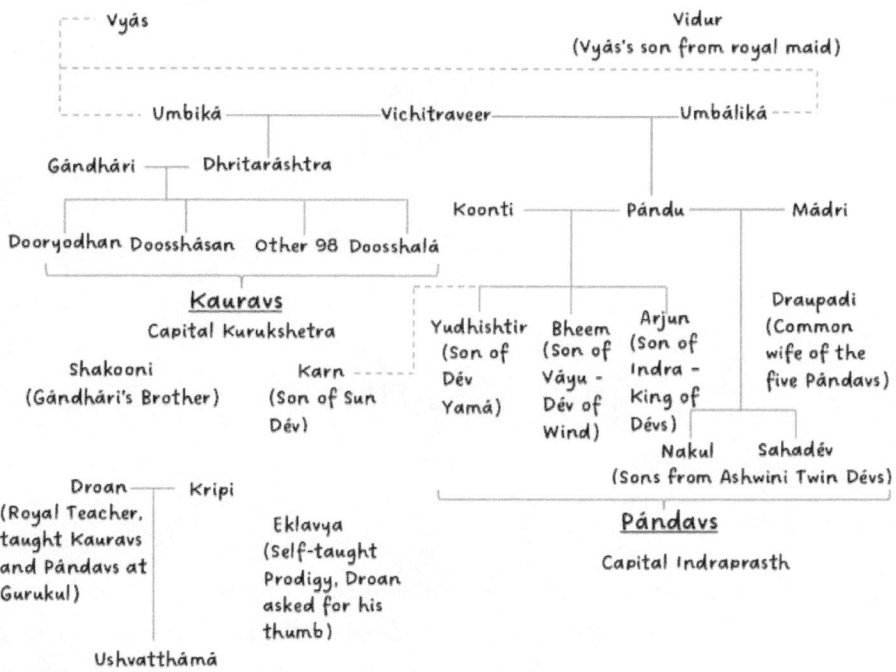

CHAPTER 55

The Memorial

Nálandá, Bihar, India

"I don't get it." Saira held her temple between her forefinger and thumb, slowly squeezing till they met at the glabella. "It doesn't make any sense. We used all the tools in our bag. Aerial surveys, LiDAR mapping, I personally dragged the Radar around the ruins and beyond, spent hours scavenging with the magnetometer, scanned for days with the conductivity meters, but still nothing." She moved her hands to her hips, staring at the map on the wooden desktop. "We freakin' excavated adjoining rooms from the chamber, scanned and scanned, but nothing. At the very least, we should've found some artifacts or relics from these new chambers. The only things we have are the carvings of temples on the walls and the sculptures we found near Nagpur. Nothing more."

"You forget, Saira." Dr. Pradhan stood beside her. "These premises and the monasteries were plundered, destroyed, and put to the torch by the generals and troops of the western invader, Muhammad Khilji. Enough evidence in historical and geological records persists on that."

"But weren't these chambers uncovered recently? Khilji is estimated to have destroyed Nálandá around 1200 CE, right?"

"That's right, but even in Egypt, when researchers opened new chambers from underground, in and around the Valley of the Kings, they were already plundered. So, the thieves got to them years ago, perhaps centuries, and nature pulled back its cover of sand and dirt over them all the same."

"Agreed, but this area is quite fertile. There is no desert around. There has never been a desert in the past. Also, unlike in Egypt, where the chambers were plundered for gold, the main reason for the destruction here was the aim to destroy anything un-Islamic. Besides, we find ash deposits around the ruins, but none are inside these chambers. So, maybe they weren't opened during the invasion."

"You make a compelling point, Saira. Perhaps we should pause the field analysis and venture into a literature review. See what we find in written history."

"That was exactly my thought."

The next few months were spent scavenging museums and libraries, ingesting countless journals, manuscripts, and books. But it was too much.

"I- am- exhausted." Saira packed her backpack after spending a whole afternoon at the library. "I really need a break."

"Me too." Dr. Pradhan closed the book he was reading.

"I'm going to the Begampur wetlands for a walk. You want to come?"

"Sure, I'll come."

They dropped their bags at the guesthouse and went to the lake. The breeze was comforting. There was greenery everywhere. Birds of various kinds chirped, while some fished in the lake with their long beaks. In an hour, the sunset was on the horizon, leaving bronze trails in the sky. After a calm few hours, they walked back toward the guesthouse.

"Gosh, are we ever going to find anything about those temples in the carvings and sculptures?" Dr Pradhan's shoulders drooped about midway from the wetlands. They had searched for months, but there was no breakthrough.

"Perhaps we're looking in the wrong place."

"What do you mean?"

Saira halted, staring at the Xuanzang Memorial Building.

Dedicated to the Buddhist monk Xuanzang, the building had a peculiar Chinese architecture that was not particularly found in India.

"Oh yes, how did I forget about Xuanzang?"

They both rushed back to the library that instant.

"Well, look over here. According to these manuscripts, Xuanzang, the seventh-century Chinese monk-scholar-traveler-translator, spent around two years in Nálandá under the tutelage of Shilabhadra, the head of the institute in those times. It says that Xuanzang returned to his hometown with around seven hundred Sanskrit texts, two hundred relics inside five hundred cases."

"That's intriguing."

"So, you mean—"

"That we need to check out China."

CHAPTER 56

Boon & Curse

Near Yemeni Peninsula

The five men slept for about seven hours, dreaming of Sánchez's story. When they awoke, a hearty supper greeted them in the dining area. There was freshly baked pita, grilled goat, chicken biryani, and salads. When they gathered again on the top deck along with Sánchez, the sweet smell of caffeine filled their noses as freshly brewed qahwa was served.

Sánchez smelled his coffee, took a sip, and picked up the story from where he had left off. "In the beginning, everyone adhered to the code of war and fought according to the strict rules written in the code," he began. "But battles don't just leave their marks on bodies and minds. They also squelch principles." Sánchez tapped his forehead with his index finger. "As days passed, rules withered. Both sides twisted them to suit their situation."

"Duels and battles spanned in all directions across the never-ending landscape. Blood flowed like water. The thirsty soil soaked it all until it could soak no more, intermittently spitting out puddles of red. A torrent of arrows filled the sky. Elephant thumps shuddered the earth. Horses galloped for as long as one could see, some dragging chariots with fighters along. Thousands perished.

Despite the carnage, however, the first nine days of the war did not see either Kauravs or Pándavs taking a decisive lead. Pándavs tried hard to gain the upper hand, but Dévavrut played true to his reputation. He commanded the Kaurav battalions with spectacular precision and countered with aggressive strategies. No one, not even Arjun, could do anything.

The only good news for Pándavs was that Dévavrut loved them as much as he did the Kauravs. It was only because of the sheer sense of duty toward the ancestral crown and Dooryodhan's relentless compelling that he decided to fight at all. His heart, though, was split on either side. He made sure not to cause much harm to the Pándavs while he was the leader. As a result, the war did not swing to any one side. It stayed balanced. Dévavrut thought both sides would fatigue by the impasse and eventually negotiate a truce.

"This war will continue forever as long as Great Uncle Dévavrut leads their forces. We must do something to get him out of the battleground," Sahadév reasoned.

"But how?" Yudhishtir asked. "Have you forgotten his boon? Only he can decide when he will die. Besides, who can take him on? He can't be defeated."

"Did I say anything about killing him? There are other ways to get him out. I have an idea. But you may not like it, brother."

Sahadév and Yudhishtir stared at each other in silence.

"Speak," Bheem intervened.

"We all know that our great uncle is a man of principles, steadfast about the rules of combat, old-fashioned. He also has his own rules." Sahadév paused, looking at Yudhishtir.

"We're listening."

"One of these rules is to never fight a woman. We can take advantage of this. That's the only way we can take him down."

"How the hell can we get a woman to fight?" Bheem asked.

"It's against the rules. I won't allow it," Yudhishtir protested.

"Hear me out first." Sahadév paused, staring at the others. "How about we have Shikhundee steer the chariot when Arjun fights our great father?"

"Absolutely not! As I pointed out, that's against the rules," Yudhishtir shouted. "Women are not allowed on the battlefield. It's like stabbing someone in the back. I will not cause adharma by deceiving anyone like that, even if I have to pay for it with my life?"

"Is it really deceiving, big brother?" Sahadév argued. "Shikhundee is only born a woman. Everyone knows Shikhundee considers himself a man. He dresses, behaves, and acts like a man. Haven't we considered him a man ever since we have known him? Isn't he here because we all consider him a man? It's not his problem that our great uncle fails to recognize this."

Yudhishtir was speechless.

"I don't see a problem with this," Kryshná said. "You would be disrespecting Shikhundee by not allowing him to fight."

Yudhishtir was uncomfortable but gave his assent.

The plan succeeded. Dévavrut refused to attack Shikhundee. Arjun grabbed the chance. He pierced Dévavrut's entire body with arrows. The patriarch looked like a man on skewers, ready for the fire. This was the defining event of the war. An event that turned the tide. Sometimes the Pándavs gained the upper hand, while other times the Kauravs."

Sánchez swallowed. The five men stared at him impatiently.

"Dévavrut's defeat was a major blow to the Kauravs," Sánchez continued, looking at their eager faces.

"Those cheating bastards," Dooryodhan shouted. "They broke the rules."

"Guru Droan, you'll take charge of the Kaurav army. Avenge our great uncle."

"As you command."

Droan stormed his way through the battlefield. He didn't have the same reservation or soft spot for Pándavs. To him, winning was all that mattered. Despite Droan's carnage, Pándavs minimized their losses by always shielding high-value targets. As Dévavrut was out, Karn entered the war.

"Stay beside me. We cannot dominate them unless we trap Arjun. He's their strength. Taking him out is half of the job done. They'll lose their morale," Droan said to Karn. "You are the only one who could defeat Arjun. I've heard of the celestial weapon you possess."

"Yes, it has Arjun's name written over it from the day I got it."

"Very well."

Lord Kryshná, who participated in the war only as Arjun's charioteer, had knowledge of this weapon. He kept Arjun far away from Karn," Sánchez said, his tone excited. "Taking advantage of this, Droan and other Kauravs trapped the remaining Pándav brothers within a circular battle formation. They attacked the four brothers from three hundred and sixty degrees with all their might. Arjun was the only one who knew how to counter this battle formation. He had learned this from Droan himself, but his being away put the Pándav brothers in grave danger.

Fortunately for them, Arjun passed this knowledge to his eighteen-year-old son Abhimanyu. Abhimanyu, though, had never fought before; he could remember it only partly. Along with his company, he attacked the circular formation in the manner Arjun taught him and entered with his battalion, creating an open side. The four Pándav brothers exited from this end while Abhimanyu's force provided cover fire with arrows. Droan countered and sealed the weakness, but the Pándav brothers were already out by then. Abhimanyu, on the other hand, was trapped within.

Frustrated by the loss of this opportunity, Droan and the other Kauravs attacked him ruthlessly. The young warrior found himself in a firestorm of arrows from all directions. He had none to help him. All his men had perished.

The arrows paused. He continued fighting with whatever he had, but he was no match for the gang. The Kauravs savored their kill. It was the first high-level Pándav casualty."

"Goddammit. It isn't fair. He was just a boy," Darren screamed.

"Fair and war go as well together as water and oil," Sánchez said. "No matter what the rules, when blood spills on the ground, fairness goes with it. Besides, Pándavs abandoned the rules first."

Shock seized their minds.

After a few minutes, Sánchez continued.

"I feel for your loss, but the war is not over yet," Lord Kryshná said. "As long as Droan and Karn are fighting together, we have no chance. We've got to do something about it."

"Droan's only weakness is his son Ushvatthámá," Sahadév said. "He keeps him safe at all times."

"A son for a son." Bheem's menacing eyes showed a longing for vengeance.

"Control your emotions, Bheem. Nakul and Arjun, you both will engage Ushvatthámá with your battalions, take him away from Droan. Arjun, you'll take him down," Yudhishtir ordered. "The rest of us will attack the Guru."

But Ushvatthámá proved to be a hard coconut. Unable to kill him, the Pándavs spread a rumor about his death. Although untrue, amid the confusion, Droan could not find his son. He tried to confirm the news but had no luck. Adding to the cacophony, an elephant by the same name had perished too. When one of the foot soldiers mistakenly confirmed the death, thinking Droan was asking about the elephant, Droan accepted the worst. He lost concentration, focus, and motivation. Right at that moment, the Pándavs struck.

Filled with grief, Droan did not respond, closed his eyes, and dismounted his chariot. The next minute, Dhrishtadyumna swung his sword, beheading him. A frown overtook Sánchez's face. "It was time for the Kauravs to feel the burn. Dooryodhan was furious."

"Karn, I want you to command," he said. "You possess the power, the skills, and a celestial weapon. I have high hopes from you, brother."

Pándavs devised all kinds of plans, but unlike in the case of Dévavrut and Droan, they did not succeed. Karn shared their blood. He was a son of Koonti, a Pándav. Their eldest brother. Born in the same fashion as them, from the sun god. They didn't know all this. They didn't have an answer to his strategies. Finally, bending the rules of the war again, they used a Rákshas.

"Rákshas?" Darren asked.

"Yes, Rákshas. They were among the many mystical beings that fought the war. They were similar to what we call Giants; bigger, powerful, monstrous, and had horns on their heads."

"This Rákshas cleared parts of the Kaurav army like a tornado."

On the word tornado, Darren stood up. "Tell me more about the Rákshas," he demanded.

"Well, a Rákshas draws power from the darkness. As the night grows, their power increases," Sánchez replied. "At times, they move at such speed that they appear like a small twister."

Was that a Rákshas? It must be, Darren thought. He had experienced a weird incident involving a twister in his past in Kansas. He had shared his story with the other four in Barcelona.

They exchanged looks in silence.

"Another rule of war was that it would be fought only during daylight," Sánchez interrupted. "Although the Kauravs had Rákshas in their army too, they were introduced only during dusk. Pándavs countered with their own Rakshas army leading to a stalemate. This particular Rakshas, though, was a halfbreed. He was born of the union of Bheem and a Rákshas woman he had met during their thirteen-year exile. His name was Ghatotkuch.

As Ghatotkuch was half Rákshas and half human, he could fight during the day, a trump card of the Pándavs. With his barbaric powers, Ghatotkuch caused havoc. Thousands of Kaurav soldiers died from his single blow.

"Use your special weapon," Dooryodhan pleaded to Karn.

"But it's for Arjun and Arjun alone."

"We have no choice, brother. Look how the Rákshas massacres our men. Please, I beg you."

Realizing there was no other way, Karn launched his one and only celestial weapon toward Ghatotkuch. It was more powerful than anything used till now in the war. It struck the beast in his chest like a bolt of lightning.

The ground shuddered as the Rákshas perished."

Sánchez paused, breathing heavily. He had narrated very fast.

"Despite this loss, it was a moment of opportunity for the Pándavs," he said. "With the special weapon gone, Arjun could now fight the mighty Karn!"

CHAPTER 57

Charioteer

"So, did Arjun kill Karn?" Ojoré was eager to find out Karn's fate.

"Well," Sánchez said as he yawned. "Even with the celestial weapon gone, Karn was stronger than Arjun. He kept the momentum on his side. Bheem was desperate to avenge his son Ghatotkuch's death. He attacked Karn from every opening he could find or create. Karn not only blocked him every single time but also returned his moves with cuts and scrapes. Every wound enraged Bheem.

"Bheem's desperation concerns me," Yudhishtir told Arjun, Nakul, and Sahadév. "You three focus only on Karn, even if some of our factions are unprotected."

"Bheem, leave Karn to these three, attack the other Kauravs," Yudhishtir ordered.

"I have to kill Karn. I can't rest until I've had my revenge."

"Brother, I understand," Yudhishtir reached to touch Bheem's shoulders, "but, you can't defeat Karn like that. He is too strong. Use that frustration to fight Doosshásan. Don't forget that he humiliated our wife in front of the entire court. Remember that ungodly game of dice. Remember how he dragged her by the hair from the palace? Don't forget your oath to kill him. You promised Draupadi his blood."

Bheem roared. He stormed toward Doosshásan with all his barbaric might. The battle was vicious. After hours of trying, Bheem broke through the circle of soldiers that protected Doosshásan and, with one blow from his mace, knocked Doosshásan off his chariot. He seized him, knelt, and placed him on his thigh facing down. With his bare hands, piece by piece, Bheem ripped out Doosshásan's limbs. The blood sprayed over his body and onto the already-drenched earth."

Diego's eyebrows rose in shock. "Wow, I wouldn't want to be on the wrong side of Bheem. His wrath is scary, gave me the chills."

"I freakin' loved it." Darren grinned.

Sánchez did not pause further. "On the other side of the battlefield," he began. "Karn resisted attacks from the four Pándav brothers with ease. The Pándavs had to do something. He was the only great warrior standing between them and Dooryodhan.

The following day, they all attacked Karn at once. That didn't work either. Karn defeated all the Pándavs except Arjun, who, at the right moment, was charioted away by Kryshná. It seemed like the end for the four defeated Pándavs. They waited for death at Karn's behest. But much to the disappointment of Dooryodhan, Karn spared their lives.

"Why? Why the hell would you spare their lives?" Dooryodhan questioned. "Explain right now, or else I'll consider it treason."

Karn sighed. "I never wanted anyone to know this. But I'll tell you now." He stared at the ceiling of the tent. "The mother of the Pándavs came to me some days back and," he swallowed,

"And what?" Dooryodhan shouted

"She pleaded with me to spare their lives should I ever defeat them,"

"And you agreed? Just like that?" Dooryodhan shouted again, his temper shooting up like a geyser. "Knowing very well that they are our enemies."

"I did." Karn closed his eyes and sighed again. "But only partially."

"Partially? What does that mean?"

"It means I agreed to spare the lives of all the Pándavs except Arjun. Arjun is my nemesis."

"But why the hell did you agree to spare their lives at all?"

Dooryodhan's face was like a hot iron pulled out from the kiln.

"Do you understand that we almost won the war had it not been for your stupidity? Tell me," he shouted frantically. "Tell me why you did it?"

Karn cleared his throat and spoke in a heavy voice. "Yudhishtir is not Koonti's firstborn. He's not the eldest Pándav."

"What are you saying?"

"I am the eldest Pándav. I am Koonti's firstborn."

He paused. "I was born before her marriage to Pándu."

It was as if the earth was pulled from under Dooryodhan's feet.

"My mother Koonti was desperate and pleaded with me to join them and fight against you, as I am, according to the rules, a Pándav. But—but I refused. I could not betray you. You're the only person who accepted me for talent, disregarded my common upbringing, and considered me a true friend." Karn closed his eyes. "Even though she abandoned me as a child, I agreed to spare all the brothers except Arjun to repay the nine months of labor she endured for me. But only once."

He stepped forward. Held Dooryodhan's hands in his.

"Now that the debt is repaid."

"But, but—" murmured Dooryodhan, still processing this revelation.

"I stayed because my allegiance lies with you. As long as I live, I will fight for you. I'll accept any punishment you bestow upon me with a smile. Including death."

Silence hung in the air like a sword about to behead.

Dooryodhan did not know how to react. He couldn't punish Karn, nor could he abandon him.

He closed his eyes for several long minutes.

"I trust you. That's why I forgive you." He paused.

"Now," Dooryodhan said as he stared into Karn's eyes, "go, get me your brothers."

"To defeat Karn, Kryshná and Sahadév devised a plan. They had placed a mole in the Kaurav army. The mole was Nakul and Sahadév's maternal uncle Shalya's squire," Sánchez continued. "Shalya had gone to Dooryodhan, defying his nephews. He was a good friend of Dévavrut and wanted to take his side. Trusting this friendship, Dooryodhan agreed. Karn, though, disliked Shalya. The loathing was mutual. Shalya believed Karn did not belong in this war, fighting at the same level as the royals, let alone commanding the entire army. He did not know Karn's story and wanted to be the commander himself."

"Instigate a fight between Shalya and Karn," Sahadév told the squire.

The pawn did as commanded. Not only did Shalya quarrel with Karn, but he also humiliated and insulted him. Dooryodhan intervened.

"Karn is your commander," he told Shalya, "you better accept it. And to make sure you understand it, I am going to make you Karn's charioteer for the day."

Shalya stormed out of the tent. "I am going to walk away and join the Pándav army," he told his squire. "Make arrangements."

But the squire reasoned against it. "My lord, your friend Dévavrut's gone. They have no reason to spare us if we go against them. If they get wind of this, they'll slaughter us before we get back to the Pándavs. Besides, the Pándavs will not take us back now. We defied them at the start of the war. I'd suggest you become the charioteer tomorrow and cause problems for Karn while he is engaged in battle."

Shalya took the squire's advice. The news reached the Pándav camp.

"Excellent!" Kryshná cheered. "Tomorrow's our chance to kill Karn. Shalya's ego will create an opening for us."

The next day, after confirming Shalya as the charioteer, Arjun attacked Karn. He had avoided doing it till now. The other Pándavs kept the Kauravs from coming to Karn's aid.

Karn was all by himself.

The fight was fierce. Arjun gave it his all but still fell short. Both of them chased each other, taking their chariots all over the battlefield. After several hours of attacks and counterattacks, Shalya sensed his opportunity. There was an unsafe patch a few meters from the chariot. He purposefully drove into it.

It worked. The chariot got stuck. Shalya refused to free the chariot. A furious Karn stepped down and attempted to free it himself.

Right at that moment, looking into his back, against the rules of war, Arjun grabbed all the arrows he had in his quiver and, one by one, launched them toward Karn. They pierced his back.

Finally, in the most cowardly manner, the great warrior of the Kaurav army breathed his last."

CHAPTER 58

Banishment

Arabian Sea

A cool breeze caressed the yacht deck as the five digested Karn's demise. Matthew entered the top deck and interjected in the intense conversation. "I wanted to get out of that bed."

"Oh, how are you, my friend?" Ojoré stood up and ran toward him. "We didn't realize you were awake."

"I've been awake for hours," he said. "I'm doing much better now. It sounds like you all lost track of time."

"Yes, Sánchez revealed a lot of information to us. We're still struggling to absorb all of it," Diego added.

"We're so glad to see you out of danger." Ojoré smiled a cheerful smile.

"Thanks for saving sun." Liang shook his hand.

"No problem, mate. I came to tell you all I'm fine. Get some fresh air." He smiled. "Do you guys mind if I stay?"

"Not at all. Take a seat." Ojoré offered his own.

"When I say this, I'm sure I echo all," Aarno said. "We're so relieved to see you recovered, Matthew. We all felt guilty about what happened in Barcelona. We'd still have chains on our bodies and drugs in our veins if it were not for your help."

"You don't have to feel guilty. I did it for my child."

Matthew sat down beside Ojoré. "Please continue, pretend I'm not here."

"What happened next?" Darren asked, looking at Sánchez, impatient to get back to the story. He wanted to find out how this bizarre story related to him. They all did.

Sánchez looked at Matthew and grinned. Matthew charged toward him in anger but was held back by Ojoré.

"You're weak now. You'll get your chance."

"Oye, continue, or shall I get up?" Darren shouted.

"Okay, okay. I was just waiting for you guys to exchange courtesies. But before we proceed, I need a break to freshen up a little."

"Let's take you downstairs." Darren walked toward him, pulled him up, and nudged him to walk.

Matthew watched them descend the stairs, walked up to the taffrail, and leaned. The air was crisp. Ojoré joined him. They both stared ahead.

It was a night without a moon. The sky dazzled with starlight that had traveled through the cosmos for countless light years. Miles away from civilization, the arm of the Milky Way appeared breathtaking. In the scarce light, waves of the Arabian Sea appeared menacing and mysterious, as if made of mercury.

"For a while, we thought we lost you." Ojoré turned to face him. "What you did for us, for me, I couldn't sleep—"

"Wouldn't you do the same if you were in that situation?"

There was silence for a while.

"I don't know how to say it or whether to say it all." Ojoré moved his hand over the taffrail nervously.

"Just say what's on your mind."

"I- I feel this deep connection with you. Maybe because of our horrible pasts or something else, I can't understand, but I really do."

Matthew smiled a wide smile. "I do too."

He held Ojoré's hand. They stared into each other's eyes.

"When this is done. When we get away from these people."

"I would want nothing more—"

The moment was spoiled by Sánchez's loud clearing of his throat as he and Darren returned.

Darren pushed him to the floor. "Alright, enough now, continue the goddamn story."

Sánchez closed his eyes. "Where was I?"

"Karn had died," Liang reminded.

"Yes, yes—" He sighed. "So, Dooryodhan was devastated by Karn's demise. He, though, did not notice Shalya's foul play in Karn's death. Besides, Shalya was the only king left on his side. Dooryodhan made Shalya the commander. With Karn gone, the Pándavs attacked the Kauravs like a pack of wild dogs."

"After a prolonged battle, Yudhishtir killed Shalya with his spear. On the other side of the battlefield, Sahadév killed Shakooni, the one responsible for the Pándavs' exile by the game of dice. Dooryodhan was the only Kaurav remaining. He knew that Bheem had vowed to kill all one hundred Kaurav brothers by himself. He used this pledge. It was his last attempt to salvage something from what was left.

"I challenge Bheem to a duel. If I win, I'd be spared and allowed to rule Hustinápoori," Dooryodhan said.

"And why would we entertain that offer?" Yudhishtir half laughed. "All your brothers are dead. Your commanders are dead. You've lost."

"Bheem, I know you have pledged to kill all the Kauravs. I'm sure you don't want anyone else killing me."

"He's mine," Bheem bellowed. His ego didn't allow him to concede.

"We accept your condition." Bheem agreed without consulting the others.

"But Bheem—"

"Big brother, you took your chance with the dice. Now it's my turn. But unlike last time, we will not lose."

Yudhishtir could not reason with his rage.

A ferocious battle ensued, a battle of two enormous beasts.

"Bheem had underestimated his opponent. Dooryodhan was clearly an expert in the mace. Not only did he fight with brute power, but he also endured mighty blows from Bheem's mace. No one knew that Dooryodhan had only one weak point on his body," Sánchez added. "They say that when he fought, Dooryodhan's body turned into a mesh of crystals above the waist and below the knees. It was a blessing that his mother granted him with her sacrificial powers of blindness. It made those parts of his body unbreakable."

Who are you to the blind whose gaze can make one's body as strong as the strongest thing in the world? Gustáv's question from Paris rang in Sánchez's head as he told the five men about Dooryodhan's mother's powers of blindness. Drágosláv and Gustáv didn't understand the meaning of this question back then, but Sanchez did.

"What happened then?" Darren interrupted Sánchez's thought.

Sánchez swallowed. "The only one who knew about this was Kryshná," he continued.

"Hit him below the waist and above the knees," Kryshná advised Bheem.

"But it's against the rules," Bheem replied. "I'm no coward."

"Rules were the first thing to die on this battlefield, my friend. The eldest Pandav died because Arjun's arrows pierced him from behind. Was that not cowardly?"

"Do what needs to be done." Kryshná patted his back. "The enemy, the time, is not for chivalry. There's only one way to defeat him, and that's this."

"Bheem did as suggested." Sánchez coughed as he talked. "It worked. Dooryodhan screamed in pain as his thighs cracked from the mace's impact. The Pándav camp was filled with joy in their victory. Pándav flags flapped all across the battlefield. For miles and miles, the winners reveled loudly. They raised their arms toward the sky in triumph."

"That's like it," Darren cheered with his glass raised.

"They left Dooryodhan bleeding and dying on the battlefield where he fell. But it was a mistake." Sánchez ignored him.

"Ushvatthámá—Droan's son, was the only prominent warrior still alive from the Kaurav camp. After the Kauravs officially conceded defeat, he stealthily approached the dying Dooryodhan.

"My Lord, what have they done to you!" Ushvatthámá held Dooryodhan's hand.

"It's over, Ushvatthámá, we've lost the war." A tear rolled down Dooryodhan's eye.

"I'm still alive. I won't let your death go in vain."

"You are alone, my friend."

"Alone I may be, but I will avenge my father, Karn, you. I have a plan."

"What- is- it?" Dooryodhan's voice cracked in pain. He had only a little time to live.

"Indraprastha. The Pándav children and women are in the palace. I'll kill them all."

"There's no- valor- in it."

"I don't care about valor. The treachery, the deception they used to kill my father, did it have any valor? No. I want revenge. I will have it. If we don't win, neither will they."

Ushvatthámá succeeded in his plan, and all the Pándav children perished in that horrendous attack. The only one to survive was the unborn grandson of Arjun, who was still in his mother's womb, away from Indraprastha.

"I want his head," Bheem screamed.

"Yes, he cannot stay alive. Let's go," Yudhishtir marshalled everyone.

"Wait," Kryshná said. "You need to forgive him."

"How can you ask us to forgive the man who killed innocent children, women?" Bheem shouted. "He needs to die."

"I did not say he will go unpunished."

"What punishment can be worse than death for him?" Yudhishtir asked Kryshná.

"A miserable life," Kryshná replied. "I promise you all. He will endure a punishment worthy of his crime. He will beg for death, but he won't have it until he has repented for his deeds, unless the time is right."

Kryshná severed the red ruby from Ushvatthámá's forehead. It was like his soul was taken away.

"You will live a cursed life till the end of this era," Kryshná declared.

He banished Ushvatthámá from civilization. "You will have to live hidden from the world, old, wrinkled, and weak," he said. "You will live this curse for eons. You will endure this until the time is right for you to return and redeem yourself for this cowardly act."

Sánchez went silent. He looked at the five men.

Not an eye wandered from his face.

"They say he lives even today, somewhere in the deep corners of this world, waiting to live again. Waiting to finally die."

CHAPTER 59

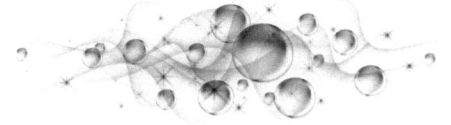

The Cursed One

Somewhere in the world

It had been a torture of the worst kind. Not for decades or centuries, he had suffered for millennia. Visions from the past stormed into his mind. No one who ever existed had undergone a punishment like this.

All those people who seek immortality don't know how horrendous it is. How it is with everyone you know gone, not able to talk to anybody, the White Ghost thought.

Memories of banishment engulfed him like dark clouds. He remembered how the deceitful killing of his father, Droan, and the death of all one hundred Kauravs enraged him. He recalled how desperate he was to kill all the Pándavs, how he attempted to end the Pándav lineage. He thought of how the Pándavs humiliated him in front of the entire kingdom and how they sentenced him to death amidst the cursing and mocking court. He recalled how Lord Kryshná convinced the Pándavs otherwise and saved his life, how an alternate punishment was declared, and how he had to endure it for millennia, living like a corpse.

Most of all, the last conversation he had with Kryshná rang in his head like a temple bell. Only Kryshná had known the real reason for the war, the world's most important truth. Before Ushvatthámá was dragged out of Hustinápoori, lord Kryshná spoke into his ears one last time.

You can only redeem yourself from this curse when this all starts again, the words echoed inside his brain. *When the great cycle ends millennia later, only then will you find your gem, only then will you know the truth, and—only then will you know what to do.* The words had tormented him for thousands of years.

Tears rolled down his cheeks.

But now, he was closer, closer to redeeming himself, closer to washing himself of that cowardly sin.

And only after you accomplish your mission, you will be forgiven and allowed to die, were Kryshná's last words to him.

He sighed.

"Before I take another step outside this cave of yours, you have to explain what's happening. Tell me the entire story. All of it," Aroon interrupted his chain of thoughts.

The White Ghost took a deep breath, swallowed, and narrated the grand old story. Like with Sánchez and the five men, it went on for days.

He told Aroon about the entire Kuru ancestry, right from the days of Emperor Bharat, about the vast empire that the dynasty ruled over, about the great and magnificent cities of Hustinápoori and Indraprastha, the way of life in those days, and about all the wealth that the empire amassed.

He told Aroon about his father, Droan, and how he taught the princes. He spoke of the Kauravs, of Kryshná, of Karn, and finally the Pándavs. He spoke of Yudhishtir's honesty, Bheem's strength, Arjun's skill and determination, Nakul's handsomeness, and Sahadév's intelligence. He recounted the constant tension between the two sides and how it all led to the greatest war ever. He described the war in great detail, including each battle and each warrior. He revealed the truth about his banishment and the curse.

"My name is Ushvatthámá," he declared, "and I am the cursed warrior."

And in the end, he disclosed the biggest shock to Aroon. "And if you're still wondering where you fit in all this, you, my friend..." He paused, then spoke, "...are the great warrior Karn. Reborn."

"Me? Me? I'm Karn!" Aroon shouted. "No. Are you insane? Me? Really, me?"

"Didn't I show you the vision?" the White Ghost said, referring to the vision Aroon saw in the Kashmir Mountains. "Believe it or not, but the truth is—you are him."

Aroon didn't know how to respond. He could not comprehend it. The revelation froze his mind, and it took him several minutes to compose himself.

"So Kryshná told you that this would all start again?"

Ushvatthámá nodded.

"But why?"

"That's the great truth, isn't it? The holy grail of humanity."

The White Ghost smiled after a long time. "I will let you process this first."

Aroon did not press him hard on this. The truth swamped him.

"My foster parents were Muslim," Aroon said. "I'm Hindu." He stared at a corner inside the cave. "Although I never read the epic, I knew the story a little bit. But not in my wildest dreams did I ever think that I am Karn. Even now, I can't and don't believe it."

"You will when you lift the Vijaya again." Ushvatthámá stared into his eyes.

"Vijaya?"

"Yes, Vijaya. Karn's weapon, your weapon, the mighty bow."

Aroon's brain was not ready.

"A bow in today's world? There are automatic guns and nuclear weapons out there."

The White Ghost grinned. His expression was that of an adult talking to a kid who knew nothing but believed he knew everything.

"All these weapons fail when you cross the ice-cold portal, my friend. There are even enormous weapons and counter-weapons."

"So, guns and bullets can't hurt me?"

"They can, for now, in this nascent state of yours."

"Nascent?"

"A warrior is not really ready without his armor and weapons, is he?" Aroon was quiet.

"Once you have your Vijaya bow and don your golden armor, no ordinary weapon will harm you," Ushvatthámá said. "Till then, we must be extremely careful."

Aroon's mind drifted toward the ice-cold portal. He closed his eyes for several minutes.

"You murmured several times about The Confluence, what is it?" he asked, "and the bubbles, I am still confused about them, how they appear, how we access them. And—" A chill went down Aroon's spine thinking about the creatures that attacked them. "—the things who attacked us, who are they?"

"That's a lot there." Ushvatthámá walked to the cave's entrance. "But I will try to explain as much as I can."

A cold breeze hit his face, carrying the freshness of the lush, green jungle. He closed his eyes, drew a deep breath. "Didn't I say that the cycle of time is the most powerful force in the universe?"

Aroon walked up to him, stood beside him, and nodded.

"We're all tied to it, to the great cycle." Ushvatthámá opened his eyes and turned toward Aroon. "Have you heard of the Yugs?"

"You mean the four Yugs?"

Ushvatthámá nodded. "What are they? How are they part of the great cycle of time?"

"I know only their names." Aroon rubbed his chin with his hand. "But I don't understand anything else."

Ushvatthámá returned to the cave. Aroon followed.

Ushvatthámá picked up a small piece of partially burned wood from an old bonfire at the corner. "The existence of us humans and non-humans, of our worlds and other worlds, of everything around us, is because of cycles." He walked to the wall near the stone bed, which had a big, flat face. "And each of these cycles are made of smaller parts, with distinct characteristics."

Ushvatthámá drew a big circle on the wall. "Our day here is a cycle broken down into morning, afternoon, evening, and night." He drew a straight, vertical line that divided the circle into two halves. "Our year is made up of seasons." He crossed two more lines passing through the center, one from top-left to bottom-right and another from top-right to bottom-left. "And there are many more cycles like that, some of which we perceive and some—" he added two more radii on either side at the bottom, "—are beyond our perception." The circle was divided into eight sectors. Two sets of four different sizes.

"And the grandest of them all is the Mahayug, the cycle of the four Yugs."

Ushvatthámá stepped back to look at the wall, making sure everything was symmetrical.

"First of the four is called the Kritá Yug." He wrote inside the first pair of sectors on either side of the vertical diameter.

"Second is called the Tretá Yug." He wrote inside the next two sectors on either side.

"Next is the Dwápar Yug." He wrote in the following two sectors. "And the last is—"

"Kali Yug," Aroon interjected.

"That's right." Ushvatthámá nodded as he wrote into the last pair of sectors. He went back once more, and both of them stared at the wall.

"But what do they mean?" Aroon asked

"The Yugs are different ages of our world, of our history," Ushvatthámá replied. "Together, they make the Mahayug, the grand cycle of time which repeats itself every twenty-four thousand years."

"Twenty-four thousand years?" Aroon was dumbfounded by that number.

"Yes, twenty-four thousand years." Ushvatthámá nodded, moved closer to the wall once more.

"One half of the cycle is made of the Ascending Yugs, and the other half is made of the Descending Yugs." He drew two arcs around the circle on either side with upward and downward-facing arrows and wrote the words ascending and descending.

"Why are they of different sizes?" Aroon stared at the diagram on the wall.

"Because each Yug lasts for a different number of years. Kritá Yug lasts for forty-eight hundred years." Ushvatthámá wrote the number on the wall.

"Tretá Yug lasts for thirty-six hundred years." He wrote the next number. "Dwápar Yug for twenty-four hundred and Kali Yug for twelve hundred."

"What do you mean by ascending and descending?" Aroon leaned closer to the wall.

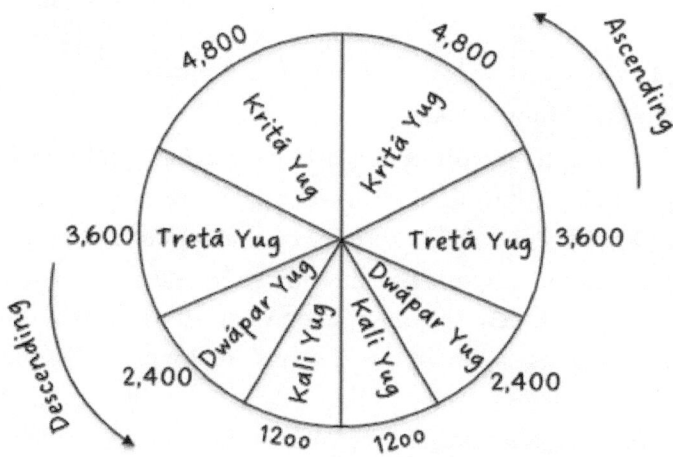

"I am telling you what I know. In my days, I was a warrior, not a scholar. I know not the reasoning behind it." Ushvatthámá finished writing and stepped back to stand beside Aroon.

Aroon stood in silence for a while, looking at the wall.

"So, coming back to my question," he said, "how does this link to the bubbles, and what is The Confluence?"

"Before I tell you about The Confluence, you must understand The Diffluence."

"The Diffluence?" Aroon's head was spinning with so much information.

"Yes, The Diffluence." Ushvatthámá paused. "It is said that the Kali Yug is the age of darkness," he continued. "You know why?"

Aroon shook his head.

"Because it begins after The Diffluence," Ushvatthámá answered his own question.

"But what is the Diffluence?" Aroon was getting impatient.

"Disintegration."

"Disintegration of what?" Aroon narrowed his eyebrows.

Ushvatthámá moved close to the wall once again. Aroon followed, stood beside him.

Outside, clouds gathered in the sky, casting a dark shadow over the jungle. Gusts of wind howled through the trees. Lighting flashed. Thunders roared.

"The place we go to when we enter the bubbles—"

"What of it?" Aroon asked.

"—It is a completely different world from this. A realm rather, realm of the Nágs," Ushvatthámá said. He went to the corner, lit a fire with the powers of his ruby. The cave flickered from the light of the dancing flames.

"And there are other worlds, realms like that." He lifted a small burning piece of wood, held it near the diagram on the wall. "Realm of the Upsarás, Realm of the Yakshas, Realm of the Rákshas, Realm of the Gundharvs and more."

"Each of these realms is distinct in nature, inhabited by different beings with special abilities—special powers. Each is governed by different rules and customs, some civilized, others barbaric," he continued. "During the last Dwápar Yug, all these worlds were one. The Great War I described to you, our war, was fought by these beings, too. Some sided with us, and some fought on the other side. But—" Ushvatthámá swallowed.

"But?" Aroon's face lit up in excitement.

"—But after the war ended, when Kryshná died, slowly and steadily, the worlds broke apart. It is during this separation that the bubbles appeared. For years, people used these bubbles to move from realm to realm. They are like holes in a fabric, like portals." Ushvatthámá paused, looking at Aroon. Aroon did not speak.

"As time passed, only a few could see and access them, and there came a day when the worlds parted for good. This whole phenomenon, this whole time from the appearance of the bubbles to their disappearance, to the final isolation of the worlds, is called The Diffluence. That is when the Kali Yug, the dark age, began." Ushvatthámá moved the burning wood from one hand to the other. "For all of this age, the worlds remained in isolation."

"Until now," Aroon said with a stern voice.

"Until now," Ushvatthámá repeated.

"And the coming together of the worlds is called The Confluence."

"Precisely."

"Does that mean the Kali Yug is over and the Dwápar Yug has just begun?"

Ushvatthámá's happiness showed on his face. Aroon was understanding it, believing in it. He needed Aroon to believe in himself, believe in his destiny.

"The Dwápar Yug must have commenced a few centuries back. I know it because that's when I got visions in my head of my lost gem."

Ushvatthámá brought the fire close to his face. The Black Prince's Ruby on his forehead twinkled in the firelight.

"I am sure that outside this cave, the bubbles must have reappeared. Although I was in hibernation, in my visions, I could see my ruby passing on from one to another. But I had to wait. Kryshná had told me not to act until there was a sign. And then, one day, my vision gave me a sign. A man somewhere had risen, and I felt the urge to awake, a compulsion to seek my gem."

"So, what will happen to the bubbles?"

"Right now, I can conjure and access the bubbles with the powers of my ruby. That's why we use them. They create shortcuts for us when we travel."

Ushwatthámá coughed from smoke as the fire in his hand died.

"They can randomly appear anywhere, but ordinary folks can't see them," he continued. "Special ones like you can see and accidentally pass through them occasionally but can spend only a little time in other realms. As years go by, they will be able to cross the bubbles when they wish and stay for as long as they wish. Eventually, all the worlds will merge into one, and the bubbles will disappear. The Confluence will conclude."

"And then?"

"It is said that The Great War repeats once in every Dwápar Yug."

Aroon did not speak. Standing here beside the White Ghost, in this jungle, inside this cave, his life in Kashmir, his parents, his foster parents, everything felt so distant.

It feels as if I have slept all along, dreaming, and have just awakened. He stared at the Mahayug cycle, trying to make sense of it all.

"You said Kryshná died," Aroon said. "But he's the almighty, isn't he? How can he die?"

"Whoever is born must die." Ushwatthámá smiled. "The truth is more complicated than we can comprehend."

He put the firewood back, walked toward Aroon. "But now, we're getting late. The time's just right."

"Right for what?"

Ushvatthámá held Aroon by the shoulders.

"The time is right to retrieve your weapon, the majestic Vijaya, and your golden Armor."

CHAPTER 60

The Five

Somewhere in the Arabian Sea

The five men rose from their cozy, top-deck seats one after another. The salty sea breeze hit their faces, and anticipation filled their minds. Somehow, they knew they were close to the revelation.

"So, after the war, Pándavs ruled the empire together?" Aarno asked

"Yes, they did," Sánchez answered, "but not for long."

"Why not?" Diego asked

"It was tradition to relinquish all worldly pleasures, retire, and go on pilgrimage when your descendants were ready to take the baton. Pándavs left the empire in the hands of their only surviving grandchild-Pariksheet."

Liang flexed his fingers. He had written nonstop.

"After all, it was a power struggle, like in so many dynasties worldwide," he said.

"In a way," Sánchez replied.

"What do you mean?"

"Every story is a power struggle. Life itself is one. Struggle amongst people, between man and nature, between the heart and mind. Sometimes you're the master, many times you're the pawn."

Sánchez paused.

"Dooryodhan was power hungry, but the Pándavs waged war only for Dharma-the righteous path, the rule of justice and fairness, the universal law of balance. The Pándavs did everything they could to avoid war. They suffered exile, humiliation, and treachery. But in the end, they waged war. They had to. They had to establish Dharma across the empire, they had no choice but to fight. As a royal born, establishing order, justice, and balance was their duty."

Silence.

They pondered the entire story for several minutes, trying to make sense of it all.

"I'm having a hard time recalling who did what to whom." Aarno scratched his head.

"Yup. It's a mountain of information. Other than the five Pándavs and Dooryodhan, I don't recall a damn name." Darren stretched his neck.

"Here, I've noted it down. It's not all, but most of it is there." Liang held out his notes.

They placed it on the bar counter and gathered around. The royal family tree branched several times and stretched to almost two sheets. Important names in the story were noted in neat handwriting and connected with lines. The information was still huge. When they were done reading, Liang folded the papers and shoved them in his pocket.

There was only one thing they wanted to know. How did this all relate to them?

They wanted to know what in this story was the reason for their abduction.

They listened for several days and tried to analyze it, but none of them understood how it related to them. Nothing in the story explained why Drágosláv and Sánchez restrained them in that fashion.

Aarno walked toward Sánchez.

"Enough of it now. It's time to tell us what we want to know," he said. "We've heard your story patiently, even Darren here behaved himself. Now, you better tell us how this all relates to us."

Darren cracked his knuckles like a boxer waiting for the sound of a bell.

"I thought you guys would've guessed it by now," Sánchez smirked. "Isn't it obvious?"

A wicked grin spanned across his face.

"No one? Really? Not even you, Liang?"

"Don't mess with me, I tell ya," Darren shouted. "Don't make me come there."

"Alright, alright. Let me give you all a clue," Sánchez said loud and clear.

"There were five Pándavs." He paused

"And there are five of you."

CHAPTER 61

Trackers

"You nuts? You mean the five of us are the Pándavs?" Diego's face looked puzzled.

"You think we're fools?" Darren lunged toward Sánchez and seized his arms. "You thought you'll tell us any crap, and we'll believe it."

"I swear, I swear, I'm telling the truth," Sánchez screamed in agony.

"Darren, Darren, hold on." Aarno patted Darren's shoulders. "Let's hear him out."

"Not this time. I have had enough of his lying."

"Please, just once, won't you listen to me?"

Darren let go with a jerk.

Sánchez steadied himself, moved away from Darren, and stood facing them all. "You," he said as he stared into Darren's eyes, "why do you have such extraordinary strength, so much so that you have to hide it to seem ordinary?"

"Don't you feel that you're just like Bheem, that it was your own story?"

Sánchez turned to face Aarno. "Why do you think you can't tolerate injustice, become uncomfortable if you have to say the tiniest bit of lie, even if it's for the good? Why are you a champion with Javelin, just like Yudhishtir was with the spear?"

"And you," Sánchez said as he turned his head toward Liang, "why are you so good, so fast at learning anything, remembering everything? Have an instinct to know when you'll be in trouble, just like Sahadév?"

Sánchez paused. Lifted his glass. Gulped down his drink, looking at Ojoré.

"Arjun was master of the bow and arrow," he continued, "he was a genius at aiming anything at any target." Sánchez walked toward Ojoré. "Any reason you have such a good aim at anything you pick, just like Arjun?"

He smiled. Turned toward Diego.

"Nakul was handsome, diplomatic, and an expert in Ayurvéd—the ancient knowledge of medicine, herbal medicine in particular. Can't you relate to that?"

They were dumbstruck. Although it sounded absurd, somewhere deep down, it resonated. They couldn't comprehend how to react. Their hearts pounded like those of a warhorse on a battlefield.

A long silence perched on the deck.

"Let's say we are the Pándavs—reborn," Liang said with hesitation, as if in two minds whether to accept it or not, "but that still doesn't explain why you abducted us?"

"That's more like it. Now you're thinking." There was enthusiasm in Sánchez's voice. "For that, you must know what happened after the Pándavs went on their pilgrimage."

He once again occupied his seat.

"As I said earlier, Pándavs left the kingdom with Pariksheet—Arjun's grandson and the only surviving heir after Ushvatthámá's massacre. Pariksheet was still in the womb when the massacre took place." Sanchez swallowed. "So, when they departed, they took their celestial weapons with them. Arjun took his divine bow, Yudhishtir his spear, Bheem his mighty mace, Sahadév his sword, and Nakul his dagger," Sánchez said excitedly. "On Kryshná's counsel, they also took the weapons from the warriors they defeated. Kryshná had given them the locations where they were supposed to leave the weapons before beginning their pilgrimage."

There was restlessness in his tone. Perhaps it was the thought of weapons.

"After traveling several hundred miles from Hustinápoori, one by one, at the exact spots where Kryshná had commanded them, they parted with their weapons."

Sánchez sighed.

"And that's why, my friends, we need you. That's the reason we abducted you. Only the Pándavs can retrieve their weapons again, which means only you can retrieve them."

Sánchez's eyes lit up as he told them about the weapons. "They're among the most powerful weapons of the world, they have magical powers. They have names. Some say that they have souls."

The excitement in his tone was like that of a child daydreaming about his birthday presents. "Only their original owners can retrieve them. Only the deserving can possess them." He stared at them with a smug expression on his face. "We know you all possess extraordinary powers. So, with the help of Matthew, we kept you drugged, temporarily paralyzed."

"But how did you find us? How did you know we are the Pandavs?" Liang asked.

Sánchez did not reply.

Darren twisted his arms again.

"All right. I'll tell you, but please let go of my hands. Please."

Aarno nodded. Darren let go. Sánchez breathed hard.

"Some time ago, I collapsed at work and went into a coma. While in a coma, I had visions, visions about you, I can't explain them, but that's how I came to know about you and the weapons."

"But how did you know our locations?" Liang asked again.

Sánchez told them about his job at the National Medical Research Laboratory and how he used the tools he built to track them down. He also told them about the biometric and identity database he developed for US intelligence and how he used online surveillance tools to locate them.

It was as if a scandal broke out.

"I can't believe it!" Diego shouted.

"It's the damn governments. They lay their freakin' hands on everyone," Darren replied. "A goddamn database of biometrics, genetic markers, bodily fluids, smart device locations, and god knows what else."

"That's insane," Aarno shouted.

Liang did not bother. The only thing on his mind was the weapons. "So, since you abducted us, you must know where the weapons are now, isn't it?"

"That's the part we haven't figured out yet," Sánchez lied. "So far, we focused our energy and resources on finding you five."

He knew. He knew everything. After all, he was the one who had set the wheels in motion.

"Guys, I think I should go back to my cabin," Matthew interrupted. "I feel weak."

"Shall I come with you? Help you get down?"

"Very kind of you, Ojoré, but I'll be fine. You guys continue." Matthew returned downstairs.

The five men were so shocked by the revelation that they failed to realize that their smart devices were still on the yacht and could be tracked.

CHAPTER 62

The Giant Pagoda

Xi'an, Shaanxi Province, China

A pleasant afternoon breeze hit her face as she exited The School of Cultural Heritage and walked through the massive Northwest University campus alongside her host, Xue Ting Li. Saira had traveled to Xi'an two months after visiting Nálandá in India and had already spent a little over three months in this city.

On either side of them were weeping willows whose long, flowing branches danced with the breeze, carrying the scent of spring.

"Beautiful day, isn't it, Dr. Solanki?" Xue Ting paced to keep up with Saira, whose normal walking speed was quite brisk.

"Marvelous, couldn't have asked for a better day. I hope there's no crowd. Please call me Saira. No need to be formal, Xue Ting."

"It's a weekday afternoon, I think we might get lucky on that. But you never know."

They came to a halt at the passenger pickup area, where a cab pulled up. Both women entered from either side and clicked the belt.

"Where to?" the cabbie asked Xue Ting in Mandarin.

"Giant Wild Goose Pagoda," she answered back in Mandarin. The driver nodded, checked his phone for traffic, pressed a button, and the meter ran.

"I'm glad you are accompanying me, Xue Ting. It's a lifesaver when there's a Mandarin speaker to help out. Thanks a lot."

"Please, Saira. It's my privilege. I have followed your research since you first corresponded with our department head last year." Xue Ting's face beamed as she spoke. "I was away from the university because of some urgent needs of my parents in my hometown. Otherwise, I would have assisted you from the day you arrived."

"Really? I had no idea. What intrigues you about my research?"

"Well, my research focuses on the interactions between ancient cultures, finding how it has influenced religion, philosophy, and traditions across regions, especially in China. I have read a lot about Vedic thought and philosophy lately. The fact that you let the ancient scriptures guide your archaeological study is so exciting."

"Isn't it? That's what has kept me going so far. The last few months have been quite challenging. I have reviewed countless manuscripts, theses, and artifacts at Northwest University. I went through the entire collection of Xuanzang at the museum, but we found no sign or clue of the sculptures we found in central India. The carvings at Nálandá were the only reference we found of them anywhere. I was so hopeful when I landed here. Now, I'm at a dead end."

"Don't worry, I'm sure we'll find something."

"I wish I had planned my visit better. When I left India, I wasn't aware that they closed the Pagoda for renovation."

"Oh, it was an unplanned repair project. The structure is quite old. They feared its integrity when they discovered one part of the wall was damaged. So, you wouldn't have known about it when you planned."

Saira nodded. "So, they finished with their repairs?"

"Not quite. The premises are open to the public, but no one's allowed near the Pagoda."

"Then?" Saira's face fell.

"Don't worry, my uncle is leading the restoration team, so we kind of have a special pass." Xue Ting winked.

"Ohh, that's such a luck."

The cab took its sweet time through the traffic before reaching its destination. "Looks like we're here."

Saira and Xue Ting retrieved their bags, which held cameras, scanners, and other gear, from the trunk of the car. Next minute, they wheeled them toward their destination.

A beautiful gate with an expansive roof made from terracotta tiles, curving its pointy corners toward the sky, greeted them. The doors were painted maroon and inlaid with black and gold carvings.

A weird sensation passed through her body as soon as Saira entered the gate. She knew something was calling her, like she had experienced in the Tadoba - Andhari National Park. She looked around. A statue of a woman stretching in a martial arts form, with extended arms, holding a sword, stared at her. For a second, she swore the woman seemed to beckon her.

I must be hallucinating.

She followed her instinct and walked. Xue Ting and she went past lush green gardens, fountains, and several big and small buildings, some housing statues of Buddha or the King. Outside, the statues of monks and Xuanzang himself stood tall and peaceful. She stared at each one for a long time as if asking for clues. They seemed to smile at her.

This can't be true; I must be imagining things.

"You know, Saira, some of these statues were brought here from India by Xuanzang himself. According to what I have researched so far, he brought around six hundred sutras and texts. They were in Sanskrit and other ancient languages. We digitized the ones we could find. You must have gone through those at the university."

Saira nodded without looking; her mind was still on something she could not comprehend. "What else is here? Are there any other things Xuanzang brought from India besides the statues and texts?"

"Yes, there's a bell."

"Where is it?"

"Inside the Pagoda."

"Take me to it."

They marched toward the seven-story building, which stood tall against the clear blue sky. The Sun shone happily above it, enhancing its brick-red color. The area around was barricaded, with a few men standing guard. Xue Ting called her uncle, who came out and escorted them inside.

As they entered, Saira's eyes followed the central shaft through its many levels all the way to the top. But all she wanted to look at was the bell Xue Ting had mentioned. They climbed the levels one by one. Beautiful murals adorned the walls, depicting Buddhist events and teachings. Delightful views of the city peeking through the windows distracted her as she climbed. The walkway narrowed, and the murals became smaller as they ascended.

"This is the seventh level. It's never opened to the public," Xue Ting's uncle told them. "And there's the bell you wanted to see."

A brass bell housed inside a glass casing was placed on a pedestal at the center. About a foot in height, it looked ancient and withered.

Saira felt the bell beckon her. She walked toward it and stood in front.

No sooner did she do so than the glass casing shattered, its pieces falling to the ground, exposing the bell to her.

She stared intently.

The next second, the bell rose in the air.

Bands of text appeared one by one on it from bottom to top.

The party of three stood dumbfounded. Xue Ting's gasp echoed through the walls.

Saira recognized the Devanagari script on the text bands that had emerged on the bell. She circled it, reading each of the seven hymns. At the end of each, the bell rang loudly, spreading its chime far and wide. After each chime, it went quiet as if waiting for the next one.

On completing the seventh hymn, the ringing continued nonstop. The three of them could feel the vibrations running through their nerves. Each time, it became louder and stronger.

Xue Ting's face showed nervousness in her mind. Her uncle, too, looked scared.

The vibrations were so strong that the pagoda walls shook.

Saira's eyes were transfixed on the bell.

Xue Ting held her hand and pulled her along. They ran downstairs, exited the building, and stood facing it.

To their disbelief, the Pagoda disintegrated level by level in front of their eyes.

"Oh, no. I can't believe it. What's going on?" Xue Ting's uncle fell to his knees.

The next second, the entire building came crashing down, and some of the dust settled on them.

The bell, which was still floating mid-air, stopped ringing and fell on top of the rubble.

A strong wind circled it. Tiny metal particles from the debris and dust floated with it, starting to coalesce together. The rest of the rubble moved around them.

Saira did not blink.

Slowly and steadily, layer by layer, a copper pot formed in front of their eyes. It floated mid-air, pulling Saira toward itself.

She walked toward the pot, extended both arms, and held it. No sooner did she do that than her eyes shut. Pieces of scenes she had never known before flashed through her mind.

Though it felt like a dream, she knew it was not. Scenes of palaces, courtrooms, courtyards, gardens, fountains; of jewelry, dresses, sarees; of chariots, elephants, and horses.

Finally, the scene in her mind paused on a woman. Her face was hidden behind a veil.

As Saira moved closer in her vision, her heart beat harder.

Slowly, she raised her arms and lifted the veil covering the woman's face.

What came next was beyond disbelief.

The face that came before her was not alien to her at all. On the contrary, she had known that face all her life.

The face she stared at was none other—than her own.

The shock knocked her out of the vision. She stood inside the swirling cloud of dust and debris, holding the pot in her hands. A tiara adorned her head out of nowhere.

Xue Ting and her uncle were on the ground, scared like sheep. Saira could not comprehend what had transpired.

The next second, the pot transformed into a shield.

As Saira examined it front and back, inscriptions appeared on the concave side.

She read them on and pointed the shield's convex side ahead. To her amazement, pictures of the same temples she had found during excavations were projected on the curtain of the encircling dust. It went on for a few minutes as each temple showed itself ahead.

Finally, five faces appeared before her.

Faces of Aarno, Darren, Ojoré, Liang, and Diego.

For the first time since the excavation, it all made sense. She knew what she had to do.

She had to find the five men.

CHAPTER 63

The Swimmers

Somewhere in the Arabian Sea

Under the mercurial waters, cutting through the docile waves, two swimmers approached the yacht. They swam two rounds across the perimeter, scouting for the best climbing spot. On finding one, arrows tied to ropes shot from their guns. The hooks locked precisely where they were intended.

One of them was Alexis Birdwhistle. She ascended, entered the lower deck. She removed the fins from her feet, undid the mask, and the scuba unit. Unloading the weight from her shoulders, she pulled up an extra scuba unit floating underneath the water. They had carried it from their submerged vessel. The vessel had brought them undetected near the yacht.

The deck was deserted. After pulling the package, Alexis gestured to her comrade, Castello, with a thumbs-up.

The five men and Sánchez were on the topmost deck. The captain's cabin was on the middle deck. It was after dinner, and the chef, crewmembers, and medical staff rested in their respective cabins below this deck.

Castello climbed to the deck. Both retrieved their handguns, fastened them with silencers.

Faint voices came from the top deck. Alexis advanced toward the top deck, signaled Castello to follow. Like predators, they placed their feet carefully on the stairs, followed the voices. On reaching the second deck, they surveyed. The deck was empty. The conversation was taking place above them.

Instead of the top deck, they walked toward the cabins. One by one, they scanned the doors, looking for someone to take hostage and get some leverage over the five men. Drágosláv had repeatedly reiterated not to hurt the five men at any cost.

One cabin had the door just a crack open. They pushed it open.

Matthew stood in front, staring at the protruding gun barrels.

Castello went behind Matthew, handcuffed him. He pointed his gun at the side of Matthew's head, poked him to move.

The three of them climbed toward the top deck. In a swift movement, Alexis revealed herself and aimed her gun at the five men. Castello followed her, with Matthew in between.

"Everyone, raise your hands above your head," Alexis shouted. "Be good, gentlemen. No one gets hurt if you obey my orders." She pointed her gun at Matthew.

"I'm so sorry, fellows." Matthew's face was depressed.

Ojoré felt helpless. He didn't want Matthew to suffer again. "Ahhhhhh—" He slammed the bar counter.

There was anger. There was guilt. They had so painstakingly escaped from Barcelona. Matthew had put his life on the line for that. Now, again, he was in danger.

"That's him. That's the man who abducted me pretending to be from Manchester United," Diego shouted, pointing at Castello.

"A single movement, and I'll shoot," Alexis said, looking at Diego and Ojoré.

They stood still.

"Mr. Li," she said, pointing at Liang, "uncuff Dr. Sánchez."

Liang stared at the machined barrel placed on Matthew's head. He obeyed. He felt guilty, too. Matthew had just recuperated and still had a bandage on his gunshot wound.

As the handcuffs were undone, Sánchez rubbed his wrists. A wicked grin spanned across his face once again.

"Aaaha, looks like the tables have turned." He winked at Darren.

Darren grunted like a wild dog.

"The diving gear is on the bottom deck, Dr. Sánchez. The vessel is only a few feet away from the left side of the yacht, looking backward," Alexis said.

"In case you face any resistance downstairs." She withdrew another gun from her jacket pocket, handed it to Sánchez. "Tell the master we have the yacht and will meet him at the decided location."

They shook hands. Sánchez hurried down to the bottommost deck, fastened the diving gear. As he was poised to escape, the six hostages stood up on the deck, looking at him.

"I think I should give you guys some consolation," Sánchez shouted at the top of his voice, "reveal some more information."

"You know now that you are the Pándavs, but you don't know who I am, or who we are—"

They wondered the same.

"Any guesses?"

When no one spoke, he shouted again. "I am Shakooni reborn—Dooryodhan's maternal uncle, Gustáv is Doosshásan—second of the Kaurav brothers,"

He took a moment for the last revelation.

"—and Drágosláv—" He swallowed.

"—is Dooryodhan himself."

Sánchez waited for the information to sink in. He fixed a fin onto his right leg. When both fins were attached to his feet, he shouted again.

"The greatest war the world ever saw is about to begin again. But this time, it seems, it's our turn to win."

Sánchez checked the diving gear one last time.

"Without the weapons, you all are nothing, and," he said, "you will help us in retrieving them."

Sánchez completed his sentence, sat on the deck's steel railing, and, leaning backward, plunged into the waters below.

They stared at the ripples left behind by his dive.

Alexis confirmed that Sánchez was gone. "Did Dr. Sánchez tell you how many Kaurav siblings were there?" she asked, pointing her gun at the five men.

"One hundred," Diego answered.

"I asked siblings, not brothers." She smirked, shaking her head.

"One hundred and one," Liang said.

"Correct, Mr. Li. The one hundred Kaurav brothers had one sister. Her name was Doosshalá." She waited for a second, "and I am her, reborn."

No one spoke. The wind howled on the top deck.

"Anyways, you," Alexis pointed at Diego with the barrel of her gun, "I need the captain. Go fetch him."

Diego clenched his fist but did not resist. Matthew's life was on the line.

As he walked toward the staircase, Diego noticed two empty whiskey bottles rolled away on the deck. They were stuck near the base of a seat.

He looked at Ojoré. Their eyes met.

He motioned with his eyes from himself to the bottle.

Ojoré nodded.

"Quick," Alexis shouted.

Diego was not near the bottles. He decided to try it when he returned to the deck with the captain. He went downstairs.

Ojoré was restless. He looked at the bottles. They were far from him, too. He had to wait.

A few minutes later, Diego returned with the captain. This time, he stood in the right spot, facing away from Ojoré, covering the bottles from the mercenaries.

Diego's back faced Ojoré. He moved his arms back, showed his index finger, making a one.

"I need you to turn the ship around. We are going back," Alexis told the captain.

Diego pulled a second finger, signaling a two.

The captain looked at Aarno.

"Do as she says," Aarno told the captain.

As Diego's third finger came out, he slid sideways, kicked backward.

A glass bottle shot out, curved through the air, and landed in Ojoré's left hand.

Ojoré was ready. Diego kicked the second bottle. It hit and dislodged the gun from Alexis' hand. Aarno dived.

Ojoré smashed the bottle in his hand, launched the broken piece toward Castello's head. The glass ripped his nose. Blood sprayed like water from it.

Darren launched himself onto the two mercenaries. It was easy. The two were subdued.

Darren and Liang searched, retrieved all weapons, and handcuffed them to the railings. Nobody was hurt. It took them only a few seconds. Their coordination was stupendous. The five experienced the connection that had existed between them millennia ago. It was as if their minds were connected. They were able to read what each of them was thinking.

"Radio Drágosláv. Tell him you're bringing us in, but it will take some time because of technical issues with the yacht," Aarno ordered Alexis. "Everyone else, get into the operating theater downstairs where Matthew's surgery was performed."

One by one, they collected all the phones, tablets, and watches on the yacht and tossed them in the ocean.

"Captain, speed up the yacht. I want to put as much distance as possible between us and them."

They sailed for hours, keeping their guards on. Only when they thought they were far away, they sat down. Darren pulled out four glasses from under the counter and poured some cognac for everyone except Aarno. No one said anything for a while. Liang pulled out the paper from his pocket.

They all looked at the tree of royal lineage once again.

"I freakin' don't understand why we have to fight this war." Darren stared at Bheem, scribbled on the paper. "But if we gotta, let's give them the fight of their lives."

The five men looked at each other. Deep within, they knew that they could trust one another.

"We are in this together, whether we like it or not," Aarno said.

He placed his right hand in the center. One by one, they all placed their right hand on top of it.

"I understand now why they're after us." Liang rubbed his palms. "The celestial weapons."

"Our celestial weapons," Darren reminded.

"Our celestial weapons," Liang nodded, "but what of those bubbles, those strange encounters, those worlds?". He paused for a second, shaking his head. "There's something more at play here, not just Drágosláv and his gang."

They stood deliberating on what Liang had said. No one knew what to say.

Tiny hints of rays lit up the sky. The mercurial water began regaining its bluish color.

As the light increased, they spotted a tiny island on the horizon. It was one among the many pieces of the beautiful Lakshadweep archipelago. They were in the Indian subcontinent.

After millennia, the Pándavs were together again.

CHAPTER 64

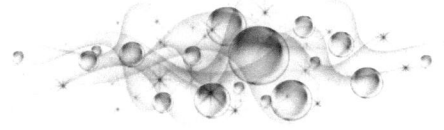

The Lost Temple

Konark, Odisha, India

Satellites, drones, and radars projected cyclone Veena heading toward the state of Odisha.

"Konark is the likely place where Cyclone Veena will make landfall," meteorologist Vicky Kumar announced on News 24x7 TV broadcast. "As you can see on the screen, it's circling in the Bay of Bengal as a category four storm. Our computer models predict winds close to 210 km/hr at landfall."

A pink-colored, funnel-shaped storm trajectory overlaid on a map appeared on the TV screen.

"The storm is quite unusual if you look at it in detail." Kumar zoomed in on the radar image of the cyclone. "Although it's rotating very fast, the bands around the eye are tiny. It has to be the smallest diameter cyclone I have seen so far."

He paused as an animation played on the screen.

"Now, I know it's not cyclone season, and the storm organized itself in no time, taking us all by surprise, but we must be careful. The state government has issued evacuation orders for the following areas."

A map of affected areas highlighted in yellow appeared on the screen.

"If you have not done so already, please, please, please evacuate to the nearest storm shelter. Veena is very dangerous. Please do not take it lightly. All maritime activity in the Bay of Bengal is halted. Airports are closed, highways are packed, and there are long lines, so please don't use your own vehicles. The state government has brought in the Army to help with evacuations. Assemble at these muster points." He pointed to the screen. "And Army helicopters will take you to the closest storm shelter."

After hours of painstaking efforts, all residents were evacuated. Konark was deserted, and so were the usually crowded Sun temple and its pristine grounds.

Amid panic and anticipation, Veena made landfall at the forecasted location. Everything in its path was gone; trees uprooted, houses leveled, power lines damaged, crops destroyed, everything. Everything except the Sun Temple. Its great pillars and walls stood firm as the storm unleashed its fury.

After hours of carnage, it all stopped. Calm. The small town was under the eye of the cyclone while torrential rain pounded surrounding towns.

Inside the storm's eye, at the entrance of the Sun temple, a giant floating bubble emerged. Two men emerged from within.

"Where are we?" Aroon asked, rubbing his eyes

"Konark," Ushvatthámá answered. He took a few steps ahead. "This is the Sun temple."

Aroon gazed at the desolate place. Not a single body was present in the premises, nor a leaf moved on the trees surrounding it, but small branches and twigs had fallen around, and the temple grounds were drenched with puddles everywhere.

"Looks like it rained quite a bit here," Aroon said.

"Well, right now, we're inside the eye of a cyclone." Ushvatthámá's eyes were fixed on the structure ahead.

"What? Are you serious? Cyclone?" Aroon's eyes popped in disbelief.

"Don't worry, the eye will stay over Konark until we are done," Ush-vatthámá replied without moving his gaze.

"But—"

"We don't have much time. Follow me, quick." The White Ghost pulled Aroon forward.

They walked toward the stone steps at the entrance.

The Sun temple was shaped like a colossal chariot, resembling the Sun god's chariot in Hindu mythology. Lions sculpted in stone greeted the entrance of the temple while massive pillars with delicate carvings stood behind them. A tower-like structure called Vimana once stood on these pillars before it gave in to time's great cycle. The primary structure, however, still stood strong. Twelve pairs of gigantic wheels were carved on the sides of its platform, while seven horse sculptures in front appeared to pull the entire chariot forward.

"I learned about the Sun temple in school, but never got a chance to visit. I recall it was built only in the thirteenth century, but the events you told me happened thousands of years before, isn't it? So, how is it possible that the Vijaya bow is here?"

The White Ghost grinned. "That's because you don't know the entire history of this place. The temple you see in front was indeed built recently. But before it came into being, there was another Sun temple here."

"Really? When? Who built it?"

"Lord Kryshná's son Sámbá," Ushvatthámá replied. "To please the Sun god, he built a greater temple thousands of years before this one," He paused, began walking around the temple, as if looking for something, "but the real reason for it was something else."

"What? What's the real reason?"

The Ghost did not answer. He ran his hand around one of the gigantic wheels carved on the platform.

"If you remember the story, Karn—your former self, born of the union of Koonti and the Sun god."

He walked to the next wheel, placed his hand at its center, and spoke, "The original temple was built to house the weapon of Karn, the Vijaya bow, your celestial bow."

Aroon could not contain his enthusiasm. He had studied the history of this place in high school, but never knew about these secrets. "What happened to the original temple? Where is it now?"

"It still is in the same place where it was built." Ushvatthámá deliberated on his next words. "The temple you see is just a cover to hide the original temple's existence."

They reached the back of the temple. There were no wheels on this side.

"The real temple still exists. Watch."

As he spoke those words, Ushvatthámá closed his eyes. He conjured the powers of his forehead ruby. Red light shot out and focused on the center of the platform. A small circular disc emerged. Yellow rays like those of the Sun radiated from it.

"Go." The Ghost gestured to Aroon.

"Where?"

"Press the disc and rotate it. Only the person whose weapon resides inside can unlock what's within."

Aroon walked toward the disc, covered his eyes with his right palm, followed The Ghost's instructions, and retreated.

No sooner did he do that than the rays vanished. It initiated a chain reaction. The pillars at the front section of the temple sank into the ground. The wheels of the chariot-shaped temple came to life, and so did the horses. They pulled the behemoth forward.

As this happened, ripping the earth apart, another structure arose in its place. The existing temple was nothing compared to the size of this new megalith. The ground shivered. The process continued for several minutes as layer after layer emerged.

After a few moments, the transformation was complete, and an entirely different temple stood in front of Aroon.

"After you." Ushvatthámá extended his right hand.

Aroon walked toward the newborn temple. When he placed his left foot on the first step, the entire structure came to life. The pillars and walls of the temple seemed as if on fire, spreading their illumination for miles across. Like the Sun, the temple dazzled and shot out bright light. If anyone were watching, they would be blinded. Aroon and Ushvatthámá, though, were unaffected. They could see everything.

Aroon climbed the stairs, unable to believe his eyes. After passing through the doorway, he noticed that the inside was all opposite. The contrast was striking. Outside, it dazzled, while inside, it was pitch black.

"Please step forward."

"I can't see anything."

"Take a leap of faith."

Aroon moved ahead. A small, stepped pyramid, about a couple feet high, came to light at a short distance. It was made of three layers of brick-like sections and was hollow in the middle.

A small, docile fire emanated from its hollow central portion. Beside it, on the ground, were several mud cups, each containing a different substance.

Aroon looked at Ushvatthámá.

"Is it what I think it is?"

"Yes. It's a havan kund."

"So, am I supposed to perform a fire sacrifice?"

"What else can it be?" Ushvatthámá motioned Aroon to sit in front of the havan kund.

Aroon had not done this ritual before.

"Remove your clothes."

Aroon obeyed and sat on the ground in a lotus position in front of the kund. He picked up the first mud cup and held the powder in his right palm. He launched the powder into the fire on the White Ghost's insistence. As particles of the powder kissed the flame, it amplified high toward the ceiling. The light illuminated carvings on the sidewalls. There were nine celestial deities. Surya (the Sun), Chandra (the Moon), Mangal (Mars), Budha (Mercury), Guru (Jupiter), Sukra (Venus), Shani (Saturn), Rahu, and Ketu, together called the Navagrahas.

Ushvatthámá knew what was needed. "Continue."

Aroon picked up the next mud cup containing ghee. A beetle leaf was kept on its side. He poured the ghee into the fire using the leaf. At that instant, Ushvatthámá began reciting the hymn, nine specific hymns for the nine objects.

"Palasha Pushpa Sankaasham

Taarakaa Graha Mastakam

Rowdram Rowdraat Makam Ghoram

Tam Ketum Prana Maa Myaham."

When he uttered the last word of the first hymn, a chariot wheel appeared at a short distance from Aroon. It was suspended mid-air and had eight beautiful arms connecting the center and circumference. It rotated clockwise.

"Hymns for Ketu," Ushvatthámá explained.

Aroon repeated the process while Ushvatthámá recited the next hymn for Rahu. A second identical wheel appeared behind the first one, suspended in a similar fashion. It spun anticlockwise.

One by one, this continued till nine wheels corresponding to each of the nine objects emerged from the darkness. Their rotation alternated between clockwise and anticlockwise. The first eight wheels shared the same axis. The last wheel for Surya—the Sun, illuminated, and did not rotate. Its center was on a different axis than the first eight. Though the Sun wheel did not rotate, it revolved with its center following a circular orbit at the midpoint of the radii of the other wheels.

"What am I supposed to do?"

"Hit the center of the last wheel, of course."

"With what?"

His question was answered before Ushvatthámá could reply. A small, antique-looking wooden bow floated mid-air between the havan kund and the first wheel. A red-colored line surfaced right below the bow, indicating the mark from where Aroon was supposed to shoot. A quiver with a single arrow was floating next to the bow.

"Is this the Vijaya? It looks very ordinary."

"This is not the Vijaya. This is the bow you will use for your test."

"Test?"

"To prove you are Karn, worthy of the Vijaya. Only Karn can retrieve his bow."

Aroon had just one shot. Still, it didn't scare him. Everything was crystal clear. He lifted the bow and mounted the arrow. He kept his right foot on the red line below, stretched out the bowstring with the arrow using his left hand, concentrated on the last wheel, and sighed.

Apart from the alternating rotations of the first eight wheels, the speed was also different for each of them. Aroon focused. He had never felt so alive before. He closed his right eye, fixed his left on the last wheel's center, and concentrated. It was tough.

After a few minutes, he found the spot. There was only one position where all the wheels were aligned in such a way that there was a straight, unobstructed path to the target. But this alignment lasted only for a fraction of a second. The speed and release of the arrow had to be precise.

Aroon took aim. He was in harmony with the bow, with the arrow, with the wheels, with their rotations, with their speeds, with everything around him. It was peaceful. He had never felt like this before.

He sighed and launched the arrow.

It passed through the first wheel, then the second, the third, and on and on, right through the gaps, and finally, it hit the dead center of the Sun wheel.

The next second, all the wheels shattered into pieces, their debris vanishing into the darkness. At the end of the hallway, on an elegant stand, was the grand Vijaya. It seemed that it was made of gold. The bow shone mesmerizingly in the twinkling light of the havan fire.

"There it is, waiting for you."

Aroon proceeded.

On reaching the dais, he bowed to it with a namasté and picked it up.

A sharp current shot through his arms. Slowly, a gold-colored shining armor embraced his torso. Two earrings hung from his ears; a Sun-shaped tattoo appeared on his forehead. For the first time since he saw the White Ghost, Aroon felt that he belonged in this world. He knew it was all real.

The temple ceiling disappeared, revealing the sky. The eye of the hurricane was still on Konark.

Aroon mounted the Vijaya with an arrow that appeared in the accompanying quiver out of nowhere, pointed it toward the sky, and launched it into the darkness above. Vibrations from its strings emanated thunder. The arrow sped like a bolt of lightning and illuminated the entire sky. The thunder went for miles and miles.

Hundreds of miles away, on the other side of the Indian peninsula, over the Lakshadweep archipelago, the spectacle unfolded in front of the five men. In Xi'an, Saira's eyes were transfixed on the sky, too. Thousands of miles away, on the other side of the Arabian Sea where their vessel was docked, Sánchez, Gustáv, and Drágosláv witnessed the same.

"The first weapon is retrieved, Your Majesty." Sánchez stood, looking mesmerizingly at the sky above. "It's only a matter of time."

"THE GREAT WAR IS ABOUT TO BEGIN — AGAIN!"

~ Intermission ~

PLEASE LEAVE A REVIEW

If you enjoyed the book, please leave a review on Amazon
using the QR code below.

About the Author

V. S. Edwár is a fantasy fiction writer whose storytelling roots trace back to a tale penned at age ten and the spellbinding evenings spent around his grandmother's rocking chair. Her stories—woven from myth, magic, and memory—ignited a lifelong passion for narrative wonder. From childhood to parenthood, storytelling remained his compass, guiding him across continents and life chapters with books as his constant companions.

His debut series, Reign of Pawns, distills the essence of every tale he's heard, read, and imagined. It's a tribute to the generational magic of storytelling—bridging past and present, folklore and fantasy, through richly imagined worlds and lyrical prose. For Edwár, crafting fiction is more than writing—it's a way of honoring legacy, conjuring beauty, and inviting readers into realms where wonder reigns.

To know more & connect, please visit
www.vsedwar.com
or scan

or write to me at
contact@vsedwar.com